IMPERFECT LOVE

ISABELLA WHITE

FIREQUILL PUBLISHING

Imperfect Love: #1 The 4ever series

Cover Design: Regina Wamba from Mae I design and Photography

Fire Quill Publishing
www.firequillpublishing.com

Formatting by FQP Design
Manufactured in South Africa and the USA.
First Fire Quill publishing edition July 2015
ISBN: 978-0-9946641-0-5 (Print)
978-0-9946536-3-5 (e-copy)

DEDICATION

To my best friend, Thea Smith-Richards; the inspiration behind Holly's character. Your light shines even in death. You taught me so much in your short time here on earth, and you inspired me. I will miss you till the day when we'll see each other again.

xoxoxo
Isabella

ACKNOWLEDGMENTS

First and always, thank you to my Father who lives in Heaven, Who once again guided me through yet another story. I couldn't have done this without You. I will always, always love You, until the end of time.

To my family; Heinrich, your love and patience with me while I spent endless hours writing these words has made me only love you more. I couldn't have done any of this without your loving support.

To my two beautiful girls, still too young to delve into mommy's world—one day you will know why some of the play dates had to be postponed. Love you beyond what words could ever describe.

To my mom, sister, mother-in-law, dad, and Vinique—my twin in so many ways—thank you for your support and words of encouragement, for listening to all my ideas and helping me to carry on when things got too much.

To Hillery, my ghostwriter/editor/friend. Although the stories are mine, your words make them so much stronger.

A special thanks to my content and copy editor, Sandra Valente. Where have you been all my life, woman! Your love for words, sentence building, descriptions, and emails after emails with questions upon questions has definitely made me a better writer. I absolutely love your ability to look beyond an editor's perspective and see what the reader would question and want to see more of. Your descriptions have made Imperfect Love, better, stronger, and a real page turner in my opinion. I will treasure your friendship forever and look forward to working on more projects with you.

To all my proofreaders. A big thanks for diving head first into another story of mine.

To Fire Quill Publishing, and the team, you are simply the best and your hard work and endless support will always be treasured.

To my cover designer/photographer, Regina Wamba from Mae I Design, and the models who gave an amazing visual to my story, Ripp and McKenzie, it was a real honor to work with you.

Thank you all so much. Words cannot express how I truly feel.

To Dr. Morgan Clond who is currently working in Israel, a new journey for me has started and I'm so glad that you are going to be part of it. You really made the medical side of this novel so much more. Thank you so much for taking the time out of your busy schedule and delfing into this make believe world of mine. If only there was something like the P47 then so many women might not have to suffer.

Lots of love,

Isabella White

ALSO BY ISABELLA WHITE

IN THE 4 EVER SERIES

SECRET LOVE

ENDLESS LOVE (2018)

What If Novels

(coming soon)

Fatality

Fortuitous

Luck

From a Jack 2 a King (2018)

Whatever our souls are made of, his and mine are the same.~Emily Brontë

ONE

HOLLY SCALLANGER LOOKED at the email in her hands.

That son of a bitch. How could he do this to me, and only a week prior to our wedding?

She had given him everything. Had stood by him in his time of need, having fulfilled the vows she hadn't yet made before God. And what had he done? Her fiancé had slept with the woman he'd promised never to speak to ever again; Donna Sinclair.

That little stunt had ripped her heart out and tore it into a million pieces, like a wolf with a fresh kill. He had decimated her without a second thought.

Their relationship was the price demanded of one tramp in a push-up bra, and paid with the wink of an eye.

Donna had always been a thorn in her side, the kind that wedged in deep like a tick, burrowing in deeper and deeper the more you tried to remove it.

She should have left him when that bitch first made her appearance in their lives, but she had innocently believed his rotten tongue.

Not only that, she had taken into her heart the poison he'd

fed her with every "I'm sorry" and "It will never happen again". She'd believed that he loved her more than anything in existence, and that he'd made a mistake.

Tears welled up in her eyes and her stomach knotted.

But if he loved me, why'd he sleep with that skank only a month ago?

A part of her knew that Brandon was aching for Donna. They were the same, both liars—cheaters. They belonged together. She just wished Brandon had had the balls to break up with her. Maybe she could have saved all the money she had poured into their farce of a wedding.

Better now than too late, she thought.

She should have known that Brandon Morgan would never change his ways. There was a saying her mother always used: "A fox may change its fur, but never its color."

Holly sat in front of her computer and began composing an email to Donna. She pounded away at the keys until the screen before her illuminated a vicious, scolding letter. Pausing, she deleted it, re-typed different cuss words, but eventually deleted that, too.

"You've won," she said out loud, as her fingertips tapped with resigned beats on the letters that spelled the two words on her keyboard and pressed the send button.

Composing herself, she gazed around the polished wooden desk that housed her computer. As her eyes swept over the books and various notes, they rested on the small, black device like a beacon of her misery. Her phone was going to ring in the next couple of minutes and she knew who it would be. Brandon, of course.

Holly wasn't stupid, knew the two secretly messaged each other, but she'd been too in love and blind to truly see Brandon's weakness.

As she looked around the small bedroom, her eyes focused

in on the dark wood of the closet door. Her suitcase was pushed way to the back.

Unable to control herself, she kept running over and over in her head what the hell she was going to tell her mom. God knew, Jane Scallanger didn't have money but had nevertheless spent—more like wasted—a fortune on a wedding that would never take place.

Pulling her legs up to her chest, she silently made a promise to herself and to whatever god happened to be listening. She would repay every penny, even if it took the rest of her life to do so.

Holly got out of the plush chair and gingerly walked across the soft carpet. Grasping the metal handle, she opened the closet door with a flourish and pulled out the suitcase. Flapping it open, she began arranging all her clothes haphazardly. Lucky for her, it was a big suitcase. When she bought it, she'd known the size would come in handy one day, she'd just never thought that it would be used for the situation she now found herself in.

Pausing in her frantic packing, she fell back onto the white carpet, letting her hair swirl around her, reflecting the tornado of emotions swirling within.

How could he have done this to me?

They'd had so many dreams. They could have been such a great couple, if he would have just kept his dick in his pants. Heaven knew she loved Brandon, but she refused to marry Donna, too.

Tears began streaming down her cheeks, leaving a hot path that burned into her very soul. She inhaled deeply, trying not to lose it as she pushed her hair back. She knew that as soon as his Audi pulled into the driveway, he was going to start with his begging again. Especially now, a week before the big day.

She had to stand her ground. She owed it to herself and deserved so much more than that two-timing whore. Yes, Holly was sick of double standards; if women were called whores when they slept around, men should be labeled in the same manner.

Suddenly, her phone began buzzing frantically. She reached out a hand to grab it off the floor, where she'd placed it when she started packing, and looked at the polished glass screen. A beautiful picture of him and her smiling, greeted her.

Damn... we look so happy.

"Yes?" she answered.

"Hey, Holls. What are we going to eat tonight?" his deep honey voice asked.

Just hearing his voice caused a wave of emotion to roll through her body, which almost sent her phone flying toward the closet's door. She knew he wasn't calling about the evening's menu. Donna had probably called him as a result of the message she'd sent half an hour ago.

"You know what? Eat whatever you want to eat. Hell, eat Donna, for all I care." Angrily, she punched the red disconnect button on the screen.

Her phone rang again a second later, the same picture flashing on the screen. "What do you want, Brandon?"

"You okay?" he asked.

"Am I okay?" She gave her 'you're unbelievable' snort, wanting to hang up on him yet again.

I'm so sick and tired of playing this game with him.

"No, I am not okay, but I will be, Brandon," she bit his name out with pure venom.

He cussed. "Is it that time of the month again?"

"You know what? Go fuck yourself. I can't do this anymore... you, you sleazeball, you two-timing piece of shit." She took a deep breath. "I'm leaving you. And I think it's better we do this now, rather than waste two years of our lives with each other."

"Wh-what? Just wait for me, Holls, okay? I'll be right there. I love you, baby."

She knew the minute she spelled it out for him that he'd cottoned on to the fact that she knew he'd slept with Donna, and then the lies would start all over again. He would begin by telling her his soppy version, and ultimately manipulate her into staying by telling her that it would never happen again. Except, that this time, she had proof.

The dead line signal beeped in her ear before she could tell him not to bother.

If she wanted to be rid of his sorry ass, she had to move fast. Where he worked was only a twenty minute drive to her place, and in an emergency, ten.

Holly got up off the floor, grabbed the rest of her stuff, shoved it into her suitcase and hauled it to her pathetic little Beetle, unceremoniously chucking the suitcase into it. She didn't own anything else, because he had everything. Another thing he'd manipulated her with throughout the years.

She backed out of the garage of the million dollar mansion her now-no-longer-to-be-daddy-in-law had bought them as a wedding present three months earlier. She knew she would never find that kind fortune again, but money couldn't buy happiness, she knew that now.

Her phone was on the passenger seat.

She had no idea where to go, except to Bernice's, her best friend. They'd had a falling out a month ago, and although Bernie had warned her to not go crying when he hurt her, she knew her friend hadn't meant it in that way.

They had been friends since they'd been in diapers. Bernie would understand. She'd tried and failed to tell Holly, repeatedly, that Brandon was a dick, but Holly hadn't listened. At that time, the reality of not being with him had been unbearable.

Now the only thing she saw whenever she closed her eyes,

was Donna on top of Brandon in some classy hotel he'd never taken her to.

Holly resolutely dialed her friend's number; thanking God she hadn't deleted it when he'd asked her to. It wouldn't have mattered anyway, as Holly knew Bernie's number by heart. The phone rang three times before Bernice answered.

"Never thought I'd hear from you again," Bernie huffed in an unimpressed tone.

"I did it," Holly blurted without a greeting, and then promptly began to cry. She'd kept most of her tears back for way too long.

"What?" Bernie sounded surprised. "Where are you now? Shit, I hope you're not driving."

"I had to get away. I only have my suitcase and no idea what I'm going to do!" she bawled.

"Calm down, okay? Pull over, or better yet, go to the mall. I'll meet you at Madley's. Just don't drive, please," Bernie begged.

"Okay," Holly uttered, so softly it was barely audible. She disconnected the call, dropped her phone onto her lap and quickly wiped the tears from her eyes and face before she ended up causing an accident. Thankfully, the mall was a five minute drive from their home. She didn't think Brandon would go looking for her there. At least, she hoped he wouldn't.

Holly ordered a regular coffee, since Madley's was a non-licensed coffee shop, and waited for Bernie. She went over in her head how she was going to beg her for forgiveness and ask to be given another chance, and possibly a room until she was able to save up enough money to afford a place of her own.

The waiting was excruciating. For Bernie, it wasn't a five minute drive to Madley's like it was for Holly. It was more of a half an hour drive.

As she waited, her mind wandered back to the day she'd met

Brandon. She remembered how his blue eyes had set her heart on fire in a downtown bar. Neither of them was supposed to have been there that night, but fate had intervened. And as far as Holly was concerned in regards to fate—it didn't fucking exist.

She should've seen the signs. She wasn't even fond of blond guys, but for Brandon she had made an exception. His personality had transformed all his flaws right before her eyes and turned him into her dream guy. At the time, she never had a clue he was a living, breathing replica of her father. Just thinking of the comparison upset her.

Charles Scallanger, she whispered, the name leaving a bitter taste in her mouth. She hated men like her father, yet there she'd been, on the verge of marrying his carbon copy.

Growing up, Holly's mother had worked two jobs, one to put food on the table and pay the bills, the other to pay her father's ass through university so that he could fulfill his dream of becoming an architect.

These weren't men. They were boys who never grew up. And what had Charles done when his ship finally sailed in? He'd dumped her mother and married his blond bimbo secretary, Gabriella, who he'd known for less than three months.

No, Holly didn't want a life that remotely resembled theirs. In the end, her mother hadn't gotten her father, and to this day still lived alone.

Maybe there was no such thing as a good husband. Maybe they were all cheaters, and there would always be a *Donna*.

The two men she'd once loved and worshipped had proved that. What was said by many was true; you always ended up marrying your father. She almost did.

Feeling herself being pulled down into a spiral of depression, Holly forced the good things about Brandon to the front of her mind. He had really made her feel like a million dollars at times, but the reality of those emails to Donna quickly made her feel like she had never been worth a dime to him.

How could I have been so stupid?

As much as Holly hated Donna, she had to admit that the bitch was really good. She'd had her sights set on Brandon ever since the day they'd met on that stupid website everyone was making such a big fuss about. Perhaps, stupidly, Holly had thought love would prevail and conquer that devil spawn. Thank heavens she found out sooner rather than later that love didn't have that kind of power. It didn't conquer all if there was no respect and trust.

She pulled the printed email out of her purse and read through it again. There wasn't any forwarding email address with her name attached to it. And it wasn't from Donna either, but somehow it had managed to get to her, a week before their wedding. There were even entries that went way back, even after he'd promised he would never speak to Donna again. She'd read through those a million times.

Fire burned inside her again as she took in every inked word. She had never felt this kind of betrayal or humiliation in her life, not even when her father left.

Brandon had written to Donna about how beautiful she was, and the words 'miss you' popped up a couple of times. What hurt the most were the emails where he told Donna how he felt trapped in his relationship with Holly. Now that she thought about it, she'd never actually had Brandon all to herself. Guys like Brandon would never know what they had, until it was too late.

Bernie suddenly dropped her skinny ass into the chair across from hers. "Sorry I'm late." She had cut her long, summer blond hair to shoulder length and it looked really good.

Holly didn't say anything, but slid the twenty-four page email in front of Bernie.

Grabbing the pages up from the table quickly, her piercing blue eyes scanned through them, as if earth's existence depended on the information she held in her hands. "That fucking asshole," she whispered, and continued to read. She gasped now and then and gave her 'I don't believe it' snort here and there. "What did he say?" Bernie asked, halfway through.

"He didn't say a thing. I just told him I'm leaving and that was that."

"He didn't even put up fight?" She looked at Holly with raised eyebrows.

"I didn't give him the chance. You know what he's like, Bernie. He'll manipulate me and tell me that it's not him, and you know how naive I can be."

Bernie looked at her, eyes huge and round. "Holly, after this, no way he'd be able to bullshit you again," she huffed. Shaking her head gently, she closed her eyes for a beat. "And, you can't be that stupid."

Holly inhaled deeply, knowing that Bernie was right. But her ex-fiancé would have found a way of talking her into making the biggest mistake of her life. Brandon was that good. "You know what he's like, Bernie," she repeated, fresh tears forming in her eyes.

Looking across the wide table at her friend, Bernie knew how tormented Holly was. She had a weakness when it came to Brandon Morgan. "Just think about these emails, Holly. No one in his or her right mind would take someone like that back. If you like, you can stay with Leonard and me. You'll just have to purchase a pair of earplugs for the nights Sam keeps me up. He's teething and it's driving me insane."

Holly hugged her friend awkwardly across the table. "Thank you, Bernie."

"You're doing the right thing, Holls. He doesn't deserve you. Be happy that this happened now, instead of two years down the line when there'd likely be little feet running around the house."

Holly nodded. Bernie always thought about others, especially children.

They decided to have lunch while Bernie wandered off to place a call to Leonard, updating him on the change of plans involving Holly. Sam stayed with Leonard's mom in the mornings, so Bernie had a chance to catch up on all the chores around the house. Luckily for Holly, it was a Saturday and Brandon had to work, or so she'd presumed. For all she knew, he could've been at Donna's. Thinking about that made her blood boil, leaving her no choice but to agree with her BFF that Brandon didn't deserve her.

When Bernie returned, they both ordered a hamburger and chips—traditional comfort food. In the end, Bernie paid the bill, which Holly hated but her friend had been adamant.

Out in the parking lot, they split up to collect their cars respectively. Bernie had parked on the opposite side of where Holly's car was, so she waited patiently in her Beetle.

Removing her phone from her handbag, she noticed that it had somehow switched to silent while they had been talking and eating.

She had wondered why it hadn't rung, although she couldn't remember making the switch. Twenty-four missed calls were brightly displayed on her phone. Three of the messages were from Brandon wanting to know where she was, why she wasn't answering her phone, and begging her not to do this to him a week before their wedding.

She sighed, forgetting all the steps involved in canceling a wedding. All the people she had to phone. Aunt Suzie, as well as Lorinda, would give their condolences and say that they'd always known Brandon wasn't the right one for her. She had gotten so sick and tired of that saying of theirs: Beautiful men belong to multiple women. This task would require a bottle of vodka.

She read the last message again.

DON'T DO THIS TO ME, PLEASE!

Blah, blah, blah.

Holly chucked the phone onto her back seat. *Do this to him, indeed!* She couldn't help but giggle. She'd almost felt bad thinking that she was doing *that* to him a week before their wedding, but then he should have thought about what he was doing a month ago when he'd rolled into bed with that slut.

She had to find another job, since the five-star restaurant where she currently worked as a full-time personal assistant didn't pay enough to support herself. Thinking of her job made her heart sink. She loved working in the food industry and needed the people who always looked out and cared for her.

Holly's boss and her husband were darlings, and they'd offered to help her financially ever since she'd started working for them. However, Brandon had always had more than enough to support them both.

Just then, Bernie's SUV pulled up and Holly quickly started her Beetle. But when she turned the key in the ignition, a loud whining noise emitted from under the hood. The car backfired and she couldn't help thinking that if he had really loved her the way he'd always said he did, he would've bought her a safer car —one that didn't die at every stop light.

Tears filled her eyes again. No matter how hard she tried to push him off the pedestal she had placed him on so many years ago, he was still on it, standing just as tall as he always had.

"Please, God, give me the strength to let him go," she whispered. Her faith had always held strong, but lately it was beginning to wane, probably because she hadn't gone to church in months. However, Holly still prayed at night, which didn't detract from the fact that she still felt bad in knowing how she had chucked God away, like a discarded toy. He was the only constant in her life, and she was banking on that constant to pull her butt through the torturous week that awaited her.

TWO

THE PAST TWO months hadn't been easy for Holly. But while everything else seemed to be crumbling around her, she was lucky to still have friends like Bernie and Leonard.

Brandon had called her ten times, if not more, begging and pleading for a chance to make it up to her, if only she would give him another chance. She couldn't. A part of her really wanted to forget everything he had done, but then again, it was the blue print of manipulators and the one thing that made them such brilliant liars.

He'd even bought her flowers, the expensive kind, and Holly knew that Brandon wasn't the flower buying type. He saw it as a waste of money, however, the gesture made it hard not to forgive him.

She had to keep reminding herself of that email and Donna's naked body on a hotel room's bed, right next to his. She ended up giving the flowers away, because Bernie would have just burned them if she had taken them home. And they'd been too beautiful to be burned.

When he realized that his begging wasn't going to work like the last time, his mom, Cynthia, tried her luck. She even gave

Holly the speech about how one should 'forgive and forget', which only made Holly's blood boil.

"I did forgive him and now I am busy forgetting him, too," she yelled into the mouthpiece, before slamming it back down onto the table. She knew it was probably not what the *good book* meant, but when it came to Cynthia, she understood why Brandon was the way he was. His mom would always stand up for him, because she used to do it with his father, too.

His dad was another story. They knew Holly couldn't say no to him but they tried, anyway. When she began to cry, he stopped. After all, he knew exactly what she was going through and what an idiot his son was for having treated Holly that way.

Unbelievably, Brandon tried one last time before the big day. He was drunk, of course.

"Please, Holls, I love you so much," he sobbed.

"Then why the fuck did you sleep with Donna? Go to her, Brandon. I'm giving you to her, because I can't do this anymore." What she wanted to say was that she didn't want him anymore, but she didn't believe that yet. She still loved him, but would never trust him again. Trust was more important than love, to her, anyway.

"Holls, I fucked up, please don't do this. Donna means nothing and is nothing compared to you. It is you I want. I'm not going to give up. I will wait for you at the altar. Please, forgive me just once?"

"Brandon, I forgave you more than just once. I can't do this anymore. I'm not going to be there tomorrow."

"Damn it, Holly. We have paid a shit load of money for this wedding, you can't leave me now."

She laughed, not the 'ha-ha' kind, but a 'this guy is unbelievable' kind. "I didn't leave you today. I left you a week ago, Brandon. You had more than enough time to call off the wedding, but you probably thought that you could screw me over one more time, lie to me, and make me come back. Well, not this time. I'm moving on with my life, I suggest you do the same, and please don't ever phone me again. Oh, and by the way, you didn't pay for the wedding, my mom did. Go spend our honeymoon with your slut."

She didn't say goodbye. He wasn't even worth that. Sadly, she'd never felt so alone. Even when Bernie was comforting her, she felt that she could never trust another man, ever again.

Holly would probably end up like her mother, a drunk with fifty cats. Thinking of that wonderful furry future, she couldn't help but wonder that a mini zoo would still be better than what her life would have been with Brandon, or so she hoped and prayed.

Why couldn't he just love me? Wasn't I enough?

It was that part that she struggled with the most, not being enough.

When the day of the wedding dawned, she drank an entire bottle of scotch she'd found after scouring the cabinet in the kitchen. It belonged to Leonard, but he was a big teddy bear and a sucker for Bernie, so there wouldn't be much of a fight over the illicit bottle. All it took was one look and he would give her whatever she needed. And the scotch was needed.

Holly was fine on the Sunday, except for a huge hangover. And as far as Monday was concerned, she was okay too, until Bridgette, one of her so-called bridesmaids phoned her and sent her reeling. The wedding had still taken place. Apparently, his mother had made a few adjustments to the seating chart. One that removed Holly's family and replaced it with Donna's.

As she listened to the words crackling through the phone, she felt her knees give in and the room seemed to become a lot more active than it had been only moments before. She felt the smooth wood of her chair under her left hand become hard and painful, where it had once been soft and inviting, as her fingers clutched it tighter. Holly was bowled over by this news and could hardly believe what she was hearing. To think he'd still been pleading with her on Friday night. She couldn't help but think about what would have happened if she'd shown up. It could only have resulted in further humiliation. Brandon had not one ounce of remorse in him, and she felt ten times worse than she had on the day she was supposed to get married.

With her life slipping through her fingers, Holly started to drink again. It lasted for about two weeks and she was glad that Jerry, her boss, had given her the two week honeymoon she was due.

As she stared into the bottom of yet another martini glass, she wished that she could be like Brandon and fuck every womanizer lurking in the bar she was currently at, but she couldn't. It wasn't who she was.

When her vacation was finally over, Bernie was the one who was there to pull her out of the powerful and miserable web she had woven around herself.

"Get up!" Bernie yelled. "You smell and believe it or not, life goes on, Holly." Bernie pushed her off the bed with all her strength.

Holly fell on the floor with a thud and just lay there, moaning. In the distance, she could hear bath water running.

Bernie returned and somehow managed to pick Holly up, carrying her—all the while cussing—to the bathroom. She chucked her into the cold bath, which made Holly gasp as the icy water hit her body sending a shockwave into her very core. "You've got to snap out of this, Holls. He's not worth it." Bernie swiped the hair out of her face.

Holly began to cry. "We could've been so happy, Bernie," she bawled.

"He's a dickhead, and 'could have' isn't a guarantee. Stop second-guessing yourself!" she yelled back. "How is it possible that he's still on his pedestal, Holls? You are in love with an idea, not the real thing. The Brandon in your head doesn't exist." Bernie sighed. Her arms and shirt were wet from the splashes when she'd thrown Holly into the bath.

She stared at her best friend, lying hopeless in a bathtub, clothes clinging to her frail body. Reaching out, Bernie took a wisp of hair that clung over Holly's face and moved it gently away from her eyes. "You might not see it now, but it's the best thing that has ever happened to you, sweets. And let's be honest here, do you really think Donna would have stayed away after you guys married? It would've been ten times worse. You did them a favor. He's a smelly cheat, and you my friend do not deserve that. Donna is going to realize pretty soon what a dick-head he is, because believe it or not, he's going to cheat on her, too." She was out of breath after her grand speech, and her eyes pleaded with Holly for some understanding.

"Do you know what happened the night of my party?" Bernie asked.

Holly just looked at her through puffy eyes. She remembered the party vividly. It had been Bernie's 24th birthday, and Leo had invited a bunch of friends over for a barbecue, as well as some work colleagues. "What?" she asked, still lying in the cold bath, fully dressed.

"He cheated on you. Everyone saw it, except you," she said.

"What? Why didn't you tell me?" Holly shrieked.

Bernie gave her the look. "What... did you think our fight came out of nowhere? I saw the idiot checking out one of Leo's colleagues. They disappeared fifteen minutes later and when asked about it, he said he wasn't yet married. Men like that will never be married, Holls. You don't need him or any of your so-called 'mutual friends'." She finger quoted the last part.

Holly started to cry again. Knowing that the scum bag had cheated on her more than once made a small part of her glad that he had married Donna, instead. They truly deserved one another.

"You need to go on with your life. When you are ready to get out of this yucky, cold bath and really want to move on, let me know. I have some pretty great ideas."

"Oh, please, give me strength," Holly complained. She didn't have the strength for Bernie's ideas just yet.

Bernie giggled. "Strength is what you are definitely going to need, my friend."

Holly didn't like Bernie's answer. It usually involved other men she had absolutely no interest in whatsoever. She knew from experience just how wonderfully these ideas tended to work out. If it hadn't been for Collin breaking up with her, she would have never been in that bar the night she met Brandon.

Thinking about what Bernie said, she drained some of the cold water and turned on the hot water tap. Bernie was right, she really did need a bath and a long one too.

When she was done, dry and fully dressed, Bernie eagerly told her about Steward. Holly rolled her eyes at the mere thought.

"I am not saying you should marry the guy, just go out and have fun, Holls."

"Fine, whatever will get you off my back," she mumbled.

Holly went back to work the following Monday; her colleagues' faces said it all. Thank heaven they had stopped with the 'sorry about Brandon and you deserve better' speeches. She heard them often enough from Bernie.

By Wednesday, she realized that life really did go on and that time didn't stop for anyone in order to get over a broken heart. A date or two wouldn't kill her and if Leonard approved, she figured Steward couldn't be that bad.

Friday couldn't have come soon enough. Holly knew she wasn't ready for another relationship, but Bernie had told her that she needed to have fun, and try to find herself again. It was easy to lose oneself in a relationship where only one half of the couple gained from it, and Holly had had plenty of those relationships. She just figured she now knew how to pick them.

They decided to meet at the closest bar to Bernie's house. Brandon had refused to set foot in this bar, because according to him it wasn't classy enough. He would rather go to the lounges where men paid big money for cognacs and cigars.

Steward had told her that he would be wearing a black T-shirt and jeans so she could easily recognize him. With Bernie's help, she had settled on a beautiful emerald top that flowed around her curves, skinny jeans, and high boots that hurt the living bejeebers out of her toes. It was one of the things Brandon loved; Holly in skinnies with boots covering her calves. She had the ass and legs for it.

A couple of men turned in their bar stools as Holly took a seat on one of the high chairs. Every single guy that looked her way was wearing a black T-shirt and jeans.

Just great!

"Holly?" a blond guy queried.

Holly smiled. *Why, for once, couldn't they be dark-haired and look as if they'd just walked out of a Hugo Boss advert,* she silently wished.

"You must be Steward," she finally said, deciding to give him a chance, knowing she owed it to herself to be nice and see how this date would end. But she already knew what the outcome would be.

"Bernie wasn't kidding when she said you were beautiful," he complimented her, making Holly blush.

"Thanks." She couldn't remember the last time Brandon had said those words; that she was beautiful.

"Can I get you something to drink?" he asked, already halfway onto the chair next to hers.

"Whiskey and water, please." She smiled again, as he raised his hand to grab the bartender's attention.

Quite a number of men were staring at her, which made her uncomfortable. She decided that they'd have one drink and then move on to another place. Holly didn't like the bar; it was full of men with greasy hair and dirty clothes who did nothing but sway on their chairs.

She had to admit, Steward wasn't a bad looking guy. He didn't have Brandon's looks and if he worked with Leonard, he didn't have the wealth either, but it didn't bother her that much. The only thing she couldn't understand was why on earth she always ended up with blond guys. Blonds weren't even her type. She like the tall, dark-haired, handsome type, but everyone she knew who happened to fit that description was either married or taken, and she didn't believe in taking another girl's man. It had happened so many times, she didn't have it in her to inflict that kind of pain on anyone, not even Donna.

They started off talking about their professions and where they worked. Holly was easy to chat to and she was quite clued up on a range of topics. Conversing was one of her favorite things and if Bernie were here, poor Steward wouldn't get a chance to say anything.

"Could we go someplace else?" she asked, after one of the drunks near them refused to stop staring at her.

"Where do you have in mind?" he asked with a sly smile on his face.

She knew he was thinking about his home, or worse... his bed, but she smiled politely and mentioned the mall. It was more her scene and she hoped that Brandon would still be on his honeymoon. If she ran into him tonight with Steward by her side, Donna would surely love the fact that she had won the prize.

"Sure. You aren't going to dump my sorry ass now, are you?"

he joked, which made her giggle.

"No, I just don't want to be here." She gestured to the crowded bar, pointing out the fact that they had to scream to hear the other talk.

"Fine. Madley's?" he queried, to which she nodded.

She hoped her ex wouldn't make an appearance, seeing as it was five minutes from his house, but the mall was big enough for both her and Brandon, so there wasn't much of a chance she'd bump into him. Besides, she knew Brandon would rather take Donna to a casino, or someplace fancier than Madley's.

The drive to the mall felt long and she couldn't shake the gloom that settled over her. She felt like crying, because she quickly realized that this date was not going to be a short one. Mentally shaking herself, she knew she might as well make the best of it and forced a smile onto her frozen face.

Over coffee, Steward talked about his parents who lived three thousand miles away. She felt sorry for him and could sympathize with how he felt.

Her mother was not the type of woman who wanted people around her, either. She'd started drinking after her dad left them and when Jamie, her twin, was diagnosed with cancer which took her at the age of fifteen, Jane completely fell off the wagon. She quickly forgot about Holly and that was when Bernie's parents stepped in and raised her right up until Holly graduated. Her childhood hadn't been easy by a long shot.

After her second cup of coffee, she looked at her watch and did a quick calculation, figured that if they ran they could make the last show at the movie theater in the nick of time.

"Would you like to watch a movie?" she asked quickly and lucky for her, Steward didn't seem to care what they did.

They ended up watching a soppy love story where the girl got her guy in the end. Holly was smart enough to know that life didn't work that way. She even briefly considered what it would be like to marry Steward, which was positively stupid because he seemed like a safe choice.

Shaking the troubling thought from her mind, she knew deep down that there had to be more than that. She couldn't live a boring life where everything was the same, day in and day out. She needed adventure, passion, and a Prince Charming who fulfilled her every wish and dream, and who would be more than happy to just be with her. Why couldn't life be like that? Why was it that the hot guy who was also the good guy only happened in books and the silver screen?

In real life, the hot dude was everyone's dude. She had learned that with Brandon. Hell, if she could just get an eraser and rub out the last two years of her life with him, she would. She didn't want to feel this emptiness inside. Maybe she'd made a huge mistake leaving Brandon.

Well, it was too late now.

When the movie ended and the lights in the theater came on, Steward dutifully walked her to her car. She turned to say goodbye with a friendly handshake and thank him for the fun evening, when he suddenly kissed her fiercely. Locked lip to lip, she had no idea what to do and decided to wait it out until he was done. Holly could never tell a nice guy like Steward that this wasn't what she wanted, that she didn't feel the same way he did. Not yet, anyway, as they'd just met.

He finally broke away and looked into her eyes. "Do you want to come home with me?"

"Umm..." She didn't know how to answer that question politely. She closed her eyes and thought quickly. Not knowing Steward that well, or at all seeing as this was their first date, and she wondered how well Leonard did. "I'm really tired, Steward, but thank you for the offer. Can I take a rain check on that? It's been one hell of a week. I hope you understand."

Perfect.

"No problem. If you'd like, we could do this again. Tonight was actually fun." He smiled.

Holly couldn't help but smile back, telling herself to be polite. "Yeah, sure. I will let you know when," she replied, hurriedly jumping into her car. "Please start," she begged under her breath. It would just be her darned luck if he decided to wait for her until her car left the parking lot. She looked up. Yep, he was still there. Lucky for her, the little engine roared to life and she reversed out quickly, keeping her foot on the gas. She silently wished she could drive to nowhere and run away from everything that kept haunting her.

Once home, she walked up the driveway and noticed that the lounge light was still on. Oh, she so hoped Bernie was still awake, only so that she could scold her over what an idiot Steward was. Her thoughts ran rampant.

How could he have kissed me without even knowing if I wanted it? Seriously, if I wanted to spend more time with him, I would have asked for another cup of coffee, or even accepted his invitation to go home with him. Even though that would have been slutty.

Snapping out of her thoughts, she made her way inside, stopping only when she plopped herself down onto the sofa's soft cushion and rested her head on the edge of the seat with an exasperated look on her face. She was sick and tired of guys like Steward and Brandon, who apparently lived for the second she fell in love with them and then started treating her like dirt.

"And how was your date?" Bernie's head popped around the corner of her entrance.

Holly gave her the look.

"That bad?"

"The guy freaking kissed me!" Holly's hands gesticulated around her head as she talked, showing Bernie how disgusted she really was with what had happened. In a flash, she noticed

Leo's huge figure and bald head appearing behind Bernie's. "I didn't even want a kiss from him. Why do you men always think that women want a kiss on the first date?" she yelled, looking pointedly at Leonard.

He made his way over to the opposite sofa, while Bernie sat down next to Holly. "So sorry, Holls. I told him to take it easy. Maybe Steward was not such a great idea." Leonard looked at Bernie with a sad expression on his face.

"You think?" Bernie shot back sarcastically.

"I beg of you, don't do that again." Holly looked at Bernie, pleading with her eyes. "All he ended up doing was make me think that Brandon was the best I could do."

Bernie's eyes became huge at this last statement. "No more Stewards. Got it," she replied in a serious tone.

"No more, period." Holly took a deep breath, but didn't take her gaze from Bernie.

"Fine, no more. But—"

"No buts. I will find my own guy when the time is right," Holly interrupted, quickly saying goodnight before they could push the topic any further. She was still having trouble believing what an idiot Steward had been. *Where does Leonard meet these guys?* She knew he was a work colleague, but really she was one of their best friends and therefore he should've done his homework better.

As she got ready for bed, she was surprised at how glad she was that she didn't have a cell phone any more. She'd thrown hers against the wall after hanging up on Brandon the last time she spoke to him. Deep down she really did miss him, but knew that he was finally with the woman he deserved.

Crawling into bed and pulling the satin sheet over her head, she cried herself to sleep that night.

She hoped that someday her tears for Brandon would finally dry up.

THREE

EIGHT WEEKS WENT by since her date with the infamous Steward, and Holly's thoughts about men had changed drastically—for the worst. She flat out hated them now. Whenever a guy attempted to even talk to her, whether it was one of the guests at work or in the mall while picking up groceries with Bernie, she would give them a scolding eye until they backed off. Bernie seriously had had enough of it, and basically forced Holly to go on a weekend trip with her and Leo.

Holly hated being the third wheel every time she spent a weekend's vacation at Bernie's or Leo's parents, but Bernie had been adamant. Holly needed the fresh air, and Bernie hoped that the time away would change Holly's attitude toward men. She needed to show Holly that not all were like Brandon or Collin.

Holly was still of a different opinion about the whole matter.

They were going to some Bands of the World Bash. She'd never gone to one before, because it hadn't been Brandon's scene. The drive felt long, even though Leo said it was only a half an hour out of the city.

When he turned off the main road onto a dusty lane, Holly could hear the music equipment being tested in the background. There were tents and RVs stacked up here and there, and a feeling of fun suddenly rose in Holly.

Maybe Bernie is right. This might be the one thing I really need.

As she scanned the passing crowd, she suddenly spotted a familiar face. "Josie!" Holly yelled out the car's window.

The SUV stopped with a thud, and both Bernie and Leo turned around to stare at Holly who was already making her way out of the car.

"Where are you going?" Bernie yelled.

Holly didn't reply, and when she finally reached Josie's tent, the two friends hugged like they hadn't seen each other for years. Josie was, unfortunately, related to Brandon, who just happened to be her cousin. Still, she was one of Holly's good friends.

"What are you doing here, woman?" Josie asked, still hugging the shit out of Holly.

"Bernie." It was enough for Josie. They burst into laughter.

"George, come see who's here," Josie yelled into the tent, and a couple of seconds later a skinny, toothpick of a man emerged.

"Holly, you beaut!" Reaching toward her, he pulled her into a death grip.

"I never thought I would see you again." Holly heard Bernie's voice coming up behind her, and when she turned to look she found Bernie's arms wrapped around Josie's neck. They greeted one another, no one saying a word about Brandon or the wedding. When Josie asked if she could get them something to drink, Leo and Bernie declined.

"Make mine a double," Holly said excitedly.

"Holls, we need to set up camp."

"Then go, Bernie. I can meet you there."

"You don't know where it is." Bernie's voice rose slightly.

"I can take her back. I know where you guys set up camp every year. It's not the first time we've come to Bands of the World Bash." Josie lifted Bernie's worry slightly, or at least Leo's.

"Thanks, Josie," Leo answered on behalf of Bernie, who just stood there looking at Holly.

"Go," Holly mouthed.

"Don't stay too long, please," Bernie urged, using her motherly tone with Holly.

Leo pulled Bernie by the wrist toward the SUV. "Stay as long as you like, Holls," he said, whispering something softly to Bernie as he steered her away. Bernie clearly wanted to protest but he showed her the zip-it sign, closing his fingers over his thumb.

Bernie laughed right along with the others who'd witnessed their exchange. "Fine. Stay as long as you like."

When the SUV pulled away, Holly dropped her backside into a camping chair. George handed her a double whiskey with water, and the two girls started chatting away.

"So, how are you doing?" Josie asked, giving Holly the softest look her chocolate-brown eyes could muster.

"Bernie said that I'm going through the anger phase," Holly answered truthfully.

"Good, because that means you're making some progress," Josie teased.

Holly laughed. "I don't know if I'm ever getting out of this. Apart from the men I know, I hate the rest."

"Sweets, I can understand where you're coming from. I would hate men, too, if my fiancé pulled a heartbreaking stunt as yours did a week before my wedding."

"So... how was the wedding?" Holly couldn't help but ask.

Josie stared at her with huge eyes. "You know about that?"

"Bridge called me."

"Oh, Holly. She's a bitch. She was never your friend," Josie said with anger in her eyes. "She's become really good friends with Donna now. The two are inseparable."

"Have you seen him lately?"

"No, there is no need for me to hang out there anymore."

Holly grabbed Josie around the neck. "I've missed you guys so much."

"Me, too. I was really looking forward to becoming your cousin, but I'm glad you ditched his ass, Holls. Bernie was right. He would have only fucked you and your life up."

All Holly could muster was a sad look.

"You don't still feel something for him, do you?"

"I don't know what I feel. A part of me feels as if I'm never going to trust anyone else, or fall in love again."

"Holls, you are one gorgeous girl. I'm sure Mr. Right is just around the corner."

"You know something I don't?" Holly asked. Josie sounded so sure of herself.

"No, but I've got to warn you. If Bernie's regular gang is up here, you will meet a distraction soon."

George shook his head. "Are you talking about Jake again?"

"You're darn right I am." They both laughed as she made a face.

"Who's Jake?" Holly asked with a huge grin on her face now, all thanks to Josie and George.

"Every girl's dream, and every guy's worst nightmare," George bantered jokingly.

"He's not that bad." Josie looked at her husband with narrowed eyes.

"And how can you not remember him, Holls?"

"I don't know anyone named Jake."

"He was at Bernie's birthday party. You didn't see the heart-throb there?"

Holly rolled her eyes. "No."

"I'm sure he even spoke to you."

"I would remember if a heart-throb spoke to me, trust me. I didn't see him."

"He definitely spoke to you. You even said something back to him over your shoulder. This is a perfect example of one of the reasons why I'm glad my cousin fucked up, Holls. You never saw the beauty in this world when you were with him."

"I wasn't like that."

George opened his eyes wide and let out a small huff.

"You agree with her?" Holly laughed.

"You did speak to him, Holls," George insisted, "I saw it, too."

"I honestly don't remember."

"My point exactly. Not to worry, you will see him today." Josie had a twinkle in her eyes.

Holly just laughed. "Save his poor soul. My aunt always said that a beautiful man is everyone's man."

"There are exceptions," Josie disagreed.

"I'm still waiting to meet one of those," Holly spoke softly, but Josie heard.

She put her hand on Holly's knee. "You're going to meet someone again, Holls, we always do."

"Hey, what's that supposed to mean?"

"Drink your martini and shut up, George."

The girls laughed, while George grumbled something undistinguishable under his breath.

Holly visited with the happy couple until about five o'clock. When their friends, with whom Holly wasn't familiar, started to pull up in their twin cabs and RVs, Holly decided that it was time to go back to Bernie's campsite.

With each step Holly took, her heart thumped faster. She was nervous to meet the heart-throb Josie and George had spoken of. Both were beautiful people, inside and out, and in all the time Holly had known Josie, she'd never heard the words *heart-throb* exit her mouth.

They used to play 'hot or not' on Saturday's when Josie, Bernie, and Bridge went with Holly for coffee at Madley's. Holly hated that game; she'd always felt like she was cheating on Brandon by participating. Bernie always ended up with about forty hot guys, while Bridge and Josie made fun of her choices. Josie would end up with one and he would always be jaw-dropping gorgeous. So, yes, she was really weary to finally meet this heart-throb she had apparently already met.

As per Josie's offer to walk Holly back to Bernie's site so she wouldn't have to make the trek alone, they walked past the showers while Josie yapped away about the past three months, and what she had been up to since the wedding. Holly listened with one ear, while trying to calm her beating heart.

"Hello, honey."

Holly heard the familiar voice as they approached, which sent a shiver through her body at the memories it dredged up.

"Steward!" Bernie shouted, somewhere in the background.

Josie just looked at Steward, who was clearly smoked, and then back at Holly.

"I'm not a bee's puke," Holly said with no emotion in her voice, as Josie cackled with laughter.

They started to make their way around Steward, who happened to be blocking Holly's path.

Josie bumped Holly softly, hooking their arms together. "Bernie sure wasn't kidding about that hate phase." The two girls laughed as they brushed past him.

"Steward was a blind date that went horribly wrong."

Josie looked back at Steward. "Seriously, if you want blind dates, Holly, I have some pretty awesome friends."

"I know you do."

"You'll have to tell me about him later," Josie said as she walked up to Bernie, nudging Holly toward her.

Bernie had a funny look on her face, as if Josie had just handed her a present.

"She's all yours!" Josie laughed.

"Stay for a drink," Bernie offered, holding a cold cooler.

"Can't, sorry. Everyone is back there, but I will see you soon. Promise." She kissed Holly on the cheek, and then looked around skeptically.

"Stop it." Holly slapped her playfully.

"What! I can look." Josie grinned.

"What's this about?" Bernie wanted to know.

"Is hottie here?"

"Oh, for heaven's sake!" Holly sighed, throwing her hands in the air in exasperation.

Bernie laughed. "Yes, he's in the RV. You want me to call him?"

"No, it's fine. I have an image of him imprinted on my mind; it would be a shame to shatter the illusion."

Holly shook her head as Josie winked and then turned to walk away.

"Enjoy the distraction, Holls!" she sang.

Holly scolded her with a facial expression that made Josie and Bernie laugh. "Who the hell is Jake?"

"Someone we've tried to get over for a BBQ for the past three months, and one of Leo's childhood friends. I can—"

"Oh, hell no," Holly scolded Bernie as they made themselves comfortable on camp chairs, which had been placed right next to the RV

Bernie laughed. "You're going to beg me."

"I'm not that cheap."

"We'll talk later."

"No, we won't."

Leonard walked out of the camper first with a beer in his hand, followed by a tall guy in a baseball cap. They were both laughing about something, to which Leo shook his head at whatever the mystery guy had said.

Holly felt a thousand pins and needles wash over her body as the stranger looked up. *So that's Jake, the one everyone is freaking out about.* She looked away immediately to avoid staring, but caught Steward smiling and winking at her instead.

"Ugh." Holly looked at Bernie. "You really had to invite him, didn't you?"

Bernie rolled her eyes.

"Sorry, Holls. I promise, he won't bother you," Leo answered with a huge grin, and Holly caught the smile on Jake's face.

He was so her type. So much in fact that she was seriously considering begging Bernie to ask him if he would go on a date with her, but she knew it was wrong. The poor guy was human like everyone else, and Holly was sure that he'd had his fair share of female Stewards.

"Well, it's too late now. I can see how this weekend is going to turn out. I'm going to break something before it's over."

"Break something?" Bernie looked at her quizzically.

"Yes, on his face."

Bernie, Leo, and even Jake laughed at her comment.

"Seriously, Holly, you need to find your happy place again. This anger phase? It's too much, babe," Bernie said through a huge grin.

"What do you mean? I've hardly started." Holly giggled.

"Not all men are Brandon. You always choose the worst ones out there."

"Second you on that, angel face." Leo lifted his beer in silent salute.

"Oh, and your choice was so much better?"

"Damn it, how many times must I apologize for that?" Leo had a playful tone to his protest.

"I thought I was considered a really good friend, Leo."

"Don't start." Leo smiled, while Holly laughed.

Suddenly, Steward made himself comfortable on the chair next to hers.

"How do you get to Bee Puke?" he asked, clearly stoned.

Bernie and Leo laughed.

"Don't ever call Holly *honey*; it comes out of a bee's front... you know, same way it went in."

Steward laughed, while Holly gave Bernie the look. She hated stoned or drunk men.

"Take a hike, Steward," Jake said out of nowhere, which shocked Holly.

"Jake. Holly and I go way back."

"Dude, take a hike." Again, Jake spoke up.

"Seriously?"

"You want me to help you?" Leo asked.

"C'mon, I'm just talking to Holly."

"Not sure about the others, but I'm not in the mood for your stoned, pick-up lines, so go sleep it off," Jake advised.

Holly sighed with longing. He had the most beautiful light green eyes she wanted to get lost in, and she knew his manly, model features would make her drool for days to come. He was a head taller than Leo, with arms and shoulders that looked like they could hug ten kids at the same time.

She smiled as she thought about a possibility: What if Leo and Bernie did hook her up with him on a blind date? The guy sure seemed like the type that would do anything for his best friend, even if it meant taking out a girl to make her forget her stupid fiancé. She had to stop herself from giggling out loud as the images of this 'possible date' flashed through her mind. She wouldn't even know what to do with herself if this hypothetical date actually took place. Not to mention how she'd react if the object of her interest was lying next to her.

"It's not like you never got stoned."

"A thousand years ago, yes. I grew up."

Holly liked that reply.

"Go sleep it off. I mean it."

Steward growled and mumbled something that sounded like he was swearing.

"Thank you, I could kiss you right about now." The words just slipped out of Holly's mouth, but fortunately she knew how to handle herself after that little confession.

"She's over her anger phase," both Leo and Jake sang.

"No, I'm not. I said could, not would. There's a difference."

They all laughed. Leo just sulked.

Holly glanced over at Jake again. He had the most beautiful face, not to mention how it lit up when he laughed. Josie was right, he would surely be a distraction, and one she wouldn't mind watching the entire day.

FOUR

AT AROUND SIX, while they relaxed around the fire, a beautiful brunette arrived and sat down next to Jake, whispering into his ear. Guys like Jake always had a girlfriend lingering in the shadows, and just as girls like Holly began to daydream about possibilities, they'd emerge, crushing all their hopes and dreams.

Of course he's got a girlfriend, Holly thought. She was really stunning, though, with model legs peeking out from a skimpy, short skirt. Holly could just imagine what that girl looked like in a swimsuit.

She watched how the mystery girl showed off her beautiful, straight long hair, something Holly wished she had. Sadly, she'd been cursed with curls upon curls of strawberry blond hair. Two near perfect rows of pearly whites shone as she smiled at one of Jake's replies, right before she slapped him playfully on the shoulder. She took a sip of her light beer, making even that look sexy.

Holly sighed again. Girls like her had no choice but to date guys like Steward. She should've forgiven Brandon this once, and maybe she wouldn't be sitting with a horrible empty feeling in the pit of her stomach. She thought about the feelings she would've been stuck with if she had stayed in order to counteract her treacherous thoughts. Then again, it would have probably not been a good idea, because the situation could've been that much worse.

Sinking deeper into the bean bag she had borrowed from the camper, she felt her emotions going numb. She sat there drinking one whiskey after another, feeling the tears begin to build up behind her eyelids as she thought about Brandon.

Guess Jake isn't a good distraction after all.

Night came quickly, and at around nine o'clock she could feel her energy waning. She wanted so badly to go to bed, but Bernie wouldn't let her.

This was the one thing she couldn't stand about Bernie. Even Leo had asked her a couple of times if she was okay. She'd just nodded. Holly would have even welcomed Steward with his stoned conversation just to forget about Brandon and what could have been. Maybe she had been too harsh on poor, old Steward.

She got up slowly and began walking to the bathroom, which was located near their campsite, gesturing to Bernie that she was fine. As she walked away, she heard Bernie laughing at something one of the other girls at the party must have said, whose name Holly had by now forgotten.

Holly knew she shouldn't have gone with them, especially as she was being morose, boring, and didn't really want to be there at all.

On her way out of the cubicle, she stopped in front of the large mirror that hung above the hand basin. She barely recognized the miserable figure staring back at her. Reaching out, she turned the faucet on and splashed some cold water on her face in an attempt to try and wash away some of the pain lining her eyes. When she exited, Steward was waiting for her at the entrance. The thought she'd had a few moments ago about welcoming Steward's conversation was instantly gone at the sight of him. An unpleasant feeling began to form in her stomach as Steward opened his mouth.

"Holly, I'm sorry about earlier."

At least he's started politely.

"It's okay, Steward. I'm sorry, too."

"So, does this mean I'm forgiven?" He had a grin on his face.

She looked at him for a beat and then nodded, smiling softly.

"What about a second date, then?"

Holly's temper rose slightly at his cheek. *Why can't he just let it go?* She didn't want another stupid date with him, but for the love of idiocy he just couldn't take a hint.

"Steward, I've told you no. I don't want another date. Please, just let it go." She turned to walk away, when he suddenly grabbed her arm and pulled her back. "What are you doing?"

"I just want a date. Don't be such a bitch, Holly."

Bitch! Did he just call me a bitch? Without thinking, her mind went into autopilot and the next thing she felt was his face connecting with her fist. Something cracked and she didn't know if it came from her hand, or from his nose. Blood spilled everywhere, and a jolt of pain ran through her hand.

"Holly, you fucking bitch!" Steward cried, while Holly cussed loudly. "You broke my fucking nose!"

"You deserved it, you asshole. Be glad that's all I broke."

In a flash, as if drawn to the conflict, Bernie was at Holly's side. "What happened? You hit him?" A small laugh escaped Bernie's lips.

"It's not funny. I think I broke something!"

Leo and Jake followed quickly, along with Sonic—the beautiful brunette with legs that went on for days—right behind them. Holly had finally learned her name when Leo had walked over to refill her drink earlier.

"You go, girl!" Sonic cried out, upon seeing Steward holding his nose with cupped hands and Holly cradling her injured hand.

"Let me see," Bernie asked, looking toward Holly's hand.

"It hurts, don't touch it."

"I just want to look at it." She held Holly's hand gently in hers, and then called for Leonard.

"Is it broken, Jake?" Steward asked Jake for the verdict.

"Does it hurt?" Jake queried.

"Like hell."

"Then it's broken," Jake said, in a manner that formed sexy lines down his cheeks.

Holly groaned, lustfully, but it somehow fit with the pain she was in, so Bernie was none the wiser.

Leo pulled one side of his mouth slightly upward and had a concerned expression on his face.

"Is it broken?" Holly asked, almost in tears. The pain in her hand sure made it feel like it.

"I don't know." He inspected her hand carefully.

"I'll go get ice," Bernie said, and ran off toward the RV.

Steward swore as the small bones in his nose were yanked back into position.

"I hope you learned your lesson; never mess with an angry woman," Jake said with a smirk.

Holly sucked her bottom lip in, trying hard to suppress the smile forming. When she looked at Leo, it was evident that he, too, was fighting the grin on his face.

He called Jake over for a second opinion at the same time Bernie returned with the ice pack.

"I think you should go home, Steward." Bernie didn't sound happy, not one bit.

"If you are going to yank back any broken bones in my hand

like you did with Steward's nose, you best stay away," Holly warned him.

The corners of Jake's mouth twitched slightly upward. He took Holly's hand in his warm ones, as gently as he could, and lifted it to the light to see better.

"Put the ice pack on it for a while. It should alleviate some of the pain for now. But it bruised pretty quickly, and it's swollen. To be on the safe side, I think you should go to the hospital."

"Damn it, Steward!" Holly cussed again, moving her hand, which was still lying gently in Jake's. Pain shot through it and up her arm again and she ground her teeth. She couldn't go to the hospital. She didn't have any insurance and paying for this would set her back in her plan to pay off her mom.

Damn it, Brandon!

Bernie led her back to the tent. "You know when you said you saw how this weekend was going to end? I didn't think for one minute you meant it, Holls."

Despite the pain, Holly burst out laughing at the same time a tear rolled down her cheek.

"That does looks bad," Bernie concurred.

"No shit. I don't have any insurance, Bernie. Paying for this means that my mom won't get her money for who knows how long."

"She'll understand. Do you have any with you now?"

Holly nodded. "But I don't have enough if it's going to mean surgery of some kind."

"We'll think of something."

"I don't want to go to the hospital."

Bernie smiled patiently. "You starting to sound like a kid, Holly. Hospitals help people who are in pain. You need to go check that hand out."

Holly snorted, pulling her mouth slightly upward. "Stupid, Steward."

"What happened?"

"He called me a bitch because I didn't want to go on a second date with him."

Bernie shook her head. "I should've never said it was okay for Leo to encourage him to take you out. I'm so sorry, Holls. In any case, I'm sure he's got the message now."

"I fucking hope so." Holly didn't even care anymore whether she cussed freely or not. Her hand throbbed with pain and made her feel as if she was going to pass out. Once they'd reached the tent, Bernie went to get a new ice pack for Holly's hand. The excitement outside had quieted down. Holly couldn't help but feel a little bad when she heard that Steward had left.

But why did he have to go and be so pushy?

When Bernie returned with the second ice pack, Leo and Jake followed her into the tent.

"How did it feel?" Leo wanted to know. He had a huge grin on his face, and his eyes seemed to twinkle with humor.

"At that moment, really good, but if I knew this was going to happen I would have thought twice."

"Are you planning on breaking any more noses?" Jake crouched in front of her, gesturing for her hand again.

"No, why?"

"Just thought that maybe I should show you how to throw a punch first."

Holly laughed softly, shaking her head. "There is no need. My hooligan days are over."

Leo laughed the hardest at that remark, since Holly used to tease him about his cage fighting days, calling it his 'hooligan phase'.

"Seriously, though, you need to go to the emergency room. This doesn't look good."

"Is it broken?" Holly asked, sounding like a broken record.

"Do I look like Superman?" Jake asked.

She caught his little joke, fast, but rolled her eyes. "Well, you seem like the expert around here. What do you think?"

"I think you should go to the emergency room."

More laughter erupted.

Jake gave her a chin lift, which made her stomach flip, got up and left their tent.

"I don't want to go to the emergency room."

"Holly it doesn't cost that much. And it won't kill you," Bernie remarked.

A remark that Holly didn't appreciate much. It wasn't what she wanted to hear. Hot tears welled up in her eyes and she swallowed hard. "Do you have a pain killer?"

"I do, but let me find out if you can have one, okay?"

"It's a pain killer, Bernie."

"I don't know what they're going to do to your hand at the emergency room, Holls. Some pain killers might interact with some other drug they want to give you. Just let me check."

Bernie scurried away but came back a couple of seconds later, followed by Jake once again who was now sporting a jacket. "Let's go, hooligan."

Holly's eyes felt as if they were going to pop out of their sockets. She was going to the ER with Jake and Sonic. She really wasn't up to this.

Bernie left her no room to protest as she shoved Holly's purse into her other hand, and then helped her into her jacket. It wasn't like it was cold or anything but who knew how long they would be at the ER?

Jake jumped into Leonard's SUV, while Holly opened the rear door and hopped up onto the back seat.

Jake turned around, giving her a funny look. "So now I look like a cab driver, too? I'm on a roll."

Holly felt a grin spread across her face.

"Come, sit up in front with me."

"Isn't Sonic coming with us?"

"Sonic isn't in pain, you are," he replied.

As that made perfect sense, she jumped out onto the grass and gingerly climbed in front with Jake.

"See you later. If it's serious, I'll phone," Jake told Leonard, who was leaning into the car on the driver's side window.

"Take care, Holls."

"Thanks," she mumbled, and Jake hit the gas.

"Why did you ask if Sonic was coming with?"

"You know." Holly felt this conversation was about to turn a bit awkward.

"No, I don't. That's why I'm asking you."

"Usually, girls don't let their guys go with girls they don't know to the ER."

Jake laughed. "Sonic isn't my girl. She's just a friend."

"Oh, really?" She sounded a bit sarcastic as it wasn't the message she got earlier from their constant flirting with one another.

"Yes. I'm not dating at the moment."

"Oh, sorry. I guess I just—"

"Assumed," he said, cutting in.

"I couldn't help making that assumption, okay? For all intents and purposes, she looked like your girlfriend."

Jake laughed again. "Yeah, I think she really wants to be, too. I wasn't sure about it, but you more or less cleared that up for me."

"You're welcome." Holly smiled and stared out into the darkness.

"I didn't thank you for that piece of information. But, I'm just not into her in that way."

"Excuse me... but why not? She's really beautiful."

"Looks aren't everything, and she's an airhead."

"Airhead?"

"Meaning, she doesn't use her brain, shakes what God gave her, and makes money wearing almost nothing."

"It's a living."

"One I'm so over," Jake said quietly.

Holly rested her chin on her chest, letting her hair form a soft curtain between her and Jake. Through the curls, she noticed that the green lights from the dash of Leo's SUV lit up his face softly. Holly didn't want to look at him, scared that she might drool or something.

"Then don't lead her on, Jake," Holly finished.

"Okay, Medusa, and I'm not leading her on."

"I'm not Medusa."

"You sure about that? Because you keep hissing at me. I didn't see a forked tongue, so it must be hiding in those curls of yours."

Holly laughed again. "Don't make me laugh, my hand seems to ache more when I laugh," she complained.

"Right. I'll keep quiet, then."

SOON, city lights twinkled in the distance shortly after silence fell between them, and by the hectic turns Jake made, Holly came to the conclusion that he really knew his way around the city.

As they went around a particularly harrowing corner, the P&E Emergency sign suddenly came into view like a beacon in the night. The hospital looked like a five star hotel, rather than what it was. Holly could feel how her stomach started to twist into knots. She was positive she didn't have the money to pay this kind of ER for their services.

Another twist of her stomach made her think back to the last time she'd been inside a hospital. It was the day Jamie died; she practically lived in one during that traumatic time in her life.

Holly took a deep breath as Jake drove around a huge water feature in front of the elite hospital, pulling into the parking lot in no time. He even did the gentlemanly thing and opened the door for her, the door squeaking softly as the hinges moved. She jumped out, landing on the smooth concrete and followed him inside. Her eyes grew wide as she took in its splendor.

"Are you sure this is a hospital?"

Jake laughed at her question, but didn't answer as he opened another door that led into the emergency waiting room.

"Another emergency, Jake?" The triage nurse behind the desk handed him a board with a paper attached to it.

Jake snorted, in a good way.

Then without waiting for the paperwork or even asking what the trouble was, the triage nurse buzzed the door open and said simply, "You two can go on into the ER."

For just a second, Holly glanced back at all the people waiting and wondered how Jake had managed to fast-track her inside. She followed Jake through the door. Inside, the staff all looked up as they entered and smiles quickly formed on every female's lips. Holly knew the feeling by now. Jake lit up a room whenever he entered one.

He took her to the nearest bed and gestured for her to hop on while he filled in the information sheet. She had to give him answers as to her birth date and social security number.

"So, how much is this five star service going to cost me?"

He grinned while looking at the board, which he was still completing.

"Nothing."

"Jake, you're not paying for this."

"No one is paying, Holly. It's free."

"This doesn't look like the 'free' kind of hospital."

"Don't worry, it's taken care of and it is free."

"What, you have access to freebies here?"

He grinned fully now. "Something like that." He continued to ask her boring questions, scribbling them down as he went along.

Holly couldn't stop looking around at all the occupied beds. An invisible weight pressed down on her chest; she felt herself begin to feel woozy. Finally, a doctor in his mid-forties came to her rescue. Upon seeing Jake, he too began grinning from ear to ear.

"Henry Scallanger," the doctor read off the chart.

"No, it's Holly," she corrected.

The doctor smiled at her. "Okay, Henry, what might be the problem?"

Frowning, she said once again, "It's Holly." She grabbed the chart out of his hand and saw Jake's handwriting. It was unreadable for a normal person, but lucky for her it was clear. She looked up at Jake. He had indeed written Henry. "How do *you* spell Holly?"

Both Jake and the doctor barked with laughter.

"What is the problem, Holly?" The attractive doctor wanted to know.

"I hit an idiot and no, it wasn't Jake. Another idiot." A twinkle was evident in her eyes.

This brought about more guffaws from the two men. The doctor picked up her hand, which now resembled the color of an eggplant. He watched carefully as he directed Holly to close and open her hand and then spread out her fingers. She complied gingerly. Lowering it after the quick inspection, he reached for a syringe and a small bottle of liquid.

"No one said anything about an injection. I don't do injections."

"It will help with the pain and swelling."

"I can't stand injections. Please," she started to beg, "can't you just give me a tablet or something?"

"Holly, are you scared of needles?" Jake asked.

She almost felt like crying. If only he knew how scared.

"It will be over before you know it," the doctor promised.

A single tear rolled down her cheek.

Jake took the doctor's place, directly in front of her. "I get that you are terrified when it comes to needles, but it will only help you with everything, Holly." He held her hand gently while he continued talking to her.

"It's going to burn and hurt like hell. I don't like injections." More tears started making their way down her face.

"It will hurt for a little while, that's true, but it's worth what you'll feel afterward. Trust me."

She felt a quick wet dab of alcohol on the back of her hand and then a burning sensation shooting through it at that precise moment. Biting down hard on her teeth, she burrowed her head in Jake's shoulder.

"It's over, Holly."

"But it's still sore." She couldn't help the whine.

"Give it a few minutes. It doesn't work instantly."

"For this kind of pain it darn well should," she moaned at the after-effect. It was still burning, a tiny bit, and for a person with a strong pain threshold, Holly didn't do so well with injections. They were the bane of her existence.

"You are such a drama queen," he said, while the doctor told him to take Holly to the X-ray room.

"I have an injection phobia. I'm sure there is a term for that; anti-hospital, or some such."

He was clearly laughing again when he pushed the door to radiology open for her.

"So, what's the deal with you and this place? Are you here on some sort of regular basis?" she queried.

"Something like that," he mumbled, one side of his mouth tilting upward with humor.

Leading the way, Jake walked past Holly, which had her running after him to keep up with his long confident strides. Her hand had started to feel slightly better, but not enough for her to forgive the distraction with the injections a couple of minutes ago. He knew he was good-looking; she just couldn't show him how much it bothered her, not like she had done back in the doctor's consultation room.

The woman behind the desk saw Jake and Holly a mile away, and a grin grew slowly on her lips.

"So, who do we have here, Jake?" she asked, tilting her head to one side.

"Working tonight, Agneta?"

"Baby, I'm always working. This is what nurses do," the short, African-American motherly nurse stated. She looked at the chart and then up quizzically. "Henry?" She looked at the chart once again, then at Holly, and then at Jake who had a huge smile plastered on his face.

"She don't look like no Henry to me, Jake."

"Agneta, you know how she gets. Please. Just say it was a Henry."

Holly raised an eyebrow at Jake.

"I'll explain later, just go," he practically shoed Holly away.

"All right, I'm going." She followed Agneta who continued to look at him skeptically.

"So, what happened, baby?"

"I hit an idiot." She looked down at the nurse. "And no, for the second time, it wasn't Jake."

Agneta laughed. "That boy is far from an idiot, but he sure is playing at death's door bringing you here."

"What's the deal with him and this place?" Holly asked as they entered a small room.

Agneta put a heavy, bulletproof-looking vest on Holly to protect her from radiation during the scan, and gently positioned her swollen hand on top of a big plastic cartridge. She aligned the head of the X-ray machine over both the hand and the cartridge.

"The P&E sign outside?" she said, and Holly nodded. "The P belongs to Jake's family," Agneta shared just before she ducked out of the room. The X-ray machine emitted a short beep as it snapped its picture and Agneta returned once more.

Holly looked stunned. "Really?"

"You didn't know that?"

"I just met the guy. He's good friends with my friends and offered to bring me in when I hit a really stupid guy. I normally don't do that kind of thing."

Agneta smiled cheekily. "You sure don't look like the bimbos he used bring in."

"No? I'm not an airhead, then," she stated more to herself than to Agneta, who was in the process of removing the cartridge in order to transfer it to another machine. "So, who is this person he's referring to?"

"His mother. She's one hell of a doctor but when it comes to her children, she's a bit crazy."

Holly's eyes crinkled at the corners. *Better a crazy mom, than no mom at all,* she thought. She cringed at that thought, though. Jane was really trying hard to reconnect with her, but she was being the hard head. Still, she should've never accepted that money from her for that stupid wedding.

Agneta looked at her with a tiny smile.

Holly started to feel slightly uncomfortable, what with those big brown eyes scanning the length of her body. "I just have to say *thank you.*"

"Why?" Holly sounded confused.

"He hasn't smiled this much in a long time."

Holly snorted, wondering where this was leading. She'd only just met him, but he didn't seem like the 'I'm-depressed-kind-of-guy'.

"All done," she uttered, first removing the heavy vest, and then taking her back through the maze of hallways to where they left Jake waiting.

"You take care now, honey bunch, but before you go, wait for the X-rays so we can find out what the next step will be."

"I'll do that, Agneta. Thank you so much, and you take care, too." She parted ways with the nurse who slipped behind the desk again to fill out yet more forms. She found Jake sitting patiently on the sofa in the waiting area.

"Henry?" Holly shook her head at him.

He just smiled.

"So what are you, some sort of a mamma's boy?"

He raised his eyebrows in question, but replied with a "No, I'm not." This was followed by a glare he directed toward Agneta. She wasn't paying attention in any case. "My mother is opposed to us having relationships during our studies. She regards studying as being essential, and believes that one should always give a hundred and fifty percent. My sister only got married last year, after she graduated."

"I get the picture, but what does this have to do with you helping someone?" Holly was genuinely curious.

Jake smirked. "I usually don't bring girls in, other than the ones I'm dating."

"Oh, I see. So you are basically scared that she would think I'm someone you're dating."

"I'm not scared of my mother."

Holly tilted her head to one side and said but one word, "Henry." Raising her eyes playfully at him, she added, "Sure you aren't."

This only made Jake chuckle.

A short silence followed this exchange, so Holly decided to say anything just to get rid of the zinging in her ear. "I take it you're studying at the moment?" she asked.

He gave her a huge frown, which inevitably turned into a small grin. "Yes, I am. In fact, I'm going to be working here soon."

"Oh, really. As what?"

"Who works at hospitals, Holly?"

"Well, lots of people do," she huffed, but looking at him with narrowed eyes she asked, somewhat surprised, "You're studying to be a doctor?"

"Is it so hard to believe? My entire family consists of doctors, so... yes. I'm just following in their footsteps."

"Good for you," she commented, making Jake laugh while simultaneously shaking his head.

Agneta returned with a huge, yellow envelope in her hands, as well as an unreadable face. Holly knew what the envelope held—her results from the scan.

"You guys sure are fast," she commented, stating the obvious.

"Not really. They're just scared that the boss' son is going to spill on them," Jake joked.

Agneta slapped him playfully. "We are quiet tonight but as is the case, I'm sure we will pick up around eleven o'clock when all the inebriated fools attempt to make their way home."

"Thanks, Agneta. Such a pleasure meeting you." Holly gave her a hug.

"Drive safely, Jake, and no more hitting guys, young lady," she said in parting.

Holly grinned sheepishly. "She's nice," Holly remarked as they walked out into the corridor they'd come through.

"I've known her for a long time. She can be quite feisty when she wants to be. She used to yell a lot for some reason when I was younger."

"I can't imagine why, Jake."

Jake chuckled, finding humor in her playful sarcasm.

Holly followed him into a small room, which was filled with boxes that were attached to the wall. He flipped a switch and bright lights illuminated every single one. Holly's heart bounced inside her chest as he pulled the X-rays out from the envelope, and then slid them onto the uppermost part of the lit up box. She closed her eyes and began to pray.

Please, don't let my hand be broken. I swear, I'll never do this again.

"So, do you want to hear the good news or the bad news first?"

"Is there any good news in these types of situations?"

His smile lit up his eyes, which made her knees wobble. She was suddenly thankful that she'd had the good sense to sit down.

"There is always good news."

"Fine. You're the soon-to-be doctor. Give me the bad news, then."

"It's going to hurt like hell for the next couple of days."

"Guess I'll have to live with that. And the good news?"

"Exactly what you've been hoping for. It's not broken, only cracked. You see that little line there?" he asked.

Holly hopped from the stool that she'd tried to make herself comfortable in, and took a closer look at where he was pointing. "That's a crack?"

"That's a crack. Luck was on your side."

"Thank you, thank you, thank you," she practically sang, which was followed by a small prayer to God.

"It will teach you that you either have to learn to throw a punch properly, or leave the beating for the guys."

"He deserved it, though," she mumbled.

Jake just shook his head. "Let's go back to the doctor. Best we make certain you're allowed to go back to work with that hand."

The doctor sighted them immediately as they returned to the bustling emergency room. He met them at the bed where they had started.

"I saw the read from the radiologist," the doctor started.

"Hairline Bar Room fracture in the fourth metacarpal?" Jake suggested.

The doctor's expression showed he was impressed. On the other hand, Holly swooned at the sound of Jake's medical jargon. It was so professional, and so damn hot.

"You were able to notice it? You're getting good. I'm glad I'm not in radiology or you'd have me worried about my job." The doctor gave a chuckle that sounded genuinely relieved.

"Are you right-handed?" the doctor asked Holly.

She nodded.

Without skipping a beat, he scribbled something on his prescription pad and passed it to Jake. Jake excused himself, saying that he would be back shortly.

"And you're working next week?"

She nodded again and the doctor scrawled a quick note.

"You need to give this to your employer. That hand needs to rest for at least two days. On Monday, call this number and make an appointment at the orthopedics clinic for Tuesday; you need a checkup. Take it easy, Henry."

Holly nearly choked on the laughter that bubbled to the surface. "I will, thank you." She barely managed to get those words out.

Jake wasn't gone long at all, and as she was done led her toward the exit.

"You guys don't hand out pain killers in this place?"

"Already taken care of, they're right here." He showed her an orange tube he'd put into the pocket of his jacket.

"They just better work," she mumbled.

"Okay, Medusa. You can relax those snakes now."

She merely smiled.

Inside the SUV, Jake gave her two of the small, white tablets, which she immediately placed in her mouth and swallowed.

"Take one now, and another one when you wake up."

"You couldn't have told me that prior to handing them to me?"

Jake gave her an odd look. "You swallowed them both?"

She nodded, looking pitiful.

"Holly, those things are really strong," he chuckled.

"My immune system is strong. Pain killers don't usually..." she trailed off, feeling warm and content and sleepy, and suddenly slumped sideways in the passenger seat. And that was the end of their conversation.

FIVE

WHEN SHE WOKE, it was dead silent. Her head still spun, but the aching in her hand was the worst. She started to cry. After what could have only been minutes, she found Bernie crouching beside her airbed.

"You okay?"

"My hand is killing me!"

"Here, take one," Bernie suggested, picking up the same orange tube Jake had given her before she blacked out.

Holly took the tablet from Bernie, swallowing it without any water.

"I don't know how you can do that," Bernie commented, shaking her head.

"What happened? The last thing I remember was driving back here from the hospital."

"You passed out from taking two of these beauts. This shit is really potent, Holls."

Holly emitted a loud snort. "Yeah, that sounds just like me."

Bernie giggled. "How are you, really?"

"They booked me off for two days. Marabella is going to love this."

"Marabella will understand, once you explain to her what you did."

"I beg to differ."

"You stood up for yourself, Holly. That woman is all for self-defense; karate, judo, you name it!"

Holly agreed. Marabella was that type of woman, one who believed that women had just as much of a say as men did. Perhaps Bernie was right, and she really would understand.

The tablet had begun to do its job. This was clearly evident when Holly fell back onto her pillow.

"Just yell if you need anything," Bernie whispered in her ear, leaving her friend to rest.

BIRDS CHIRPING woke Holly for the second time that day, and deciding to get up went after a quick shower. The water felt refreshing as the tiny droplets ran over her aching body, which was probably due to having slept so much and most likely in the same position. She slipped into her sweat pants and a tank top, rolling her hair into a messy bun. As she walked out of the public restroom, she looked up at the sky. It was around five o'clock, too early for anyone to be awake yet, but she knew Josie would be.

Having reached Josie's campsite, she found George sitting on one of the camp chairs with a cup of coffee next to him on a small portable table, and his laptop opened and perched on his lap. George worked for an international company, so having meetings via Skype on a daily basis with people all over the world was the norm.

"Hey," she greeted when she finally reached him.

He looked up and smiled, but it soon disappeared when he saw the bandage around her hand. "What happened?"

"I hit a stupid guy."

He laughed, throwing his head back. "Did you at least break his nose?"

"Yes," she giggled. She was actually very proud that she'd done what she had intended to do. And then the darn guilt rose up again when she thought about how it all could've all gone horrible wrong. What if it had shifted up and spiked into his brain? She'd heard about noses being broken that way, with the person ending up brain dead. It had been a stupid thing to do and she should've apologized to him.

"Holly, don't overthink it. The guy deserved it, otherwise you wouldn't have hit him in the first place."

She smiled. They knew her so well.

Josie emerged from the tent, hair standing on end and pointing in every direction. "Hey you! You're up early." On noticing Holly's hand, she freaked. "What happened?"

"I hit Steward. And I broke his nose."

"Holly," she said, a tinge of pity evident in her tone. "Did you go to the ER?"

An almost uncontrollable grin broke out on her face. "I did, and Jake took me."

Josie laughed. "I told you he was a heart-throb. If I wasn't married—"

"Okay, we get it. You would do things to him that I could only dream of."

"That's not true. I do them all with you, my big toothpick," she teased, leaning over and kissing George loudly.

"Too much, people. Still angry over here," Holly cautioned, pointing at herself.

"Still?" Josie asked with an incredulous 'huh' look on her face.

Holly just chuckled.

George got up and poured both Josie and Holly a cup of coffee.

"So, did you guys chat? What does he do?"

"He's studying to become a doctor. Did you know that?"

"Seriously?"

Holly nodded.

"Could that man be any more perfect?"

"He's not. His mom is apparently crazy when it comes to him."

Josie's expression dropped from the daydream smile that had been plastered on it, to the 'surely you jest' kind of look. "You're kidding?" she finally managed to say.

"Nope. He put my name down as Henry on the hospital form, just so his mom wouldn't find out that he'd taken a female there for treatment."

"Henry?" Josie could not contain her laughter.

Holly went ahead and recounted the entire story of how they kept calling her Henry. She had to admit that Jake hadn't known where to look or how to act, but she was really digging the guy and looked at him the way she had before she'd assumed that Sonic was his girlfriend.

At around nine o'clock, everyone began to wake up; it was coffees all around. Holly met a couple of Josie's friends, whom she'd never met before even though she'd been with Brandon. Every single one congratulated her for leaving his ass, adding that someone better would come along.

An hour later, breakfast was on the grill. The smell was divine, but Holly knew she needed to head back to Bernie's. However, Josie talked her into staying and having breakfast with them.

This went on until noon when a familiar ache told Holly that her pain medication had worn off. When she mentioned it to George, he said that he had something even better for her pain. He got a bottle of South-African *mampoer*, a name she couldn't pronounce, which brought about bouts of laughter when George kept repeating it and she kept getting wrong. However, the contents of the bottle were no laughing matter. It was really strong and went straight to Holly's head. She'd had about four shots and was feeling dizzy but not the bad dizzy Jake's medicine had left her with, this was a good dizzy.

Everyone started to whistle when Josie began chatting about her fantasy.

Holly attempted to get a clear picture of how Josie perceived Jake, but it was hard.

"C'mon, Holls, you can do it."

"Do what?" Holly shrieked.

"Kiss the living crap out of him. He doesn't have a girlfriend."

"No, that is your fantasy."

"It's yours, too! No fibbing."

"Okay, fine, it's mine, too. But I'm not going to admit it."

They all cracked up again at Holly's reply. She just rolled her eyes with a huge grin plastered on to her face.

"Do it, Holls, take one for the team." The girls began to chant, "Do it, do it, do it!"

"Okay, I'll do it."

"Woohoo!" Josie clapped her hands excitedly and cheered.

A fifth round of *mampoer* came around, and one by one the girls passed out. Josie stumbled to her bed and collapsed. Holly had to admit that her head spun faster and faster and she felt as if she needed some air, even though they were outside.

"Let's get you back to Bernie's," George suggested, throwing Holly over his shoulder.

"I can walk," she slurred.

"No, you can't. You'll pass out before you get there."

It seemed like the trip back was taking ages, so Holly sang

all the way in her precarious position hanging down George's back. He chuckled at some of her words, singing along to some verses he knew.

"What the fuck?" Bernie shouted, when she saw them.

"Sorry, Bernie," George apologized.

"She's drunk."

"I'm not drunk." Holly lifted her body as best she could, turning her head in Bernie's direction.

Bernie looked at her, not at all impressed. "You are drunk."

Holly giggled.

"She had a good time, Bernie."

"Your wife is a bad influence, George."

"I know, that's why I love her so much."

Bernie shook her head, but couldn't prevent grinning. "Put the alcoholic down."

"I'm not sure if she can walk."

Swatting George on his head, Holly slurred, "I can walk. Plus, I still need to do that favor for Josie."

George's shoulders vibrated with apparent laughter. "This, I've got to see."

"What favor?" Bernie was doing the hands-on-hips, what-are-you-on-about stance.

When George finally placed Holly down gently, she inhaled deeply as her head still seemed to be spinning. He caught her as she started to sway backward.

"I... am... fine." Holly managed to make those three words seem like a whole sentence, it took that long to say.

"Like hell you are," muttered Bernie.

Holly ignored that comment and instead made her way toward Leonard and Jake on wobbly legs. But when she saw him sitting with a beer on the step of his RV, a picture of her leaping on him and falling off before she could kiss him played like a movie in her fuzzy head. She snorted—in a very unladylike manner—and walked back toward her friends, not even attempting to walk anything resembling a straight line.

"Nah, it's not my fantasy." She looked at George who was trying his damnedest to cover his smile.

"Coward."

"Whatever," she mumbled while stumbling to her tent.

"One hour, Holly, and then I'm going to wake you up," Bernie yelled.

Holly pulled a face, mimicking Bernie, and collapsed onto her air bed. The world spun and she felt like throwing up, but thankfully that didn't happen. A couple of seconds later, followed by a few good spins, she fell asleep.

"GO AWAY. You had her the entire day." Bernie's voice pierced Holly's ears.

She opened her eyes, everything was still spinning. Closing them again, she breathed in deeply trying to settle herself. She could hear Bernie and Josie speaking softly, but couldn't quite make out what they were saying. Hell, if she were honest right about then, she didn't really care.

Out of nowhere, Josie gave her overpowering shrill laugh. "You coward!" she yelled into the tent.

Bernie would probably ask Josie what was going on, and Josie would tell her for sure. And that's exactly what must have taken place, because a minute into their continued whispering, Bernie burst out laughing.

"Wake up, coward." Josie kicked her air bed.

Holly growled. "Leave me alone."

"I'm not leaving you alone, we had a deal."

"It's your fantasy, not mine."

"Whatever, Holly. Get up, or else I'm going to ask Bernie to throw water on you."

"Do what you want, just leave me alone."

The girls apparently thought this was extremely hilarious.

Not five minutes later, Holly was soaking wet, drowned in ice-cold water. Gasping for air, she felt her body jerk back to life. "You bitch!" she screamed like a banshee.

"Josie did warn you, Holls," said Bernie, a satisfied look on her face.

Gasping, she reasoned, "B-b-but, I didn't think she meant it, and I didn't believe you'd do it!"

"Well, I did. Get. Your. Ass. Out. Of. Bed!"

"Coward, coward, coward," Josie sang.

She could honestly be such a pain sometimes.

"If you want it to happen so badly, why don't *you* go kiss him?"

"I'm married, so I can't. And I do have morals, I'll have you know."

Holly could in no way be upset with these two, so just ended up shaking her head and smiling.

"I'm not going to live out your fantasy. Poor guy, in the state I was in, he would have probably ended up in the ER himself."

With all three giggling, it was quite a sight to behold.

"I'll give you five minutes to get out of this tent, or else I'm sending Jake in." Bernie's finger was in Holly's face now.

"Fine, you win," Holly stuck her tongue out. "Just let me put on another shirt. This one is soaking wet."

"Leave it on. It looks like you've just taken part in a wet T-shirt contest. The boys will love it."

"My boobs are seriously not wet T-shirt competition worthy."

"Holly, you can always make them bigger."

"No, thanks. There is a reason why they are so small. I'm not going to tamper with that."

"Four minutes, Holly, and counting." Bernie wiggled her eyebrows and exited the tent.

Without wasting another second, Holly got up and started looking for a shirt in her bag. It would be just her luck if Jake walked into her tent after three and a half minutes, asking her what she wanted.

Sometimes, her friends annoyed the crap out of her, but they both had good hearts and would always have her back, no matter what. She found a black shirt, one that went well with her mood and slumped out of the tent. The sun was beginning to set, but the light still hurt her sensitive eyes.

"Over here, you coward," Josie yelled from the direction of Jake's RV.

She would kill her if she'd told him what she'd planned to do a couple of hours ago. She took a seat on a camp chair next to Bernie and promptly closed her eyes. It felt as if someone had blown sand into them.

"Holly, why are you a coward?" Leo asked.

"Josie is the coward, and a permanent pain in my ass."

"Whatever, coward." Josie kicked Holly's chair, and it almost collapsed. She managed to keep it upright, but just barely.

"Your balance is good, for someone who is drunk," Jake commented.

"I'm not drunk."

"Holly, you sang, upside down of all things, when George brought you back. You were out of your rocker." Bernie said.

Holly laughed. "Okay, a tiny bit, maybe."

"You sang!" Josie shrieked.

"Oh, shut up, already." *Please, God, make them stop.*

Josie started to sing Holly's drunken song, and was quickly joined by Leo and Bernie who sang right along with her.

Jake's shoulders shook with humor.

Holly looked at Josie. "Something is wrong with you, seriously. You should get your head checked out." Suddenly, Holly gasped. "Maybe Jake can check it out for you. I'm sure if he tweaked some things up there, you would finally be somewhat normal."

A fair amount of sniggering and giggles followed this statement.

"Jake can tweak my head, anytime," Josie flirted.

"Ugh! That sounds so disgusting coming from your mouth," Holly mumbled.

"Am I missing something here?" Jake had a puzzled look on his face.

"No, trust me, you're not. Go home, Josie."

"Fine, but you are still a coward."

"Go home!"

Josie winked at her, then made her way back to her camp. "Coward," she couldn't help but part with.

"So, why are you a coward, Holly?" Leo asked again.

"That is our secret. You guys are keeping a secret from me, so deal with it," Bernie answered for Holly.

"That must really be killing you." Holly looked at Bernie with a mischievous grin.

"Ha-ha. Be nice, or I'll tell."

"Tell. It's not my fantasy."

"Seriously?"

"Yeah, go ahead."

"What fantasy?" Jake piped up.

"Josie has some pretty crazy fantasies. Ones that George can't fulfill." Everyone found this pretty funny. "She's mental, really, a few steps away from the nut house."

"What did you have to drink?"

"Something I still for the life of me cannot pronounce. That stuff burned all the way down. It lit up all my organs, even in places I didn't know organs resided."

"Well, you should really sober up because we're going to do shooters tonight," Bernie said excitedly.

"If I smell any more alcohol, I will puke."

Jake stood and left. Bernie looked at him for a while. Her gaze soon affixed itself on Holly, who was also staring at his back as he walked into his RV.

Bernie sighed. "You are a coward, Holls."

"Shut up. I'm getting tired of that damn word."

He walked back out just as quickly as he'd entered, and making his way to Holly handed her a Coke. "Drink this."

"I don't drink Coke."

"You want to feel better? It will help."

"Is that a doctor thing?"

"No it's a general knowledge thing." He smiled.

"Fine." She opened the can and the bubbles prickled her lips before the cool liquid tingled her tongue. The sweet taste felt good, and she finished the entire can in seconds. As soon as she was done, everyone looked at her disbelievingly. "What? I was thirsty."

"Don't drink Coke, my ass. For someone who doesn't drink Coke, you sure poured that down your throat in record time." This was the first time Sonic had spoken to someone other than Jake.

"She seriously doesn't drink Coke." Bernie, good friend that she was, rushed to her defense.

"Uh-huh," Sonic mumbled.

Holly knew that Bern was going to have a fit as she disliked anyone who answered in that manner.

"Ignore it, please," Holly murmured softly to Bernie.

"So, Sonic. How long have you been back in Jake's life?"

"Bernie..." Leo warned, and Holly sighed.

"What? I'm just asking her a question."

"About two months, and it's got absolutely nothing whatsoever to do with you."

"Uh-huh," Bernie mocked with a raised lip.

Holly kept a straight face.

Sonic got up and stomped into the RV.

"Was that really necessary?" Leo asked.

"Leave it, Leo. Bernie's got a point," Jake said.

"Thank you, Jake, just as long as you remember that."

Jake only smiled. "Did you really think I would go for someone like Sonic?"

"Jake, I love you like a brother, but you are still a guy. And that in there, is a piece of ass."

Holly was riveted to their exchange.

"Can we please not speak about this kind of stuff around Medusa?"

Holly was thankful she'd finished the Coke before his comment or she would have, without a doubt, spewed it all over herself from laughing so much. "I'm not Medusa."

"Well, you hiss."

Bernie and Leo exchanged grins.

"I hiss, because I'm fucking tired and my hand fucking aches. Speaking of which, I'm almost positive I'm not going to be able to convince you to give me a painkiller due to the fact that I have more alcohol flowing through these veins than any human probably should. I'm also pretty sure that if I tried to swallow one of those fire pills, I would explode. I hope that sums it up for you." Narrowing her eyes, she looked at Jake.

Bernie, Leo and Jake couldn't for the life of them contain the laughter that erupted.

"I don't ever recall hearing you swear that much, ever," Bernie stated with a fake, shocked look on her face.

"Zip it. You're the reason for my foul mood."

"I think it's shooter time, so you zip it and go pour us a few." Bernie cocked an eyebrow.

"That's why you woke me up?"

"You are the only one who knows how to concoct an entire list of shooters, Holls. Why do you think I brought you along?"

"You're evil, and you have the audacity to call yourself my friend."

"I do, because you love me to bits."

"Yeah? And how do you suppose I'm going to prepare the shooters, Einstein?"

"Ask Sonic, it will give Jake a couple of minutes away from her."

Jake snorted. "Yeah, ask Sonic, please. I'm begging you."

"Why did you bring her?" Holly asked on a whisper.

"It's a secret," Bernie whispered back, sounding really sarcastic.

Clucking her tongue, Holly teased her, "It must be so hard."

"Shut up. Shooters, now."

"Fine." Holly got up. "I don't think Sonic likes me very much after Bernie's really mocking lesson. Could you please ask her if she would like to help me?" Holly asked Jake.

"Sonic!" Jake yelled.

"Seriously, you couldn't get up to ask her?"

"Yes?" Sonic's head popped out the doorway.

Pathetic, Holly thought.

Jake's shoulders shook, as if he'd heard Holly's thought.

"Would you help Holly prepare some shooters, please?" He gave her his super smile, the one Holly didn't want to look at because it would make her turn into a pile of goo.

"Sure, come." Sonic gestured to Holly to join her in the RV.

They spent the next couple of hours preparing shooters, managing to remain relatively civil to each other. Jake sauntered in from time to time, usually as they were close to finishing up and flirted with Sonic. She handed him a shooter; both threw their heads back at the same time on numerous occasions, letting the mixture trickle down their throats. Holly felt like she was intruding on their moment and walked out.

"Not want her, my ass," Holly ground out, irritated after the umpteenth time it happened.

"He's really not into Sonic, Holls," Leo spoke quietly next to her.

"Whatever."

The night went on and all she wanted was to go to bed, but again Bernie wouldn't let her.

Holly started a countdown to Jake's eventual appearance just as they finished pouring another shooter, and just as she'd predicted he walked in and had an extra one with Sonic.

"You want to make me drunk?"

"Sure I do," Jake replied.

Holly left the RV. All she had had to do was look at Leonard to set him off bursting into laughter.

"He's not," Leo mumbled.

"Let's bet. I say he's going to grab her before the night is over," Holly challenged Leo.

"How much?"

"A hundred dollars. Deal?"

"Deal."

A couple of rounds later, Jake's gaze didn't waver from Sonic, who really didn't look like she could handle one more shot. "I think it's time you go to bed, missy." He pulled her up gently and helped her to the tent situated directly in front of the RV. He ducked, lifted the green canvas flap and ushered them both inside.

Holly watched this turn of events with eagle eyes.

"Pay up, loser."

"He's not going to do it."

"Oh, please. What do you think they're doing in that tent?"

"Holly's got a point. You lost."

"I didn't lose."

Just then, Jake re-emerged.

"That was fast," Holly smirked.

"What was?"

She merely scrunched up her face in reply.

"I told you I'm not interested in Sonic. I just never thought she could drink that much."

"Pay up, loser." Leo was sporting the hugest grin ever, as well as having a hand on his forehead, thumb in the horizontal position and index finger in the vertical; the universal sign for loser.

Jake turned and looked at Holly. "You bet on this? You're mean."

"So, sue me. There were a few times I had to get out of there. Your RV isn't big enough for all that love."

"Oh, please. I just gave her a shooter, woman."

"Pay up," Leo cut in, snapping his fingers.

"There's a hundred in my purse. I'll get it for you later."

"A hundred bucks? At least I'm not considered a cheap bet."

"Oh, shut it. You were supposed to grab her."

"I...don't...want...her," Jake said, slowly enunciating every word.

"Uh-huh," Holly replied.

"Don't say that. Only stupid people say 'Uh-huh'.

"Uh-huh," Holly repeated, looking at Bernie. Of course, all she was doing was mimicking her.

"Ugh. Go make shooters."

"I can't, you guys just poisoned my assistant."

"Take Jake."

"Now *I* have to make the shooters?"

"You poisoned Sonic. Entirely your fault, now go."

"Yes, ma'am," he grumbled.

"Do you even know how to pour one?" Holly asked, tongue in cheek.

"Sure I do. I've watched Cocktail. Can't be that hard to figure out." With a wink thrown in Bernie's and Leo's direction, Jake moved toward the RV. "Let's go, Medusa! Shooters wait for no man, or woman, as the case may be."

Holly sighed while simultaneously rolling her eyes. "This is going to take a long time."

"I'm sure it will," Leo agreed, adding his two cents.

"What do you want this time, Your Highness?"

"A Jelly Baby."

"Seriously? It's his first shooter."

"Holly, is it going to be today?" Jake yelled from the RV.

"Keep your pants on, I'll be right there."

Leo roared with laughter as Jake mumbled something from the RV.

"What is with you?" She looked at Leo, not the least bit impressed with him.

"Nothing, just go."

"I can't promise it will look like what you are expecting," Holly warned as she walked up the RV's steps. Jake had already put the shot glasses out.

"I'll have one, too. This is my favorite," she smiled at Jake.

"What is it?"

"It's called a Jelly Baby."

Jake looked at her quizzically, but Holly knew he was faking it. For someone who could drink as he had and still stand on both feet, sound and sober, she knew he'd had them before.

"The one with layers," she explained, arranging the different bottles of liquor she'd need for it.

"We have to pour all of them in one glass?"

"You've had shots before, and I know you know what a Jelly Baby is."

"I drink neat shots, not fancy ones."

Holly giggled. "Right. So, pick up the spoon and hold it like this," she said, showing him how it was done.

Jake got it right the first time. It was perfect.

"Hmm, maybe I can work with this," she whispered.

Jake was none the wiser.

SIX

THE JELLY BABY shot had indeed been great, for an assistant who had apparently never prepared one before. Bernie had been excited when she saw them, and happy that Holly had taken one, too.

Holly had silently thanked the heavens that Bernie hadn't requested another immediately thereafter. She was tired of preparing shots, even if it had meant spending time with her yummy new assistant.

"So, can I ask you a question?" Holly looked at Jake.

"Is it Sonic related?"

"No."

"Then, shoot."

"How on earth did a hooligan and a doctor become friends?"

The laughter that followed was roaring loud. Holly had clearly missed something, but when she noticed tears streaming down Leo's face, she put two and two together.

"You were into cage fighting, too. You hooligan," she teased Jake.

"Now that was a long time ago."

"That used to be the shit," Leo said defensively.

"What, beating people up?" Holly asked.

"Never had the time to beat them up," Jake explained. "It took a mere round or two to knock them out, stone-cold."

"Always?" she looked at Jake.

"No, not always."

"How did your mom feel about that?"

He chuckled. "Didn't like it one bit."

"I'll bet," she said. "Why did you stop?"

Leo gave Jake a concerned look, which in turn made Holly feel like crap.

"You don't need to answer. Forget I asked..."

"Why not? It's fine. I got badly injured. So badly that the doctor told me I'd never walk again."

Holly could feel this was a very sensitive topic and she wanted to kick herself for bringing it up.

"But thanks to Leo and Bernie, I'm walking again."

"Seriously?" She looked at Bernie.

"I'm a good friend," Bernie sang.

Holly chortled. "Yeah, you're okay."

"And that's when you became a doctor," Leo stated.

"Yeah, there are more important things to live for."

"Like a married woman."

Bernie, Holly and even Jake gasped.

"Thanks, Leo." Jake was none too pleased about that faux pas.

"Sorry dude, it slipped out."

"I knew it would come out when the shooters started flowing." Bernie looked at Leo and sniggered, "You, my angel, can't keep a secret."

"Shut up." He sounded really upset, but then Jake started to laugh.

"You're a home-wrecker, too?" Holly asked him, incredulously.

"Not in the least. I didn't do a damn thing."

"That's the reason we haven't seen you for the past three months," Bernie asked.

"It was hard, okay?" He looked at Bernie.

"Jake, we help each other, always have."

"I know, and I'm sorry I didn't come to you guys."

"Do we know her?"

Holly knew that once the secret was out, Bernie would interrogate them.

"No, you don't," Jake replied, quickly.

"I can't believe you didn't come to us."

"Seriously, you had me to deal with. I really wouldn't have liked it if Jake was there, too," Holly joked.

Jake looked at Holly with a comical expression.

"See? I just had a feeling you already had a sad situation at your place."

"Oh, can it." Holly wished she could have slapped him with her left hand.

"I'm dead serious," Bernie told him, after she got her laughter under control. "You should have come to us."

"I know. I should've."

"Sorry, dude," Leo mumbled.

"Don't worry about it, Leo." Jake was sporting a huge grin.

"What happened? You guys have an affair?" This from Holly.

"No. I don't even think she knew I existed," Jake answered."

"That's boring," Holly stated.

"They said their vows before God, Holly. You think I would break that?"

"To be honest, I don't know you that well, Jake. But that's very moral of you," Holly finished.

One of Jake's eyebrows shot up.

"What? It is. Just think, if everyone had Jake's morals there might not be any Donnas."

"No. Because then there would've been a Molly, or a Sarah, or..." Bernie trailed off, anger lining her voice.

Holly thought over her words. "True."

"Brandon was a dick, Holly. You need to see that," Leo said.

"I did. Why do you think I left him?"

"Then it needs to sink in," Bernie said, adding her two cents worth.

"That takes time. But I'm sure it eventually will."

"It needs to sink in faster," Bernie practically growled.

"Rome wasn't built in a day, okay? I'm getting there."

"Time for another shooter!" Leo clapped his hands together, breaking the tension.

"Sure. What would you like?"

"Something with Sambuca, please."

Holly got up. "You coming, home-wrecker, or am I going to do this by myself?"

At least Jake was finding humor in this situation, because he grinned in her direction. However, he could deal as well as he got.

"I wasn't a home-wrecker, and for that you can do the prep work yourself. Call me when it's time to pour."

Holly could hear Bernie speaking to Jake the minute she entered the RV. She knew there was something odd about Jake, but couldn't quite put her finger on it.

No man is that perfect, and to think he's the male version of Donna! Did he really not interfere the way Donna had? Her thoughts were running rampant. That was definitely the question of the day.

She arranged the shot glasses neatly in a row, but as she turned around one of the Sambuca bottles went skittering toward the floor. Holly tried to save it with her good hand, her legs and basically every body part she could in order to soften the bottle's landing, but it shattered and the bright blue liquid spread quickly across the RV's floor.

"Shit!" she shrieked, scrambling to clean up the mess.

"What are you doing?" Jake came in after he heard her scream. "I told you to call me when it was time to pour."

"It wasn't. I knocked it over by mistake." Angrily, she crouched to pick up the pieces of glass, while Jake ran to the cabinet where the dishcloths were kept. He got to work soaking up some of the liquid. Holly watched as it began to turn a dirty blue.

"Oh, shit. This is going to stain the floor."

"My mom's going to kill me."

"I'm so sorry, Jake." Holly felt like crap.

Jake chuckled, instead. "I'm just kidding, she won't mind."

"You idiot," she yelled.

Truth be told, she desperately wanted to smack him with her left hand but after giving it some thought, realized he was pure muscle and didn't want to break her other hand in the process. Forcing herself to calm down, she gingerly showed him the bits of glass she had picked up and asked him where she should put them. He gestured with his head to where the bin was located.

Once she'd disposed of the sharp pieces, she said, "Go, I'll clean up the rest."

"It's no problem. More hands make light work."

"This is my mess."

"Breakage, Holls," Leo yelled from outside.

"Yeah, yeah," she yelled back. "I'll replace it later!"

She could tell from both Leo's and Bernie's chuckling, how easily it was to entertain them.

Holly picked up some of the smaller pieces she'd noticed

shining in what little blue liquid still remained on the floor. If she'd had the use of her now injured hand, the clean-up would have gone a lot quicker.

Jake was at the stainless steel sink, rinsing the cloth. That was followed by more crouching and yet more cleaning. Holly could only watch helplessly when he mopped up what was left after they'd made sure no further glass fragments remained. However, to lighten mood, she joked about wanting to lick the rest up with her tongue.

Jake barked with laugher, shaking his head as he looked at her. "You sure Josie isn't the only one that needs a few tweaks?"

"No. Believe me, Josie is bad. She needs it more than me."

With a big smile on her face she crouched down, pointing at a tiny bit of Sambuca Jake missed. Jake, too, crouched but twisted around her to pick something up. It was a large piece of glass neither had seen. He moved back and stopped, his face inches from Holly's. They stared at one another intensely for a few seconds, barely breathing.

Jake exhaled, long and hard, and the next thing she knew, he'd pulled on her T-shirt and slammed her into him while he kissed the living crap out of her.

Somewhere in the distance, Holly heard the piece of glass fall to the floor before she was pulled up onto her feet and pushed against the wall. Jake's kissing started to make her ears zing as their tongues danced love steps inside each other's mouths.

Ironically, her mind brought up the conversation regarding the married woman. Somehow, she managed to pull away, hard as it was.

With her eyes still closed, she barely whispered, "I can't and won't do one night stands."

"You're not a one night stand, Holly," he uttered softly, claiming her lips once again.

Holly knew she wouldn't be able to pull away again, so simply succumbed and enjoyed the dizzy feelings kissing this heart-throb, home-wrecker, and hooligan were giving her.

"Are you guys making the alcohol?" Bernie's voice came at them from inside the RV, forcing them to break their kiss while laughing.

"Does she not have a pause button?" Jake asked softly into Holly's neck, which made her body break out in a million goose bumps.

"Unfortunately not," she snorted. Best we pour the Sambuca and get going. Luckily, you have another bottle. Blue, red, who cares, right?"

Winking, Jake turned away from her, rearranged the shot glasses on the table and opened the Sambuca, pouring the red liquid cocktail-style over each shot. Red Sambuca spilled everywhere, but the shot glasses were finally filled.

Holly had watched the entire 'operation' with a lopsided grin.

When Jake looked up, he pointed the bottle at Holly, saying, "Told you I watched Cocktail."

"Jake, look what you've done. You'd never say we just cleaned the floor and counter," she groaned, all the while looking at him with a smirk.

"So what. We can clean it again."

Holly's heart sped up, and her legs trembled slightly. She knew exactly what kind of cleaning Jake had in mind. "Go. Give them the Sambuca. And stay there. I'll clean up." *I sound almost robotic!*

He merely shrugged and walked out, but not before she saw the mischievous glint in his eyes.

"Finally! What on earth took you so long?" Bernie yelled. Clearly, she had way too much alcohol in her system.

"We had to clean up," Jake explained.

"Red Sambuca? What, there was no time after cleaning up to prepare a proper shooter?" Leo asked.

Next thing Holly heard was from Jake.

"Drink, or you can bloody well go make your own next time."

She quickly cleaned the counter and almost floated out of the RV. "Don't smile," she said to herself softly. Bernie knew her extremely well, and Holly knew that what had just happened would be written all over her face.

"What took you so long?"

"Jake was acting like Tom Cruise, but has nowhere near his skills."

"Well, I'm sure Tom Cruise doesn't have my skills, either. Not even close."

"He could, if he got a role as a doctor. I would be shocked if he hasn't already played one."

Jake only grunted at their verbal exchange, taking a sip of his beer. "Yeah, that's called *faking it*."

Holly looked at Bernie, noticing that her friend had started to contemplate her next shooter.

"Seriously, woman, haven't you had enough?"

"No. I want a shooter."

"Fine. I'll pour you one and you'd better drink it."

"Whatever, baby."

"This will be your last one. I'm not cut out for Cocktail shit," Holly grumbled, already walking up the RV's steps.

"Wait up, before you break another bottle," Jake yelled to her back as he followed her inside.

As soon as they'd cleared the doorway, he pulled her into the corner and they started kissing. Not two minutes in, her ears started zinging again. What was it with this guy and his kisses? She could kiss him forever. Holly only hoped that the feeling was mutual, and not just the alcohol flowing thickly in his veins.

As if reading her mind, his hands slid down her butt and when they reached her thighs, she was lifted up. Of their own accord, her legs wrapped around his waist. She felt herself being pushed back against the wall, hard. Her hands became tangled in his hair as their kissing turned frantic and more demanding. She breathed through her nose rapidly, her heart rate elevated, and the butterflies in her stomach felt as if they were going to burst free. She'd never felt like this before, not even when Brandon had kissed her for the first time. This was like an out-of-body experience; something she just didn't have the words to explain.

His rigid shaft pressed hard against her core, making her moan softly through their kissing. One thought stuck in her mind during the euphoria she was experiencing. *Should I go all the way tonight? Can I? Hell, yes, I can and I will,* her mind screamed eagerly, without giving it further thought. Holly decided she would become the slut in those movies where the couples had sex on their first date, even though she'd always hated those kinds of girls.

"I want my shooter," Bernie yelled once again, bringing their intense moment to a halt.

Jake chuckled, while Holly complained.

"Just make her something strong so she passes out, please," Jake begged.

Holly inhaled deeply, struggling to settle down. "I'll hit her with a baseball bat if she doesn't stop with this."

Jake grinned, kissing her softly on the tip of her nose before putting her down.

Begrudgingly, Holly poured half the shot glass intended for Bernie with Stroh Rum and the other half with black Sambuca. The color changed to black, making it look like it was only black Sambuca. She filled the other shots glasses with only the black. Jake merely winked. He arranged the drinks on the shooter tray in such a manner so that he wouldn't accidentally hand Bernie's shot to one of them.

"Enjoy," Holly sang to a giggling Bernie.

"You're making boring shots now?"

"I'm tired, and my hand is tired. Deal with it," Holly said as she watched Bernie down hers.

Holly kept an eagle eye on Bernie, and it became quite apparent the second the rum started to do its job and work through her system. She began closing her eyes for brief periods of time, as if she were trying hard to stay awake.

"Another one, Bernie?" Holly asked.

"No, thanks. I think I've had enough. I'm going to lie down." She looked at Leo who winked at her.

"So, does this mean I can finally sleep?" Holly yelled after Bernie.

"Do whatever you want. Sleep, grab Jake, I don't care."

"You stupid cow," Holly said, which made both Leo and Jake chortle in unison.

"*That* was what you wanted to do this afternoon?" Leo asked.

"Josie put me up to it," Holly answered. "It's her fantasy."

Jake cleared his throat.

"Oh, shush." Holly shot him a look.

Leo did nothing but look from one to the other. "Uh-huh," Leo said and got up. "Who knows, maybe I'll get lucky tonight, too."

"Seriously!" Holly hissed, looking at Jake, while Leo wandered off to join Bernie.

Jake's face lit up in a broad smile. "What? Leo is one of my best friends, believe me, he already knows."

As soon as they were alone, Jake wasted no time in pulling her closer by grabbing her shirt again. Their lips met and before

Holly could count to ten her ears had started to zing again. Through the tongue duel taking place, Jake lifted and placed Holly on his lap. Her body turned to mush as she let herself go, loving every moment of getting lost on top of him.

SEVEN

HOLLY HAD no idea how long they'd kissed for; she only knew that she didn't want it to stop. Their breathing escalated, and both had a reluctant hunger that clawed within them. She'd never thought that she would feel this way ever again, and silently prayed that by morning things wouldn't be awkward.

She really liked Jake and had fallen hard for him, like a wrecking ball crashing into a skyscraper. If he would... No, she couldn't think about that now, she would deal with it tomorrow and enjoy whatever it was that was happening between them that very moment.

They finally broke apart, struggling to catch their breath.

Jake was the first to speak. "You are one hell of a kisser."

"Yeah, so I've been told."

Flinging his head back, Jake barked with laughter, and then sent tingles all the way to the very tips of her toes by giving her another juicy kiss, gently scraping her bottom lip with his teeth.

Holly was all hormones; she just wanted more. She also knew that Jake must have sensed it, because he growled seductively and so deeply in his throat, all it did was drive her even crazier.

"Spend the night with me," he finally asked, hope lighting his eyes.

Holly tensed at his words. It was a reflex and one she didn't really want to give into. Spending the night with Jake could only mean one thing, and God alone knew she'd never spent the night with anyone like Jake before.

"I didn't mean it like that, Holly. We can talk and get to know one another better and if you fall asleep, it will be right next to me," he said, sensing the panic in her eyes.

She smiled, feeling like an idiot that her body had signaled the opposite of what she wanted to do with him. She couldn't tell him what she really wanted now or he would think she was cheap, and that was the last thing she wanted Jake to think about her.

"Okay." It was the only word that passed her lips. Her mind was raging with all sorts of possibilities and her body was riddled with lust, constantly thinking about how it would feel to have him inside her. *Stop it,* she reprimanded herself as she climbed off him.

He took her hand gently in his and led her into the RV.

She felt like a giddy young girl on prom night, one who was going to have sex for the first time. Nerves nibbled her stomach. She dearly wanted to take a deep breath but was scared he might misinterpret that, too.

Jake locked the door behind them, pulled her into his body with one arm and gave her another sumptuous kiss. "Do you want something to drink?"

"Water, please," she said, carefully.

He kissed the tip of her nose and grumbled.

It made her giggle. *Oh, man, what is tomorrow going to bring?* She closed her eyes and hoped with her whole being that this would not be a one night stand. Holly feared that she would never recover from this.

Jake handed her a glass of ice-cold water, which she immediately began to sip. The cool water simmered in her already warm body as she took in the man standing before her. Jake fell down onto the bed, while Holly made herself comfortable right next to him, with her back resting against the wall. She looked down at him.

"So, how many doctors are there in your family?"

"Quite a few," he replied. "My dad is a gynecologist, one of the best in the US. Mom is a really good heart specialist, and my sister is a therapist." He made his eyes really big on that last comment.

Holly got what it was he was saying. Her mother used to say that it took a loon to be able to work with loonies. She smiled, but nodded for him to continue.

"Her husband, Armand, is a pediatrician. The only non 'ist' in the family."

Grinning, Holly opened her mouth to say something.

"Then there is—"

"There's more?" she asked, disbelieving.

"There are. You see, apparently, my parents couldn't keep their hands off each other," Jake replied with a saucy grin.

"I can imagine that!" She could, especially if Jake's dad had the same charm and looks as his son; it would be difficult not to want to have children.

Jake's chest rumbled. "Robin is in her second year of medical school. Lisa is sixteen, but I'm sure she will enroll in medical school, too. My pappie, on my mom's side, was one of the best heart specialists in the county, and on my father's side both my grandparents were in medicine."

"How many siblings do you have?"

"Sure you wanna know? Jake wiggled his eyebrows. "I'm the eldest of six."

"Six!" Thank goodness for small miracles, because Holly

nearly spilled the contents of her glass all over Jake's bed. To avoid that from really happening, she placed her glass on the side table.

"Told you the old folk couldn't keep their hands off each other." He winked. "Now, Amelia, the therapist, is ten months younger than me; Robin is about a year and a half younger than Amelia; Lisa is turning sixteen; Kimmy is about eight, and Ben is five." He pulled himself up and rested his head on his hand.

"You have a five-year-old brother?"

"I do. But I do believe he's the last one. At least, I hope he's the last one."

Holly laughed so much and so hard, she nearly cracked a rib. She couldn't but think how sweet it must be to see him and Ben sharing a milkshake.

"What about you?" He started doodling with his finger on Holly's arm.

Holly swallowed the lump in her throat. Her arm was covered in goose pimples, but she wasn't complaining. "I'm the only one. I used to have a sister, Jamie. Twin actually, but she died of cancer at the age of fifteen."

His smile disappeared immediately.

Before he could say anything, she continued while looking down at the print on his T-shirt. "I guess it's one of the reasons I hate hospitals. We practically lived in one." She looked up him again. "My mom is a nurse, so we have something in common."

"Your mom's a nurse?"

She nodded.

"What type cancer did your sister have?"

"I would have rather you asked where didn't she have cancer."

Taking her hand, he rubbed circles on her palm with his thumb. "I'm so very sorry, Holly. I can't imagine what it would feel like to lose one of my sisters or little brother. Not to mention one being a twin. Were you identical?"

Holly nodded again. "She had the personality, and all the friends. I was more of the quiet one, reading books and always studying. Bernie used to be her best friend, and when she died, well... Bernie was the only one who stuck around and I sort of took Jamie's place."

"Wow. Then I must thank her for sticking around."

That made Holly smile.

"Where does your mom work? Hospital, clinic?"

"I don't know," she answered softly.

Jake frowned at her words.

"I must sound like a hopeless case. We don't talk that much anymore. When Jamie died, my mom fell into a rut and forgot that she had another daughter. Bernie's parents basically raised me, made sure I had everything I needed. I saw my mom as a roommate as I literally just went home to sleep. My mom's trying, though, but I'm the hard ass."

She wasn't going to make him privy to the fact regarding the booze and the nights her mom had tried to kill herself. However, thinking about it brought tears to her eyes.

"I'm a dick. I'm sorry." He leaned over and gave her a hug.

Holly giggled and sniffed simultaneously. "You're not, okay? I just don't have happy family stories. You want to know about my dad?"

Jake gave a nervous chuckle. "Did he die?"

"No, he walked away to live a new life with his secretary when we were about five."

"Noooo!" Jake protested playfully, which made Holly chuckle.

"Now, that's a dickhead, and that's my story."

"People can be so horrible. You can have mine."

She liked that idea a lot.

"They are plenty and annoying, but I love 'em. For some reason, they like to expand... in huge proportions."

Holly slapped him on the arm. "Were you really a cage fighter?"

"I was," he answered, quite excitedly. He turned over to lie on his stomach, with his upper torso resting on his elbows. "I was actually good, won trophies and everything."

"There are trophies for hooligans?"

Jake lowered his head, but his shaking shoulders were a dead giveaway. When he looked up, his response was the funny kind. "Well, I'm not the one with the injured hand."

"Ha-ha."

"But to answer your question, yes. And then four years ago, I met my match. He was huge and way bigger than me, and all the way from Russia."

"A Russian." Holly couldn't imagine that and her eyes raised slightly, trying to form the picture in her head.

"The fight went on and on, and I'm not even sure for how many rounds we pounded each other. Eventually, though, he grabbed me in a death grip and almost tore me to pieces."

"Oh, my word."

"I was depressed for a while, wasn't interested in anyone and didn't want anybody around me, much like your mother. So, I began to eat and didn't stop. I lost my toned body, lost my friends, lost my girlfriend of five years and became a huge, fat blob."

"I'm sorry." Holly understood now why Leo had acted uncomfortable when she'd asked about his cage fighting days.

"I wanted nothing more than to be in that cage for the rest of my life, even thought of opening a club later on, you know, stuff like that. When I couldn't carry on, Leo quit, too. Gave a stupid reason about Bernie not wanting him to get hurt, but I know he did it for me."

"They are awesome people."

Jake nodded his agreement. "It was Leo who started me walking again. He was the only one who didn't give up on me, even when I pushed him away. He just kept returning. When I did start walking again, somehow my anger escalated. We actually beat the living crap out of each other a couple of times. My mom freaked."

"Who won?"

Jake laughed. "Well, I was much bigger at that time, so I could've won easily if I'd just sat on him."

Holly laughed.

"But, Leo was much faster than me, so he found a way to get the upper hand every time. I only found out years later from my sister when she graduated, that the punches between him and me were some sort of therapy. After I finally managed to control and get rid of all my anger, he picked me up every morning for a two mile run. I owe him my life and getting this back, of course." He pointed at his body, in a very elaborate manner.

Laughing and shaking her head, Holly asked, "And that's when you decided to become a doctor?"

"Yes, I tried so badly not to walk in my family's footsteps but I became intrigued with the brain. It's truly one of our most fascinating organs, and that is what I ultimately want to specialize in."

"So, you're studying to become a neurologist?"

He nodded, a huge grin illuminating his face. "I thought you knew because of your previous statement regarding Josie's head."

She laughed. "Wow, I'm impressed. I take it you're smart, too?" Holly rolled her eyes in a dramatic way.

Jake just shrugged in an 'I guess so' manner. "I did plenty of sexual favors for professors so that they could teach me everything they knew, you know, having started my studies so late and everything."

Holly's eyes rose. "What?"

He laughed. "I'm joking, you really think I would do that? No, I have a photographic memory."

"Ugh! That just sucks," Holly complained, which made him chuckle again. She started wringing her hands nervously, only because of what she wanted to ask next. Trying to look nonchalant, she forged ahead. "So, this girlfriend of five years, was it Sonic?"

Jake smiled. "No, her best friend, Melanie. They're not friends anymore."

"I can't imagine why," she replied sarcastically.

"You sound like Bernie now," he answered on a grin.

"Well, maybe she has a point."

"Yeah, maybe she does. I learned my lesson with Melanie, though. I'll never go for an airhead again. They don't stick around when you need them the most, and Sonic only started speaking to me again when she bumped into me two months ago."

Holly shook her head. "Not everyone is like that."

Jake gave her the eye, the one that meant he totally disagreed.

"You dated that many?"

"Holly, if only you knew. There was a time when Bernie hated me. Seriously. I was not one of the nicest guys around, and my morals were way out of place."

"At least they are in place now," she said, glancing around the room. "I hope."

"They are." His tone was seductive.

He tugged on Holly's shirt again, until she finally gave in and leaned forward. Their lips touched, and the butterflies in her stomach turned into tiny fire crackers; it felt as if she were going to explode. She'd never experienced anything like this, and with all the stories about his life swimming in her head, she knew she was done for.

She had somehow crashed into love with him.

His hand cupped the back of her neck gently, his thumb rubbing the side of her neck, and the kiss grew in intensity. It felt as if she couldn't get enough of this man, and the urge to dispose of his clothes rose up inside her gut.

But, Holly couldn't do that. She needed to be sure about his feelings for her first. Tomorrow, it could all be over and she would be left in the dumps again. Jake was far from safe when it came to getting over Brandon. Heck, she didn't even think that Brandon would be able to help her get over this, if it turned out to be a one-night stand.

They were both out of breath when they finally broke away.

"I could kiss you forever," Jake told her, his eyes still closed.

Holly smiled, both on the inside and out, as she felt exactly the same. "It takes two to make kissing a success."

He nipped her bottom lip in reply.

"So, this Brandon guy..." he started asking.

"Who?" Holly queried, making him grin.

"Never mind," he said, his hand touching the back of her head again. His fingers tangled themselves up in her hair, pulling her down so she could lie down on the bed next to him. When she complied, he moved his body over hers, lowered his head and their lips met.

Holly's legs moved of their own accord and locked around his hips, while her feet rubbed up, down and around his calves. They were insanely lost in their kiss. One so feverish, it felt like Holly's hormones would be messed up for good.

When Jake began to rock slowly on top of her, she thought she was going to pass out due to the pure, carnal lust that had taken over her body.

He stopped, trailed his lips to her neck and growled, making her shiver. "Woman, you have no idea what you are doing to me."

If only he knew what he is doing to me!

He kissed her neck, but all too quickly hoisted himself up. "I promised, and I think I'm going to take a quick shower."

Holly's skin broke out in goose bumps. If she had acted on her desires, he wouldn't that minute be making his way to the bathroom. But she let him, because that was just the kind of person she was. She wouldn't change her morals, despite what she'd thought earlier, and become like the girls who gave themselves to a guy on the first night; not even for Jake. She continued to ponder her situation and what she would do if it indeed turned out to be a one-night stand.

Tears pressed against her eyelids at the thought. She'd wanted a guy like Jake ever since she'd noticed boys. Now that one was right there with her, available and clearly interested, it scared the living shit out of her. She had nothing to offer him, except her sex and her body.

She laughed when a memory hit her. Her sister Jamie had called her private bits Viola, which Holly had thought stupid, but didn't think so now. She would give anything to hear her sister saying it again the way only she could.

One thing she definitely didn't have was a huge bank account. She was in fact still in the red, trying to pay back her mom for the money she'd borrowed for the stupid wedding. Money she never should have borrowed in the first place. Holly didn't even have a place of her own, either.

Breathing out a ragged sigh and listening to the sound of the water in the shower running, she giggled to herself again. *So what if this is a one-night stand? At least I won't be crying over a jerk like Brandon anymore.* However, tears threatened once again and she closed her eyes. She should've enjoyed it for what it was.

Hearing the shower stop, she decided to pretend that she'd dozed off, even if it was very far from the truth. Her uppermost thought was that she needed to protect herself from whatever tomorrow brought.

As she lay there unmoving, she heard the door open and relaxed her body completely. If there were two things Holly did well, it was fake an orgasm and fake sleep.

When Jake walked over, stopping at the foot of the bed, obviously contemplating her sleeping form, she thought she heard him sigh. It was a sigh Holly knew well, one that was always connected to the gorgeous smile he had which in turn transformed his face into a Greek god. She, herself, fought the urge to smile in that moment.

Holly heard Jake move around. The lights went out, and his cold body slid in right next to hers. Goose pimples danced over her entire body, but she kept pretending to be asleep. As much as she wanted to chat to him a little while longer, she had to prepare herself for the worst.

Ever so gently, Jake's lips touched her shoulder, followed by a soft kiss he planted on her neck. Her entire being demanded that she turn around and put her lips to his. But no, she couldn't do that. Tomorrow was another day. The day Jake would reveal his true feelings for her.

EIGHT

HOLLY WOKE as the birds began twittering in the brisk morning air. It was silent in the RV, except for Jake's soft snoring. She smiled down at him, while the reality that the night before might not have been real played inside her gut like a jackknife.

She gently lifted and removed his arm, which was firmly tucked around her waist and got up. Placing the pillow she'd slept on in her spot, she grabbed her flip flops and tiptoed to the door. She thought he would wake up when she unlocked the door, but he never even moved. She stepped out, closing the door behind her. Tears threatened to roll down her cheeks, just imagining that that might be it. He would most likely leave or ignore her later on, now that the alcohol was gone from his mind and system.

Get a hold of yourself, Holly, she reprimanded, and walked out.

Luckily for her, Bernie and Leo were still fast asleep when she reached their tent. She tiptoed softly past them, making her way to the back—a separate section of the tent—where her air mattress had been placed. She struggled to fall asleep once she'd made herself comfortable, and when she finally did the clock read seven in the morning.

IT WASN'T LONG before Holly's eyelids fluttered open once more. Her hand had started to ache, the pain unbearable. Why she hadn't felt it the night before was a mystery, but now it was killing her. Wondering if she could get past Bernie and Leo again without disturbing them in order to get her medicine, Holly heard whispering. Bernie was talking to Leo. She couldn't hear what Bernie was saying, but she could tell it was some sort of interrogation.

"Good morning, sleeping beauty," she heard Bernie say, but it wasn't to her. That greeting was followed by a grunt, which sounded none too pleased.

"Why did you sneak out?" Jake's voice suddenly filled her side of the tent, making her jump.

Holly looked up at him. The feeling of rejection she had had minutes ago melted away like snow in the warmth of the sun. "Good morning to you, too," she huffed. "If you must know, my hand was aching and I didn't want to wake you," she lied. There was no way on God's green earth she would tell him that she'd felt insecure.

His foul mood changed in an instant.

"Holly," he sighed, making his way toward her. When he reached her, he sat down beside her on the floor.

"Sorry," she mumbled.

"You have no idea how much you scared me," he said softly.

"So, I take it we will be seeing you a lot now?" Bernie's voice came from the entrance. Approval laced her tone.

"Yes, you are."

"Here." She handed Holly a capsule, which she swallowed dry.

Jake just smiled while Bernie shivered. "I still don't know how you can do that, Holly."

"It's an art. Besides, water gives it an aftertaste."

Rolling her eyes, Bernie announced, "I'm going to take a shower."

She left as Jake bent down to kiss Holly good morning. "Don't ever sneak out again, please."

Holly blushed.

He'd already showered and was sporting clean clothes; a pure white shirt, and a pair of shorts that reached his knees, making him look like some sort of Olympian god.

"I have to leave early today but I will see you later, okay?"

"Okay," she mouthed.

He kissed her on the tip of her nose, winked at her—which made her melt again—and left. She could hear him speaking to Leo, who still sounded as if he was in bed.

"So, what time will we see you?"

"Soon," Jake replied and left.

"Holly, Holly, Holly."

"Shut up," Holly said, making Leo laugh.

"One thing I know for sure, Bernie is not going to stop hassling you today."

"Nothing I can't handle."

He chuckled.

WHEN HOLLY EVENTUALLY MADE HER way outside, Jake's RV was nowhere to be seen. Her eyes gazed at the spot where it had been parked; she felt empty again. She hated the fact that Sonic had gone with him, and she couldn't help the jealousy that rose inside her. *Stop it!*

At around ten that morning, they were all packed up, too, and had already said their goodbyes to the others.

"I'm just going to quickly say bye to Josie. I'll be a minute, promise," Holly said as she started making her way toward Josie's camp.

"One minute, Holly," Bernie yelled after her.

When she got to Josie's, they were still enjoying breakfast. Holly was grinning madly upon seeing Josie.

"What happened? You're glowing."

"Shut up," Holly grumbled, embarrassed.

"Share, Holly. Now!"

"As it turns out, Jake had the same fantasy as yours."

"He made a play for you?"

Holly nodded, biting her lower lip.

"I want to hear every single detail. All of it."

"I don't have much time, Bernie and Leo are waiting. But... it was hot."

Josie shrieked in excitement.

Speaking as quickly as she could, Holly shared in record time. "I thought that it was a one-night stand at first, although he did say it wasn't. They had so much to drink last night, but this morning I did what I do if I'm not sure over certain situations."

"Please, tell me you didn't sneak out?"

"I did," Holly replied, wrinkling her nose.

"What now?" Josie asked in a serious tone.

"He stormed into my tent at around nine, wanting to know why I'd snuck out. I'm seeing him later today."

Josie let out a wolf-whistle, well, something resembling one. "You deserve it. He just better treat you right. We should do something later on."

"I don't have a phone, Josie."

"Still?"

Holly nodded. "But you do have Bernie's number, so when I eventually get a new one, I'll let you know."

"Deal."

"Bye, Josie. It was so nice seeing you guys again."

"We'll stay in touch. I'll give you a call." She gave Holly a huge hug before making her way back to the SUV.

"So did you tell her the news?" Bernie's face was one huge, big grin.

"Bite me."

"I want details, Holls."

"I'm sure Leonard has you all caught up."

Leonard laughed and started the car as Holly jumped in and closed the door.

"I'm so happy for you, Holls."

Holly shrugged, but nonetheless content.

Bernie beamed. "He'll take good care of you, I can promise you that."

"Let's see. Too early to tell yet, although he passed my little test this morning. But I hope you're right, Berns, because I have no idea how I'm going to get over this one if things go south."

Leo snickered.

"You just shut up, you hear me?" Holly said, pointing and wagging her finger at him.

"I won't say a word. Bernie would kill me."

"That would be a first. You can hardly keep a secret."

"You better keep your mouth shut, Leo. I mean it. I don't want him to know that he's already got some leverage."

Leo roared with laughter. Turning to face Holly, he said, "You're hilarious, but I'll keep my mouth shut. Promise."

"Thank you."

The drive home went quicker, but that was usually the case.

Once home, Holly helped Bernie pack everything away, while Leo went to pick up Sam from his mom's.

Holly couldn't stop smiling, and noticed Bernie giving her the eye every now and again.

"Stop looking at me."

"Holly is in love."

"Yes, I am."

"We tried to get him to come to a BBQ, Holls, but he kept declining. He wasn't even going to come this weekend. Leo had to threaten him."

"Then I should thank Leo."

Both girls laughed.

"Can I ask you a question?"

"Sure."

"What the hell is his last name?"

"Holls, you spend a night with a guy and you don't even know his last name?"

"We didn't do anything."

"Sure you didn't."

"I'm serious. Believe me, I wanted to, but he was a gentleman."

"Peters," Bernie finally answered.

Holly Peters. It sounded good. Better than Holly Morgan, had she married Brandon. *Okay, I'm getting ahead of myself here. We've practically just met!*

"So, what's the deal with his mom? Everyone sure made her sound like Cruella at the hospital."

"She's not that bad, really. She just doesn't want her children to fuck up while they study. Other than that, I won't say she's Cruella... she's more of a psycho mom."

Holly's eyes rose. "Are you serious?"

"Leo would beg to differ, but I saw her with one of his girlfriends before. He's not a momma's boy, though. Once, he ignored her for like six months because she interfered."

"I guess that means she'll have a problem with us dating, then."

"Maybe not. If it doesn't interfere with his studies, I can't see how she would not approve. I mean, really, the guy does need someone."

Holly chuckled and glanced at her watch. It was already eleven.

"Stop looking at your watch. Sundays are family days at the Peters' home, so everyone is expected for lunch. As we don't usually see him, for the precise reason I've just told you, I was extremely shocked when Leo said we'd see him later on."

That piece of info made Holly feel like a million dollars. She was finally worth someone's time and not just anyone, this Olympian-god-of-a-man's-time.

"He's perfect for you, Holls."

She smiled again. "To be honest, he seems too good to be true and I'm waiting to wake up any minute."

Bernie pinched Holly, hard.

"Fucking ouch!" she yelled in Bernie's face, while rubbing her arm.

"I was just proving a point. See? That was real; you're awake, so now you know."

The girls couldn't have laughed any harder or louder than at that exact moment. It was precisely then that Leo entered the front door with Sam.

In an instant, Bernie sobered up and ran toward Sam, and in an animated tone began lavishing him with love. "You are such a big boy," Bernie cooed, taking him from Leo. "Yes, you are. You spent the entire weekend with Nana. My big, little man," she sang, giving Sam a hug.

The sound of a car pulling into the driveway made her stop

As for Holly, she didn't bother wondering who it was. She knew it wouldn't be Jake so continued with the task of packing the camping stuff away.

Leo opened the door and guffawed, "I wish I could have been there to hear what the hell you told your mom."

Holly froze when she heard Jake's laughter.

"I told her the truth."

"Sure you did," Bernie interrupted, still holding Sam in her arms.

"Hello, Sammy," greeted Jake, taking him from Bernie and proceeding to throw him a couple of times in the air. The one-year-old cackled with glee.

"No, seriously, bro. How did you get it right?" Leo really wanted to know.

"It's not a big deal. I just told her I had other plans and that was that."

As much as Holly loved that Jake was there, she didn't like that he'd forgone lunch at his parents just to be with her.

"Hey," Jake greeted, nodding in Holly's direction.

"I should send you back home," she playfully scolded him.

"Why?" he asked, through a huge grin.

"It's family time at the Peters'."

Jake grinned. "My family isn't going anywhere. You and I can only see each other on weekends, so deal with it," he said, still holding Sam in his arms.

"Hey, sexy," she whispered to Sam as she kissed him on the cheek. He automatically leaned forward and opened his arms for Holly. She took him from Jake, who stared at Sam with a serious face.

"What's this?" Jake asked Sam.

Bernie and Leo looked on lovingly as Holly hugged Sam, and he in turn had both his little arms wrapped around her neck.

"You will lose every time when it comes to Holly, Jake," Bernie stated.

"Seriously, buddy? You're swapping me for a chick?"

Sammy giggled. "Holly."

"That's it. I'm your Holly."

"My Holly," Jake teased Sam.

"Mine," he said back to Jake.

They all chuckled.

"I'm your Holly, okay?" she said, planting another kiss on his cheek.

Sam laughed delightedly, which was the sweetest sound in the world. Mischievously, he threw his arms out in Jake's direction.

"Oh, now I'm somebody again."

Grabbing him, he flung Sam over his shoulder and they started to play.

"You staying for lunch?" Leo queried.

"No, I just came to pick up Holly."

"I'm not going to your mom's if that is why you're here."

"As if. That's not what I'm picking you up for. You think I'd want to go back there now?"

Leo roared. "So, something did happen."

"She was shocked, and as for the rest? Well, who knows?"

"Your phone hasn't rung."

"That's because it's off."

"Jake!" Holly yelled. "Your mom's going to hate me when she finally meets me. I already struggle where moms are concerned."

"Why?"

"Well, I wasn't sure before, but I think I know *why* now."

Amused, Jake tried to reassure her. "My mom won't hate you. She'll love you." He put Sammy down on the couch and walked over to give her a hug.

She didn't look pleased.

"I'm not going back."

"Fine. I'll go get my purse." On her way to her room she could hear Leo's voice, but not what he was saying. Her room still looked like a mess; she hadn't even unpacked her stuff from the weekend. She'd have to get to it when she returned.

Grabbing the purse closest to her, Holly tossed in her wallet, a lip gloss, and a tube of hand cream. She never left the house without either of the last two. Just as she was about to exit her room, she reached out and grabbed the deodorant from her nightstand, chucking that in there, too.

The first thing she noticed as she walked back into the lounge was Jake's megawatt smile, aimed in her direction. Her heart skipped a couple of beats, but that was normal now. She still couldn't believe that he wanted anything to do with her, but there he was and she wouldn't complain.

Mentally shaking her head, she realized she'd forgotten her keys and not knowing how late they might return, she hurriedly went back to her room to retrieve them.

"You done?" Jake asked in a playful manner.

"Yes, we can go." Holly rolled her eyes.

"See you later," Bernie sang.

Jake took Holly's hand and they made their way out the house. Upon noticing her ride—a gray BMW parked in the driveway—Holly raised an eyebrow. Looking at Jake, she playfully said, "You drive a BMW?"

"You betcha," he replied through a huge grin. "You have a problem with BMWs?"

"I just didn't take you for one of those."

He laughed. "One of those? Best you get in, before I change my mind." He winked.

He started the car and reversed down the driveway. "So, pray tell, what do you have against BMWs?"

"Not against the car as such, but BMW drivers think they own the road."

Jake roared with laughter. "What can I say? It's a car made to be driven."

It was such a typical answer all Holly could do was roll her eyes once more. "Exactly where are we going, Jake?"

"You'll see." He had a mysterious tone to his voice.

Jake ended up taking her to a small diner where they chatted about how he'd told his mom he wasn't going to stay for lunch. Holly still wasn't comfortable over the fact that he had done that, not one bit. Although she was grateful for the extra time she was spending with him, she felt her stomach turn into knots at the thought.

I'll make it my life's mission not meet them, she thought, trying to calm down. She knew that Jake would get over whatever it was they had and fast, while it would linger with her for years to come. She'd convinced herself that she didn't have what it took to keep a guy like Jake all to herself.

There you go again! Negative thoughts continuously jumped into her mind. *Insecure much,* she admonished herself. Holly hated being insecure, she wasn't really the type but now, she had no idea how to keep her insecurities at bay.

A busty waitress with long, blond hair walked over and handed them each a laminated menu. Holly watched the girl's face go through an array of expressions. She was trying to figure out if Holly was Jake's sister, a friend, or a handful of other possibilities. It was quite evident that the wheels in this woman's head were turning at breakneck speed.

Holly composed herself, giving the waitress a small smile whilst clearing her throat softly; all to stop from bursting into laughter.

"Could you give us about five minutes?" Jake finally asked.

It was one of those awkward moments, where the person

being spoken to seems to be on a different planet altogether. Eventually, the waitress came back down to earth, managing to mumble through her fluster.

"Uh... yes, of course. Sure. See you in a bit."

As soon as Holly thought it safe, she giggled softly, hiding behind her menu. "Awkward," she said, releasing a small breath. "Is it always like this?"

Jake's grin reached his eyes, it always did, forming vertical dimples on his cheeks. "I'm sure I have no idea what you are talking about."

"I'll just bet you don't."

Jake chuckled.

"What's good here?"

"They do a mean steak, egg and fries. It's my favorite."

Holly was sold. When the waitress returned exactly five minutes later, she addressed Jake only.

What, I'm invisible now?

"What would you like to drink?" Jake asked her, his tone sweet and gentle.

"Hmm, I'll have a light beer, thanks."

Jake stared at her, his expression somewhat shocked.

"A beer?"

"What? Girls can drink beer. It's not written in any manual that we can't have beer."

The waitress, amazingly, giggled slightly. Turning to her, Jake said to make it two beers.

When ordering their meal, the exact same thing happened.

"I'm not one of your FHM swim models, Jake. I don't do salads with a dry, crisp glass of wine."

He chortled at the smirk on her face. "This is going to be fun."

Ignoring him, Holly told the waitress how she wanted her steak done, all the while seeing Jake cringe from the corner of her eye. Turning her attention to him, she sighed. "I don't like steak well done. It's too dry, rubbery and feels like you need three beers just to swallow it down."

"Holly, it doesn't have to still be alive, either."

"I like my steak bleu, okay? It's nice."

Once their orders had been placed, Jake began telling her more about his family and how close he was to his sister, Amelia. She was the psychiatrist, and her husband, Armand, worked as a resident in the children's unit of P&E. It sounded to Holly like Jake had the same kind of closeness to Amelia as she had had with Jamie. She missed her sister so much, but she had gotten used to the fact that she was on her own now. Jamie was in a better place, and pain free.

During the course of the afternoon, conversation turned to Holly and her family. Jake was curious. All she could really say in answer was that she didn't have any. Both her mother and father had been only children. Therefore, there were no first cousins for her; only her mother had cousins—a few times removed—who were more like aunts to Holly. The closest she'd ever come to a family was Bernie's. They treated her like she was one of them, and for that she would always be grateful to her best friend.

Jake's expression had been one of sadness throughout her explanation. Holly loved the fact that he could empathize. It showed that he wasn't all rock, and that deep down within the confines of his beautiful body was a kind heart. She just prayed that it would stay kind.

"You ever think about forgiving your parents?"

Holly hadn't expected that question and it made her think for a couple of seconds.

"Sorry, I didn't mean to pry."

"No, it's not that. It's just that nobody has ever asked me that before. But, I have thought about it... I guess I'm scared of them leaving again when I become attached." That was the best way she could have described how she felt about Charles and Jane.

"You should give it more thought, Holly. I can't imagine not being able to speak to my mom. I mean, she drives me up the wall sometimes, but I would die for that woman."

Another thousand points for Jake. Her nana used to say that when the time came and she starting dating, to look at the way the guy treated his mom and she would know that that's how he would treat his wife. Jake spoke very highly of his mom, even though she sounded a tad over-protective.

Their waitress, who was carrying two steaming plates and a couple of cold beers, interrupted them a short time later. They took their time, eating slowly while Jake told a few jokes. Holly found herself laughing so much that she could barely eat her food. Jake earned another thousand boyfriend points at that meal. Making her laugh was always a good sign.

A while later, when their plates were almost devoid of food, Jake looked at Holly with a smile. Obviously, the meal had lived up to his recommendation and he was pleased. Before he could ask Holly if she'd like dessert, she held up her hand, as if she'd read his mind.

"I'm honestly stuffed, Jake. I won't even bother looking at the dessert menu. You're more than welcome to have if you want."

"No, I'm good, too. Let me settle the bill." Jake looked around for their waitress and when he caught her eye, waved his hand in the air.

"So, where to now?"

Jake wiggled his eyebrows. "Wait and see. You're an impatient one, aren't you?" His expression was one of playfulness, which made him look even sexier.

In the car, they mostly listened to music, with Jake playing her all his favorite songs. There was plenty of hard core bands in the mix, which made Holly cringe.

"Dude, this is seriously angry music," she joked.

Affronted, Jake grumbled. "It is not, it's awesome. Don't you like it?"

"Not really, no. I love my ears too much. But don't change it on my account. Your car, your choice. Just don't be upset if I feel like punching out a window or something."

Jake's one eyebrow went up. He said nothing, though, and instead turned off onto a dirt road. Holly's heart started to bounce as a beautiful farmhouse popped up directly ahead. She gave him an intense look.

"Oh, for crying out loud. We're not at my mom's place. Out with you."

She found she could breathe again after that welcome bit of news. Plastering a smile on her face, Holly climbed out of the car.

A middle-aged woman came out to greet them. "Jake, is that you?"

He grabbed the woman around her waist and swung her around the large, front porch. She was small and could have easily passed for his mom, but he'd said that that wasn't where they were going and she believed him.

"They still here?" Jake queried, head cocked to one side.

"They are, although they're a bit bigger now and will leave us soon."

Holly had no idea what they were talking about, so she just stood there and listened.

"My apologies, Leonora. This is Holly." He winked at Holly.

"Nice to meet you, Holly. I wondered where Jake's been all this time."

"I promise you, it wasn't with me," Holly joked, making Leonora laugh while simultaneously giving Jake the eye.

"It's a long story. One we don't have time for now."

"Fine, just as long as you don't wait weeks before you show your face again."

Holly wondered about that. Was he really that depressed over his supposed affair with the married woman? And what would it mean if she became available again? Would he leave her in order to reunite with this woman? Holly's insecurities soon washed away as she followed Leonora and Jake to the backyard. Her heart started to pound softly when she saw a huge cage housing three lion cubs. Apparently, it was play time as they rolled around inside, pawing one another.

NINE

"HOLLY, I'd like you to meet Jake, Leo, and Amy," Leonora proclaimed, as one of the lion cubs wrapped his paws around her arm. He was still a baby, but not as small as one would have imagined.

"How old are they?"

"Approximately two months. The wildlife rescue organization gave us permission for them to stay until they found a permanent home for them in Africa. They will be leaving us soon," she sighed, looking sad while she watched Jake wrestle with one of the cubs.

"That one's Amy," Leonora offered, pointing at the feline Jake was wrestling. "When she was tiny, Jake used to sit for hours feeding her from a syringe. They have a special bond." This last part she whispered softly.

"I can see that."

One of the other cubs came rambling up and climbed onto Holly's lap. He was strong and managed to push Holly back against the cage with his soft paws.

Both Leonora and Jake laughed as Holly let out a small, involuntary shriek, followed by giggles.

"Come here, Jake." Jake pulled the lion cub's tail and suddenly the lion cub by the same name started playing with him.

"It looks to me like both Jakes are crazy about you, Holly."

Before Holly could utter a single word, someone joined them.

"Jake, is that you?" a male voice asked.

The man, who looked to be around Leonora's age, opened the gate. Jake got up and shook his hand with a smile on his face.

"Holly, this is Chris. He's Leonora's husband."

"Nice to meet you, Holly," the older man greeted her, a twinkle evident in his eyes.

"It's nice to meet you, too." Holly nodded.

They spent another delightful hour with the cubs, after which they made their way to the house for a much needed cup of coffee. As they settled around the large, oak table that served as the family's eating area Leonora recounted the sad story of how the lion cubs came to be at the farm.

Apparently, a nearby neighbor had kept lions without a permit. One night, a storm hit and lightning struck a large tree on the edge of Chris' and Leonora's farm. When Chris went to investigate the damage, he saw the lions roaming their pasture.

The storm had blown down the rickety fence their irresponsible neighbor had constructed to keep the lions caged. Chris had immediately phoned the authorities, who arrived in record time in order to remove all the lions. Days later, Chris found the three cubs tucked inside a hollow tree near where the lightning had struck. He brought the three malnourished cubs back to the farm, and applied for a temporary permit to care of them until a suitable home could be found.

Holly still didn't know if Leo was named after Leonard, or Leonora.

Leonora continued with the cubs' story, explaining how the

minute the cubs were safe on the property she had given Jake a call. He'd raced over in a big SUV, Amelia with him. Brother and sister had sat with the cubs for weeks, feeding them and playing with them.

Another thousand points for him, because anyone who loves animals has a good heart.

"We couldn't have cared for all three if we hadn't received the funds to do so from Jake and his family."

"You are too modest. Anyone would've done the same."

"I wish that was the truth, Jake," Chris said honestly, getting up to pack their mugs in the dishwasher.

Holly and Jake stayed and visited with the couple until three, then decided it was time to go.

"That was amazing!" Holly said as they got into Jake's car, thinking that she probably would never see wild animals up close ever again.

"I thought you might appreciate that." Jake had both a look of sorrow and peace on his face.

"Are you sad they are leaving?"

"A little, but this isn't the right place for them. They belong in Africa."

"I agree."

"You should have seen them when Chris and Leonora found them. They were literally starving. The vet provided us with a special formula to feed them, and we slept with them for days."

"Who's we?"

"Me and Amelia."

"I can't believe how stupid some people can be. I mean, you have to be pretty insane to keep grown lions in your backyard. Although, I'm sure nobody ever broke in there!"

Jake laughed. "That's one way to look at it. But, I agree, they were pretty stupid."

Silence took over for a while before Jake spoke again. "So, Leo tells me you don't have a phone."

Holly shrugged. "I don't. I smashed mine against the wall after the last time I spoke to Brandon."

"Remind me to never piss you off."

They chuckled. Holly couldn't remember the last time she had laughed and enjoyed herself so much, and the thought made her sigh a little with happiness. They drove for about twenty minutes before Jake pulled up at the mall. Clasping her hand in his much larger one, he dragged her into the first cell phone store they came upon. Her protests didn't help one bit as he shoved a brand new Samsung smartphone into her hand.

Holly eventually accepted it graciously.

After that elaborate purchase was made, they walked hand in hand into Jake's favorite clothing store. Curiously watching him pick through what was on offer, Holly couldn't help but think how much she loved his taste in clothes as well, and pondered once again why a guy like him would be interested in her.

A satisfied Jake paid for his purchases, and once again taking Holly's hand they decided to go watch a movie. Of course, the genre was action, something she didn't really care for but didn't complain as the venue allowed her to sit very close to a certain heart-throb hooligan who had stolen her heart with one glance.

It didn't escape Holly that when they entered the dark theater, he led her to the back and settled them into chairs at the end of the aisle, against the back wall. The theater wasn't particularly full, but at least twenty or so people occupied the chairs below them.

Talking was kept to a minimum as loud voices rang out from the speakers right above them, followed by the dimming lights. As always, previews of upcoming movies didn't grab Holly's attention even though she'd hoped they would, because she was totally distracted. She couldn't stop thinking about Jake. The theater's darkness, coupled with the heat, started to wash over her body and it began to feel like they were stuck in a heat-wave.

Ten minutes into the movie, Jake lifted the armrest dividing their seats and pulled her closer. She rested her head gently against his shoulder as his right arm wrapped around her body. When he began to draw circles on her upper thigh, Holly thought that she was going to pass out.

Turning his head, Jake gently lifted Holly's chin, and when she looked up her lips were inches from his. He kissed her softly, making her stomach knot, and when the kiss deepened their tongues dueled and moved in an age old perfect rhythm. A foreign feeling she was sure was lust, moved up her chest and flushed her face. Holly started to kiss him harder and by the way he'd moved her on to his lap, told her that he didn't mind it one bit.

Her hands became tangled in his hair, and his were moving from her ass to her legs, pulling her harder against him. She was on the verge of complaining but then remembered where they were, as loud noises from the shooting scene playing out on the big screen filtered through. Holly couldn't help the smile that spread across her face. There they were, necking in the back of a theater like a couple of teenagers, only the action was of a different kind.

"What is it?" Jake whispered in her ear.

Her body riddled with goose bumps. "Nothing important, just the movie. Is this the reason why you chose it?"

Jake chuckled. "Busted." He closed in on her lips and kissed her again.

Holly had no idea for how long they'd been kissing, but when music started playing she looked up and saw the white lettered credits rolling on the screen.

"That must be a record," she said.

"I could kiss you forever, woman."

Likewise, she thought, but smiled instead.

Holly climbed off his lap and pulled her shorts back into place.

Shit, this has never happened before.

When she'd retrieved her handbag, Jake took her hand as they made their way out of the theater, both feeling quite satisfied.

The drive home was too short. It seemed like they'd just left and Jake was already pulling into Bernie's driveway. The clock on the dash showed that it was just after ten in glowing red letters.

"So, I won't be seeing you this week. Weeks are strictly for studying. But, I promise that I will phone you every day, a dozen times if I have to. However, I will see you first thing on Friday."

Holly looked at him. "This is going to be one long week," she confessed.

Jake leaned over, placing his hand on the back of her neck, while looking intently into her eyes. After what seemed like eons, he pulled her closer to him and drove his lips against hers for another long, juicy kiss. Somehow during their kiss, she had once again ended up on his lap with the steering wheel pressing hard into her back, but she didn't mind. All that mattered was that she was kissing him; everything else was soon forgotten.

All too soon, Jake broke the kiss, rested his forehead against hers and sighed. "Go, before I do something I shouldn't." He patted her on the ass and opened the door.

An awkward exit was on the cards, and she was soon proven right when she stumbled and nearly fell flat on her face. Righting herself in case anyone was watching, she asked Jake to reach over for her handbag.

"Thank you, Jake. I had an awesome time." Holly was mortified.

Jake smiled broadly. "Believe me, it was my absolute pleasure, Holly." He took his sweet time in drawing out her name.

Holly felt hot and bothered all of a sudden, but then Jake knew exactly what he was doing.

"Put your phone on charge. I'll be calling you soon."

"Yes, dear," she mocked, walking toward the front door followed by Jake's laughter. She noticed, ecstatically, that he'd waited until she was safely inside before leaving. Looking out the window, Holly felt an utter loneliness fill her gut as the lights of his car faded away.

She'd sat by the window for a while, letting the events of the day wash over her, welcoming the touch of the cold glass against her forehead; it helped in cooling her raging libido. It was then she realized that she'd forgotten to phone Marabella, her boss, to explain what had happened with her hand. She jumped up and made for the landline in Leo's office. Her new phone was still charging.

The two spoke for almost half an hour, with Holly having to answer all of Marabella's questions as to why she'd hit Steward. After that tale of woe had been shared, she then went on to tell her about Jake. Marabella's laughter had echoed down the line throughout her explanation, which only served to make Holly sigh dramatically. Nevertheless, she moved on to describing Jake, knowing her boss could be overly nosy when it came to men. However, despite that tiny flaw, Holly did confide in Marabella about Brandon and his trunk-load of shit. Her boss had retaliated with "Dump his sorry ass!" on numerous occasions. Still, she had always been nice to Brandon when he'd come to the lodge, which in all honesty had been the right thing to do.

When their call came to an end, finally, Holly noticed a light flashing on her cell phone. A missed call; Jake.

"You going to dream about me tonight?" he asked, in a very seductive voice when she called him back.

"Why dream about you? I was under the impression that I already had you," Holly replied with confidence.

"That's my girl. Well, I'll definitely be dreaming about you, and next weekend."

Holly felt herself blushing as her mind imagined what all Jake was planning.

"You do that. At least I don't have to come up with the fun stuff anymore."

He chuckled. "Sweet dreams, Holly. I'll give you a call tomorrow."

"Sweet dreams, Hooligan."

He snorted and bid his final good night. The line went dead in her ear.

That was one thing Holly would never be able to do, disconnect first. Sighing, she put her phone down but as she did so, it beeped with a message. Smiling happily, she opened it.

Jake: That was extremely hard, ending the call.
Holly: LOL. I will never be able to do that.
Jake: Night, hon.
Holly: I'm not a bee's puke!
Jake: You're my bee's puke. Deal with it. ☺
Holly: Night, hon.

Holly's last reply mimicked Jake's, but the messaging stopped. She let out another satisfying sigh and sank into the couch's soft, plush cushion.

Hell, I must be the luckiest girl in the world right now.

TEN

HOLLY WOKE around ten the next day when the sun's brightness forced her from her dreams of Jake.

Sighing, she stretched languidly. Her hand was still tender, but not as painful as it had been when she'd hit Steward. *Why on earth shouldn't I go to work?* She despised taking sick days off, because all that happened was that her work piled up and then by Wednesday when she was due back, it would be so humongous it would take her at least two days to sort out.

She smiled as Jake crept back into her mind. *What a nice way to wake up.* His piercing green eyes were the only thing Holly could see when she closed hers, as well as the warmth of his lips when she thought about his kisses. The butterflies in her stomach had gone crazy again just thinking about it.

Deciding it was time to get out of bed, she made her way through to the living area where she found Bernie watching The Real Housewives of Beverly Hills.

"So, this is what you do when we are at work?" Holly teased, making herself comfortable next to her friend.

"I love this! You see the blond? Her name is Brandi and she is a real *want it all, have it all* type of woman. She is also the bitch of the lot. The other blond, Lisa, is her friend. They had this huge fight and now she refuses to accept her apology.

Holly shook her head as Bernie tried to update her on the whole season, it seemed. To be honest, Holly didn't give a shit who was who. She couldn't stand phony reality shows like those anymore.

"Bernie, do you honestly believe that that's what their lives are really like? The producer brings them a script every morning, or some such. There is no way people's lives are that interesting."

"Gah! You sound just like Leo now. I don't care. It's freaking entertaining." Bernie started laughing as the one blond punched the other one in the face, real hard.

Holly got up from the couch, leaving Bernie to enjoy the catfight being played out on TV, and made her way to the kitchen. She grabbed the cereal box out of the cabinet; Bran Flakes were her favorite, the one with bits of dried fruit, and she always made sure that she ate a good portion of it for breakfast before she went to work.

When she'd consumed the contents of her bowl, she tidied up and headed off to shower, all the while thinking about her date. She knew Bernie was probably going to ask her about it sooner or later, so she wanted to be prepared.

Forty-five minutes later, she was dressed and once again joined Bernie on the couch. Not five minutes after the show ended, Bernie started asking Holly about her date with Jake. They chatted for almost an hour before Holly remembered that she needed to phone the hospital to confirm her checkup, which was scheduled for the next day.

The woman on the other end of the line sounded as if she'd already had a really hectic Monday, and Holly was put on hold for about four minutes. When the woman finally returned, she informed Holly that her appointment was for three o'clock.

Bernie grabbed a piece of paper and wrote down the address of the doctor's office as Holly repeated it to her.

"Three o'clock?" Bernie queried.

Holly nodded. "Why?"

"I'll need to arrange for my mom to look after Sam tomorrow a little longer. It won't be a problem."

"Bernie, I'm sure I can drive myself. It's doesn't hurt as much anymore."

"How are you going to work the shift?"

"Easy," Holly said in a slightly higher octave.

"And let Jake have a go at me when he finds out? No, thanks. I'm taking you and that's it."

"Fine, whatever."

Just then, Holly heard a car's tires on the gravel right in front of Bernie's house.

"Who the hell can that be?" Bernie got up and peeked out the window; the driveway was in perfect view. "You've got to be shitting me!" A huge smile spread on Bernie's face as she looked at Holly with a raised eyebrow, which told Holly exactly who it was.

"Are you serious?" Holly jumped up just as the knock on the door sounded.

"Coming!" Bernie sang, opening the door a couple of seconds later.

"Can I help you?"

"Ha-ha," Jake mocked, pushing Bernie gently out of the way to walk in.

"What happened to 'see you Friday'?" Holly asked, using air quotes.

This only made Jake laugh. "It's too far away." He suddenly grabbed Holly around the waist and gave her one hell of a smacker.

"Should I leave?" Bernie joked.

"No. I brought food."

"I have food, thank you."

"You don't have McDonalds."

"That, I don't have."

"Aren't you supposed to be in some class or other?"

"Not right this minute. As I have a couple of free periods, I thought I'd pop in. You want me to leave?"

"No, but I don't want you to get into trouble, either."

"With who?" He frowned at Holly.

"Your mother."

He barked with laughter. "She's my mom, Holly, not my boss."

"The way you said 'she doesn't like me messing around on weekdays' tells me otherwise, momma's boy."

"I'm not a momma's boy." He pulled her shirt until she smacked into his torso and planted a kiss on the tip of her nose. Jake let her go and went to fetch the food from his car.

After they were settled into chairs around Bernie's dining room table, each enjoyed a Big Mac and Coke while discussing Holly's appointment tomorrow.

"I'm off. I can take you, but I can't go in with you. My mom would throw a fit."

"I don't know. I'm too scared to even contemplate taking that chance," she teased him.

"Funny! I'll take you." His tone was full of authority and Holly knew that she couldn't protest. Not that she wanted to, anyway.

Just then his phone rang, and after taking a quick look at his screen Jake put his index finger to his lips. He answered it on the fourth ring by just saying his name. He listened for a couple of seconds.

"How did she find out?"

Holly froze as his face looked suddenly serious.

"Fine, change it," he said, disconnecting the call after he thanked someone named Leslie.

The name rang a bell. She'd spoken to a Leslie that morning, the one she'd thought had already had a very bad Monday.

"My mom found out about Friday."

Holly's eyes grew bigger. "And?"

"Nothing. She is extremely nosy and has been asking everyone behind my back what you look like. Plus, she knows your appointment is tomorrow at three, so I just changed it to ten."

"Jake?"

"No, Holly. My mom could have simply phoned me and asked me directly. I hate it when she snoops around behind my back."

"Who told her?" Bernie asked.

"It doesn't matter," he spoke low, and in a tone laced with irritation.

Holly could only imagine who it could be; probably someone who wanted Jake and hoped to get on his mom's good side. That's what she would have done if she'd wanted him. Or would she?

Jake stayed until about three. When he was ready to leave, Holly walked him out to his car. As soon as they reached it, he swung her around against the driver's door and kissed her passionately, the cool metal at her back pressing against the thin fabric of her shirt. As before, her ears started ringing as the kiss became more aggressive and the butterflies in her stomach felt like they wanted to break free.

And just like that, Jake abruptly stopped, broke the kiss and rested his forehead against hers. Straightening, he kissed her on the tip of her nose. "Talk to you later, and I'll see you tomorrow." He climbed into his car slowly and put his sunglasses on, which made him look extra hot.

"See you tomorrow, Hooligan," Holly finally said.

"I'm not the one with the injured hand."

Holly giggled and waved as he drove off. She sighed again. She was really a lucky girl.

HOLLY WOKE EARLY the next morning, had a shower, applied her makeup, and at around half past nine was ready to leave. Jake pulled up in his BMW five minutes later.

Holly met him outside and got in. She had barely made herself comfortable when Jake leaned over, grabbed her around the neck gently and pulled her in for a kiss.

"Good morning, sunshine."

"You are a morning person, aren't you?"

"I'm a morning, afternoon and evening person."

She smiled at him and Jake drove off.

"I'll drop you off in front of the hospital, and then I have to find a parking spot as far as possible from the entrance."

Holly laughed. "Are you that scared or that devious, Jake?"

Chuckling, he replied, "The latter."

Holly did the only thing she could think of to do right then, shook her head.

Leaning forward, she turned up the volume as she heard her favorite song playing on the radio. Jake thought it extremely funny as she sang along, mimicking the words with facial expressions and hand gestures. It was one of her trademarks when it came to singing along with some of her favorite songs. Holly wasn't bothered that he laughed. She loved the fact that she could put a grin on his face, too.

Jake hadn't been kidding about dropping her off right in front of the hospital. But before Holly climbed out, she removed her bandage, just in case she ran into his mom. That way she wouldn't be able to put two and two together.

Jake quickly pecked her on the lips. "Phone me when you're done, okay?"

"Yes, boss."

"That's my girl," he joked.

Holly merely clucked her tongue at him. "You would be so lucky."

Jake grinned broadly, winked, and drove off as soon as she got out.

Once inside, she made her way to the elevator. When it finally arrived, she was the only passenger. This was short-lived, because directly after pressing the button for the third floor and as the doors began to close, a hand appeared to stop them from closing fully. A male nurse entered, followed by a few more staff members. Holly stepped back to accommodate them. She felt her hand twinge, but without the bandage it felt that much better.

The door finally closed and the elevator began its ascent.

"Mara, I'm sure it's just some sort of fling." The two women directly in front of her began chatting.

"It had better be. He knows how I feel about relationships while studying."

"Oh, he knows. You've raised them well."

"When did you say her appointment was?" the woman, who she was sure was Jake's mom, asked.

"At three."

Holly stretched her neck forward as she tried to see what his mom looked like, without making it too obvious, or falling over in her attempt. The two women continued talking until the elevator stopped and its doors opened on the second floor.

Luckily for Holly, his mom got out with the other woman who was wearing a doctor's coat. His mom didn't look anything like him;

she had blond hair, streaked with low lights and a long, oval face. She was tall and skinny, but didn't really look like she was old enough to be Jake's mom. Not to mention the fact that she did not have the figure of a woman who had given birth to six children. Quite the opposite. She made a point to ask Jake what his mom's name was.

When the metal doors opened one floor up, Holly got out. She found the doctor's suite quickly and entered through two glass doors. Sitting behind the reception desk, an older woman was on the phone so Holly had no choice but to wait until she was finished, and hoped that she didn't need to fill out any further paperwork. If Bernie had accompanied her, she could've helped.

"Sorry about that," the lady apologized, a beautiful smile adorning her face.

"Not to worry," Holly replied, politely. "I have an appointment for ten o'clock. I'm Holly."

The receptionist simultaneously smiled and winked. "And I'm Leslie."

Holly giggled. "Ah. Thanks for moving my appointment."

"You're so very welcome. I didn't think you would've wanted his mom to corner you out in the hallway."

Holly nodded. "Not in this lifetime," she whispered. She didn't like the picture everyone painted in regards to his mother.

Leslie snorted. "It will happen one of these days, but for now you're safe. Have a seat, Holly. The doctor should be with you shortly."

"Great. Thanks, Leslie."

Holly's wait lasted ten minutes. Finally, when the doctor came to collect her, it was the same gentleman who had tended to her on Friday.

"Ah... Henry. And how are you today?"

Holly laughed.

"Henry is feeling much better, thank you."

"Happy to hear that. But come, let's have a look."

Holly followed him into his office, and after making sure she was comfortable he began inspecting her hand.

"Is it sore when I move it like this?" He twisted her hand gently.

"A little, but it's not excruciating."

"Right answer. I just wanted to make sure you weren't lying."

Holly chuckled.

Just to be sure all was healing as it should, he sent her down for a few more X-rays. On arriving, she noticed they were quite busy. Taking her phone out, she sent Jake a text.

HOLLY: HAVE BEEN SENT FOR MORE X-RAYS. IT'S FULL. GOING TO TAKE FOREVER!

JAKE: NO WORRIES. HAVE TEXTBOOKS WITH ME.

SHE GIGGLED as she read his message.

HOLLY: IS YOUR MOM'S NAME MARA?

Holly had to know just to be sure before she mentioned anything else.

JAKE: YES. SOMETHING HAPPEN?

Replying as quickly as she could in order to set his mind at ease, Holly punched out an answer using her thumbs.

HOLLY: NO. NOTHING. BUT I'VE NOW SEEN HER. WE SHARED AN ELEVATOR.

JAKE: GOOD THING YOU REMOVED YOUR BANDAGES! CLEVER GIRL.

She smiled again. A hundred messages later, Holly's name was called.

The X-rays went pretty fast, but the wait for the processing took a bit longer. By the time she got back to the doctor's office it was already eleven o'clock.

He took the envelope from Holly and began examining them thoroughly against the light fixture molded to the back wall of his office. After much deliberation, he looked at Holly and stated, "I would like it if you rested your hand for another day or two if possible. But if you are not able to, you must at least take it easy at work."

"So I can go back?"

"Yes, if you must."

"Thank you so much, and I will take it easy, promise."

"It's improved substantially since Friday night. Is the guy you hit okay?"

"I think so, but I haven't seen him since. I do know that Jake fixed his broken nose, though. As for his shattered ego? I don't know."

The doctor laughed. "Off with you then, young lady. Take care, and do tell Jake he owes me one. His mom is going to be livid when she storms into my office this afternoon."

Holly covered her nervous laugh with her good hand. "Sorry. I'll tell him."

Holly gave Jake a call, letting him know that she was finally done and more than ready to leave. After listening to his directions of where she should meet him, she disconnected and made her way outside.

Jake picked her up about a hundred meters from the entrance and drove back to Bernie's house. He wasn't able to spend any more time with her as he had a class to attend, but Holly was grateful for his help and the time, however short, they got to spend together.

As soon as Jake left, Holly started to dissect his mom's words. Would she really be that upset that Jake had met someone, or would this be another broken heart episode? Was what they had only to be a fling, where when Jake had had his fill, he would waste no time in getting over her and moving on with his life?

The butterflies in her stomach were silenced as Holly pondered her dilemma. Surely, his mom wouldn't be so callous as to request he break up with her. Would she? Then again, Jake did say they fought on a regular basis. She just hoped and prayed that this time mommy dearest wouldn't get her way, and that Jake would choose to remain with Holly, come what may.

Feeling drained, coupled with the headache that was making itself known, she took an aspirin and decided that the best thing to do right then and there was have a short afternoon nap. Naps were more often than not a good remedy for life's little disturbances.

ELEVEN

WAKING UP FROM HER NAP, she felt a whole lot better. And with feeling better, decisions were always easier to make, so Holly decided to hell with her insecurities. She hated feeling insecure about stupid stuff and was determined to go with the flow and enjoy whatever they had right now, no matter what.

When Holly got to work, the first thing she did was go in search of her boss, Marabella. Cindy, her daughter, who also worked at the lodge, happened to be in her mom's office.

Once the welcome back greetings were out of the way, all three made themselves comfortable. Mother and daughter listened attentively as Holly recounted her wonderful weekend, as well everything and anything that had taken place during the past couple of days. Holly glowed and Marabella continued to compliment her on that the entire day.

On Thursday, Holly found herself in a conundrum. Jake wanted to take her to a fancy restaurant on Friday, but Marabella had asked her to fill in for that particular shift. Cindy couldn't do it because she had a function she had to attend with Mark, her boyfriend, and none of the other hosts were free.

Having had no luck, she had no choice but to give Jake a call that night.

"I've got bad news." Holly almost felt like crying. She couldn't wait to see Jake again and now she had to work.

"What's wrong?" His tone dropped a few octaves, which made him sound as depressed as she felt.

"I've got to work Friday night. None of the others can fill in for me and Marabella really needs me. I couldn't tell her no, I'm so sorry."

"It's fine, Bee Puke, there's always another day. What time do you finish? I'll pick you up."

That put a smile on her face. "Eleven-ish, although the restaurant doesn't stay open that late, so guests usually leave around ten-thirty."

"I'll see you at ten-thirty, then."

"I can't wait," slipped out. These little confessions had started to happen on a daily basis now. The other night she'd had to bite her tongue, or she would've said *I love you.*

They chatted for a while longer about the test he had taken that day. It had been a hard one, according to Jake, and one he hadn't expected. But as doctors in training, they needed to be prepared for anything at any given time. Jake, however, came across as the prepared kind of person.

He also went on to tell her that the lion cubs had finally gotten picked up for their transfer back to Africa. Holly could sense a tinge of emotional tension in his voice, but didn't say anything. She loved that about him, that he loved animals. They said goodbye around ten, and after her bath she went to bed.

FRIDAY TICKED BY SLOWLY. She couldn't wait for ten thirty to come so that she would finally get to see Jake again.

At around twelve, a delivery was dropped off at the lodge for a Mr. Frabriusa, an extremely difficult guest who was going to celebrate his anniversary with his wife later on that evening. It was one of the biggest bouquets of flowers she had ever seen. The arrangement was made up of tiger lilies, huge leaves and the most beautiful, salmon pink roses. The whole thing was covered with brown paper and bound with raffia. It also happened to be Holly's absolute favorite kind of flowers, too.

Mr. Frabriusa had phoned Holly about three times a day all week to make sure that everything would be ready for that evening. He had some sort of European accent, but she couldn't place the country.

The one thing she did know was that Mr. Frabriusa was extremely difficult and Holly didn't like difficult, especially in people. Thank heaven she was working as a host tonight, not taking orders like Marabella and two of the head-waiters.

The phone rang just as she was about to place a call to Mr. Frabriusa in order to let him know that his flower arrangement for his wife had arrived.

"My flowers there?" Mr. Frabriusa asked, and Holly cringed at how rude he was. *Hello* wasn't a foreign word.

"They've just this minute arrived, Mr. Fabriosa. I—"

"It's Frabriusa," he corrected, cutting her off.

Holly rolled her eyes. "My apologies, Mr. Frabriusa."

"Everything set for tonight? You've got all the arrangements in order?"

"Yes, sir. Marabella has everything you asked for."

"Hmmm, we'll see about that."

He slammed the phone down, making Holly want to scream. What could be so horrible in this man's life that he had to be so rude?

Five o'clock finally came around, and Holly went to the bathroom to change into a beautiful black suit. She loved her outfit and only wore it on special occasions, or when she needed to work. It was a pantsuit that connected the top to the pants at her waist. The pants fit her hips perfectly, and the sleeveless top hung loose and went all the way up to her neck. Marabella loved it. She always joked that it made Holly look professional and sexy at the same time.

Slipping on her black heels, she was grateful that she wasn't going to have to stand all night; she'd be working in the restaurant. One of her tasks was to ring up bills for every waiter, as well as make sure everything was punched into the computer correctly and that every bill was paid in a timely manner. Not a job anyone could get right, except for someone who could multitask.

At six, some of the guests began to arrive. Those who were waiting for friends were led to the bar with its comfy chairs and African décor so they could enjoy a drink until the rest of their party arrived. Couples were taken directly to their table, unless they specified they'd like a drink at the bar first.

Marabella was a queen when it came to running her restaurant. She treated her guests like they were gems, and that was one of the reasons both the restaurant and lodge did so well.

Holly tried her hardest to be friendly to every single guest, but found it damn hard as all she could think about was Jake, and that she could've been spending this time with him.

Closer to seven, yet more guests poured in and the phone rang non-stop; there were always those who hadn't booked but tried their luck nevertheless, hoping to get a table.

Holly had just placed the phone down when she heard Mr. Frabriusa's accented voice greeting Marabella. She took a deep breath and closed the reservations book while he continued to discuss all his requests with her boss. Holly tried to pretend she was none the wiser and kept herself busy with absolutely nothing. She did, however, try to keep from looking up.

Anything in order to avoid having to speak to the arrogant bastard.

"Holly, would you mind escorting Mr. Frabriusa to his seat?" Marabella asked.

Fuck! Holly plastered a smile on her face, finally looked up and pinned the idiot with her eyes. Her heart skipped a beat. Jake was grinning from ear to ear. "You're Mr. Frabriusa? I'm going to kill you!" She stood up and pinched him playfully. "Rude bastard."

Jake laughed. "Good surprise?"

"Enjoy your dinner!" Cindy sang as rounded the corner.

"You set this up?" she asked Marabella, who was still watching them with a genuine guilty smile on her face.

"He begged me so nicely."

"I could really kill the both of you. And you..." She pointedly jabbed in Jake's direction, but all he did was pull her into a hug.

"Come on. Admit it... it's a good surprise."

"Whatever. Rude bastard."

Both Jake and Marabella shook their heads, but Holly could see they thought the whole situation funny. She suddenly remembered the flowers. "The flowers are mine?"

Marabella nodded.

"They're gorgeous!" she squealed, and went to retrieve them from behind the bar.

When she returned, Jake and Marabella were chatting, while Cindy was escorting guests to their table. When Holly got close to Jake, he put his arm around her waist and followed Marabella to their table. She couldn't stop smiling, thinking about how many times she'd wanted to swear at the stupid idiot, who'd turned out to be her romantic idiot.

Their chairs were pulled out by waiters and Marabella placed menus in front of them.

"What may I get you to drink?" Marabella asked in her professional voice.

"I'll have a champagne cocktail, please," replied Holly.

"Cocktails?" Jake pulled a face. "No, thank you. Make mine a Chivas on the rocks."

"Certainly. Enjoy your evening." She gave them her super smile.

"She's nice," Jake whispered when she walked away.

"Oh, she can be a pain in the ass sometimes, but I love her."

Jake smiled broadly. "So. This is where you work."

"This is the place you wanted to bring me?"

"You said it was one of the best restaurants in the city. I hope you don't mind?"

"Are you kidding me, not at all! I love this place. I could eat their food for the rest of my life."

"Good. So what's up with all the African décor?"

Holly laughed. "Jerry has something for Africa. He goes there once a year on a hunting trip and apparently, just has to be surrounded with everything he can get his hands on that resembles his favorite activity."

"I take it Jerry is her husband?"

"Yes, and the chef."

"Oh, wow." Jake seemed impressed.

Peter, one of the waiters appeared with their drinks. He was one of their best, and that had been the reason why Holly had placed Mr. Frabriusa on his list. Nobody complained in Peter's section. He chuckled when he saw Holly.

"You knew about this, too?"

"C'mon, Mrs. Kensington couldn't keep her mouth shut if you paid her to."

"You could've told me, Peter. I thought that's what friends did."

"I wanted to, but then I would've ruined everything this young man here worked so hard on."

"Appreciate it. Thank you, Peter," Jake said with a friendly slap to the arm and a handshake.

"You are so welcome, sir."

"Jake, please. I'm too young to be a sir."

Nodding, Peter began reciting the evening's specials. He was good and extremely professional, and one of the reasons why Holly didn't mind hanging out for dinner at the restaurant in her free time. It was as if they treated her extra special simply because they worked side by side.

"You going to go for the steak tartar?" Jake asked.

"Ha-ha. No, I don't like steak tartar. It's raw."

"So, you like raw."

"Not *that* raw. I like the fact that when I'm hungry, my food doesn't get up and make a run for it."

Jake chuckled and took a sip of his Chivas. "Your turn to enlighten me. What would you suggest I order?"

"Everything's good here. But if I had to pick something for you, I'd suggest the smoked duck with nectarine coulis for your starter, or the crocodile tail—it's pretty damn good. I'm going to have the first. And for my main course, I will have a ladies steak with mushroom sauce. The Springbok shank is a really fast mover here, too."

"I was just thinking about that. The way Peter described it, sounds amazing."

Holly smiled at his words.

When Peter returned ten minutes later, they ordered their starters along with their main course. Jake ended up having the crocodile tail, while Holly enjoyed her smoked duck breasts.

Between bites, he kissed her hands about a million times, as they talked everything and anything; her future plans, as well as what he'd like to accomplish. Holly could listen to him for hours.

She was also impressed with how good a head he had on his shoulders, especially when he started talking about his family again. She only wished that she'd had the opportunity to know what it would be like to have lots of siblings. She'd give anything to meet his family. However, her fear where his mom was concerned and what she'd said in the elevator on Tuesday, still weighed heavily on her mind. It was one of the reasons why she wasn't yet ready to meet them.

The evening was amazing. They'd chatted, drank and laughed so much that time was forgotten. When Holly finally looked around the restaurant, she noticed that they were only one of two couples who still lingered.

She didn't want the night to end, and that made her wonder why on earth time always flew when one was having fun.

Jake broke into her musings. "There is no way I'm going to be able to drive tonight," Jake said, rubbing his eyes.

Holly's amusement showed; she knew exactly what he meant. Her head had that spinning feeling, but it felt good. She'd let all her worries go, even if that only happened when she spent time with Jake. He really made her feel free and alive.

"Do you think they still have rooms available?" Jake asked, a huge smile adorning his face.

"You want to stay the night?"

"Why not? I'm the responsible sort, and it doesn't hurt that I always carry an extra bag of clothes," he hiccupped, bringing Holly to tears.

Was he really drunk?

Jake guffawed right along with her.

"I'll go find out," she said, scraping the chair backward. When she stood, she felt somewhat unsteady, and as she made her way to the restaurant's reception her legs started wobbling.

She immediately grabbed one of the chairs at another table to steady herself. This brought about more laughter from the both of them. The couple at the other table, however, didn't find it the least bit humorous and looked from Jake to Holly like they were mad.

"Please accept my apologies." Holly nodded in their direction. Professionalism and politeness had been drilled into her—into all employees—by Marabella. She couldn't let her boss down, no matter what the occasion.

She stumbled, although she tried her best to keep her back straight, all the way to the front desk where Cindy still sat. She was playing games on the computer while she waited for the remaining couples to leave.

"Sorry. We're keeping you up," Holly mumbled.

Cindy gave her a huge smile. Leaning in, eyes huge, she whispered, "You never mentioned he was *that* gorgeous!"

"I know, right?" Holly smiled from ear to ear. "Do you know if there are still rooms available? We are horribly drunk and in no condition to drive, plus, we'd probably get lost either way."

Cindy snorted, raising an eyebrow and giving her the 'look'. "Are you going to score tonight?"

Holly blushed but pulled herself together, fast. Too much alcohol never ended well. "Stop it," she hissed.

Winking, Cindy said, "I'll phone and find out." Her finger hit the button so fast that Holly wasn't sure if she dialed the front desk's number correctly.

"Do we still have any rooms available?" she asked. "For two... okay, great... almost done, yep. It's for Holly." Whatever the comment on the other end of the line was, it made Cindy laugh.

Hanging up, she beamed at Holly. "Lynette says there are a lot to pick from, but that you make sure you guys are out before ten. We are fully booked tomorrow."

"Great! Will do, thanks, Cindy." Holly turned, but this time took her shoes off before making her way back to Jake.

She heard giggling at her back. "Enjoy," Cindy teased.

Holly waved her off. When she neared their table, she noticed that Jake had just settled the bill and was chatting to Peter.

"Holly is like a sister to us, so please take good care of her."

That's so sweet. "Thank you, Peter." She made her way to his side and leaned on his shoulder.

"Any time. Did you enjoy yourself tonight?"

"Too much. Thank you." Holly practically fell into her chair.

Sniggering, Peter thanked Jake for the tip and bid them both a good night.

"Okay, it's sorted. Luckily there are a few rooms available. Only drawback is that we have to be out before ten tomorrow."

They got up to leave, but Jake paused to rub hard at his face. "I haven't been this woozy in a very long time. I hope I'm not coming down with something."

"You should've stuck with what you had to drink the first time. Mixing is never good."

"It's your fault," he accused her.

Lifting an eyebrow, she asked, "Did you have a good time?"

He looked at her, frowning. "That's a no-brainer."

"Then I'll take the blame."

Jake chuckled, shaking his head.

"I think it's best we call one of the valets to sort out your car," Holly stated.

"They do that here?"

"Of course. We go the extra mile." She smiled.

"Be right back." Jake turned and headed toward Cindy. Holly followed and when she reached them, Cindy was on the phone. She looked flushed, but Holly knew it was because of

Jake's presence. He had that kind of effect on women, including her.

Jake wrapped his arms around Holly and rested his fore-head on hers.

"All sorted. Leave your keys with me. Holly knows where the room is. It's not a long walk down, but I could organize you a golf cart if you'd like?" Cindy addressed Jake, batting her eyelashes at him. She was such a flirt.

"Great, thanks. But there's no need to disturb anyone. We'll walk. It's not like we don't need the fresh air." He took his keys out of his pocket and dropped them on the desk. "Thank you for tonight, it was really amazing, and please let Marabella know I said thanks for everything," Jake spoke over his shoulder on their way out.

"I sure will."

Holly just gave her the eye, glancing over the same shoulder. She knew Cindy too well and it was a given that she'd have something to say in parting, something that would make Holly blush horribly.

Cindy bit hard on her lip to suppress a smile, but Holly winked. "Bye, Cindy."

"See you Monday."

TWELVE

THEY WALKED ALMOST to half a mile to the lodge. Holly laughed as Jake stumbled slightly over rocks and other debris scattered along the path.

"You seriously that drunk?" she asked, holding her hand out for him.

"Did you really have to take me through the canyon?"

"It's not that bad. It's a short cut, unless you want to walk for half a mile that way." She pointed in the opposite direction.

"Canyons are fine."

Holly shook her head slightly, while Jake used his phone's screen light to see where to walk. Unfortunately, she completely missed one of the rocks. Her shoes flew into the air, and a shriek left her mouth as she fell over the rock. She'd always hated that rock and had told Marabella many, many times that someone was going to break his or her neck one day.

"It's not near a path, Holly, so if you are too lazy to walk around, break your neck." Marabella's voice echoed her usual answer every time Holly had complained about it.

Jake picked her up. "Are you okay?"

"You can laugh," Holly said, "I've seen my ass so many times over that stupid rock."

Jake chuckled. "You want me to carry you?"

Holly broke out in a fit of giggles. "You want us both to break our necks?"

"I'm not that drunk." And to prove it, he picked Holly up and threw her over his shoulder as she shrieked.

Her knee ached; she knew it had been scraped, and she'd probably ruined her beautiful black satin number, too. It had cost her a fortune, so if it truly was ruined she would cry.

"Which way, Miss Shortcut?"

"Go left," she mumbled while hanging upside down. See could see a huge welcome sign surrounded by rock and African décor right outside the entrance.

Jake put her down gently and just before they walked inside, he bent down to look at the huge hole the rock had torn in her pants. "We should look at that."

"Just as long as it doesn't hurt, you can do whatever you want," she said without thinking, blushing the minute the words left her mouth. Thank heaven she'd stepped in front of him and had walked a few steps.

"Me? Hurt you? Never!" he admonished in a playful tone as he followed her inside.

Lynette's eyes looked like saucers when she saw Jake, but then she smiled at Holly, which soon turned into a chuckle on noticing the huge hole in her pants.

"You must be Jake. I'm Lynn." She held her hand out to Jake. He took the proffered hand and shook it gently.

"Manly hands, too. They can rub over my body any time," Lynn mumbled under her breath, but not so low that Holly didn't catch every word. Lynn got they eye in return.

"Okay, here is key fifteen." She handed Holly a huge key

holder with three keys dangling from it. "You do know where fifteen is, Holls?"

Holly's expression changed to thoughtful as her mind tried to remember, while simultaneously pointing her finger every which way possible; like she was having a discussion with herself.

"That way." Lynette eventually pointed in the right direction. "How much, exactly, have you had to drink?"

"Oh, shush. Like you don't get wasted every weekend."

"Whatever. Enjoy," she said.

Holly grabbed Jake's hand and pulled him back out of the main entrance.

"So... it's not a room?"

"We call them rooms, but they are actually chalets."

"Is there a shortcut for this one as well, or are we safe?"

Holly burst out laughing again. "We can wait for Luke, if you want. He's usually parking all the cars this time of night." She stretched her neck out. "He should be coming this way any minute now with your BMW."

"You say that like it's a crappy car. For your information, it's a really awesome car."

"Whatever."

Upon seeing headlights approaching, Holly waved. Luke pulled up and stopped, but all you could see through the windshield was a pair of very white teeth. He loved pretending that he was some rich boy behind the steering wheel.

"You want a lift?" he asked, when he'd rolled the window down.

"Just unlock the door, Luke."

"Fresh air is good for you, Holly." He then looked at Jake. "Awesome ride, man."

"Thank you. At least somebody appreciates a good car."

Luke chortled as both Holly and Jake climbed into the back. "Holly is very hard to please."

"Ha-ha," she said sarcastically.

"Appreciate the head's up," Jake joked.

It took all but a short turn to the left and they arrived at the chalet.

She looked at Jake, whose eyes were slightly raised.

Whistling, he said, "Impressive."

"Yeah, it's okay."

"You see?" Luke peered at them in the rear-view mirror, making Jake laugh.

"Thanks for bringing the car around, Luke." Turning to Holly, he said, "What's the hold up, Bee Puke? Let's go."

She rolled her eyes, but climbed out nevertheless. Luke bid his farewell after handing Jake his car keys, and then jogged back to the front office.

Holly had already tried two of the keys before she finally found the right one and opened the door.

The chalet was beautiful, and someone had already lit a fire in the fireplace. She dropped the key onto the table, when Jake's hand grabbed her elbow. He turned her around and picked her up in one swift motion, placing her gently onto the table. She looked up into his face and his ice-green eyes bore into hers. She could feel her mouth becoming dry and swallowed hard.

"Now, let's take a look at that knee."

She wanted to groan. Jake had such a magnetic pull on her she'd forgotten all about her accident earlier.

"Do they have a first aid kit here?" Jake asked.

"I think there is one in the bathroom." Holly pointed in its direction. She all but drooled watching him from the back. Almost as if Jake could hear her slobber hit the ground, he looked over his shoulder and winked.

Jake returned a few seconds later with a small first aid bag under his arm pit. Unzipping it, he selected what he needed.

Holly twitched when he first cleaned her wound with some kind of antiseptic, and then applied ointment. And when Jake bent lower to blow softly on her knee, hot flushes coursed over her entire body.

"That should do it," he stated seductively, whilst looking at her from beneath unbelievably thick lashes. He straightened and leaned closer, their lips barely an inch apart. Her heart beat erratically.

Jake brought his hands up, touching her lips with his thumbs as his fingers feathered over her cheeks. Holly felt like she was on the verge of combusting; her heart beat in her throat, ready to run for the hills, but then she felt herself drown in his amazing eyes.

Jake's hand slowly reached around the back of her neck. With a slight pull toward him, their lips met, and Holly's ears started to ring again as his tongue gained entry into her mouth and began a dance as ancient as time itself.

It seemed as if her blood was beginning to boil, and in the pit of her stomach it felt like a bomb was going to explode.

Holly's hands had gained a life of their own and found themselves tangled up in his hair, but before she could think about what she was doing, her legs followed suit and curled around his waist. She could feel his cold hands on her thighs, but they scorched her flushed skin all the same.

Through the thin silky material, his touch felt like a thousand tiny kisses caressing the side of her leg. She let out a small groan as he pulled her closer to him. His hands squeezed her ass, hard, which made her grab him around the neck, maneuvering herself even closer.

Suddenly, Jake lifted her off the table and began walking them toward the bedroom. He stopped at the foot of the bed and threw her playfully onto it. This made Holly laugh but when her eyes met his, her insides twisted into knots. His scorching eyes and wicked smile made her burn all over, and when he started unbuttoning his shirt, she didn't think she could have gotten any wetter.

Holly felt her mouth become dry. Jake was taking his time and she couldn't stop staring at his perfectly built body, toned muscles and beautiful six-pack that had been hiding beneath his shirt.

She swallowed past the hard lump in her throat as he took the two steps he needed to reach the bed, and once his shins touched the bottom, he placed one knee on the mattress and then the other and began crawling toward her in a predatory manner. When their faces were but a breath apart, time stopped as they stared at each intensely.

Seductively, he parted her legs at the knees, moved between her thighs and lowered his body onto hers. Toying with her, he winked.

Holly could feel her teeth biting the inside of her lip as she tried to control her emotions. *Please don't pass out,* she kept begging in her head. Not that anything of the sort was likely to happen, but this felt like a dream; a fantasy she didn't want to own up to, and she was scared that it would all puff up in a billow of smoke and disappear.

Jake's face hovered over hers for a second, and then their lips touched softly. The kiss started off slow, gentle, erotic, but it became aggressive and the lust within Holly wanted her to rip off her own clothes, as well as the rest of his.

All she wanted was to feel his naked body on hers and, hopefully, finally, him inside of her. Thinking in this manner would've made her blush for secretly wanting him this badly, but thanks to a margarita, a mojito and some kind of Shiraz, modesty flew out the window.

Holly's hands explored to her heart's content. They brushed over his pecks and moved gently over the lines of his abdomen. *He must work out a couple of times a week. Could he be any more perfect?* Her legs, of their own volition, began curling around his waist again, and he finally closed the gap and rested his body on hers.

His hands stroked up her legs, all the way to the sides of her hips. She groaned again as goose bumps shot up all over her skin.

As the kissing intensified so did their shortness of breath, yet neither wanted to pull away. Holly moaned as his erection rubbed against her core and pressed herself harder into him using the strength of her legs.

His hips began to grind, allowing her to reach another kind of ecstasy, the kind that was dangerous. Holly knew she wasn't going to stop this now.

Jake's lips finally left hers, moving slowly to her neck, and as his hands played over her hips she let out another groan. Jake reciprocated by grinding even harder.

Shivers ran down the length of her body when his lips went to her ear. "Do you like this?"

She nodded. "Yes," she whispered, surprised the word made its way out.

Jake kissed her again, tugging and sucking on her lower lip with his teeth. It was driving her insane. His hands left her hips and traveled along the side of her body, moving down and up, and then slowly feathering over her breasts.

Abruptly, he rolled them over so that she was on top. Her lips automatically ran a line down his chest, planting soft kisses everywhere before making their way up to his neck, and then taking his lips again.

Jake spread her legs to either side of his hips and pushed them both up into a sitting position. Giving Holly a smoldering look, he fiddled with the buttons at her throat. When he'd succeeded in undoing the last one, the top part of the suit slid off, revealing her strapless bra.

Jake was a pro at unhooking bra clasps and in under a minute, naked chest touched naked chest, forcing another groan from Holly. She felt her eyes close—simply couldn't keep them open any longer.

Jake moved them once more, and she ended up on her back again. His lips began worshipping her body, softly kissing and nipping down her breastbone, to the left and right of her ribs, and further down to her stomach. This was repeated on the way back up again, but this time he rubbed both his cheeks first over one breast and then the other, sucking gently on her nipples in between.

Holly loved the fact that it wasn't a tug-of-war, the way Brandon used to play with them. Her body was on a high, and she didn't think she could take much more when Jake swiftly moved down again and kissed her on the navel.

An involuntary groan escaped her lips, which only made him chuckle. The hands that had been cold when they'd first entered the room, were now flaming hot. The mattress shifted, and when she looked at Jake from under her eyelashes, he began removing the rest of her clothes ever so sensually. She was just thankful she'd worn her sexy panties and not the ones she had wanted to originally. She had secretly hoped that something like this might happen tonight; he had said he would stop by later that evening.

Holly had been watching Jake's face so intently that when she heard something hit the floor with a dull thud, only then did she realize he'd swept her clothes clear off the bed. Her eyes bulged wider when Jake lifted himself off her and sat back on his haunches, because the only item of clothing that still remained on his body were his boxers.

How the heck? The thought bounced into her mind.

When he saw her looking at him in question, he bent forward and kissed her again. This time, though, it didn't start off gently. Their tongues performed some sort of tango, one that made her breathing escalate feverishly fast. She felt as if she was drowning, hating that she was weak in his presence.

Jake's hands found their way to her breasts, rubbing in circles, not hard but not gently, either. It was perfect, so much so it only served to make Holly ache for more. A jolt of heat and hunger rose in the pit of her stomach, moving down to her core as his warm tongue sucked gently on one nipple again.

Jake groaned softly, too, and the vibration of his voice against her skin wanted to make her tear out of her body. His hands slid down the side of her breasts, past her ribs, and then over her panty line.

She felt the lace fabric being pulled down by his expert hands, at the same time his tongue drew circles on her stomach and licked its way down toward her navel again. This time, though, it didn't stop at her navel, but went lower and lower until her toes curled and her back arched as his tongue found her swollen clit.

By now, Holly was panting. That unexplainable itchy, out of this world feeling erupted from inside her and moved up toward her belly. Her teeth bit hard on her lower lip as she tried to hide her level of pleasure.

She'd never reached an orgasm this fast in her life. Sadly, it had usually taken hours of foreplay and hard sex afterward, for at least half an hour, before she could reach one. Jake hadn't even started and she was already feeling like she wanted to explode.

She let out a squeal, grabbed Jake by the shoulders and pulled him up toward her. And just like that, she convulsed beneath him uncontrollably, every muscle within her pulling and releasing. Holly had the good grace to blush when she saw the look on his face.

Thankfully, Jake chuckled. "Why are you taking all the pleasure away from me?"

"I'm not. How the hell did you do that?"

He smiled, his eyes traveling up and down the length of her body.

She laughed at his facial expression.

Jake became serious for a second. "I need to tell you something."

She swallowed hard, hoping it wasn't bad news. "What is it?"

He cocked his head slightly to the left with a lopsided smile. "I struggle to orgasm. So... this could turn into an all-night thing. Don't feel bad if I don't get there. It's normal."

Holly felt sad for him. "You don't get orgasms?"

"I do, but not through sex. I seem to have no problem all by myself for some reason." He chuckled and looked away.

"Don't. This is something we'll have to work on. It's not fair I experience one and you don't."

"Bee Puke?"

Holly laughed.

"Don't, you are going to drop dead, and what am I going to do then?" he joked.

"Shut up," she said, reaching for him again.

The fact that he'd told her meant the world to her. He was that someone who deserved to have an orgasm. She couldn't understand how in the world Jake wasn't able to reach that pinnacle. What was worse was how any girl would be okay with that. Holly was nothing if not determined, and she wasn't going to give up until Jake reached that same kind of ecstasy.

What followed happened pretty quickly. As soon as Holly kissed him it turned feverish again, and this time Jake pulled his boxers down with one hand, kicking them off the rest of the way with his feet. Nudging her legs apart with his knee, he guided his shaft into her wetness. Holly moaned and whimpered loudly, while Jake grunted and groaned as he thrust inside her.

It was the most amazing sex she had ever had. Jake just happened to be of the size most guys dreamed of, and she seemed to be turning into one of those girls who scratched the guy's back and bit their necks when they wanted more.

Jake didn't complain, though. In fact, he groaned every time she did that. But it wasn't a disapproving growl by a long shot; more of a guttural *I'm going to fuck you even harder because of it* groan.

Holly's core pulsed and she could feel she was becoming wetter as Jake moved inside her, if that was even possible. She couldn't keep her voice at bay and moaned louder, begging for more. And then when her climax reached its peak she screamed, which turned into a funny type of sex laugh, the kind where you are out of breath. Her body shivered when Jake rolled off. "Holy crap, that was amazing!"

Jake chuckled and shook his head slightly.

Holly's hand moved across his chest and rested on his shoulder.

He bent and looked at her, and then kissed her softly on the tip of her nose.

She was tired, but didn't want to break her promise. Jake was going to have an orgasm, even if it was the last thing she did. "Again," she begged, pushing Jake over and onto his back.

When Jake's eyes questioned what she was doing, she threw a leg over his hips and sat back, slowly rubbing herself back and forth on his shaft.

"Holly?"

"Shush," she whispered, and then kissed him.

It turned into another wrestling match where she ended up

getting another orgasm. By the fourth one, all sorts of Kama Sutra positions jumped into her head.

She'd always wanted to try them, but had never felt the trust she needed with any other guy to carry them out. However, this time was different. She was sure she could do most of them; her body was made for it, and with four years of yoga under her belt, she could practically contort into any position.

This time, she turned around, with her back to him, and guided his shaft inside her. Jake filled her up like no one else ever had, which made the hairs on her body stand on end. She let out another groan, wondering if there would ever be a time she'd tire of having sex with him.

She arched her pelvis forward, bending his shaft against his erection. Jake groaned deeply, and when she began to move the groans became louder and more frequent.

When he grabbed her hips and his movements escalated and thrusts became deeper, she knew she was onto something. She hoped it was stimulating his shaft at just the right spot, which would in turn drive him as insane as he was driving her. That still remained to be seen, but Holly was hopeful.

With Jake's help, the movement became fairly easy. She started to voice her moans again and couldn't stop them, and no matter how hard she bit her lip they just poured out her mouth.

He was fucking her brains out, and all she wanted was more. Holly was on the verge of hyperventilating as she reached yet another orgasm. But this time, Jake didn't stop.

"Holy fuck," he growled, lifting her higher and plunging her down harder, faster, and deeper onto him.

In the next instant, Jake pushed her forward and onto her belly, falling on top of her. He growled as warm liquid squirted over her back.

Holly, relieved, giggled softly.

Breathing hard and fast, Jake chuckled in awe. He pulled

away from her back as they were in an awkward position and rolled onto his, taking her with him.

Holly slumped to the side, breathing just as hard.

"How the fuck did you do that?"

Smiling, she lifted her head and grabbed his chin with one hand. "Now that would be giving my secrets away," she said softly. She was beyond tired, but it was the fantastic kind of tired. Holly winked, leaned forward and placed a kiss on his chin, and then his lips, right before she got up to take a quick shower.

It was no-brainer that he joined her and had one last session in the shower.

Holly felt as if she was barely going to make it to the bed, but to her surprise she did. The cold shower and the warmth of the linen felt amazing on her body, and when she placed her head gently on Jake's chest and his arms tucked around her, she closed her eyes.

She felt his lips brush the tip of her nose softly, and then she passed out.

THIRTEEN

"WAKE UP, SLEEPING BEAUTY," Jake's voice sang softly in her ear the next morning.

Holly's eyes seemed to burn when she forced them open, the light making it worse. Grabbing the pillow, she pulled it over her head. She could hear him chuckle and when she moved her legs, pain stabbed the inside of her thighs. Memories of the night before filled her mind. She couldn't help but grin, pretty chuffed with herself for having given him an orgasm on their first sexual experience.

Jake peeked beneath her pillow. "We need to get going, it's already nine-thirty."

"You're kidding! Why didn't you say so before?" she yelped, jumping up and out of bed, not giving a damn if she ached all over. Grabbing the duvet, she high-tailed it to the bathroom and into the shower, but right before she turned the taps on, she heard Jake laughing in the background.

Dropping the duvet on the floor, she stepped into the glass shower stall. The lukewarm water felt heavenly on her muscles. Relaxing with her hands flat on the wall in front of her, she tilted her head backward, letting the water run down her face and hair.

Flashbacks of the previous night started playing through her mind; his lips, the way his green eyes burned right through her skin and directly into her soul. *Damn! Jake is so hot and beautiful.* But that ever present fear of losing him emerged in the pit of her stomach again. She'd promised herself that she would not be so insecure, but it always found a way to creep into her mind.

Holly really didn't want to think about that any more, but apart from the sex, what else was there for her to offer him? She just hoped that Cosmopolitan was right about men and how important sex was for ninety-nine percent of them. She prayed that Jake wouldn't fall into that one percent.

A soft knock on the door made her jump. She shied away, shimming up against the wall, scared that he might see her buck naked in the shower, but then giggled inwardly. She'd just spent an entire night squealing like a pig, scratching him like a cat, purring like a lioness, and pretending to be the queen of Kama Sutra, as well as share a shower with him through all of it. Yet she was feeling insecure over what Jake would think of her naked body still.

"Yes?" she shouted, over the water's noise.

The door opened and Jake stepped in. She could feel his eyes on her, but he uttered not one word. When Jake's eyes finally met hers, he was grinning lustfully. His eyes gave nothing away besides the evident longing. He dumped her bag on the floor. "This was dropped off earlier. Thought you might need it in here."

Shyly, she mumbled, "Thank you."

When Jake left, closing the door behind him, she was blushing over the way he'd looked at her.

Holly wondered if she was really that beautiful to him. Nobody had ever looked at her that way, until the gorgeous hooligan of her dreams had walked into her life. He was so the last man she'd thought would ever look her way, not to mention looking at her the way he so blatantly had a few seconds ago.

Coming back down to earth, she turned the taps off, stepped out, grabbed the towel she'd also unceremoniously left on the floor outside the shower door, and draped it over her body.

The bag Jake had thoughtfully brought in contained her toothbrush and toothpaste, which she usually took with her on the days she worked double shift, as well as the clothes she'd worn yesterday during the day shift.

She pulled on a tank top that clung to her body like latex, thinking that it felt good to not wear a bra. Over that, she wore her lace top with a beautiful ribbon that weaved through the fabric underneath her breasts. This was followed by pulling on a pair of black shorts over her naked body. As for shoes, she stepped into her wedges, fastening them around her ankles with laces.

Holly applied a small amount of makeup with the sole purpose of trying to mask her puffy eyes in order to make them appear normal. And finally, she tucked her long, curly hair into a bun, fastening it with a clip. She had to admit that she looked good, good enough to face him, at least. A smile played over her lips.

When she opened the door and walked out, Jake's eyes rolled over her like a scanner.

"You look beautiful. Is this how you look every day?"

"Thank you, Jake," she said, shyly. "But, yes, I have to. I constantly deal with guests, so I need to look pretty and well put together at all times."

"Lucky guests."

She snorted as she picked up the clothes that had been discarded the night before, chucking them into her bag. When she straightened, Jake's arms wrapped around her, and his lips kissed hers gently.

"Thank you so much for last night, Holly. Who would've thought?" It wasn't really a question, at least one where an answer was expected.

Holly just smiled and kissed him softly. "We should really be going," she advised against his lips.

Jake grunted in return.

Once they'd made sure they had all their possessions, they walked out hand in hand toward his BMW. It was a gorgeous morning and the air was pleasantly cool.

They drove down to the front office, where Holly dropped the key off with Petra—the weekend girl, while Jake waited in the car for her. She was in such a hurry, she simply waved at Petra without any form of greeting and rushed back out.

"Where to?" he asked, when she'd gotten in.

"Bernie's, please. I need to get underwear. I don't know how some people find it freeing not wearing any at all."

Jake's entire body froze. It looked as if he was in some kind of pain, making her wonder if she'd somehow hurt him last night.

"Are you okay?"

Jake cleared his throat. "I'll be fine," he said, his voice sounding hoarse.

"You don't sound fine. Tell me what's wrong"

He gave her a sideways look when he stopped at the red light. "You not wearing underwear, is imprinted right here." He tapped the left side of his temple. "You just over-stimulated my left anterior cingulate cortex. If we were not in this car right now, missy..." He grunted, which made her laugh out loud. "And now you are laughing."

"Sorry, I didn't mean to," she said, through obvious snorts.

"You should count yourself lucky we are on the road and

not in my room," he mumbled, but leaned her way anyway to give her another juicy kiss.

Someone blew their horn, breaking their little intimate moment. When Jake took a peek in his rearview mirror, the driver behind him was waving his hands in the air and mouthing what were obviously swear words.

Holly tried very hard, not really succeeding, to suppress her laughter.

Jake rolled his eyes but stepped on the gas pedal, mumbling something while looking in his rearview mirror.

"See, what did I tell you? You BMW drivers think you own the road."

Jake roared with laughter. "You are so lucky for another reason, smart mouth. If it weren't for other drivers on this road, I would've shown you what BMW drivers are really like."

Holly laughed but not out loud. It was evident in the shaking of her shoulders.

The drive to Bernie's was relatively short. She left Jake to explain where they had been the night before, while she snuck away to put on some underwear, exchange her wedges for flip flops, and her black shorts for a pair of jean shorts. The beautiful lace tank top was replaced by a bright, yellow summer top adorned with sparkly stars on one side.

Bernie gave her the eye when Holly joined them in the living room.

"What? I'm old enough to take care of myself, thank you, mom."

"I didn't say a single thing," Bernie retorted.

"Oh, you didn't have to. Those eyes of yours speak a language all their own."

Harrumphing, Bernie ignored her comment and asked, "Well, what are we doing today? Sam is at his grandparents, so we've got the whole Saturday to ourselves." Bernie clapped her hands excitedly.

"Do we want them with us?" Holly asked Jake.

Affronted, Bernie gasped.

"I'm joking, Berns. You're so sensitive sometimes."

"Sure you were, Holls," Bernie replied sarcastically.

Holly could see her friend biting her lip to stop herself from saying what she really wanted to. Eventually, Holly and Jake chuckled; they knew her that well.

Bernie just smiled askew, knowing exactly what they'd been thinking.

"That's right, keep it to yourself," Holly warned her playfully.

"I'm just teasing you. I'm glad you have started living again." Bernie leaned on Holly's shoulder.

Leo joined them not a short time later.

Jake caught him up on current events, and then they started discussing the day's possibilities.

"I'm starving. Shall we go have something to eat?" Jake asked.

Agreeing to start with breakfast, it was decided they'd eat at the same diner Holly and Jake had had lunch at a few days back. Holly ended up ordering a farm breakfast of bacon and sausages—not that she hadn't had enough sausage to last her a good couple of weeks the night before—accompanied by hash browns, jam and toast, grilled tomato, and mushrooms on the side.

"Shit, Holls, how do you stay so thin?"

"I work out," she snapped back at Bernie.

"When, apart from last night, have you been to a gym these past three months?"

Holly gasped. "Bernie!"

Jake and Leo both pulled their lips in tightly in an effort to not laugh. They must have been making one hell of an effort with their teeth, because both looked like they were in pain.

"I'm just saying." Bernie shrugged.

Blushing, Holly couldn't stop herself from giggling. And she couldn't hide behind a menu, either, as the waitress had literally taken them away not five seconds before.

Jake's phone rang. He looked at the screen and sighed before answering. "Jake," he barked.

Holly was all ears, and it was evident by the shrill tone of a woman's voice on the other side that all was not well.

"None of your business, Amelia."

Holly relaxed as she knew it was one of his sisters.

"Nothing."

Jake's answers were short, brooking no discussion. But after the next few back and forths, a smile spread across his face as his eyes caught Holly staring at him. "When I feel it's the right time." Jake looked at Holly and winked. "Stay out of this Amelia, she's already terrified of meeting Mom."

Holly immediately knew what Amelia was asking; when were they going to meet her. She had to admit, it made her feel all warm and fuzzy inside, but Jake was right. She *was* terrified of meeting his mother.

Jake chuckled. "Paintball." He made gestures with his hands, accompanying the conversation he was having, and played with his eyes. Holly found herself smiling. Amelia babbled so fast on the other end, Holly couldn't make out one word. "Fine, but we go to the one on Heathcliff Road."

Holly could hear Amelia protest by the loudness and tone of her voice, but Jake stuck to his guns. "Heathcliff Road or nothing, Amelia. I don't play at any other place."

Amelia had one more thing to say, and then Jake disconnected.

"You are so going to get your ass kicked." Bernie's finger was in Holly's face.

"Shut up. Paintball?" Holly asked, looking at Jake.

"Don't worry. I'll protect you."

Leo gave Jake a look. "So we're not teaming up on the girls anymore?"

Jake chortled. "Nope." He shook his head, his eyes huge and round.

Holly giggled.

Leo looked at her accusingly. "What have you done to my paintball partner?"

"Would you really like to know?"

Leo closed his eyes, sighed, and then shook his head fervently. "Err... that would be a no, thank you."

At that, everyone smiled stupidly.

WHEN THEIR FOOD ARRIVED, they dug in, famished, with all four thoroughly enjoying their lovely meal. Once the bill was settled, they walked out to Jake's car. Jake took a moment to place a call, speaking to someone named Steve.

He asked him to keep the Vendetta course open, and that they would be there in approximately half an hour. He also told Steve that Amelia would probably check in first and that he wasn't sure at that stage how many would be joining, but that it would most definitely turn into a war.

Jake laughed at something Steve was saying, while simultaneously opening the door for Holly. He really knew how to make a girl feel special.

Holly was silent on their way to the paintball place, wherever Heathcliff Road was. She'd never played before, and coupled with meeting his sister for the first time was making her stomach turn into all sorts of knots. She was brought out of her thoughts over how bad this day was going to turn out, when Jake startled her by putting his hand on her leg.

"Why are you so quiet?"

"I've never played paintball before. Is it true you walk away with bruises the size of tennis balls?"

He laughed. "Don't worry, nobody will hit you today, and if they do they will regret ever having made you a target."

Holly smiled at him and laid her head on his arm. She felt his lips and breath on her hair just as they pulled into a parking lot surrounded by hundreds of tires stacked up against its fence. She couldn't see the play areas as they were covered with nets, but she could see the tops of wooden towers, which once again sported tires and lots of hiding spots. Seeing that made her feel somewhat better, not having known what to expect.

They made their way inside, where Jake greeted a big, bald guy whom she assumed to be Steve.

"Holly, Steve. Steve, Holly." Jake made the introductions.

Holly greeted him with a handshake and a smile. Jake then led both Holly and Bernie to the locker room's entrance, where the women changed into a one piece suit, like an overall. Holly's heart bounced when she heard laughter coming from within the change room.

"Have you met his family?" Holly asked Bernie.

"Only Robin, but it was like for a couple of seconds. Leo knows all of them, since he was practically part of the family growing up."

Taking a deep breath, Holly followed Bernie inside. A group of women were yelling playfully at each other, making jokes and laughing. Bernie and Holly each picked a suit from the closet, choosing the opposite corner furthest away from them.

"So, he's coming." A tall brunette in her mid-twenties asked another woman with black hair. When the girl turned around, she had the same ice-green eyes as Jake, as well as the same beauty, and Holly knew it could only be Amelia.

"Yes, and don't even think about it, he's seeing someone now." She gave the brunette a smile, one that would make any guy's knees wobble.

"I don't give a shit. He's not married yet."

Bernie's posture changed. Holly put a hand on her arm, stopping her before she uttered a single word.

"Please, don't. I really want to make a good first impression," Holly begged her softly.

"Fine, but that bitch is going down," Bernie snapped under her breath, which made Holly suppress her laughter. Poor girl, she had no idea what she'd just unleashed on herself.

Amelia chuckled at her friend. "Good luck with that. He's spending like every minute he can with her. Mom is really starting to worry about the situation. It's so annoying."

"Do you think he brought her with?" the brunette asked, skeptically.

"I don't think he would be here if she was free. She works at some sort of lodge and something tells me she works weekends."

"Bonus," the brunette shouted.

"You are going to see your ass, Ash. Don't say I didn't warn you. He's head-over-heels for this one."

"Puhleease! Jake's crushes are like seasons. Constantly changing."

"I'm not so sure. This one's really got a hold on him. He's never missed a Sunday lunch before, and last week..." Amelia didn't finish her sentence.

Holly was still a little upset that he'd left what was clearly family time in order to spend the day with her.

"Yeah, right. Just like he was madly in love with that married woman. Got over her, didn't he?"

"That was different. At least he's opening himself up to

romantic possibilities again."

"Whatever. It's my time, sister. I haven't worked at losing my fat ass for nothing."

Bernie gave Holly a stern look. The kind that pulled her jaw muscles tight from not lashing out.

Holly only smiled at her friend. She was still worried about this married woman business and by the sound of Amelia's tone, it had been and was something difficult for Jake to let go of. She wasn't sure that she wanted to know how hard.

The women walked out soon after, while Holly struggled with her goggles.

"That girl is going to wish she'd never lost her fat ass, today," Bernie threatened, making Holly giggle.

"Don't pay any attention to her. Jake is so over airheads, and that my friend, is an airhead."

Bernie snatched the goggles from Holly and yanked the straps tighter. When she gave them back, Holly placed them on her head to see if they fit.

Satisfied, both left and followed the exit signs. They could hear people talking up ahead. One stood out; the brunette's voice became sweet as honey.

Holly's belly twisted again just listening to it.

"C'mon, Leo can partner up with someone else today. I need someone to protect my skinny ass."

Jake laughed. "Leo *is* partnering with someone else today."

She gasped excitedly. "See! Then where is the harm?"

"Sorry, but I've got my own sexy, skinny ass to protect."

Holly smiled from ear to ear. That was the sweetest thing anyone had ever said about her.

"Your ass is anything but skinny."

Someone's laughter bounced off the walls.

"Gee, woman, you think I'm that full of myself?"

Holly and Bernie finally walked into the room, and immediately caught Jake's attention.

"Really, missy, you are killing me," Jake smirked, wrapping his arms around Holly.

"Seriously? It's a paint suit. Nothing gorgeous about this," she retorted.

"You make everything look gorgeous."

Holly rolled her eyes, albeit sporting a huge smile on her face.

Jake eyes twinkled as he kissed her softly.

Throughout this exchange, she could practically feel daggers being thrown at her back. A throat was cleared, loudly, and when Holly looked up, brunette-chick did not look the least bit impressed. Her lips had been drawn into a thin line, almost as if she'd just eaten a lemon. When her eyes met Holly's, though, she instantly looked away.

"And who is this?" Amelia stepped closer, looking pointedly at Jake.

Jake looked up at the ceiling, as if he was praying for patience, earning him a smack on the arm from Amelia. This made a dark-haired, bear of a guy laugh out loud.

"Amelia, Holly. Holly, Amelia. Happy now?" he mocked. He continued with the introductions. "Holly, this is Armand," he said, pointing at the same guy who'd laughed.

He looked like a geek with a pair of glasses resting on his nose and so not Amelia's type, but neither was she Jake's and she got him.

"And this is Ashley."

Ashley, being the brunette. She waved once in the air and in no particular direction, but gave Holly a fake smile and stare. The rest were introduced as Victor, Mark and Paul. Jake looked at the one guy, clearly not remembering his name.

"Herschel," the guy said, while giving Holly a real smile.

"Watch out for Herschel," he whispered in Holly's direction, which made those closest to them snigger.

"The rest are my sister's friends, whose names I can't remember. Sorry guys."

"Shame on you, Jake," a blond yelled.

Just then a buzzer went off, and guns housing fairly large sized balls appeared on the wall. The first two were green, which Jake immediately took possession of. The second pair pink, and yellow the third. All the colors she could think of were in bags with guns right next to them. Teams of two now shared the same color gun. Jake handed one to Holly, its paint balls also green.

"How do you use it?" Holly asked, accidentally hitting the trigger, sending a paint ball into Jake's chest. He grunted and closed his eyes in pain. She could see the pain reflected on his face.

This obviously made for a funny situation, especially when Holly tried to apologize. *Shit! I'm really so clumsy at times.* "I'm so sorry, Jake."

He rubbed the side of his torso where a huge splatter of green inked his suit. "You are supposed to hit them, not your own teammate." He looked like a little boy.

Holly, on the other hand, forced her lips tighter and tighter together to prevent herself from laughing. But when Jake couldn't keep it in any longer and threw his head back with laughter, she followed suit.

"I'll be fine, but it's going to cost you extra loving care tonight."

"Now *that* I can do," she replied, loud enough for Ashley to hear.

Clapping loudly, Leo shouted, "Pep talk, people." Looking at Jake, he questioned, "Jake, you up for it?"

"You betcha, dude," Jake shot back, his voice sounding like that of a team leader on one of those PlayStation games.

Leo went on to relay the rules and regulations of the game. They formed two lines as Jake walked with the gun over his shoulder, reminding Holly of a really badass soldier. He gave a really nice speech about how this was war. That really made Bernie and Holly want to laugh at how serious he sounded. Plus, he kept looking at everyone's guns; almost memorizing which ones belonged to whom.

"And," he continued, still in a serious manner, "if I find any color on that woman's body after the game," he pointed in Holly's direction, "you are going to wish you'd never heard of paintball."

"That's not fair," the blond shouted, whose name Jake couldn't remember.

"I don't play fair, cadet. It's war, and that was a friendly warning." Jake was all serious again as he walked back to Holly's side and winked. When he reached her, he lowered her goggles. "When the second buzzer rings, we run like hell. I've got a funny feeling a lot of people are going to aim at us."

Holly felt like crying, but she kept her poise. She really wasn't looking forward to the paintballs hitting her. As soon as the second buzzer went off, Jake pulled her in one direction. She ran as fast as she could.

When a third buzzer went off, paint balls flew past her, with two or three painfully hitting her on the butt and legs. It made her stop and rub at the sore spots, when more hurtled their way. She lost the grip on Jake's hand in the process of trying to protect herself, but felt him grabbing her arm just as two blue paint balls hit him on the butt.

"Just run," he shouted, turning around and firing back.

Holly waited for him behind a wooden bunker. When Jake darted past her, she ran behind him. She was it again, but this time she kept on running, even though her back and ass were throbbing in pain.

Jake grabbed her hand again, breaking right and around another bunker to a huge, wooden watchtower. He looked around him quickly, and then kicked one of the poles, hard. Something on the ground shifted open and she noticed stairs leading down.

He maneuvered Holly in front of him, allowing her to go first. She stumbled down the stairs as she couldn't see properly, and because her legs and practically every inch of her body ached. The stairs led to a small room with holes cut into the wall. She looked through one and saw grass and bushes.

"What is this place?"

"It's my payback spot. Take off your suit. I need to look at your bruises."

Holly looked at him incredulously.

Sighing, Jake raised his eyebrow. "They can't see us down here, Holly. Now do as I say. Take it off."

She unzipped the front of the suit and stepped out of it. Huge blue and red marks were tattooed on her legs and butt, aching like a bitch. She also had two bruises on her back that hurt like hell.

"I'm true to my word. I'm really sorry, Bee Puke." Jake kissed her softly before he climbed onto some sort of bunker on beams. He pulled the trigger, and cries of pain followed. His name was yelled numerous times, which satisfied Holly. He finished both their paint balls in under half an hour.

"Now what do we do?" Holly asked, worried that if somebody found them, they were going to be in big trouble.

"Now, you're mine." He winked, pulling her into him. Jake proceeded to kiss her shoulder, as well as every single bruise he could find on her body, including those on her butt. They still hurt, of course, but the tingling feeling he left her with replaced some of the aches.

With her bruises taken care of, somewhat, it was time for

some lip on lip action. It wasn't long before they seemed lost in another world, and Holly knew that if she hadn't gotten hit they would have probably done it right there on the dirt floor.

When a buzzer went off again, Jake groaned and pulled away, but not before imparting with one more quick kiss. It took another ten seconds for Holly to think straight and for the ringing in her ears to stop.

"Let's go. The game is over, so now we see how many people we've injured."

They exited through a different door and walked out into the sunlight. It was an entrance on the opposite side of where they'd entered. Once everyone had gathered back in the same room, Holly started to feel awful. Those whose colors were splattered over Holly's overall, hadn't been left with the bluish overalls they'd all worn into the arena. They were now green.

"Did you really have to be so violent?" yelled the girl with blond hair.

"It's only a game, Candice," Amelia interjected.

Jake chuckled.

"You okay?" Bernie asked Holly.

"Yeah. I'll live."

The party broke up and headed to the change rooms respectively. Holly could feel Ashley's eyes boring into the back of her head as she cleaned up, and if looks could kill she would've dropped dead.

She couldn't help but wonder if all women behaved in the same manner when it came to Jake Peters. If one thought about it, he was training to be a doctor, had a good head on his shoulders, not to mention the looks that made women's knees wobble.

But Holly knew different; there was more to Jake Peters than just a pretty face. He was exactly the type of man she had been waiting for her entire life.

FOURTEEN

IT HAD BEEN DECIDED that everyone would meet up at a nearby restaurant. Holly's stomach grumbled and growled in such a way, it would have seemed she hadn't had breakfast that morning. Burgers was the chosen meal, and Holly was the one every girl around the table stared at.

Amelia smiled and tried to strike up a conversation. "I love the fact that you are different from the girls my brother used to bring home."

Holly smiled. "In what way?"

"They only ever ate salads, accompanied by low calorie wine." She rolled her eyes. "So annoying."

"What's wrong with salad?" Ashley asked. "We like to take care of our bodies."

"Oh, please, Ashley. Three months ago you were stuffing your face with McDonalds. Now it's only low calorie food, and all it does is make you miserable. You should eat what you want; everything in moderation, of course."

"That's easy for you to say, Miss Perfect. You've never had to deal with a slow metabolism. I just look at a potato and it goes straight to my hips."

The men were engaged in their own discussion, which more than likely involved anything with an engine, while Amelia and Ashley talked about food and calories. Holly hated the conversation, but agreed with Amelia's reasoning. After all, there was only one life to be lived, so eating whatever made a person happy, in moderation, wouldn't do any harm.

Holly found herself giggling inwardly as the two girls bickered. Still, she couldn't help but like Jake's sister. She was really beautiful. Her lips were just as succulent as her brother's, and she was sure that had she been attracted to women in that way, she would've definitely gone for Amelia.

She also had the kind of laugh that made everyone want to join in. Holly loved the way Jake and her husband, Armand, teased her about how she'd ran and ducked for cover as different colored paint balls flew through the air.

They parted company at around three, which saw Holly walking like a cripple to Jake's car. Her legs seemed to be pounding and she felt like crying from all the pain. "Don't ever ask me to play paintball again. I'm not cut out for this," she told Jake, deadly serious.

His expression was one she'd never seen before. It was as if he could feel her pain and winced on her behalf. It made Holly feel a different kind of pain, the kind where she needed to be patient, even though it hurt.

"I'm so sorry, Bee Puke. I should've protected you better."

Bernie and Leo looked at each other, grinning like mad things. They obviously thought his nickname for Holly was hilarious. She had to admit, though, that the way Jake said it sounded special.

They dropped Leo and Bernie off and bid their farewells after Holly grabbed an overnight bag.

The ride felt long, or maybe it was just exhaustion from the day's adventure. Her eyes flew open when Jake slowed down, turned into a driveway, and stopped in front of a garage to a double-story house. It wasn't fancy or anything, but it was huge. Tall windows took up most of its front, and a small garden caught Holly's eyes as one of the garage doors opened. Music blared in the background. She couldn't tell if it was coming from the house itself, or one of the neighbors.

Jake pulled into the garage and crawled to a stop. He sighed, more out of exhaustion, Holly thought than anything else.

"Home, sweet home," he sang in a seductively gruff voice. He was also giving her the beneath-thick-lashes look when he leaned in toward her. Their lips lingered a breath apart for a couple of seconds, her heart beat rapidly.

Jake's hand went to her face. His thumb and fingers touched her cheek softly, and she felt as if her heart was going to bounce right out of her throat at the same time as she drowned in his ice-green eyes.

Holly felt his hand slowly moving around to the back of her neck. With a slight tug, their lips touched. Her ears started to hum as his tongue danced around hers, gently sucking. This was the mother of all kisses; she felt amazing, and could feel herself slowly floating away in pleasure.

Before long, her hands had tangled up in his hair, and without too much thought she swung one leg over the shift gear and across Jake's lap. She winced as reality hit on her blue and purple bruised leg, but she didn't stop. She could feel his cold hands rest firmly yet gently on her thighs. Her skin was on fire.

Holly let out a small groan when Jake pulled her closer to him and away from the steering wheel, which had kind of been digging into her back.

His hands slid down to her butt, gently kneading, back and forth, and up and down.

She grabbed him around the neck and shifted even closer, wincing again as her leg bumped against the side of his door.

This made them both laugh because she was complaining under her breath.

"The car is maybe not a good idea at the moment?" he said, burrowing his face into her neck. His lips lightly touched the skin on her neck, and she felt as if she would melt like butter on a hot summer day.

How on earth can one man make me feel all of this?

Their lips found each other again and she moaned as Jake sucked her lower lip.

"We should really get out," he whispered, through half-moon eyes.

Sitting back on Jake's lap, Holly looked down at her legs, splayed weirdly either side of his hips, the steering wheel digging into her back once more. "How?"

Jake grinned. His hand reached down the left side of the seat. With a jerk, the seat suddenly moved backward.

The motion happened so quickly, she shrieked, nearly head-butting him when the seat abruptly stopped. Jake shook with laughter, while opening the door.

Trying to get up and off his lap proved to be really tricky. When Holly attempted to move her leg over his hips, she lost her balance and dug her knee into his groin.

"Argh," Jake growled, the sound making its way from deep in his throat. "I deserved that."

The pain he desperately tried to hide, told her she'd really hit bull's eye. She prayed she hadn't maimed him in some form or other, and hoped that it would still be able to perform in a more private setting.

Holly snorted whilst trying to regain her balance, apologizing all in one go. When she eventually managed to clamber out, she nearly stumbled again as pins and needles rushed up her legs and pain pulled on her muscles. She grabbed the door to regain her balance.

"Please, don't take out my door," he joked on a huge grin, revealing a perfect row of teeth and sharp edged canines, the ones Holly loved and one of the features that made his smile extra sexy.

Look away, she rebuked herself. She turned her head, clutching her bag in her arms, and made room for Jake to get out. An arm snaked around her waist, pulling her closer to him, before he opened the door leading into the house.

They walked into the living room, where a long L-shaped couch greeted them. The room had a modern vibe feel to it; rich, dark brown and red colors accented it, and a huge TV was mounted against the wall. A fluffy, white carpet stuck out from underneath a coffee table, and tall orange lamps had been placed at two corners.

The dining room was just as gorgeous, with a huge, wooden table and high-backed chairs placed dead center. Jake steered her to the left and they entered a hallway. There were so many doors leading to other rooms as they walked down the hall that for a second, she thought she was in a maze.

She saw the kitchen and through its many windows, saw lights and people having a good time. Now she knew where the extremely loud music had been coming from, his back yard.

"Sorry about the noise, this literally happens every weekend, thanks to Robin."

"Your other sister?"

He nodded. "Yes. I now have the privilege of living with her again."

Holly giggled as they reached the end of the hall. An iron gate met them and Jake unlocked it.

Holly just looked at him.

"Don't give me that look. This is for my own safety."

"Your own safety? What about the rest?" she asked, thinking about burglars entering the house at night or something.

"Not that kind of safety. If I told you how many times I've woken up with Robin's friends in my bed—and I wasn't drunk by the way—I would need all my hands and toes, and probably yours, too. This gate has literally saved my life from further awkward situations."

Holly grabbed the handrail and started to climb the stairs, laughing. She could hear Jake locking it behind him and his footsteps followed right behind her. When she opened the door, she found herself in a very organized room, too organized to belong to a guy.

Her eyes fell on the king size bed covered in a black duvet and matching pillows; it looked extremely comfy and inviting. She felt his arms wrap around her as the door closed.

He slowly turned her around to face him. Jake grabbed her ass softly and guided her backward toward the bed, and when the backs of her knees hit the end, he picked her up gently and lowered her onto it. As the kiss broke, their eyes met. Holly's insides twisted into knots; his bedroom eyes and sly smile made her blood boil.

Jake took a step back and started to pull his shirt up and over his head.

Holly's mouth turned into a desert. She couldn't stop staring at his body, her eyes traveling up and down the length of his perfection, until they noticed the green and purple bruises on the side of his torso where she'd accidentally shot him. Her mouth pulled down as she stared at the spot.

Reaching out, she ran the back of her hand over them. "I'm sorry, Jake" she whispered, without taking her gaze from the bruises.

"I'm a big boy. I can handle it. Besides, you'll make it up to me."

Holly blushed a very deep shade of red, but Jake was having

none of it. He looked serious, seductive, and most obviously turned on.

She swallowed hard.

His face lingered only inches from hers, the intensity of his stare all-consuming. Jake maneuvered his legs between hers and winked.

Holly felt her teeth grind in anticipation.

Their lips touched, lightly. The beginning of the kiss was slow and tentative; it was gentle yet hungry, so much so, all Holly wanted to do was rip off her clothes. She not only wanted to feel his naked body on top of hers again, but she needed to. And she no longer cared about the unsightly bruises dotting her body, because just thinking about Jake and wanting him with her whole being made her shiver. It was still hard to accept the fact that for now, he wanted her like no other man ever had. For now, though, he was hers, and she was equally his.

Almost shyly, Holly ran her hands over his chest, pausing to allow her fingers to brush his nipples teasingly, moving lower over the lines of his abdomen, and then softly over his bruise. She really felt awful, but of one thing she was sure, and that was that she couldn't keep her hands off his body, off him.

Growling low and deep, Jake slid his arms around her back, lifting her slightly so she could wrap her legs around his waist. She complied, and once she did he placed his right knee on the bed and then his right arm in order to support them both, bending her backward gently until she was flat on her back. He ran his hands down her sides, over her stomach, and around to her ass. Gripping her butt cheeks, he pushed her further up the bed. And then, crawling on his knees, he covered her body with his.

For a few beats, Jake's eyes wandered over her body, making her slightly uncomfortable. Women tended to always think their bodies were flawed in some way, and sadly couldn't help wondering how they compared to previous lovers. As quickly as these thoughts entered her head, they left, because Jake's masterful hands had started an erotic stroke up her legs and over her denim shorts, before sliding softly under her top.

Holly inhaled sharply in anticipation. At the same time, a fair amount of contractions were taking place between her legs. She couldn't stop herself from groaning out loud into his mouth. The kiss became more demanding, hungrier, needier, and breathing for both become labored.

Almost as if Jake could read her mind, he started to rock back and forth, rubbing his groin where she ached the most. Instinctively, Holly hooked her legs around his waist, forcing Jake's shaft to rub at her center in an almost rough way. If she died now, before any penetration even took place, she'd die happy.

So intent was she on matching him stroke for stroke, she never felt his hand move down to the button on her shorts.

Looking into her eyes, he undid the button, grabbed either side of her shorts and pulled them down as gently as he could. Even though Holly felt like she was in another dimension, she helped him by wiggling her hips. Unfortunately, she was still sensitive to touch. But, she wanted Jake more than what her body ached from the bruises so bit her tongue to stop herself from making any sound, even if it meant she'd bite right through it. No way in hell did she want him to stop.

By now, they were both too far gone to even contemplate foreplay. In unison, both had a good go at removing the rest of their clothes; almost like they were competing to see who'd be naked first. As soon as Holly discarded her underwear, Jake shoved her onto her back, taking care not to hurt her, slid up her body, spread her legs with his and guided his straining shaft to her eagerly awaiting and beyond wet entrance.

Holly couldn't stand to wait a second longer and decided to

take matters into her own hands. She gripped his ass and squeezed.

Jake got the message, loud and clear. He rubbed her mound with the tip of his shaft, up and down, circling her clit over and over, before he guided it down once again, this time ramming it to the hilt; again and again, and again. The feelings Jake was invoking in her were out of this world, so magnificent, the hairs on her face stood on end.

Had Holly been able to curl her toes any further, they would have surely broken off. This was exactly what she'd been hoping for the second she'd opened her eyes that morning.

Whimpering, she flung her head from side to side, not able to remember the last time she'd acted this wanton—it seemed to fuel Jake even further. He leaned slightly back and without breaking contact, grabbed her ankles from around his hips and threw them over his shoulders. His hands slid down her legs until he'd gotten a firm hold around her thighs, crossing his arms over them. Their position now was hotter than hell, primal, guttural and raw. Jake pumped harder, deeper and with such force, Holly's head slammed into the headboard on occasion. Not that she felt anything, really. She was in nirvana. Totally and absolutely.

All too soon, that familiar feeling started to build up at the pit of her stomach, increasing to a fever pitch she wasn't going to be able to control anymore. Hanging on for dear life, she dug her nails into Jake's back.

Growling, he pumped harder and harder.

"Jake... don't stop. Oh. Fuck!" She couldn't believe how much of a wildcat she turned into every time he was inside her.

Her orgasm was nearing its peak and she knew she'd lose control soon. She rammed her pelvis into his and that was all it took. Holly's entire body convulsed into spasms and shivers as the best orgasm she'd ever had to date ripped through her very soul. Whimpering as the last of the aftershocks rippled through her, she collapsed like a rag doll.

Jake bent over her, rubbing his nose on hers tenderly. "I take it you liked that?" he asked in a seductive tone.

Forcing her eyelids open, she grinned. "The screaming and the scratching not enough evidence that I did? Jake. Pay attention. That was pure, out of this world, pleasure."

His canines appeared when his lips spread into the hugest, sexiest grin. This only made Holly groan. She wanted him again and made no bones about it.

Inhibitions had no place in that bed. When she reached her third orgasm, she decided it was Jake's turn. Taking charge, she rolled him onto his back and climbed on top, in the exact same position as the night before. And then, as if her life depended on it, Holly rode him like a mechanical bull, not that she'd ever been on one before.

This time, though, it was different. Noises were coming from Jake she never knew a man could make, turning her on even more if that was even possible, and it wasn't long before he gained control of her movements.

When Holly orgasmed, so did Jake—so strongly, he ejaculated time after time until he, too, collapsed, completely spent. His breathing was ragged, and sweat had beaded on his forehead. Watching him, Holly couldn't help but feel good in knowing that she'd done that to him again.

Jake didn't pull out this time, however, but wrapped his arms around her back and held her tight. As they lay side by side, noses almost touching, Holly could still feel his body shivering slightly.

Breathing deeply, Jake made eye contact. And then grinning he said, "What the hell you are doing to me, woman?"

"Now, Jake. If I told you, I'd have to kill you," she retorted, in such a serious manner, they both burst out laughing.

FIFTEEN

THE FOLLOWING MONTH flew by fast. Holly spoke to Jake every day, but hated the fact that she only got to see him on weekends, which always ended up turning into lengthy fucking sessions. They could not get enough of one another. One thing she had never thought would happen to her was the fact that she was so open to trying new things sexually.

Amelia had started calling her about once or twice a week, just to chat. Holly really liked Amelia, and for some reason reminded her of her twin, Jamie. She'd had the same kind of personality as Amelia's and they got on like a house on fire. It was as if she had suddenly gotten her sister back.

Holly's greatest fear was that if her relationship with Jake didn't last, she would not only lose him—the man of her dreams—but she would lose his sister, too. There was a lot at stake, but deep down she knew that Jake Peters was worth it.

They lay in bed that night, both out of breath and exhausted, but not the sleeping kind of exhausted. This exhaustion was different. Holly didn't want to go to bed early; her time with him was already frustratingly limited.

He brushed a loose curl from her face gently. "Holly, my

mom really wants to meet you. She asked if you'd like to join us for our Sunday lunch."

Holly's eyes grew somewhat bigger. "I can't Jake, it's your family time."

"So, it's the perfect time to meet everyone, then. I mean, you haven't even met Robin for crying out loud and she lives with me."

Holly laughed, but sighed all the same.

"I promise not to leave your side. Not for one second."

She looked at him and swallowed, hard. "Fine, but I'm telling you, she won't like me."

"She will love you."

"We'll see." She gnawed at her bottom lip. *Damn it!* He'd known just what to say to get her to change her mind.

THEY LEFT FOR JAKE'S PARENTS' house at around eleven on Sunday morning. When Jake pulled up in front of two huge gates adorned with twirls and curls embedded in the metal, Holly's heart stopped for a second.

He squeezed her hand, and then leaned out the window to press a button. A woman's voice, the one she'd heard in the elevator at P&E, answered.

"It's me," Jake announced.

"Just you?"

"No. Holly's here, too."

A shriek emanated from the background—Amelia—and Holly laughed softly as the gates opened. She gasped when a huge, double story Victorian mansion with six garages appeared majestically in front of her. A gorgeous water feature with a cherub in its center stood in the middle of the courtyard. Holly's heart started to take on a life of its own, it beat so fast and loud she could have sworn Jake was able to hear it.

"They are human, I promise," Jake said, reading her mind.

All he got was a grin Holly was trying desperately to hang on to. But, her posture relaxed a tiny bit.

Jake, like the true gentleman he was, opened the door for her and helped her out. He kept a hold on her hand, softly squeezing it in assurance.

Her mom used to say that a woman's match could be detected just from the first touch of a hand. If they fit perfectly and you felt safe, you'd found your soul mate. If Holly felt one thing, it was that nothing could hurt her while Jake held her hand. They fitted perfectly, and she prayed her mother was spot on in this regard.

Nearing the front door, they climbed up six marble steps and came to a halt. Jake glanced at her face, and upon seeing her expression scrunched up his nose. It was another feature of his that made Holly's legs wobble.

"Deep breaths. You know what? You don't give yourself enough credit. Trust me, you'll bedazzle them."

Holly smiled, and inhaling deeply looked at Jake and nodded.

Jake turned the brass knob and they entered the sprawling mansion. The inside of the 'house' was even more beautiful than the outside, if that was even possible. The first thing she noticed was a huge entrance with stairs that descended into a huge living room. Little cars and toys lay sprawled on the carpet, and huge, soft brown couches with matching curtains made her feel welcome.

A very intricate chandelier hung from the ceiling, and a huge fireplace took up on corner of the room. A thick, luscious carpet, which when she stepped on made her pumps disappear, softened the entire lounge area.

Against another wall, a huge wall cabinet with a big screen TV stood regally. And as far as the windows went, they were as tall as the wall, as were the sliding doors that opened onto an outside patio. As she gazed out, she could see people sitting around a long glass table, one that had already been set.

"Jakey!" A young boy, who resembled a much younger Jake, ran into Jake's arms.

"Hey, Ben. How are you doing, kiddo? This is Holly."

The boy lowered his gaze and his face turned red. "Hi," he greeted shyly.

"Hey. So, you are the famous Ben 10, huh?"

He squealed with laughter, making Jake chuckle and knuckle rub the top of his head before putting him back down.

Holly couldn't believe that he was only five. He could very well have been Jake's, and his mom and dad had decided that they would raise the kid on his behalf. He was Jake's spitting image; thick, dark hair and dimples that dented deep into his cheeks. The only difference between them was that he had bright blue eyes, where Jake's were ice-green.

Ben ran off ahead of them. They followed suit, continuing through another area with numerous pictures of the entire family hanging on the walls. It led to a beautiful kitchen with an island in the middle. All countertops were made of granite, and the appliances were all silver and black. Above the island, pots and pans hung in varying heights.

Out of nowhere, a shout rang out, making Holly laugh. "Mommy, Jake is here with Holly!"

They walked out onto the patio, turned left, walked up a few steps, and when they reached the landing her heart started to bounce even faster as the huge table occupied by Jake's family came into sight.

"You forgot to tell your mom that Holly's super gorgeous," Jake said.

Holly lowered her head, shaking it from side to side, embarrassed by his compliment. *Your best manners, Holly. You only get one chance to make a first impression,* her mother's voice suddenly jumped into her head.

She was confused as to why it was in her mother's voice, since she hadn't gotten that advice from her mom.

"Hey, everyone. This is Holly." Jake tugged her forward from behind him so that she was visible for everyone to see. Right at that moment, Holly was glad she'd decided to wear a summer cotton dress and not a pair of shorts like she always did.

"Hey, Holls. Finally!" Amelia got up and gave her a hug.

"Jake, I taught you better manners. Introduce her properly." Jake's mom sounded stern, and she didn't get up.

Laughter and chuckles came from everyone around the table. Jake, however, had a huge grin adorning his face as he looked at his mom.

"Holly, this is my dear mother, Mara."

"Don't push your luck, Jake." She looked at him sternly.

Winking at Holly, he cocked his head to the side.

She cleared her throat and offered Mara her hand. To Holly's surprise, she shook it and began to smile. Mara had the bright blue eyes and long, golden blond hair that three of her children shared.

"Nice to finally meet you, Holly."

"Likewise, Mrs. Peters." Holly's voice broke and everyone laughed again.

"You see? No fangs, she's human."

"Oh, shut up," Holly mouthed, earning her chuckles from everyone.

"And this distinguished gentleman is my dad, Gus," he introduced. This earned Jake a slap on the back.

Holly could see that Jake wasn't exactly doing cartwheels

during the introductions, but she felt better knowing that he was trying to make it memorable for her.

"Nice to meet you, Holly. Welcome to our home." Much like Jake, he winked at her, which only served to make her blush all over again.

She shook the hand he offered and smiled. Gus had dark hair, lined with gray highlights, and Jake's eyes; much friendlier ones than his mother's. His smile was identical to Jake's.

Robin was next, as she'd already met Amelia and Armand. Robin was the spitting image of her mother, same hair and eyes. Still, she was stunning and would make any medical student's heart beat that little bit faster.

"I'm with Amelia. Finally." She got up and gave Holly a hug, too. "It's about time I meet you. You guys always leave so early in the mornings."

Holly's eyes rose, and Robin laughed. She didn't dare look Mara's way.

"What? It's over weekends," he grunted, to whom Holly assumed was his mother.

"I didn't say a thing."

"You didn't have to with that glare. Besides, I'm twenty-seven years old. Really, Mom, it's time you let me off your boob."

He didn't just say that! Holly was mortified. But she soon realized that however stern he had made his mother out to be—and Holly was sure that Mara was just that in certain situations—they obviously had a wonderful relationship. She was thankful, nevertheless, that their exchange was humorous. She was feeling more and more at ease in their presence.

The other two introductions were fairly easy, as one was in her teens, Lisa, who was too busy playing a game on her phone to pay much attention either way. It was only when Mara grabbed the device out of her hands that she noticed Holly and Jake.

"Oh, hi," she greeted, flashing a beautiful smile.

The other was Kimmy, who ran over to Holly and gave her a hug. She was eight and a beautiful golden blond haired, blue-eyed girl.

Finally, Jake and Holly were able to join the rest of the family at the table and took their seats, which happened to be next to Amelia and opposite Mara. Jake sat close to his father.

Lunch was served, but before anyone could dig in, Gus said a prayer.

"Dear God, thank you for this beautiful day, and for the food we are about to eat. Bless the hands that lovingly put this meal together. And thank you, God, for finally giving Holly the strength to meet our family."

Holly nearly snorted, she was trying that hard to suppress her laughter. It didn't help matters that she could feel Jake shaking with his own dose of humor beside her.

All the while, Gus continued with the prayer, asking God to open Holly's heart to his family, to accept them as they were—faults and all—and to please not allow Holly to break poor Jake's heart because of his wretched wife, who wouldn't let him off her boob. "Amen," he ended in a serious tone.

Tears rolled down Amelia's face as she laughed at her father's prayer.

Holly couldn't contain herself any longer, either, although she tried to hide it behind her napkin.

Jake's shoulders shook erratically, but his attempt at covering anything up was hilarious. He'd shoved his head under the table cloth as if he'd dropped something. Holly was surprised he hadn't fallen right off his chair.

As for Mara, she just gave Gus a stern look. "I'm not wretched, and Jake is *so* not on my boob anymore."

"That is debatable," Jake grumbled.

"Eat your food and stop talking crap, both of you," she shot back, wagging her finger between Jake and Gus.

Almost immediately, everyone started to eat if the sound of forks and knives clattering was anything to go by.

Holly couldn't take her eyes off of Mara.

"Holly. Just so you know, I do believe I'm the only normal one in this family." With that, Mara looked pointedly at Jake. "Don't get me started, Jake."

"No, please, do. What is so wrong with me, Mom?" He smiled.

"Let's start with the head of the house, shall we?"

Gus glanced sideways at his wife, a piece of fried chicken halfway to his mouth. "What have I done?"

"Gus, you never take anything seriously, and I won't even mention that awful prayer of yours."

"Ha. You just did. And anyway, God loves my prayers," he teased.

Mara slumped in her chair.

"Besides," Gus continued, "you are serious enough for the both of us. Someone needs to keep this family balanced."

Mara laughed. "Okay, okay."

"Jake, where do I begin?"

Jake chortled.

"The married woman, Mom," Robin piped up.

"Oh, yes." Mara's eyes were huge, and a playful smile illuminated her face.

Jake snorted. "Too late, people. Holly already knows about that."

"You told her?"

"I did."

"I'm still in shock that I went for a home- wrecker," Holly announced, concentrating on her vegetables.

Mara almost choked on her wine as she started to laugh, pulling everyone in like magnets to do the same.

"I didn't wreck any home." He looked at her.

Holly looked up and shrugged. "Whatever makes you sleep better at night."

He poked her hard in the ribs. "You are mean."

"But you still like me, so it's fine."

The exchange between them was highly entertaining to Jake's family.

"Okay, fine. I'm a home-wrecker, which by the way, I wasn't. What else?"

"You're a coward, because I raised you differently. I raised you to go after the things you want in life."

"Even if she was married?"

"You had the chance to intervene, before she got married."

"Well, I didn't, and now I've met Holly. So, it worked out exactly the way it was supposed to."

Holly's heart dropped all the way down to her stomach and bounced right back up to her chest, like a yo-yo. *Wow, that's nice.*

"What else?"

"You were a hooligan," Holly chirped in again.

"Excuse me, but I'm not the one who ended up with the broken hand that weekend, so I wonder who the hooligan is now."

Mara cut in. "I have to admit, I'm glad your hooligan days are over."

"So, I'm a home wrecker, a coward for the same reason I'm not a home wrecker, and I was a hooligan. Anything else, Mom? Holly?"

"You are plain crazy, Jake." Before he had a chance to reply, she turned her gaze to Amelia, who had been patiently waiting for her turn. "Amelia is easy. She's a psychiatrist," she proudly stated.

"And what's that supposed to mean?" Amelia yelled, while Jake, Armand and his father grinned like lunatics.

"It takes a nut to treat a nut," Mara answered.

"Well, and you can't say anything about me?" Robin asked.

"You are just like Jake, honey. Sorry. I don't even know where to start, but I can try. Let's see." She looked up at the ceiling. "Oh, yes, I knew I'd come up with something. Take the way you burst out laughing when you see a cripple."

Holly gaped at Robin.

"I can't help it. It just happens. I wish I could change it, but I can't. It's a sickness."

"I rest my case, then." Mara's hand was up in the air now. "The only ones who are anywhere near normal are Ben and Kimmy."

"Normal!" All excluded children protested, with Gus between them.

It made Holly giggle.

"You are *psycho mom*," Jake grunted, throwing his hands up in the air.

"I'm not the least bit psycho. Neither am I a 'psycho mom'." She looked at Holly. "Don't listen to him."

When it was time for dessert, Mara served up sorbet with fresh fruit pieces—simply delicious. Jake's hand touched her leg every once in a while, which always set free a million butterflies in Holly's stomach. Every time he touched her was simply magical. Holly would never get tired of it.

Once everyone was done with dessert, Mara stood and addressed Holly. "Holly, would you like to give me a hand?"

"Mom, you have a dishwasher."

"I do, and aren't I lucky? But I need help loading it. In other words, hooligan, it's so I can get to know her better."

"It's fine. I'd love to help." Holly stood and playfully stuck her tongue out at Jake.

He just raised his left eyebrow. "It's your funeral," he joked.

She slapped him on the shoulder. "Stop being so mean to your mother."

He pretended to be affronted.

"Thanks for the effort, Holly, but Jake is like that."

"You are so mean."

"Well, you still like me, so it's fine." Jake mimicked Holly's previous answer.

Holly huffed, walking away with a stack of dessert bowls in her hands.

In the kitchen, Mara rinsed off all the plates.

"Just sit there, so we can have a little chat." She pushed a chair out from the breakfast nook that connected with the island.

Holly sat down and her heart started to thump again.

"So, where are you from?"

"Here, not born but raised. My mother and I moved here when I was about four."

Mara asked Holly a million questions about her family and life in general, and for some reason Holly completely opened up. She didn't mention losing her twin, but she did tell her about her father, as well as how her mom's heart had never healed when he up and left them. It had been mostly over losing Jamie that she had struggled with, but Holly didn't burden Mara with that tale.

When Mara was done packing the dishwasher, she poured them each a cream liqueur and sat across from Holly, listening attentively as Holly recounted her childhood days. She then asked what Holly did for a living. Holly got the feeling Mara didn't really approve but wasn't sure if it was just Mara's personality, or if it was really how Mara felt about her work.

"I could've easily gone off to university. My grades were up to par, but I hadn't found a profession I truly liked so never enrolled. When I'm as passionate as Jake and the rest of your children are about something, I will enroll myself in a college or university and take it from there." She was babbling now, as thoughts of Mara approving her current employment lingered in her mind.

"Well, being a doctor is great, but you don't always have time for family. I guess that's why Gus and I were glad we were in the same field. I almost went into marketing. I'm really good with predicting situations and growth by listening to people and knowing what they want. But, becoming a doctor was always what I'd wanted to be, and I'm glad I stuck with it and I am one. Some people struggle to discover what it is they were made for, but I promise you that when you do, it's going to be the best feeling ever."

Holly smiled at the older woman, feeling relieved.

"I'm really glad you decided to come with Jake today. I've asked him to bring you so many times, and all he could do was grunt every time."

"Why is he like that?"

"It's nothing for you to worry about. I'm used to it and don't tell him this, but I do keep a close eye on him. He was the only one in my family I couldn't predict."

Holly giggled.

"So, you can just imagine how I felt when he came home from school one day saying that he wanted to learn how to fight. In a cage!" Mara's eyes were huge and she shuddered at the sudden flashback. "It was the scariest four years of my life. Although, I have to admit, I cheered the loudest on the sidelines, but I'd never been that terrified, ever. Seeing your child fight like that gave me nightmares. When he eventually got the beating of his life..." her voice broke and she shook her head gently as tears glistened in her eyes.

"He told me about that."

"It was so hard, Holly. I thought my boy was lost forever. But Leo, bless his heart, somehow pulled him through."

"They are amazing people."

"Do you know them?"

"Well, it's how Jake and I met. I'm best friends with Bernice."

"I'm so glad he met you. The married woman thing was really hard on him. He thought he would never get over it, and then he met you. I'm so grateful that you walked into his life. I haven't seen Jake laugh so much in a long time."

"Well, it's important to laugh."

"It is. And it's a good sign, too."

Silence filled the room.

Mara cleared her throat. "Can I please ask you something?" Mara looked at Holly, a frown pinching the skin between her eyebrows.

"Of course."

"I know my son is neither a saint nor a monk, and I don't want to know if your relationship is a sexual one, but I do beg you to use protection. He can't study to be a doctor, and raise a baby. Gus and I did that with Jake and it wasn't easy. I want him to graduate first. Would it be too much to ask you to go on the pill?"

Nobody had ever asked her a question like that before. Holly, as more than likely anyone else would be, should have been shocked, but she wasn't. What Mara was asking wasn't unreasonable.

"I want him to succeed in everything he does. You need to know, Mara, that I'm not one of those girls who thinks a baby can keep a couple together, and what you ask isn't too much. I'll get on it."

Mara gave her a soft smile and pulled her in for a hug. "Thank you, Holly. That is another weight off my shoulders. Just do me a favor, please." She looked at Holly again. "Don't tell him I've asked you this. He would never speak to me again for intervening."

"Your secret is safe with me."

SIXTEEN

THEIR CHAT CAME to an end the minute Jake stepped into the kitchen. He walked over and stood behind Holly, stroking her back. "So, what are you two talking about?"

"Nothing for you to worry about." Mara was quite blunt. "We're just getting to know each other. Is that a sin?"

Jake squinted at his mom, a suspicious smile playing over his lips. "No, I guess not." He didn't push, deciding to leave it at that.

The rest of the afternoon went by in a whirl. Holly couldn't remember when she'd had so much fun with strangers. She'd enjoyed meeting and spending the day with Jake's family.

His dad was funny and she'd laughed so hard at his jokes. Mara, on the other hand, was quite the opposite. She was more often than not serious, and it was evident that at times she completely missed the boat on some of his jokes. Mara's humor was of the darker variety, which meant that Holly was going to struggle to differentiate between when she was really joking and when she was being serious.

Amelia was a darling. She had a mouth on her, though, and didn't shut it for anything or anyone. Holly wished in so many ways that she could develop the strength Amelia carried in her —she didn't seem to be afraid of anything.

Her husband, Armand, reminded Holly of someone who simply tagged along. He only had eyes for his wife, though, and it was quite clear that he had a gentle side to him. When she'd first seen him at the paintball game, she'd had to look twice, because he neither seemed nor looked like Amelia's type. Armand was a bear of a man but looked like a total geek, right down to the glasses, although a really smart and super awesome person.

Robin was a lot like Mara, but in many ways like Gus. She was also a bit of a tomboy.

Lisa continuously played on her device and when she got bored, would go into the house to watch TV.

Kimmy was only eight so still loved to play with dolls, which was exactly what she did after lunch.

Ben was one hell of a cute boy and a mini version of Jake, except he had a missing tooth— something he was proud of. He'd had this long discussion with Armand while sitting on Jake's lap regarding the Tooth Fairy.

Holly had found him adorable and laughed wholeheartedly as Ben told both Armand and Jake his intricate plans to catch her.

"She won't make an appearance tonight if you mention your plans out loud, my boy," Gus chirped from the opposite couch.

"She will come," he said adamantly. "I left her Oreos, and Armand said that she has a craving for Oreos. So I figure she will eat until she's so fat, she won't be able to fly away." Ben's logic brooked no argument.

Everyone had a good chuckle at that.

"Mom did say you were the sanest," Jake said to Ben. "Hmph! I think she should re-think her words." Jake looked at the five-year-old who cackled with laughter.

Holly really tried not to laugh at their antics, but it was impossible with that family. Despite the day having been beyond amazing, all good things had to come to an end. At around five they bid their farewell. As Holly put her coat on, Robin and Amelia took turns to give her a hug.

"Okay, let her go," Jake intervened, which earned him a scold from Amelia. "Don't look at me like that. If she doesn't come back next Sunday, it's not my fault."

"Whatever. Just go. Bye, Holly," Amelia repeated.

Holly waved as Jake led her to the car.

ON THE WAY HOME, they decided to stop at the mall and caught the eight o'clock movie; a beautiful romance, both quirky and funny. They enjoyed it tremendously, especially the kissing they were able to do in the inky blackness of the theater.

At around ten, they had to say goodbye again. It was becoming harder and harder for Holly to only see Jake on weekends—at least she knew that he was studying and not fooling around with another girl.

She was sitting on his lap in the car, as she always did on Sunday nights. Weekends seemed to fly by when she was with Jake, something she hated.

"Charge your phone, missy. I don't want to struggle in trying to get hold of you."

"Are you ready for this week's tests?"

"Easy." He scrunched up his nose, pretending that passing tests was easy and had to do with blood, DNA, and other medical terms Holly never could remember. In other words, it ran in the family.

"Tell you what, for every A you get, I'll give you the best blow job you've ever had."

Raising his eyebrows, Jake asked, "Oh, really? Can we shake on that?" His voice dripped seductiveness, making Holly squirm.

"We can, if you don't want to take my word for it."

"Interesting. And for every A+?"

"Are you that smart?" She raised her own eyebrows, looking straight into his soul searchingly.

"Maybe..."

"Okay, for every A+—"she looked at the roof, trying to think of something that would make her deal worthy of an A+ "I'll give you a lap dance, an oil massage, and the best sex you've ever had and will ever have."

She leaned her head closer to his as he stroked the side of it softly. When their lips touched, it immediately turned into a burning hunger. She started to move into him, and those ever present butterflies erupted in her belly when his hands dipped under her summer dress, caressing her hips and butt.

She could kiss him forever. It didn't stay in the kissing zone as neither of them really wanted to say goodbye. When Holly finally pulled back from their kiss, they were both out of breath.

"If you tell me it's time to go, I swear I'm going to kidnap you and lock you inside my closet," he grunted in her ear.

She laughed softly, thinking about his proposal. She definitely wouldn't mind being his prisoner. "Don't temp me. But I really have to go." She opened the door and almost fell out. Hot flushes washed over her body, and her arousal made her blind. She shook her head, letting the cool air do its trick. Once she was steady, she bent down and kissed him through the open window one last time before entering the house.

He always waited for her until she was safely inside. Holly watched as his car lights faded away, until darkness replaced them.

How could I have fallen so hard for a guy in such a short amount of time?

THE NEXT TWO weeks flew by, and soon the end of the school year was upon them. Holly and Jake couldn't wait for that last week to be over. It was his final year of medical school before starting work as an intern. He was really excited yet nervous, because he knew his already limited time with Holly would be cut in half.

There would be no more free weekends; he'd have only one week of day shifts before night shifts started, with the latter allowing no one-on-one time to spend with her. This meant that she'd only see him for a couple of hours during the odd day shift. It all sounded awful. However, before that horrible period—and it would be horrible—started, Holly would be able to see him every single day for almost an entire month.

On the Sunday, they paid his family a visit and had lunch.

"So, are you in?" Amelia asked Holly while they helped Mara with the dishes again.

"For what?"

"A two mile walk. It's not so far, and it's for a good cause."

"What cause would that be?"

"Don't do it, Bee Puke," Jake warned.

"Shush," Amelia slapped the air playfully in her brother's direction, as if she was shooing him to be gone. "Anti-abortion. My dad usually does this with me, but this year he can't. He's on standby next Saturday, and I have no one to do it with. Armand is such a pee-wee when it comes to things like that. Although, everyone's always clearly stating that they are all for the cause. I need you there, Holly."

"Sweetheart, you don't know what Holly's beliefs are," Mara spoke softly.

"No, I'm against it as well. Sure, why not. How much does it cost for this amazing two mile walk?"

Armand and Jake chuckled, earning them a glare from Holly. "Okay, what is going on? Is there something I should know?"

Amelia rolled her eyes at them, throwing a napkin in their direction. "Tell her, you can't wait to, anyway." She looked at Jake.

"And spoil all the fun?"

"Tell me what?" She looked at Jake.

"The amazing two mile walk? You do it in high heels."

Holly's head snapped back to Amelia.

"Please, Holly. I really don't want to do this alone."

"Your dad does this with you?"

Through everyone's laughter, Amelia replied, "Yes. He's the best dad a girl could ask for. I'll even pay the fee, you just need to bring high heels."

"Oh. My. Soul. I'm going to have blisters the size of watermelons, aren't I?" She looked at Amelia for confirmation.

"It's for a good cause," was all Amelia said.

"Fine. Just as long as you remember this; you are going to owe me big time, missy."

Amelia clapped her hands excitedly, which made Holly laugh.

"Seriously, Amelia. You taking Holly away on one of the last few days I'm going to be able to spend with her."

"Don't give me that shit, Jake. You are finishing this Friday, so you can see Holly any day of the week."

"Fine," he said, looking at Armand. "I guess me and you are on banner duty, then."

The girls giggled. Holly could just imagine Jake cheering

her on with a huge banner that read: Go baby, go! or something like that, written in huge, big bold letters.

"This is going to be fun," Holly admitted.

"You bet, sister," Amelia concurred, lifting her hand to Holly for a high five.

Holly complied and slapped it, a warm tingling feeling spreading inside her chest. Nobody had called her sister in the past nine years.

But looking at Jake dangling his car keys in his hand, she wanted to cry. She knew their time was going to be cut short as he really wanted to study for tomorrow's test. He kissed his entire family goodbye, and it was at this moment that Holly realized she'd fallen in love with them all.

Just before they left, though, his father gave him a quick quiz. Holly didn't know if they were pulling one another's leg or not as the terms were foreign, but by Armand's shaking body and Mara's eyes, Holly assumed it was bullshit.

"You are going to ace that test, son." His father slapped him solidly on the back when they'd reached Jake's car. Gus turned to Holly and gave her a bear hug just before Jake opened her door.

Holly waved at Amelia, who'd taken Holly's spot next to her dad.

Jake honked before the car disappeared out the gates. She turned, keeping her gaze on his family until she couldn't see their house anymore.

"You are blessed, you know that?" she whispered.

"To have such a beautiful girl at my side? I know."

"No, not that, but thanks. I'm talking about your family."

"Yeah, they're not too bad, I guess."

Holly shook her head gently, but smiled at him regardless.

"Well, you are."

"I know. They absolutely adore you, you know."

"They do?"

"Please. You think my mom has ever treated any of my girlfriends the way she treated you?"

"She didn't?"

"Heck, no. She didn't even like Mel. She just pretended she did. Believe me, I know when that woman pretends, and she's totally herself when you are around."

"How many girlfriends are we talking about?"

He chuckled. "Holly, not that many. Actually, I can count them on one hand. Only two girls met my parents, and you are one of them."

"Really?"

"Of course. What did you think? That I took every stranger I came across to meet my parents?"

"Some do."

"Well, I'm not some. I'm just Jake."

Holly grinned broadly. "That you are." Becoming serious, she asked, "You scared about tomorrow?"

"No," he said, an underlying chuckle evident in his voice.

"Then why all of a sudden do you need to revise your work?"

"Oh, I don't want to revise a damn thing. It was the only way I could get you all to myself."

"Sneaky! But, really?"

"Yes. I need quality time, Holly. Not quantity."

Jake parked when they arrived at the county park and took out a blanket and a book from his trunk.

"You read?" she teased him.

"Ha-ha," he kicked her, playfully, and walked hand in hand toward the lake.

Now that she knew he didn't want to revise for tomorrow's test, she felt herself relax, glad that she would spend at least another eight hours with him before she had to say goodbye.

They looked around for the biggest oak tree they could find, closest to the lake, and after deciding they'd picked the right one, Jake spread the blanket beneath it. Making themselves comfortable, Holly laid her head on his stomach as he read William Shakespeare's Romeo and Juliet to her. She never could understand what Shakespeare had meant by *'But soft! what light through yonder window breaks?'* phrases, but the way Jake spoke every word it almost made her want to cry.

When the sun began to set, it was decided that they should pack up and go back to his place.

During the journey, Holly made small talk. "I didn't know you loved Shakespeare."

"I do, but don't tell anyone. I don't want to have to kill you."

Holly smiled at him.

"You wouldn't know what to do with yourself without me."

"That is true," he replied, kissing every knuckle on her hand softly.

Pulling up at his house, Jake parked the car, and shortly thereafter they made quick work of getting to his room. As soon as they were inside, clothes seemingly disappeared. They were like rabbits; couldn't get enough of each other. When they collapsed afterward, wrapped in each other's arms, Holly remembered Mara's request.

"Jake..." She didn't have a clue as to how she was going to explain this one to him. But it was her body, and although she would have loved to have kids before the age of thirty, she had to keep her promise to Mara.

"Yes, Bee Puke?" he replied in a tired voice.

"I really think I need to go on something." She leaned on one arm and looked down at his face.

His eyes flew open. "What do you mean... like the pill?"

Holly didn't like the serious tone in his voice, but forged

ahead anyway. "Yes, we hump like rabbits. I can't get pregnant, not now."

"Holly." He sighed, looking at her. "No." He pushed himself up on the bed, flung his legs out and when his feet hit the floor, sat with his back to her.

"What do you mean, no?"

He faced her. "I really won't mind if you get pregnant."

That took her by surprise. "Well, I would," she lied.

"Listen, your sister died of cancer. I just don't think you should be exposed to the extra hormones. There's a lot we don't understand, like what causes cancer." He was adamant, yet it was something Holly didn't understand one bit.

"But, Jake. I can't get pregnant, not now," she repeated. "So, whether you like it or not, I'm going on the pill."

"Then why the hell did you tell me?"

She couldn't believe this. They were going to have their first fight over the pill. Usually, roles were reversed, but she couldn't break his mother's trust, not after he'd told her that Mara really liked her.

"Gee, I don't know. Because, maybe, just maybe I really don't want to do anything behind your back!" she yelled as she got up, grabbing her clothes and stomping to the bathroom. She locked the door behind her, leaned against it, and took in huge breaths.

She couldn't believe how mentioning the pill had turned out. Brandon had begged her at one stage to go on the pill. Men were typically the ones to suggest it. She had never expected this kind of reaction from Jake. And if she were honest, she never knew what she was going to get with Jake, but never in a million years had she expected him to be so totally against it. He'd reacted almost like she was a child, one who wanted a really expensive doll for Christmas, and he'd said no.

SEVENTEEN

A SOFT KNOCK on the bathroom door drew her out of the rage bubble she'd found herself in. Holly hated being treated like a five-year-old, instead of the adult she was. Not having his girlfriend fall pregnant—the one he'd practically just met—should have been at the top of his list, too.

She opened the door slowly, just a crack, and stared into his beautiful face. He'd pulled on one of those pajama slacks that hung nice and low on his hips.

She turned away and stepped clear of the door, bracing herself, because she knew she really should stand her ground on this.

"I'm sorry. I don't want to fight with you, Holly, but I'm just worried about what effects it could have on you."

"Jake, I can't get pregnant right now."

"I know," he sighed.

Deep down, she knew everything would change if Jake had to wear a condom. He already struggled to reach an orgasm, and she didn't want to think about what she would have to do then for him if he wore one.

"I'll talk to my dad. See which one is effective, but not as harsh, okay?" He stepped toward her and placed his hands gently on her face.

She was still upset that he'd treated her like a child, but she knew that when he looked at her with those ice-green eyes, her heart would melt and all would be forgiven. Their lips touched, the kiss they shared tender.

"I'm really sorry. I'm just worried about the risk, and frankly I'd rather risk us having a baby than risk the chance of you getting cancer."

Holly swallowed. She didn't like the fact that although he sounded kind of worried, according to him, either her getting pregnant or getting cancer both fell under the 'risk' factor. It seemed like no matter what, she'd be a burden to him. She couldn't help but wonder if he was even going to be in her future.

She merely nodded.

OPTING TO EAT OUT, they had a nice dinner at a small Italian restaurant, after which Jake took her home. It wasn't that late, but Jake did want to go over his notes one more time before the next day's big test. Or, that was just the excuse he chose to use. She hoped it was the truth and not Jake starting to doubt where their relationship was heading.

She lay in bed, contemplating what would happen next. They'd almost been together for two months. She was starting to worry that he would call things off now that they'd had their first fight.

On that thought, her phoned beeped. She reached over and picked it from the nightstand.

Jake: Sleep tight. I'm off to bed now. Sweet dreams. Hope I'm included in them. Love you.

She froze. *Love you.* She kept staring at those two words for what seemed like forever.

Had Jake really just told her he loved her? Her heart ached for him again. In all the time she'd spent with him in bed, he'd never even whispered those words to her softly. Now, after their first real fight, he seemed to have just blurted them out.

Jake wasn't someone who threw those words around. Granted, he showed his family and friends how much they meant to them, Holly included. He'd treated her like gold these past two months. Now that he'd said them, all sorts of emotions flooded her mind.

It went without saying that Jake was gorgeous and seemed to have everything a girl ever dreamed of in a guy, but he was more than that. He was smart, kind, and had an absolutely amazing personality. Holly really didn't want to see his dark side, if he had one, yet she couldn't recall Leo speaking ill of Jake in all the time she'd known him.

The question was, did Holly love him?

Her thoughts went to the fight they'd had that day. Would she have gone on the pill if his mom hadn't asked her? This made her think long and hard, and for a long time.

"No," she said out loud. It wouldn't even have bothered her. She did love him, a lot, so much in fact that she was sure if an enraged ex-girlfriend or someone tried to shoot him in the middle of a mall, she would jump in front of that bullet.

"Fuck!" Holly slapped her hand over her face. A part of her wanted to cry with the realization that she would take a bullet for him.

BY THE TIME Monday came around, Holly had received no messages, which she found a bit weird. She glanced at the clock on the wall and noticed that it was already nine o'clock. She'd been so busy all morning that she'd forgotten to wish Jake good luck. And now it was too late. She figured she would speak to him later in the afternoon when he called her. She was sure he would.

At around one, her phone finally beeped. She smiled, knowing that she would be able to message him back. She picked up her phone.

JAKE: YOU'RE AWFULLY QUIET. WAS IT BECAUSE OF WHAT I SAID LAST NIGHT? TWO LITTLE WORDS?

It was then that it hit her. She had been in such shock over what he'd said, she never replied. She rushed over to the land line and picked up the earpiece. Thankfully, Marabella didn't have a problem with Holly calling from work, because she knew Holly wasn't the babbling type and would be as quick as possible.

As she'd never called him from work, he wouldn't recognize the number. She prayed he'd pick up, anyway. He picked up on the fourth ring.

"Jake," he answered.

"I'm sorry," she blurted. "To be honest, I was a bit shocked last night with your message. I had been struggling to fall asleep, but when your phone beeped and I read your message, it caught me off guard."

He laughed. "That's okay. I won't hold it against you."

"No, it's not okay. I should've replied. I know one thing for sure, Jake. I hate fighting with you."

"Bee Puke, that was hardly a fight."

She giggled. "Still, I don't like it."

"Yeah, it sucks. Listen, I'm quickly going to see my dad, so I'll speak to you later, okay?"

"Sure. How was the test by the way?"

"Easy as pie."

Holly snorted.

"Bye, Bee Puke," he said, in a sing-song voice.

"Okay, love you, bye," she replied, and put the phone down.

Only when the connection was broken did she realize what she'd told him; she found herself smiling from ear to ear.

Marabella walked in and looked at Holly. "So, how is Jake?"

"He's good, why?" She frowned.

"Holly, you only smile like that after you've spoken to him."

Holly blushed. "Oh. Guess I can't help it."

"You can't. He sure is able to raise your temperature."

Holly grinned and continued doing so until Marabella left.

At three, she moved over to the restaurant. The receptionist only worked until three, so Holly had agreed to take over, answering calls for general inquiries, as well as noting reservations.

Marabella had some paperwork to finalize and with all the guests gone, it was a good place to concentrate. She had worked with Marabella in silence on numerous occasions. Besides, they were so much alike that Holly couldn't envision what her life would be without her in it. Both Marabella and her daughter were more like family to her, not just her employers.

They chatted a bit more about Jake, and Holly told her about his reaction when she mentioned the pill.

"Babes, I told you before, when you meet the right one, all morals go out the door."

Holly laughed as it kind of rhymed, but it was exactly what she was experiencing.

"Hello, gorgeous!" Marabella yelled at someone on the verge of entering the restaurant. Probably just Jerry. They had such a sweet relationship. "Talk about the devil, and then you step on his tail. How was your test this morning?"

Holly almost spat out the juice she'd just taken a sip of. *What the hell is Jake doing here?*

"Nice to know you talk about me."

Marabella got up and kissed him on both cheeks. She was such a warm person. "Your lovely is right here."

"Thanks," he said, chuckling.

Holly, too, got up and pecked him on the lips.

"Marabella is really friendly today."

"You'll get used to her."

"I heard that. Can I get you something to drink?" Marabella's voice came from the bar.

"I'm good, thanks. I've got water." Jake shook the bottle in his hand. He dropped a brown paper bag onto Holly's desk.

"What's this?" Holly peeked inside and found a circular container holding small, little round tablets. Looking up at him she said, "Well, that was fast."

"I'm a fast guy."

"What did you tell your dad?"

He gave her the look. "I'm twenty-seven years old, Holly. Besides, he thought it was very responsible of me."

"Well, thanks." She fluttered her eyelashes at him, making him laugh as it was her idea in the first place to go on the pill, which made him not so responsible at all.

"I've got to go. I still have my license to sort out before they close. Talk to you later." He kissed her briefly, but managed to nip her bottom lip all the same. It only served to make her stomach tie into a knot. "Bye, Marabella."

"Bye now," Marabella sang back.

Holly put the bag away, shoving it into her purse, and let out a sigh of relief.

"I don't know how you manage to keep your hands off that one, Holly."

Holly burst into laughter. "Who says I do?"

"Holly Scallanger!" Marabella's eyes were huge, but winking she said, "I'm so glad to hear that."

Both snickered and joked for a couple of minutes, until Marabella went back to sorting out her paperwork. When Holly had a bit of a break, she took a closer look at the object in the paper bag. It was made up of small, red pills. *Just one a day and I will be fine, eventually.*

Holly skimmed the leaflet, electing not to read the whole thing. It didn't take a brain surgeon to remember to take one pill a day. The leaflet said to start a week after her period began, but she figured the sooner she started the better. She popped one out of the container and placed it in her mouth.

THE REST of the week flew by in a whirl. She didn't know who was more excited about Friday, Jake or her. He'd finally finished with all of his tests, and was officially on vacation.

She would be able to see him every day now without worrying about his mom being upset. She would also have to fulfill some of her promises as he would be receiving his final results soon, and then it was graduation, vacation, and internship. Holly breathed out a huge breath just thinking about it.

EVERY FRIDAY, Holly took a small weekend bag to work; she now spent every weekend at Jake's. On this particular Friday, from three o'clock to be exact, time seemed to drag. It just didn't want to reach the five o'clock mark.

However, she was super excited when Jake showed up early. He looked relieved. She didn't want to think about next year, though, when he was going to have to work almost the entire week and then their time would be cut tremendously short, as if it wasn't already. But, it was what she had to get used to. She was dating a doctor-to-be and not just any doctor, but a neurologist.

At five, they finally made their way out, hopped into his car and took another route back to Jake's house.

"Are we going somewhere?"

"Yes, we need to prepare."

"Prepare for what?"

"You'll see, it's going to be fun."

"Oh, please, if it's going to involve guns and paint again, God help you, Jake."

Jake started to laugh. "No, I promise it's not that bad."

They stopped in front of a huge gate and once it opened, Jake drove into a complex. The houses within seemed to be more beautiful than the next.

They drove through another set of gates and approached a huge, gray house. It was nothing like his parents' place, but it was still huge and modern.

Jake opened the door for Holly and she climbed out. Her expression was one of curiosity.

"We are preparing here?"

"Yes. Follow me," he requested, his tone serious.

"For what exactly, Jake?"

He didn't reply, but instead led her through the main door. Inside, she found Armand and Robin kneeling in front of a huge coffee table. On it and splayed around it on the ground were rolled out banners. Holly burst out laughing when she saw both her name and Amelia's written in huge, bold letters.

"Where's the glitter?"

"No glitter." Robin pouted, looking up.

Amelia rounded the corner. "Hi, Holly. You ready for tomorrow?"

"Girl, I'm going to walk circles around you."

They both cackled like loons. She motioned for Holly to follow her. On their way to the kitchen, Amelia shouted to the banner makers over her shoulder, "Enjoy!"

"We're not helping them?" Holly queried.

"Holls, we are going to do all the hard work tomorrow. I think it's only fair they pitch in and do their bit."

Amelia set about making cocktails and when she was done she gave Robin, Jake, and Armand theirs before she and Holly sat at her breakfast nook. They chatted about everything.

Being with Amelia brought back memories, memories Holly had never wanted to remember, and before she knew it she told Amelia about Jamie. She never mentioned the fact that they had been twins, simply because people tended to ask the same stupid questions over and over, like was their bond special, where when the one twin got hurt the other would feel it, or were they identical and so on. She hated the fact that every time she looked in the mirror she would see Jamie. Or what Jamie would look like if she were alive.

Amelia had tears in her eyes when Holly grew quiet. "I don't know what it would feel like to lose one of my siblings, just thinking about it..." She shook her head. "I can't." She gave Holly a lopsided smile. "Believe me, they are annoying as hell, but to never be able to speak to one of them again is unimaginable. How do you do it?"

Holly shrugged. "Take it one day at a time, I guess."

"Well, you've got a bunch of sisters now. Jake just needs to get his shit in gear."

They laughed like typical women would.

"I can't have babies," Amelia suddenly blurted.

"What?"

Tears pooled in Amelia's eyes. "It's true. The doctor gave me the news today. I haven't even told Armand yet." She breathed deeply.

"What did the doctor say, exactly?"

"He called it premature ovarian failure. My ovaries don't produce enough eggs, and... ugh! It's so wrong and unfair."

Holly placed her arm around Amelia's shoulders, hugging her. "You can never lose hope, Amelia. There have been a million cases where women fell pregnant against all odds, and doctors weren't able to explain how. It's called a miracle. Just hold on to that."

"I am, but to be honest..." she trailed off, letting go of Holly to wipe a tear away. "Look at us, Holly. We've been bestowed with so many blessings that I don't think a miracle will come our way soon."

Holly just looked at her kindly. "You'd be surprised at the things that happen daily."

"Thanks for doing this with me, by the way. Tomorrow means a lot, and I just wanted you to know how much I appreciate the fact that you are willing to take my dad's place."

"I'm doing it for the cause, too. I don't understand how any woman could do that."

"Me, either."

Moving the conversation away from the sadness of the one they were having, Holly giggled. "So, your dad really walked two miles in high heels?"

Amelia threw her head back and abruptly brought it forward again, laughing as doubled over. The sound pierced throughout the entire house. "He dressed up and everything. I have pictures. Wait, you have to see them." She hopped down from the high chair and ran out of the kitchen, returning a couple of seconds later with a photo album—a scrapbook photo album, and it was done beautifully.

Amelia showed Holly photos of the fundraiser, which spanned over four years, and laughed at one in particular where her dad had been wearing a sequined dress with the ugliest red shoes she had ever seen.

They continued in this light, going over photographs and having a few more cocktails, while Amelia paged through albums of their life. She even saw a couple of pictures of Mel, Jake's previous girlfriend.

"She's beautiful," Holly admitted.

"She's an airhead," Amelia stated, but Holly laughed as Amelia's expression was silly.

The night flew by, much like their cocktails. At one point, Holly felt so calm and relaxed, she started singing her special song. Amelia cracked up at Holly's words, and in a matter of seconds Jake, Robin, and Armand came into the kitchen to see what they were up to.

"Bee Puke, are you drunk?" Jake asked, grinning wickedly.

"Nooo. Nope. I'm not," Holly slurred, whilst waving a finger in front of her and throwing one leg over the other. She fell off the chair.

Amelia and Holly were beyond help, and their laughter erupted amongst snorts all over again.

Jake shook his head and picked Holly up off the floor. "I can't take you anywhere. Tsk, tsk."

Armand mimicked Jake, shaking his head at Amelia, but he had a huge grin on his face, too.

"We needed that." Holly looked at Jake.

"Sure you did." He looked at her, eyebrows arched, and that gorgeous grin that revealed his canines giving him away.

Holly couldn't stop staring at them.

"Okay. I'm going to take this one home." And with that, Jake threw her over his shoulder.

"Just remember, Holly, we need to be there by eight," Amelia yelled.

"Eight is great. Eight is super. Eight is just perfect," Holly practically sang. This only served to make her giggle uncontrollably, which was soon followed by her passing out on Jake's shoulder.

EIGHTEEN

THE SMELL of roasted coffee beans filled Holly's nostrils as she lay in bed. Opening her eyes slightly, she found a huge mug in front of her nose, but as soon as she tried to lift up her head, the pain made it ache so much it dropped back down onto the pillow.

"Yeah. I don't think cocktails were the way to go."

She grunted at Jake's comment.

He chuckled close to her ear, nipping her lobe gently. "I'm going to run you a bath," he whispered.

When he moved, the bed shook, like she was on a raft in the ocean. Bile rose up in her throat, but she quickly took a sip of coffee to force it back down. It would just be her luck to hurl, right here on Jake's bed. She laughed at herself as that image jumped into her mind. *Very sexy, Holly. Not!*

Jake walked out of the bathroom while the water still ran and handed her two capsules. "For the head."

She looked up at him and smiled. "You are my life saver."

"I know," he replied, sounding really pleased with himself when he sat down on the edge of the bed.

She gulped the tablets down, hoping they would work fast.

When she eventually sat up fully, she noticed she was wearing a Van Halen T-shirt, one that was two sizes too big. "And this?" She pulled on the shirt.

"My mom taught me not to go through a woman's luggage."

"So you decided to dress me in this?"

"It was that, or butt naked."

Holly gave him the puppy dog eye treatment and leaned in for a kiss. He broke away before it got too steamy and led to something more than just kissing, which they really didn't have time for right then.

"It's already seven. You still need to bath, get ready, and eat before we go."

"Bleh! Yes, boss."

"I didn't say you must sign up."

She mumbled within the confines of the bathroom as she removed both the T-shirt and panties. Dipping her toe in, she decided that the water felt just right. She got in carefully, sat and lay back so that only her head stuck out of the foam. Sighing, Holly relaxed.

However, Jake didn't give her a lot of time to soak and knocked on the door, what seemed like only a few minutes later. She jumped when she realized she had fallen asleep and quickly washed herself.

Holly dried in record time, too, and dressed in knee-high pants, bra and a tank top. Never in her entire life had she walked in high heels on an open road.

Lastly, she brushed her teeth with one hand, while slipping on no-show socks with the other. And finally, she stepped into her high heels.

Exiting the bathroom, Jake was nowhere to be found, so Holly took the time to apply sunscreen, a smidgen of eyeliner, and lip gloss before pulling her hair through the back hole of a baseball cap. When she eventually ventured downstairs, she found Robin and Jake in the kitchen.

"How's the head?"

Holly raised her upper lip in a snarl, and that was enough of an answer.

Robin chuckled. "Today is going to be *so* hard."

"Shhh," Holly hissed, sitting down with a plate of scrambled eggs, bacon, and a piece of toast Jake had made for her.

Can this guy be more perfect?

Having had to rush through breakfast, she was glad that the drive to the starting line was a short one; it was practically around the corner from Jake's house. As far as the banners went, she couldn't help but shake her head at the terrible noise they made in the wind. Why on earth they'd brought that stuff was beyond her.

Holly eventually located Amelia, who was wearing a mini and a cut-off T-shirt, managing to look just as bad as she did. However, she couldn't help her mouth from gaping when she noticed Amelia's abs. It was probably safe to say that her friend wasn't going to see her ass today.

Amelia put her arm around Holly's neck when they reached Armand. "Last night was so much fun, but as much as I loved every minute of it, I'm really regretting it."

Holly smiled. "Just think, we'll definitely be sober after this walk."

Amelia chuckled and immediately rubbed her temples. "Oweee," she grunted.

"You want something for that?"

"She doesn't believe in tablets," Armand stated.

Amelia slapped him on the arm. "I don't drink tablets for a hangover."

"Same thing in my book."

"No, it's not. Go," she shooed him away, "the walk is about to start."

Jake comically started jumping in one spot. "Are you ready?" he yelled, with the same go get 'em attitude he'd had at the paintball game.

"Oh, hell no. Go away!" Both girls yelled at him.

Jake stopped, but continued to smile at Holly. Bending down, he kissed her cheek. "Make me proud," he whispered in her ear, while slapping her on the butt.

Rubbing her butt dramatically, Holly grunted, "I'll be lucky if I make it through this in one piece."

"Just remember that it's for a good cause, Holly. You'll be fine," Amelia said, drinking from a water bottle.

Five minutes later, a guy dressed as a drag queen climbed onto a small podium. He took the mic. "Thank you all for being here today. I know that anti-abortion is very close to our hearts." He went on to recite the statistics, as well as giving approximate numbers on how many clinics were in existence.

Throughout his talk, Holly noticed that Amelia had teared up. Shifting closer, she placed an arm around her friend's shoulders and embraced her. The girls smiled at one another and continued listening.

"Today, we will all be called Sisters in Blisters; just remember that every single one of those blisters will be for this very important cause."

Jake cheered loudly and everyone looked at him. He simply grinned.

He should be standing next to me, wearing heels and a dress, Holly thought, grinning.

All too soon, the man got off the podium and joined the other women and men who were all wearing high heels. Participants readied themselves, and shortly thereafter a gunshot went off.

At first, it was chaotic, but soon both Holly and Amelia stuck to a pace they were comfortable with. For the first ten minutes, Holly cursed herself for having signed up, but Amelia had needed her support and, as she'd said, it counted for something.

Holly felt herself becoming nauseous twenty minutes later and wished the walk would come to an end. The girls didn't talk much, so intent were they on not tripping and falling flat on their faces.

Holly kept looking at her watch, and the sun shone brighter and brighter. By now, they'd been walking for almost an hour.

How much longer is this going to go on for?

Holly was exhausted, and her toes and feet were killing her. A half hour later, she really began to feel the strain around her calves. To make matters worse, she couldn't feel her feet anymore. She was convinced she was going to die, never mind throw up.

Amelia tugged her by the arm when she started slowing down. "Keep up, Holly. What happened to you walking circles around me?"

"I was drunk, then. But now? I think I might have been stupid, too."

Both burst into giggles. Thankfully, Holly noticed people handing out water a couple of feet away. Each grabbed a paper cup as they walked past. Holly actually stopped to drink hers, but Amelia pulled her by the arm once again.

"We're halfway, so let's make this one good, okay?"

Oh. My. Soul! Holly nodded anyway and tried her very best to keep up with Amelia. *If she asks me to do this again next year, I'm going to shoot myself before an answer is required!* "How the hell did your dad do this?"

"With lots of cussing, but it was hilarious to watch," Amelia replied, laughing.

When they'd made it to the three-quarter mark, she could hear Jake and Armand yelling their names.

"Ignore them. Why on earth do they make those ridiculous banners every year? I swear it's to piss me off, or something." Amelia smiled.

"I think they are awesome."

Amelia laughed. "The banners or the guys? Regardless, they sure are a crazy bunch."

Holly pouted, stuck her tongue out, and then waved at Jake as she walked past him. She almost lost her balance due to her antics, but thanks to Amelia grabbing her arm, she managed to right herself. But when she ventured another look in Jake's direction, he was laughing his head off.

"Almost there," mumbled Amelia.

Holly bit down on her resolve and kept up, and for the last half of a mile both upped their pace.

Soon, they reached Jake and Armand at the finish line. Sweat dripped off both girls. Holly felt surprisingly good about having signed up for the walk, now that she was finished, of course.

"Two freaking hours! I do not want to know what my feet look like."

"Poor, baby. You deserve a foot rub and massage," Jake said.

"Only if she'll let you anywhere near her feet."

Holly placed a hand on Jake's shoulder and bent to remove her shoes. The white no-show socks were soaking wet. A yelp left her lips when she took off her socks to inspect her feet.

"It was worth it, Holly," Amelia said, as she too, removed her shoes.

"I guess. Mind you, it wasn't that bad." Holly looked at Amelia.

A disgruntled Jake groaned. "Oh, hell. Am I going to have to be here every freaking year with a banner?" Jake complained.

"It's for a good cause!" Amelia and Holly yelled in unison.

Amelia gave Holly a one arm hug and kissed her on the cheek. "Thank you so much, Holly. It was awesome. Next year, we can do this again."

"Deal," Holly agreed, even though her feet ached like they'd never ached before.

They made a quick stop at Amelia's house so the girls could shower, and thereafter went for lunch at a restaurant in the mall.

Holly continued to notice the looks directed at Jake every time they went somewhere, but they didn't affect her as much as before.

During lunch, Holly found herself laughing at Amelia. Armand, too, was extremely funny. Jake on the other hand showed a dry personality when he was with Armand, which Holly loved.

After lunch, the girls decided to do some shopping, while the boys watched a basketball game at the pub. Whether they watched a replay of a previous match or a live game, Holly didn't know and didn't really care, she was just happy to spend some quality time with Jake's sister.

In the interim, Amelia had taken a call; it had been Robin, who'd be joining them on their shopping spree. Shortly thereafter, Robin joined them and couldn't stop talking about her new boyfriend. Amelia didn't like him much, but the worry on Robin's face as Jake's name was mentioned was evident.

"I don't think he's going to like Quinton. He'll probably think the guy is a bore. It's only you who doesn't think that, Robbie."

"He's not a bore, okay? What he is, is a bit of a caveman, but I like that in any case."

"Our brother isn't going to." Amelia gave Robin a serious look.

Holly looked at Amelia.

"Jake made a deal with us when we were younger, to sort of be the judge and jury when it came to our boyfriends."

Robin scrunched her nose. "Amelia went through hell before she met Armand."

"It wasn't that bad." Amelia tried to look convincing.

"Pft! You had like, what, seventy thousand boyfriends before he approved of Armand?"

"I did not. I have to admit, though, it was hard for me in the beginning. At first, I didn't want to break up with what's-his-name. He was so cute. But I eventually saw what my brother did in him, and I had to admit he was right."

"So... let me get this straight, he chooses your boyfriends?"

"No, we do, but if he gives you the shake of his head—"

"Or the lip," Robin interrupted.

"Let's not forget the raised eyebrow," Amelia added, making everyone laugh. "We used to know that we were basically wasting our time with just that one look. My brother is really good when it comes to reading people."

"Yeah. Strange, because I keep wondering what the hell he saw in Mel," Robin stated.

"He was different then. It was all boobs and legs."

"Do you guys have to approve his girlfriends?"

"No, Holly. Besides, we love you." Amelia bumped her on the hip.

She liked the fact that these two women trusted their brother with something as important as choosing a guy. She would love to see the raised lip kind of disapproval snarl on him; it would probably end up being another of her favorite expressions.

The girls browsed and shopped until about five when they'd finally had enough and parted ways.

Holly hadn't bought too many things the way Robin and

Amelia had. She was on a strict budget and stuck to it as much as possible, but the clothes she had gotten, she absolutely loved.

As far as the evening was concerned, Holly and Jake decided to spend it at home, his house to be exact. He pampered her feet and took care of every blister he could find. It was infinitely sweet, especially as it wasn't something many men would do. She couldn't believe how lucky she was.

By eight, she could barely keep her eyes open.

Jake decided they'd take a shower together which, and despite the fact that Holly resembled a zombie she was that exhausted, turned into another sex marathon. They could not get enough of each other and carried their lovemaking into the bedroom.

Actually, making it onto the bed was the least of their worries; the floor proved just as useful. Completely spent, both passed out exactly where they were.

SUNDAY WAS SPENT in pretty much the same manner as the last, at his parents' house.

Mara had immediately demanded a recap of the previous week's tests to which Jake obliged, although Robin had written a few, too.

Holly began to understand why Jake was so blunt with Mara at times. She was someone who always got her way, and if she didn't, there'd be hell to pay. This was without a doubt the one side to Mara that still scared the shit out of Holly. She only hoped that she would never have to deal with that aspect of her personality. It was the only reason Holly was so adamant about staying on the pill.

Having to work the following week was not something Holly was looking forward to, as Jake would finally be on vacation. She hated saying goodbye to Jake, but with that she was also ecstatic as it meant that because Jake was on vacation he could do whatever the hell he wanted without Mara's approval. So she was going to stay the entire week with him at the commune.

After leaving Mara, Jake drove Holly home to collect more clothes for the week. Just one more week, then she would go on leave too, and she could not wait.

They'd be going on vacation with Bernie, Sam, and Leo to the family's beach house right after Jake's graduation ceremony on Wednesday.

Jake had gotten his results back, and now it was Holly's turn to deliver the goods, which she was saving for the holiday. His marks had been top notch, with most being A+'s; these had been exchanged for blowjobs. She'd laughed over this whole situation, but in the end it had been his prize for doing really well.

Having never been to a proper beach house, she could not for the life of her imagine what their beach house was going to look like. She was so excited, she couldn't wait for Friday. But when Jake picked her up every day after work, she begun to not care where they were going, as long as it was with him. They could have gone to Hades for all she cared.

IT WAS Wednesday afternoon and Jake was having a shower before the graduation ceremony.

Holly had asked for the day off as she really wanted to be there for him.

Sitting up, she got off Jake's bed and made her way to the bathroom to brush her teeth. As if on cue, the door opened and Jake stepped out wearing only a black towel around his waist.

Holly couldn't help her eyes from traveling up and down his body.

Obviously pleased by her interest, Jake smiled seductively, and with a quick raise of his eyebrows grabbed her around the waist, playfully pushing her backward. Once they reached the bed, he shoved her onto it gently. Jake followed and climbed over her, pinning down her wrists above her head.

"Like what you saw?" He looked at her with those smoldering eyes of his, and not really expecting an answer, bent down and captured her mouth hungrily before she had a chance to reply.

Holly's insides turned to knots, but she managed to break the kiss. Chuckling, she said, "You have no idea how much."

"I think I'm beginning to." He pressed his hips harder into hers.

Holly kept eye contact with him, all the while feeling the bulge beneath the towel wrapped around his hips. Breaking contact, her eyes wandered over his body; his rock hard muscles and super tight abs were starting to drive her nuts.

The second Jake kissed her again, and the second her legs wrapped around his waist, off went the towel. They were once again lost in the throes of passion.

NINETEEN

JAKE AND HOLLY SCRAMBLED, they were horribly late. When they eventually made it to the venue, Mara gave them a scolding look as everyone was already in their seats.

Giving Holly a quick kiss, Jake ran to where his classmates were already seated; the first eight rows on either side of the aisle.

Jake looked unbelievably handsome in his black graduation gown and hat, but it went without saying that Jake Peters looked good in anything.

The dean began his speech immediately after everyone had settled, and even made a couple of people laugh. He mentioned a few medical terms Holly didn't understand, but the way Armand, Robin, and the rest of the Peters' laughed she knew it was comical.

Jake's name was called. This surprised Holly as he hadn't mentioned he'd be doing a speech. She couldn't keep her eyes off him and noticed he wasn't at all nervous speaking publicly.

"Good day to our guests, who are mostly parents waiting in faith, and I'm sure praying non-stop in the hope of seeing us all graduate today." The crowd seated beneath the beautiful oak trees erupted with laughter.

"Robert Gallagher said that change is inevitable - except from a vending machine." More laughter ensued.

"As you stand on the brink of moving into life beyond these prodigious buildings right beside me, with all its amazing professors who no doubt had the faith that none of you would be sitting here, giving you lectures upon lectures about how to save a life; let me tell you that change is inevitable!

It is inevitable and indeed gratifying to see that our graduating Class of 2015 matured, and hopefully will become proficient in their skills."

Jake looked around skeptically, which made everyone chuckle. "You need to be ready to tackle and further your lifelong education. It is inevitable that structures, processes, and relationships change our day to day lives. It is inevitable that we will face new challenges, and it is inevitable that things may seem a little different in the year ahead. Yes, life is definitely going to become a little 'shaken and stirred'."

Jake spoke with his hands and Holly was transfixed.

"But as we look back, this evening is the culmination of a journey; a journey that started out with hesitant, tentative steps, and which we are now able to witness as to just how far these young ladies and gentlemen have progressed. It has been an honor and a privilege to be part of this journey right along with them, one which has been imbued with wonderful memories."

Pausing to peruse the audience, Jake smiled and then continued.

"It is these memories, ladies and gentlemen, that testify to the fine caliber of the graduating Class of 2015. I would like to pay tribute to each and every one of you. You have all left and will continue to leave an indelible legacy of excellence, achievement, and a fine ethos and tradition for generations to come. I would also like to pay tribute to the wonderful teachers, the parents, past pupils, and indeed the board of directors—you have all guided, molded and shaped these fine young people standing here tonight. Your role has been hugely instrumental in molding our youth; our hope for the future.

Our future seems destined to be in capable hands. The graduating Class of 2015 has achieved exceptional accolades, perhaps too many to highlight or single out. Suffice it to say, I believe that the vast majority of pupils strove to work to their full potential, aimed high, and set and stuck to their goals, and for the most part not only achieved them, but in fact surpassed them."

Pausing again to take another much needed breath, Jake began to wrap up his speech.

"So, ladies and gentlemen, as you face and tackle the inevitable changes, always keep true to yourself. Remember to hold on to your value system, your work ethic and most importantly, your humanity. It is these qualities that will guide you further on your journey. Today's achievements may fade, or even be forgotten. The applause may become a distant memory, and your certificates and medals may gather dust on a shelf or in a drawer. But, you will always be remembered for caring enough, for helping someone, for making someone feel special and appreciated, and for being the kind of person others enjoy spending time with. Your life is a remarkable occasion, and I have no doubt that you will rise to it!"

Jake ended his speech to a roar of applause from the crowd.

Taking a few steps back to allow the dean access to the microphone, Jake relaxed as the dean began to call out names in alphabetical order. Each graduate walked up onto the stage proudly, received their scrolls, and walked back down in the opposite direction.

Holly smiled at Jake, more than happy for him to enjoy the moment he had worked toward his entire life.

IT WAS BACK to work for Holly the day after graduation. Just one more day and she was going to be free.

She struggled to concentrate on her work as the previous night's events played through in her mind. She had to make due on her promises and gave Jake the best blow job she could. From the soft grunts coming from his lips, and by the way he grabbed her hair told her that she delivered in so many ways.

The door to reception pinged, forcing Holly to snap out of her memory and look up. The heart-throb was staring down at her, looking just as yummy as he had a couple of hours prior when he'd dropped her off at work.

She smiled, got up from her chair and gave him a soft kiss on his lips over the counter. "You want something to eat? I'm sure the restaurant can whip something up."

He smiled and ran his tongue along the top part of his teeth. "The bathroom free?"

Holly slapped him playfully on the chest when he fiddled with her blouse. "Not that kind of meal."

Jake chuckled as he raised his eyebrows playfully. "Then, no. I have a couple of errands I need to run. I'll come by to pick you up and talk about dinner."

Holly shook her head but laughed all the same.

"Have you spoken to Marabella about tomorrow?"

"What about tomorrow?" Marabella suddenly appeared around the corner, inevitably making Jake jump. She grinned mischievously.

Holly hid her giggle behind her hand.

"Geez, woman. Where did you come from?" Jake asked, one hand on his chest.

"Oh, I'm everywhere, mister. So you better be careful what you spew from those lips of yours. My bathrooms are not for your pleasure."

Both Holly and Jake laughed.

"I'm so sorry, but c'mon." He gestured with his hands at Holly. "She's extremely hard to resist and you can't blame me."

Marabella threw her head back and laughed heart-warmingly.

Holly only shook her head gently and answered the phone, which had chosen that precise moment to start ringing. Whilst trying to concentrate on the call, she managed to overhear Jake asking Marabella if Holly could get off around twelve the following day.

She'd totally forgotten to ask Marabella, but she was sure that for all the nights she'd helped out, it wouldn't be too much of a problem.

When the call came to an end, Jake gave her a quick kiss on the mouth and made his way to the door. He opened it and held it open for a couple who had come to discuss a function with Marabella. But before he exited, he turned to tell her that she was the best, which made the forty-something blond woman blush.

Holly greeted the couple, smiling at them both, as well as her boss, who was at that moment fanning herself with the front of her shirt. She knew exactly what was going through Marabella's mind; she felt that same every single time Jake was anywhere near her.

At around three, Holly made her way down to the restaurant and took over Stacy's shift. She'd started a couple of weeks ago and Holly hated every moment that she drooled over Jake.

Stacy had barely graduated from school, but Marabella had felt sorry for her and gave her the morning shift at the restaurant.

Five o'clock finally came around, but no Jake. However, her phone began to ring, and the most beautiful picture of her and Jake flickered on its screen.

"Where are you?"

"What? No... hey, my love, I've missed you so much, but when the hell are you going to get your sexy ass over here?"

Holly laughed, shaking her head.

"To which I would've replied, if you got your hot little butt out of that building and through the gate, you would see me parked right across the street."

"You're a funny man, Jake. I'll see you in a minute," Holly said, disconnecting the call.

What would I do without him? That thought was still unbearable to think of, and she prayed with all her heart that she would never have to find out.

Holly gathered her purse and waved to Marabella and Jerry on her way out.

She found Jake's BMW parked exactly where he'd said he would be. When she neared the vehicle, he opened the door for her from the inside. Smiling, she slipped into the passenger seat, leaned over and gave him the hottest kiss she could muster. When her ears started to ring again, she broke the kiss.

"Now *that* is a greeting I could most definitely get used to," Jake mumbled out of breath, before starting the car.

THE NEXT MORNING, Holly was running extremely late for work. They had packed for their holiday until late the previous evening. And when Holly, tired and sweaty decided to take a shower, Jake had joined her, trapping her within its walls. What took place thereafter was a fucking session like no other.

Holly couldn't help blushing every time she thought about his body rubbing up against hers, his shaft filling her up to the hilt, and his mouth and hands devouring every inch of her body. The sound of her screaming like a pig being slaughtered hadn't vanished, either.

The past week was everything she'd ever dreamed of. She wondered what his internship year was going to be like. He had said that it was either a morning shift or a night shift, and she hoped with all her heart that it wasn't the latter.

When they were done showering, she quickly dressed in a beautiful short skirt, a satin blouse, and stepped into her wedges before she ran down to the kitchen where all of Jake's room mates were having breakfast and waiting for her to make a fresh pot of coffee.

It was one of the things she hadn't gotten used to that past week. Their coffee was way too strong and she missed her own blend, the one she'd been making ever since she fell in love with coffee.

Two of the guys smiled broadly as she entered the kitchen.

Why she couldn't remember their names was beyond her knowledge, but they were much easier to talk to than the girls who constantly glared at her, or had *that* look on their faces, the one that constantly wondered what Jake Peters saw in her.

"I am running late, but simply need your coffee. What on earth do you put in there?" Tony, or Richard—she couldn't remember the tall, skinny, blond guy's name—asked.

"That is my secret." She chuckled, reaching for her Starbucks house blend in the cabinet and pouring it into the percolator.

She then took out her own syrup, made from nut essence, vanilla syrup, and a hint of chili, and squirted it into the coffee jug. A heap of hot chocolate joined the rest of the contents. That done, she then switched on the percolator and watched how the coffee dripped into the jug.

She started thinking about Jake's body again, pushing against hers in the shower. How he'd pressed her hard up against the cold, shower wall and fucked her the way only he could.

Holly snapped out of her naughty thoughts when the coffee stopped dripping. She also noticed Robin staring at her as she grabbed a slice of toast, handing her an empty cup.

She blushed, looked away, and began filling Robin's cup, as well as one for herself and Jake who at that moment walked into the kitchen.

"You know some of us still have a day's class right?" One of the girls, Molly—Holly thought that that was her name—asked while staring at Jake.

"And how is that my problem?"

"The way the two of you carry on each night, it's extremely hard to concentrate, Jake."

One of the guys laughed.

Jake chuckled and threw in a shrug for good measure.

Holly, on the other hand, burned with shame from deep within.

"Uh-huh," Robin mumbled, still staring at Holly.

"Shut up," Holly whispered, bending over to give Jake a quick kiss on the cheek. Just as she was about to leave, Jake pulled her back gently and gave her his Beemer's keys.

"What is this?" Holly looked perplexed.

"That Beetle of yours is running by a miracle. Take mine, I don't need it for today."

"Excuse me!" Robin stated with a surprised look.

"It's no big deal. Quinton," Jake said the guy's name in a not-so-pleased tone, "let's you borrow his Jeep all the time."

"He's not that bad, Jake."

"Uh-huh."

"Really?" Robin asked, sounding hurt and angry at the same time.

Holly knew what that was all about; they'd told her how they trusted their brother when it came to approving their boyfriends.

She hadn't witnessed the lip yet, but the look on his face at that moment was beautiful.

"Okay, see you then later," Holly said, kissing him on his cheek.

Robyn was still waiting for an explanation from her brother as to why he didn't approve of Quinton.

Holly didn't hang around any longer and ran out to Jake's car, still shocked that he'd let her borrow it for the day. She couldn't believe her luck, and by the almost choking sound that had escaped Robin, Holly knew it was a first for Jake as well. *At least he trusts me,* she thought.

She yanked her heels off and chucked them, along with her handbag onto the passenger seat. She adjusted the seat in order to reach the pedals, but jumped when she found Jake, who was still wearing his PJs and a robe, standing at the window. She rolled it down and received a passionate goodbye kiss.

"Don't scratch my baby," he growled.

Holly rolled her eyes. "I'll try my best," she joked.

Jake took a step back and gave her a stern look.

"I'm joking, relax," she said, putting one hand up. "I know how to drive. Actually, women are better drivers, I think." On hearing Jake's snort, she turned the key with a flick of her wrist and the engine roared to life.

Winking at Jake, she shifted into reverse and backed out down the driveway and through the gate Jake had opened with the remote in his hand. She honked twice as she drove down the street, feeling like an absolute diva. Never in a million years had she thought that she would ever find herself behind the steering wheel of a BMW.

WORK WAS HECTIC AS USUAL, but at noon Holly bid her goodbyes excitedly. She had a couple of weeks off, which she'd be spending with Jake, her two best friends, and their beautiful little boy at his family's beach house. It was going to be a super amazing holiday, and the best part was that she wouldn't have to say goodbye to Jake in the mornings, or just see him only over weekends again.

Holly had thought about a lot of things lately. Especially in regards to his mom being overly protective, or it could be said, possessive of him. He was twenty-seven years old, and for him to still follow her rules was a bit on the crazy side. But, Holly figured that it was better to have someone care like that, than have no one care at all. So, in the end she tried to not put much thought into it.

The thing that worried her the most, though, was that Jake would be starting with his internship soon, and that entailed shifts. With her luck, it would probably be the night shift and she would never see him at all.

All kinds of fears emerged with that, too. Number one on her list was the biggest, that Jake would find someone else who wouldn't be a hassle to see or spend whatever limited time he had with.

She wasn't a complete idiot; she'd watched Grey's Anatomy plenty of times to know exactly what took place in those sleeping quarters at hospitals. What if Jake bonded with another blond-haired bimbo and told Holly to take a hike?

She hated feeling insecure, but it was something she just

had to get used to. The conclusion Holly came to was simple; if she wanted to be in his life, she would have to trust him and hope for the best.

He wasn't a Brandon Morgan and if she were honest, she didn't really know who Jake was. Not really. The only side she'd seen of him was this beautiful, sweet guy whose personality clashed with his looks. Men who usually looked like Jake were womanizers—most of the time, and had no qualms about jumping into bed with any number of women, especially those who looked like models.

But those very women on the other hand, were her other worry. They would do anything to get into his pants. She'd seen the looks many gave him, the smiles, the drool that literally ran down the side of their mouths, and the lust in their eyes. This would all disappear in a heartbeat the second they'd see her touching his arm, or giving him a kiss. But the want never disappeared. That much she knew.

It was never hard to figure out what they'd been thinking: What the fuck was he doing with someone like her? But Holly made peace with this, too, deciding to let the next month be and just enjoy what was left of this one.

ON HER WAY to Jake's house from work, her thoughts had been so all-consuming she'd almost driven past. Slowing down, she picked up her phone and dialed his number.

"Hey," he answered in a seductive voice.

Holly smiled. "A tree jumped in front of me and I think I wrecked your car." She bit hard on her lips to keep from laughing.

Her reply was dead silence.

"Jake?"

"Are you okay?" That was all he asked and bless his heart, he really sounded worried about her.

"I'm joking! Sorry. I'm right in front of the gate. Open up, pretty please."

"Damn it, Holly, you need a hiding!"

"Oooh... you going to give me one?" she flirted.

Jake uttered not one word, and that was followed by the phone's dead tone as she watched the gates open. She drove in and saw Leo's SUV parked in front of the garage. She parked next to him and turned the engine off. She slipped her feet into her high heels and adjusted the seat to its original position. Climbing out, she began to laugh when she saw Jake emerge from the house.

"That was not funny. You have no idea how my heart dropped. It's still lodged somewhere inside of my stomach."

"Your car is fine, Jake. Really. Stupid joke, I know. I'm sorry."

"Are you serious? Do you honestly believe that I'd worry over a piece of metal?" He grabbed her around the waist and pulled her tightly against him. "I had this insane visual of you bleeding somewhere, alone."

Holly's heart melted. "Nice comeback."

"It's not a comeback, Holly, it's simply the truth." He kissed her hard on the lips, and squeezed her ass just as hard.

Holly blushed. "You really missed me that much?"

"Baby, I always miss you."

This pleased Holly no end, but not wanting to show how much, she replied, "I miss you, too. On occasion."

Jake faked being hurt by holding both hands over his heart, which only served to make Holly giggle. Chuckling, he grabbed her hand and pulled her toward the house.

Sam ran straight to Holly as soon as she stepped over the threshold. Bernie and Leo had arrived earlier.

"Hello, baby. You've gotten so big, and it's only been five days, wow." Holly praised, picking Sam up and giving him a huge hug, while waving at Leo and Bernie.

Sam babbled something, but the only word Holly could understand was 'home'. "Soon, I promise." She kissed him a couple of times on both of his cheeks and then put him down. She needed to change into more comfortable clothes.

Shortly thereafter, they left for the beach house in one car. It wasn't a particularly long drive, and only took them about half an hour to get there.

They ended up listening to all the children's songs that ever existed, laughing on occasion when Leo and Jake imitated animal noises every time 'Old McDonald Had a Farm' played. The ones Jake didn't know, he quickly learned, and by the fifth time they played he sang along with them. He really loved Sam, and Holly doubted there wasn't a thing he wouldn't do for that boy.

Veering sharply, Jake took a road hidden within a tunnel of trees.

Holly gasped as he pulled into the grounds of a beautiful mansion. It had soft, sandy colored walls, and a huge veranda that circled the entire house—simply breathtaking. Every room on the upper level had a balcony. Glancing around at the grounds, Holly noticed an old woman playing ball with a gorgeous black lab.

The woman stopped, bent ever so slightly and stroked the lab. She immediately smiled when Jake climbed out of the SUV.

Jake wasted no time in making introductions. "Dani, this is Holly."

"Holly?" She looked at Jake in a teasing manner.

"Yes, Holly," he repeated, smiling.

The old woman's gaze reverted back to Holly. Suddenly, she grabbed Holly around the neck and gave her a grandmotherly hug. Holly could hardly remember hugging her grandmother, but she assumed it must have felt similar to this woman's hug.

"Nice to meet you," Holly greeted.

"Dani lives right around the corner," Jake elaborated at the same time Leo went in for a hug, lifting the woman off her feet. "She and her husband keep an eye on the place."

Dani hit Leo playfully as he released her. Chuckling, she went over to Bernie and kissed her twice on both cheeks.

Holly sidled up close to Jake and whispered, "She seems very nice."

"She's the best," Jake stated, giving her a kiss. He excused himself and made his way toward the SUV, mumbling that they had to unpack.

"There are sandwiches in the kitchen, and I bought milk and coffee. I thought you guys might be hungry." Dani looked very pleased with herself.

Leo, meanwhile, had been entertaining the dog with Sam; he was very playful.

"See, what did I tell you? She's the best." Jake winked as he flung a bag over one shoulder and carried another in his hand. "Thank you, Dani. You're a star." He gave the old woman a peck on the cheek and walked toward the house.

"Thank you so much," Holly said, as she too, grabbed one of the smaller pieces of luggage with both hands and put it down on its wheels.

"You're very welcome. It's so nice to see that he has someone in his life again." She sighed.

Holly smiled, because she never knew how to reply when someone said that. "I'm the one who's lucky. He has been nothing but amazing these past couple of months."

"That's our Jake, all right," Dani concurred. Turning slightly on her heel, she whistled to the lab.

"It's about time, too," Bernie put in.

Leo, having heard anything relating to food, was now making his way out of the house with a sandwich in his hand.

Bernie gave him the eye. "There are bags with your name on them, buster."

Leo took a huge bite of one sandwich while simultaneously laughing. Amazingly enough, he also managed to run to the SUV at the same time, kind of looking like the lab that was running toward Dani.

As Dani made to leave, they thanked her once again and bid her a good day further. The old lady smiled, and then made her way down the driveway and out the gate.

Inside, the house was massive. They walked into a huge living room and open kitchen with a large nook area. Fresh flowers that had been beautifully arranged in eye-catching vases sat proudly on the dining room table situated just behind the lounge.

Family pictures of the Peters' hung regally on the walls, immediately piquing Holly's interest. She couldn't help but have a look. There were many of Jake as a child, and one thing Holly could tell right away was that he'd been a hunk from the minute he was born.

"This Amelia? How old was she?" Holly pointed at a black and white photo of a girl with long, black hair who looked a lot like Jake's twin, rather than his sister.

Both Leo and Bernie began to laugh hysterically.

"Shut up," Jake grumbled, turning on his heels and making his way out of the house in order to collect more luggage from the SUV.

"Umm... that's Jake," Leo said in a loud voice. "His mother went through a phase where she refused to cut his hair."

"It's Jake?" Holly doubled over, almost choking with laughter.

"Hey,"—Jake had returned with another bag, which he was

now holding up in the air, whilst gesturing in Holly's direction with it—"I was a damn beautiful little kid, even though people always referred to me as a cute little girl."

Leo guffawed. "Was that when she decided to finally have it cut?"

"I think so."

Leo placated Jake by slapping him on the shoulder. "Be glad, be very glad that that phase is long over, dude."

"There is nothing wrong with growing your boy's hair. Not anyone's fault he was mistaken for a girl. It happens the other way around, too. Or so I've been told." Holly tried to make it sound like it wasn't the most awful thing in the world to have happen to a little boy.

Bernie tapped her lips with an index finger. "So... are you saying that I can grow Sam's hair, too?"

"No. It wouldn't suit Sam," she quickly corrected.

"That was crazy, Holly," Bernie said.

"My mom wasn't crazy, Bernie. She was and still is 'disturbed' at times."

"Oh, please, Jake. Your mom is psycho when it comes to you."

"She's not really that bad."

Looking around suspiciously, Bernie asked, "You sure there are no cameras here?"

"I'm sure, or Dani would've said something if there were."

"See, even you think she's psycho mom."

"I never said that."

"She's not like that, Bernie," Holly defended.

"Thank you, sweetheart." Jake walked over to her and gave her a hug.

"Pft! She has to say that for your benefit. Then again, Holly really has no idea what your mom can be like."

Jake shook his head. "Don't listen to her. They never see eye to eye, and I guess it's because they are both so much alike."

Leo chortled and gave Jake a high five, something Bernie didn't appreciate in the least.

"Seriously, Leo? Would you like to sleep outside? 'Cause you know I can make that happen in the blink of an eye." Bernie snapped her fingers for good measure.

"Well, funny enough, I noticed that there's a hammock. I wouldn't mind."

Bernie slapped him, but was pulled in by Leo's arms for a tight hug. "You are not psycho, Bernie my love. We're only teasing you. However, if you were, you'd be my psycho." Leo looked extremely chuffed with his statement.

Bernie and Holly gurgled with laughter, but at the back of her mind, Holly couldn't help but worry about Mara.

What on earth did Bernie know that she didn't?

TWENTY

THEIR VACATION FLEW by at breakneck speed, and each day upon Holly waking up her entire body ached.

Jake was a beast and didn't seem too worried that there was an almost two-year-old in the house. It had to be said, though, that he was overtly careful.

By the end of the week, they'd almost baptized every room in the house, as well as having had sex twice on the beach, which was so not an amazing experience as sand would end up in the most awkward places. Sex on the beach was not her thing.

Jake's reasoning was that they were making up for the nights he was going to have to work.

Holly chuckled every time he said so, but dreaded what was to come in any case. She couldn't imagine only seeing him fortnightly.

Phone sex was definitely going to be on the cards when he started with night shifts.

On the last day of their vacation, Jake took Holly to an upmarket restaurant. She loved the atmosphere the second they walked in. It had the most beautifully laid out tables, draped with white tablecloths and gorgeous pewter cutlery, reminding her of their restaurant back home.

The décor had been done in soft hues and gave off a welcoming feeling, yet it was sleek and showcased numerous beige chairs.

A huge crystal chandelier hung from the ceiling, illuminating most of the restaurant. However, further light was provided by a centerpiece on each table; an elaborate wrought iron candelabra holding three candles each.

Waiters were all decked out in tuxedos, no less, and looked like penguins.

As if all of that weren't enough, Holly's eyes glanced over the orchestra playing quietly in one corner.

Feeling a tug on her hand, she looked in the direction Jake was leading her toward and gasped at the sight of the table adjacent to one of the huge glass walls. Looking out through the magnificent floor to ceiling windows, it was apparent that the view of the ocean was what they would be sharing that evening.

When they reached their magnificent table, the waiter pulled Holly's chair out. Nodding her thanks, she sat and was immediately but gently moved forward into position. Confident that she was comfortable, the waiter snapped open a white napkin with much flare and arranged it ever so lightly on her lap. Straightening, he handed Jake the wine list and upon clearing his throat—very elaborately it must be said—he began reciting the restaurant's wine selection.

It all sounded Greek to Holly, figuratively speaking. There was not a single name she recognized, but that made absolutely no difference as each one sounded super sexy, especially when Jake made a selection in a language that sounded like Italian. When the waiter left them, Jake took Holly's hand gently in his.

"This place is gorgeous," she complimented, shyly.

"Not as gorgeous as you," he replied, winking, making her blush.

Holly didn't think she would ever be able to get used to all that was Jake.

He chuckled at her red cheeks.

Embarrassed, she smiled and shook her head slightly. She'd noticed the indiscreet glances thrown their way, and how some of the women—obviously those lacking any scruples whatsoever—gaped in their direction, whether they were with a partner or not. For some reason, he always only had eyes for her, which made her feel super special.

"Look, I know you are worried about me starting with my internship."

"I am?" she joked.

"You are," he stated, smiling. "And I know this, because I worry about it myself. But, I know we can make it work, and I know we'll find a way around all the work, work, and more work."

She giggled at his answer. "So... do you have a plan?"

"I do." He wiggled his eyebrows. "You can come and visit me at night—"

Holly interrupted him when she burst out laughing, but cupped her hand over her mouth in order to not let it echo throughout the entire restaurant. "And then what? Are we going to have picnics in the cafeteria, followed by me sleeping over at the hospital? Your mother would just *love* that."

"My mother doesn't have a say."

"It's her hospital, Jake. I'm sure she does."

"Well, then, we'll just have to sneak you in."

"Oooh, that sounds so exciting!"

Jake chortled.

Holly breathed deeply when she saw him starting to pull gently on one of his eyebrows. He really was one of the hottest guys ever, and she still had no clue what she had done to deserve him.

"So, give it to me straight. How many times a week are we going to be able to see one another?"

The corners of his lips twitched slightly upward. "My shifts are either day or night shifts. Interns have to be there almost every day, but after the first year, it gets a bit easier."

Holly did the calculations in her head and came to the conclusion that when Jake worked nightshifts, she was almost never going to see him at all. "So, is it safe to say we're looking at about once, maybe twice a week, then?" It came out in a squeak. She swallowed hard, fighting the urge to cry, but it didn't sound so great. Especially now that she knew their weekends were over. However, seeing him once or twice a week as opposed to only fortnightly as she'd thought was better than nothing.

"Hey..." He touched her hand again.

"Jake, I always knew seeing you would eventually become limited, but I so don't love the fact that it's like right around the corner." She forced a smile. "But, you're right. We'll just have to make the most of it when we do get to spend time together."

"There are phones, too, Holly."

She snorted in response, "Yes, there are, but it won't be the real deal. You've spoiled me. I'm too used to seeing you every day. Guess I'll just need time to adjust to not seeing you that often."

"I'm sorry. I feel like an idiot. I knew this profession was going to bite me in the ass one day."

Holly smiled. "No, we will make it work. You are going to be a terrific head doctor."

"Neurologist."

"Whatever, you know what I mean." She stuck her tongue out. "And one day, years and years from now, we will share our story and laugh at all of this."

"That's my girl." Jake leaned forward and kissed her softly.

Just then, the waiter returned with their wine. He inquired if they'd like more time to look over the menu. As Jake had been to that particular restaurant on more than one occasion, he knew what was good, not that there was meal he didn't like.

He began describing an amazing dish to Holly, one she just had to try. As soon as she heard the word *lobster*, she was sold; she'd never had one before and there was nothing like the present.

She watched as Jake ordered, while the waiter poured the Italian wine she couldn't for the life of her remember the name of.

The evening went by too fast, just as any time spent with Jake did, but she enjoyed every minute she was with him—they laughed about a lot of things.

He also shared stories about his family and all the crap they used to pull whilst on vacation at the beach house. It held many beautiful memories for his family. She hoped that one day, when she had a child of her own, he or she would be fortunate enough to live their life the way Jake had, and she hoped it would be nothing like hers.

Nearing eleven in the evening, after dessert and two bottles of wine, Jake signaled the waiter for the check. Fifteen minutes later, they left, Jake's hand resting lightly on Holly's lower back.

They decided to take a walk on the beach. The fresh air made Holly's head spin a little, but she somehow managed to keep it together, enjoying the time she got to spend with Jake; running and playing like children, and wetting their feet in the refreshing water that washed onto the beach.

Jake would chase her, catch her, and twirl her around and around while kissing her. At one point they gasped, laughing when a huge wave crashed against their legs as they'd wandered a little farther in than expected, ending up soaking the bottom half of their bodies.

"This dress is never going to be the same again," joked Holly.

"Then we'll get you a new one," Jake countered, kissing her again.

His lips tasted salty and felt extra soft. Holly groaned as his teeth softly scraped her lower lip. His tongue dueled ardently with hers, and she began to feel lightheaded but pushed through the euphoria until her entire body felt like one huge, scorching hot coal.

Jake's hands worked their way beneath her dress and kneaded her backside. It drove her insane. He lifted her off her feet, her legs twirling of their own accord around his waist, gripping it like a vice.

She couldn't stop kissing him, not even if her life depended on it. But when she ran out of air, Jake moved to her neck, sucking and nipping on it gently. His lips moved down her collarbone toward the V between her breasts. Holly could feel her nipples hardening as the heat emanating from him was driving her body wild.

Jake's mouth trailed back up to her neck where it stopped so he could let out a frustrated groan.

Holly's shoulders shook with suppressed laughter.

When Jake looked up at her all she could tell was that he was smiling, and when their lips touched again it was a soft, sweet kiss. Resignedly, he lowered her back down to the ground. "We should get home before we catch a cold. I really didn't bargain on that stupid wave."

"It's what waves do, Jake. We shouldn't have tempted them," she teased, slapping him hard on the ass, which inevitably turned into a game of chase all the way to where he'd parked.

Her legs and feet were covered in sand, and his pants were completely soaked. She looked at him disbelievingly when he unzipped his trousers and began pulling them down.

"Jake! What are you doing?"

"What does it look like? There's no one around, and I refuse to drive with half the beach up my ass."

Giggling like a school girl, Holly grabbed one of the towels Jake had left in the car and placed it on the passenger seat. He wrapped one around his waist before jumping behind the wheel of the SUV. She suddenly felt a little chilly when a soft breeze blew in from the ocean.

Gentleman that Jake was, he noticed and immediately turned on the heat. As soon it finally warmed her feet and traveled up her body, Jake threw the car into reserve and exited the parking lot.

"This is asking to get sick," Holly said.

"Tell you what, soon as we get home, I'll park the SUV and you run us a nice, warm bath."

"Deal," she said, shuddering slightly.

"Are you really that cold?" He chuckled.

"I am," she replied, her teeth chattering.

Jake leaned over to adjust the heat, all the while smirking.

Holly slapped him playfully.

When he finally pulled into the driveway, she jumped out quickly, keys at the ready. It took her about thirty seconds to open the door, run past Bernie who was sitting next to a sleeping Leo while she watched a movie, and up the stairs.

She was still able to hear Bernie's laughter as she entered the bathroom. The bath's taps couldn't open fast enough, hating the cold that was making her freeze from the inside out. Dipping her hand in the warm water felt blissful; she figured that would have to do until the bath filled.

Jake's voice filled the house. Holly heard him speaking to

Bernie as his footsteps echoed on the wooden stairs leading to the upper area. He chuckled when upon entering, he saw her crouched down next to the bath with both arms under the warm stream of water. "It's not funny," she said, but chuckled, too.

"Let's get you out of those horrible wet clothes." He walked to her, lifted her up gently, and in one fluid movement Holly's beautiful black dress was unzipped and dropped to the floor. His shirt followed suit, but unlike hers, Jake's body was amazingly warm.

Holly immediately took advantage of that and wrapped her arms around his torso. It was her turn to laugh when he gasped for air as soon as her ice cold body touched his warm one.

"You poor thing," he whispered in her ear, rubbing her arms and back repeatedly in order to warm them up.

As soon as the bath was half filled, Holly wasted no time in climbing in. It was the most amazing feeling ever as the warmth of the water started to heat up her entire body.

Jake didn't hesitate, either, climbing in right behind her, planting kisses on her shoulders and on the nape of her neck.

Holly shuddered when he tugged her gently backward against him. Turning her head to the side, she looked right into his eyes, and like magnets their lips locked in what Holly called *Titanic* style. She loved kissing Jake, no matter the ways, positions, or circumstances. When the strain became too much for her neck, Holly twisted her body around and climbed on top of him.

Jake's hands grabbed her butt cheeks and pulled her harder against him, while his lips trailed from her jawline, down and across to her shoulder, and then farther down to her breast.

She moaned breathlessly as he gently sucked on one of her nipples, following it with a groan when she felt his manhood harden.

"You like that?" he asked, thrusting his hips upward.

"You know I like whatever you do, Hooligan."

Grinning, he kissed her again. The bathroom seemed to heat up even more, and it had nothing to do with the water's temperature. Suddenly, Jake's butt lost traction and his body slipped, splashing water over the edges. They tried but failed to not make a racket.

"Shhhh... Sam is sleeping," Jake whispered, a naughty grin evident on his face. "Are you warm yet?"

Holly nodded, still giggling, immediately following it with a yelp when Jake climbed out with her in his arms.

"Just don't slip on your way out of the bath, please," she begged him. "That would be the cherry on the top if we ended up breaking our arms or something tonight."

"That's not going to happen. I'm not a klutz like you."

"Oh, please! What happened in the bathtub a couple of seconds ago?"

"Shut up," he growled, pinching her backside. Jake wrapped her, as well as himself, in a towel keeping the warmth the bath had left them with trapped, picked her up once again and carried her through to the bedroom.

Holly dropped her towel and climbed into bed; Jake did the same but covered her body with his, pulling the duvet over his back and both their heads.

The foreplay in the bath had been enough and without wasting any time, Jake sheathed himself inside her, pulling out slowly and then plunging back in with slightly more force.

Holly's mind reeled, and her muscles clenched as heat warmed her from the inside out. She'd happily have sex with Jake every single day of her life and never complain.

Holly was a screamer, of that there was no doubt, although she'd tried on a few occasions to keep it in. She'd eventually given up and opted instead to concentrate on not being as loud. After all, one could scream internally—although still somewhat audible—in the throes of sex if one tried hard enough. In the end, it was still a struggle as Jake drove her insane time and time again.

The sweet spot between Holly's legs began to itch, and the pit of her stomach felt as if it was going to explode. Sometimes, she felt as if she would burst right out of her skin; that's how Jake made her feel every single time. She bit his shoulder to keep her squealing at bay, but the groan from Jake told her that he absolutely loved it whenever she went semi-vampire on him.

Her orgasm kept on building and she dug her nails deep into his back.

In response, Jake thrust harder and deeper, accompanying his movements with grunts.

Holly bit down harder on his shoulder, convinced she must have drawn blood, but while her teeth remained attached, her mouth opened in order to release the whimpering that had built up. "I'm close," she ground out in his ear.

Jake's response was to clamp his lips down on hers, drawing her tongue into his mouth. They dueled, sucked, retreated and teased, until Holly's toes felt as if they were going to curl backward from the pleasure that rippled up and down her body. She shoved her face into Jake's neck, again struggling to muffle the sounds of pure ecstasy.

And then it came, that over-the-top, exploding feeling that lasted, sadly, for about ten seconds. Holly rode him fiercely until she was spent, collapsing like a rag doll thrown onto a bed or dropped on the floor.

Jake stopped, pulled out gently, and rolled onto his back, breathing like a freight train.

Mustering every bit of energy she could in order to speak, Holly managed to croak, "I hope this is never going to stop."

Jake snorted. "The only time it will stop is when I'm six feet under." Pulling himself up on to his elbows, he said, "I'm damn thirsty, need something to drink. You want anything?"

"Yes, please. Just some water." She watched him get up off the bed and walk butt naked—proud of it, too—to the closet where he retrieved a pair of shorts and pulled them on.

When he noticed her ardent look, he cheekily drawled, "Wipe your mouth, Bee Puke, you're drooling."

Holly was gob-smacked. "You're full of it, aren't you? But, I'll admit... that's one fine looking ass, Mr. Peters."

Chuckling, Jake left.

Snuggling into the pillow, she took a couple of deep breaths to calm her heart.

Fuck, what on earth am I going to do?

She didn't know how she was going to cope with seeing him only once or twice a week. Her insecurities wreaked havoc with her mind, but she still couldn't help thinking about the new female interns who would work right beside him.

If Jake needed sex as much as they were having it lately, who was to say that he wouldn't...

Stop it, Holly! Jake isn't Brandon, not even close.

She didn't really believe he'd do that to her.

You just have to remind him what it is you can do that others didn't seem to get right. You just have to remind him of how you make him feel.

She giggled at her thoughts, which were kind of running rampant. Just then, Jake walked into the room.

"What are you giggling about?"

"Get your ass here, and you'll see."

"I like that, and I'll save you the trouble of having to ask twice." Jake placed the glass of water on the nightstand, jumped into bed, and pulled the covers over them.

And Holly got ready to give him another of the biggest orgasms of his life.

TWENTY-ONE

"FUCK!" Jake was out of breath. "What the hell, Bee Puke?"

Holly's grin was naughty. "Did you enjoy that?"

"Did I... What?" He looked at her disbelievingly. "Are you shitting me? That thing..."—He twirled his finger about—"...you do with your body. Is that even possible?"

She laughed outright. "I seem to be fine, so I'm sure it is."

"How do you do that?"

"Oh, no. It's a secret, mister."

He pulled a face, kissed her one more time, and then slid his arm under her body and promptly fell asleep.

THE SUN STREAMED into the room the next morning, waking them both up. Holly hadn't felt any aches last night, but she sure felt them this morning. Maybe what she was capable of doing with her body wasn't normal at all.

"Good morning, beautiful," Jake croaked beside her.

"Morning, Hooligan," she said sleepily.

Jake groaned. "How long am I going to hear that for?"

"Until the day you die."

"I need to shower," Jake mumbled, getting up.

"Go. I'm way too pooped to get up just yet."

He walked to the bathroom, smiling.

Holly heard the shower start, and if her body hadn't been pounding the way it currently was, she would've joined him. But the way she felt at that moment, she did not want to have sex for the next couple of weeks.

She laughed inwardly, thinking how that might just be their solution after all. To have crazy hot sex, sex that would leave her body aching for days, and then maybe she wouldn't miss him that much. But she knew that was a lie. Jake was so much more to her than someone to have sex with. He was everything she'd ever wanted.

Crawling out of bed, she walked like a penguin to the closet. She had approximately two minutes max to get ready, otherwise she'd make him late and he would more than likely never let her do that to him again. She grabbed a pair of shorts and a T-shirt.

Today was the day they would go back home; the holiday was over. She really wasn't looking forward to it, as Jake would start his internship the following week. Never in a million years would she have thought that she'd fall for a doctor, and not just any doctor, a freaking neurologist at that.

Holly fanned herself just thinking about it, when she felt his arms around her. She hadn't even heard the shower turn off.

Jake kissed her on the cheek, following that with a slap on the ass. "We should hurry, we still need to pack."

"Aye, captain," she joked.

"I'll show you tonight what a captain is capable of," he teased, making her laugh.

"Oooh, I can't wait."

"Don't start, we really don't have time, sweetheart."

"I'm not starting anything," she argued.

"Oh, no. You are just driving me insane." He pulled her into his arms.

"You are the one who's always starting things. I'm just an innocent bystander."

"An innocent what?" He pretended to cough.

She giggled again. "You heard me just fine."

"Right. Innocent bystander, indeed. We'll see how innocent you are tonight." He walked to the door. "I'll make us a quick breakfast. I'm starving."

"I'm sure Bernie has already cooked up a storm," she yelled after him, glad that he'd left without taking things further. She wouldn't have been able to have sex with him again in any case without showing her discomfort.

She slipped on her shoes and walked out of the room slowly. *Fuck, what was I thinking, twisting my body like that?* Maybe Jake was right; if she ached that much, it couldn't be good for her body.

When she reached the bottom of the stairs, she caught Bernie's eyes, but was elated over the fact that both Jake's and Leo's backs were turned to her. It was evident that Bernie was on the verge of saying something, but Holly shook her head. She kind of managed to continue walking in as normal a manner as possible. However, Bernie wasn't one to be fooled and chuckling went back to placing fresh bread in the toaster.

They were ready to leave at around mid-morning. Dani arrived just as they finished packing the SUV, ready to collect the keys from Jake again.

"Don't be a stranger, Holly. And don't break this one's heart, you hear?" She winked.

"Me? Never," Holly assured her.

Jake grabbed Dani and pulled her in for a bear hug. "We will see you soon, I hope."

"I'll probably see you again in five years. Doctors don't get many breaks."

"Now, Dani, don't go scaring Holly," Jake teased.

Waving their goodbyes, they got on road for the journey back home.

JAKE HAD STARTED his internship a month ago. She had to admit, it wasn't that bad. She saw him a couple of nights during his first week, even if it was only at eight in the evening, although he normally stayed until around ten. She missed staying with him and wished that she could just move in with his ass, period.

But the week that followed was tough. Jake's shift began at six, so he never visited as he was extremely punctual, which meant that Holly didn't see him for seven days straight.

The week after that things reverted back to normal, but then night shift began again.

She was missing him terribly and couldn't wait to see him—one more day to go—which would be his first full day off.

She marked the day with a huge red marker on her calendar as he'd promised that he was going to spoil her rotten, and make up for all the horrible evenings he'd had to work.

Lately, Holly had been feeling a little tired and hadn't had much of an appetite. She hoped it wasn't the flu, or something she'd caught which would ruin her night with Jake completely. That would be just her luck.

She'd been surprised when Jake phoned her at midday the next day, telling her that he'd reserved a table at an Italian restaurant that one of his father's friends owned. Apparently, the man constantly asked Jake when he was going to visit him for a good bowl of pasta.

"I don't know if it's a good idea, Jake. I... umm, haven't been feeling too good, lately."

"You coming down with something?"

"I'm not sure. It doesn't really feel like the flu, but I feel lethargic." It was the best word she could come up with.

"That's not nice, Bee Puke. But I miss you, Holly, and I promise that after tonight you will feel fresh again. Please?"

Holly snorted. "Okay, then. Pick me up around seven at Bernie's."

"You took that beat-up Beetle to work?"

"Don't insult the Beetle just because it's not a BMW."

Jake chuckled. "We'll have to do something about that."

"Uh-huh. One day," she replied.

"She you later, Bee Puke."

"Later, Hooligan."

As soon as Holly disconnected, Marabella raised her eyebrows. "Are you okay?"

"I don't know. But I do know that I don't feel well."

"How long have you been feeling like this, sweetheart?"

"A day, maybe two. I'm sure it's just a stomach bug or something."

"Nevertheless, Holly, you should go to the doctor."

"I promise I will, just not today. It's the only night we can really spend time together."

Marabella stroked Holly's back. "You have to get used to it, Holls. Doctors rarely have lives outside of hospitals."

"Tell me about it."

Bernie and Leo looked just as worried as Holly was when she slumped into the house at five-thirty. But she continued telling everyone that she would be just fine. Bernie made her a cup of coffee and she had to admit, she felt somewhat better after that.

Seven o'clock finally arrived and Jake picked her up, which

made her feel ten times better. What if she was feeling this way because she wasn't seeing him as much anymore? Perhaps that was her ailment; she'd gotten Jake fever. It sounded pathetic, even to her. Holly was of the mind to pull herself together.

Once they entered the restaurant, the first thing Holly noticed was that it was cozy and extremely Italian. Jake introduced her to Maro, the owner, and they were thereafter led to one of the tables in the corner.

The service was very personal; she noticed that quite a number of patrons knew one another. She now understood why Jake loved this restaurant so much, as everyone spoke to everyone, laughed at one another's jokes, and the ambiance was relaxing.

Alone time with Jake was minimal, as it seemed every second person stopped by their table to greet him, wanting to know how he was doing.

Holly merely watched, smiled on occasion and sipped slowly on her drink. And just like that she suddenly felt dizzy. She closed her eyes quickly, hoping that whatever was going on would pass, fast.

What the hell is going on with me?

Hot flushes traveled up and down her body. She eyed the drink she was having and taking a deep breath, placed the glass on the table, sliding it to one side, and then got up.

Placing her hand on Jake's shoulder to get his attention, she said, "I'm just going to the ladies' room. I won't be long."

Jake winked and continued speaking to a big guy who just couldn't stop babbling about his motorcycle.

Once away from the commotion, Holly entered one of the stalls and closed the door. She put the lid down on the toilet and dropped onto it. She now knew that having agreed to tonight had been a mistake, but she couldn't have canceled on him.

She'd missed him so much, and then when he'd begged... she just couldn't have denied him.

The main door opened and two women's voices filled the room. They kept yapping about their day. Their conversation turned and Holly found herself smiling.

"That guy in the corner is just simply gorgeous," the one girl said.

"I have a list of things I would like to do with him," her friend added.

Holly couldn't help but wonder why some women were always like that. She didn't mind the 'gorgeous' comment but the 'things they wanted to do with him' irritated the living crap out of her.

She blocked out their voices from her mind and concentrated on her spinning head. When she took a deep breath, the dizziness began to abate. She was sure that the drink she was having was to blame; something in it didn't agree with her.

Breathing deeply again, she opened her eyes, and taking another to clear her mind the spinning turned into a soft buzz. As this was the best she was going to feel at that moment, she decided to make her way back to the table before Jake called it a night.

Unfortunately, the two women were still in the bathroom so she figured she would ignore them, wash her hands and exit. She wouldn't look up or say a word, just do what needed to be done and leave. As she opened the door, the dizziness and hot flushes came rushing back. Her vision blurred and the buzzing in her ears got louder. Before she could stabilize herself, the room spun out of control. One of the women shrieked as she fell to the floor, and then everything went black.

TWENTY-TWO

"HOLLY." She could hear a faint voice calling her name, and felt a soft pat against her cheek. "Sweetheart, wake up."

"Here is the ice, Jake. What is wrong with her?"

Holly heard an Italian accent, which obviously belonged to Maro.

"I don't know. She complained about not feeling well," he said, shrugging. "I'm quite worried now."

"Oh, fuck," Holly croaked. "What happened?"

"Shh, don't lift your head yet. I think you fainted. Just give it a couple more minutes," Jake requested.

She could feel his hands at the back of her neck. Her head was still twirling like crazy, and every time she tried to open her eyes she was forced to close them again.

"Do you feel any other pain? Did you hit your head?" Jake asked.

The bathroom door opened. "Will she be okay?" It was a voice that belonged to one of the girls who she'd heard a couple of minutes ago, the one with her list of things to do with Jake.

"I think so, but I'll take her to the hospital just in case."

"You don't have to, we've called for an ambulance and it should be here shortly."

"Thank you, but I do have to. She's with me and I have to make sure she is okay," Jake replied, in a not so impressed tone.

If Holly could've, she would have loved to see the look on the woman's face that accompanied the "Oh, I see" following Jake's comment.

Holly finally managed to open her eyes, which soon brought on a nauseated feeling she'd never felt before, one that rose up her throat. She winced.

Clearly, Jake noticed it, because he immediately asked, "What is it? Just tell me where it hurts."

"I'm feeling sick, like I'm going to barf my lungs out," she mumbled, barely able to get those words out.

"I've never seen you faint like this before. Damn it! We really need to get you to the hospital."

"No, I'll be fine. I hate hospitals, Jake. Just help me get up, please," she begged.

Jake complied and lifted her up onto her feet.

She took another deep breath and opened her eyes again. The bile felt as if it was retreating back down her throat and it became slightly more bearable. She gave Jake a look and hoped that he was able to read how sorry she was for feeling so crappy on their date.

Jake, however, had made up his mind. "Hospital, now. I will never be able to sleep tonight if I don't know you are all right."

"Fine, a checkup only. But no needles, promise?"

Jake's eyebrows furrowed sympathetically. "All I can promise is that I'll hold your hand if there are."

Although it was sweet, it wasn't quite the answer Holly wanted. Nonetheless, Holly could see that Jake was really worried. The crappy way she felt and his sense of concern were enough to overrule her fear of needles this time.

"Deal."

He smiled, making sure he had a firm grip around her waist. He then turned to Maro and apologized before making their way out.

The drive to the hospital felt like it had taken forever. Holly laid down on the backseat, which didn't make her feel any better in the confined space, and the slight rocking motion of the car was playing havoc with her dizziness again.

Eventually, she felt the car stop, heard Jake get out, and then felt the cold air when he opened her door. He helped her out, and once she was stable on her feet, placed his hand on her forehead. His hand felt like ice against her skin.

"You're warm," he said, concern evident in his voice.

Holly felt too weak to do anything but grunt, resting her head on his chest.

They made their way inside the hospital and the first thing she heard was one of the staff members sounding really pleased to see Jake.

"Oh, my! Let's get your friend to a bed," the woman exclaimed on having noticed Holly.

"I just need a checkup here. I'm taking her to bed 6," Jake replied quickly.

"We'll call for a doctor, Jake," an older woman's voice stated.

"Thanks, Aggie."

The next thing Holly felt was Jake placing her down gently onto a bed. Her body began to shake with cold.

"Is there anything I can help with?" The eager woman from before offered her assistance.

"Yes," Jake answered. "Can you get me a monitor? I'd like to get a blood pressure reading. I'll need an IV kit and a glucose stick as well." The nurse nodded and disappeared.

"What have we here?" a male voice asked. "Jake?"

"My girlfriend, Holly. She's 24. She passed out at the

restaurant. She feels nauseous, but no vomiting. I think she might have a low grade fever. She's never had anything like this before." Jake shot out her symptoms to the man in quick succession like he was presenting a case.

"How much did you have to drink at dinner, Holly? Do you think that might be why you feel sick?" asked the doctor.

Holly shook her head definitively and then stopped because it made her dizzy. "No, I've been feeling bad for a couple of days. I only managed to keep a couple sips of wine down at dinner."

"Are you taking any medication?" The doctor continued with his checklist.

"Nothing. Well..." she paused and then whispered, "...does birth control count?"

"It does. I'll make a note of it. I'll get a nurse to insert that IV, and then I'll request blood work to be done."

The nursing aide returned, wheeling a monitor to the side of the bed.

"Great, thanks," said Jake as he began untangling the cords. He freed the blood pressure cuff and wrapped it around Holly's upper arm. While the cuff inflated, he untangled four more cords for an EKG, and another that he clipped to her fingertip.

Jake and the doctor both watched the blinking monitor in suspense. The display beeped cheerily when it arrived at its answer: 165/100.

Jake shook his head. "That can't be right. That's absurd!"

"Take it again." The doctor seemed to agree.

Jake pressed the read button and the cuff inflated, but its answer was the same.

"Where's the pharmacist? She needs a beta blocker before she has a stroke or something."

"Jake, wait. You have to do the lab work first. You know that." The doctor carefully reeled Jake back into reality.

A nurse tied a rubber strip tightly around Holly's arm.

Jake looked at Holly sympathetically, "Sorry, Bee Puke. We've got to get blood before we treat you, okay?"

Holly's heart beat fast in her chest; she felt trapped. She looked back at Jake with panic in her eyes.

He took hold of her hand.

Holly felt a prick on the inside of her arm, and then a nurse untied the rubber strip. She didn't want to open her eyes, because she knew that all she'd see was a needle poking out of her arm, filling a syringe with her blood.

"All done," said the nurse.

Holly made the mistake of turning her head in time to see the nurse putting labels on the tubes. Nausea rose in her stomach as she registered the size of the tubes.

All of that is my blood? Did they leave me any? She knew the thought was irrational, but she couldn't help it.

The nurse handed Holly a gown and a plastic cup with a sticker that said 'sterile' covering the seal of the orange lid.

"Here's a gown for you to wear, and I need you to go to the bathroom and pee in this cup."

Awkward but dutiful, Holly took the cup to the bathroom. She poked her head out of the bathroom a minute later and saw to her dismay that the ER was teaming with people.

She tugged at her gown, which was too short and didn't seem to be properly closed. She didn't think she was wearing it right. Feeling a moment of triumph, she realized the gown had a pocket. She slipped the warm cup of liquid into it before emerging.

Casually, she walked up to the nurses' station, but her cover was blown by the nurse who asked loudly, "Holly, where's your urine?" Holly blushed.

"It's in my pocket," she replied.

The nurse looked alarmed and confused until Holly produced the orange, capped cylinder and set it on the counter.

"Oh," said the nurse. "Thanks. I'll send it to the lab. You can go lie down."

Holly returned in time to overhear the doctor talking to Jake.

"It's good you brought her in immediately and didn't try to sort it out yourself. You did the right thing."

"I hope so," Jake mumbled.

The doctor disappeared into another room.

"What's wrong with me?"

"We'll find out soon, okay? Just stay tuned," Jake said with a fake-looking smile.

Even though she felt awful, his tough guy act made her giggle, or at least it was something that resembled a giggle.

"Try to rest, it is sometimes the best."

Holly tried to do what he'd asked as she listened to people rushing in and out around her. Eventually, she dozed off for a while. Slowly coming to, the first voice she heard was Bernie's. Her friend was freaking out, and true to Jake's character, she heard he was trying to calm her down.

"Jake! What is wrong with her?"

"I don't know, Bern."

"Jake." Holly heard another familiar voice. "What are you doing here?"

"I could ask you the same thing, Dad."

"I got a call out from Dr. Augustus."

"Dr. Augustus?"

Just then, the doctor who'd seen to Holly earlier cut in. "A minute, Jake."

"Why did you call my father?"

Holly froze.

"You called me for Holly?"

"Jake, you know your father is a specialist on this condition. It's his area of research. Give us a minute, Jake. Gus, please."

Holly opened her eyes.

What condition? He's an obstetrician. Please, God. No. Not that. I can't be....

She couldn't think about or even say the word, but she knew that God would know what she meant.

I can't be. I'm on the damn pill, which is supposed to be 99 percent foolproof. I will sue the company... I... Stop it, Holly! You are not, you are not.

"Holly?" Gus' voice was close to her ear. "Can you sit up for me, please?"

She did as he asked, but tears threatened. When he examined her glands, she looked up into his eyes. "Please, tell me it's not what I think it is," she begged.

Gus looked surprised. "And what do you think it is?"

It was Holly's turn to look surprised. *Why's he asking me? He's the doctor, and that's supposed to be my question.* In response, she merely shrugged feebly.

"We are still waiting for the blood work results," he said softly. "When was your last cycle?"

Great, now I have to share with my boyfriend's father when my last cycle was.

She tried to think, but really couldn't remember. *Why can't I remember?*

"I was taking the pill and then I kind of stopped getting it. I thought it was just a side effect."

"You don't remember your last period? Even just a spot?"

Holly shook her head, while a tear ran down her cheek.

"It's not necessarily the end of the world, you know."

"Excuse me, doctor. The blood work results are back," said an eager girl's voice that Holly didn't even want to look at. She handed Gus a piece of paper and left.

Where the hell is Jake?

Gus scanned the results. Something caught his eye and the lines on his face relaxed. He had found the diagnosis in the blood work. His expression told Holly right away what the cause of her sickness was.

No two ways about it; she was pregnant.

TWENTY-THREE

GUS GAVE her the news she had already seen on his face. She was going to be a mother. And then, much to her shock, he asked her what she wanted to do.

"What do you mean?"

"Holly, Jake doesn't—"

"I know!" she ground out, cutting him off. "He doesn't need this right now."

Gus frowned. "That isn't quite what I was going to say. I meant, he doesn't need to know."

She looked at Gus like he'd grown another head. How could he even suggest what he was suggesting? Holly could never do that, not in a million years. His own daughter wasn't able to have a child, and now he was proposing that she abort his first grandchild.

"I'm sorry, I truly am, but I can't do that. Correction, I won't do that."

"Holly, you may not realize the risks of trying to carry this pregnancy. Your blood pressure is much too high. I'm going to get right to the point. You are sitting on a rare case of gestational hypertension, which may be a precursor to an early preeclampsia onset. The earlier this happens, the higher the risk to you and the baby. You could have permanent organ damage from the pressure, and some mothers die.

Holly's heart dipped into her stomach.

"The only solution is to deliver the baby and," he took a deep breath, "maybe you'll be luckier on the next try."

"That's it? Try again, like it's a game? How is there no treatment?"

"Well, I promise I'm working on it, but I haven't proven anything, yet."

Holly was in no mood for some speculative research.

"Why can't you give me blood pressure medication like old people take?" Holly asked.

Gus nodded like he'd contemplated that course of action before. "The fear is that if we reduce your blood pressure, the fetus won't get enough blood from the placenta. It's you or the baby, basically."

"So, on the whole, you're telling me that I can die from carrying this baby?"

"You could. But lucky for you, I'm one of the best in the world, and I might just have something that could work." Gus tried his best to help Holly relax, if not smile with his words.

However, she was too caught up in the news and simply nodded while trying to suck up her tears.

"I need to speak to Jake, too. I'll ask Bernie to come and sit with you, all right?"

She nodded and tried to return Gus' smile, but for some reason she had nothing to be happy about. She wiped at a stray tear as he exited.

How can this be happening? She was on the pill, and one he'd recommended in the first place. He'd said it was safe, and now there she sat with a bun in the oven. It was something both her grandmother and mother used to say. It was a cute saying, except this particular bun was already making an effort to kill her. *Mara is going to be pissed!*

"Hey," Bernie's voice filled the room. "Are you okay?"

Holly shook her head, then promptly began to cry.

Bernie rushed over, folding her arms around Holly. "Shhh, whatever it is, it's going to be fine, Holls. I promise."

Holly shook her head again.

"Holly, speak to me. I think I know because Jake's dad's here, but I have to hear it from you. Are you..."

Holly nodded.

Bernie gasped. "You're pregnant?" she asked softly, grinning.

"It's not like that. I could die, Berns. What happened tonight is just the beginning. I have some sort of the beginning stages of pree-something."

"Preeclampsia?" Bernie queried.

"Yes, that. He said that at this early stage, it's called gestational hypertension. Dangerously high blood pressure caused by the pregnancy."

"Holly, most women only contract it from about around 32 weeks into their pregnancy, they don't get it this early."

"He said that too, but that it's more dangerous since it's this early. At least it explains why I feel so shitty.

Bernie rested her hand on the bed while staring at Holly with a concerned look.

"Does he have a plan?"

"I don't know."

Silence filled the room for a few seconds. "Well, he is known to be one of the best gynecologists in the world. I'm sure he'll figure it out," Bernie stated confidently.

"So, you're saying that my boyfriend's father is going to be my vagina's doctor?"

Bernie laughed, and shaking her head said, "No. He can't.

Because the baby's daddy is his son, which makes him the grandpa and pappies are too close. He'll assign you another doctor."

"I just don't want to feel this horrible."

Bernie stroked Holly's cheek softly. The last time she'd done that was when she was saying goodbye to Holly's twin, Jamie.

"It's going to be okay, Holls. You'll see. The Peters' are a bunch of kick-ass doctors. They've won awards; that kind of crap. Gus won't let anything happen to you." She gave Holly a sweet smile, but tears glistened in Bernie's eyes all the same.

Her friend was worried to death, that much Holly could tell.

Just then, Jake appeared from behind the curtain. He looked worried, too, when he sat next to her on the bed. He gently placed a hand on Holly's stomach and bent forward from the waist down to give her an awkward hug. "It's going to be okay. You'll be fine, you hear me?" He looked at her.

"I take it your father told you?"

"He did."

"How is this even remotely possible, Jake? They said 99 percent effective."

"I guess you are that special one percent," he joked.

"This is not funny." She sighed and covered her eyes with the back of one hand. "We can't be parents now, Jake. You have your internship and I—"

"Stop that. You think I'll leave you? Believe me, I won't. Not with Amelia as my sister. But I wouldn't do that to you, in any case. If you ask me, Amelia would practically take over and raise the child herself if she could. She will help out, Holls, it's going to be fine. I don't want you to stress about anything, okay."

Holly finally laughed.

"I'm here too, Holly. And you know I will never leave you. You're stuck with me forever," Bernie said softly.

Holly grabbed Bernie's hand, squeezed it gently, smiled and finally sighed. She looked at Jake again. "Your mom is not going to like this."

"Was it my mom who told you to go on the pill?"

Fuck! Lie.

"No, Jake, but I'm positive that she isn't going to be as accepting as your father."

He smiled. "I don't care if my mother is going to like or not. I'm so ready for this. I want this child, as much as I want its mother. So don't worry about mine. I'll take care of her. Your job is to stop stressing, relax and enjoy your pregnancy. That is an order." Jake gave her a lopsided smile.

"How on earth am I going to enjoy it, if I continue to feel like this?"

Jake raised an eyebrow. "Really, you stubborn woman. You don't think we have a plan to make you feel better?"

"I didn't say that," she huffed, and then as if his words had just sunk in, she asked, "You do?"

Jake smiled. "We are the fucking Peters', so of course we do."

"See," Bernie said, all-knowing. "Told you so."

All three chuckled at that.

"Jake." Gus walked in with a different type of medicine in his arms. "There are forms you two will have to sign as this is purely a trial basis."

"Dad, we're not going to sue you."

"It's not that. We have to show the trial's paperwork to the government if we want to release it to the public in the future. Holly is the type of woman I've been waiting for, to be honest."

"Fine, give it to me." Jake held his hand out for the clipboard.

Holly could hear the pen scribble on the pad.

"Holly needs to sign it as well."

"Could you explain it to her first? Like you did with me out in the hall?"

"Sure."

Bernie got up to leave. "I'm just outside, okay?"

Holly smiled and nodded as Gus took the chair Bernie had occupied seconds ago and re-positioned it closer to her bed.

Jake sat next to Holly on the bed, stroking her back softly.

He smiled, looking down at the tin of formula with a huge p47 on the label, and a picture of a pregnant woman smiling. "It's a product specifically designed for pregnant women who struggle with high blood pressure and all sorts of illnesses during their pregnancy; specifically for gestational hypertension and preeclampsia symptoms. If immediately treated, we think it might help in reducing many of these symptoms, which in turn might even allow you to have a normal pregnancy without paying the hospital too many visits," Gus explained.

He went on to tell her about the amount of vitamin properties the shake provided, and how good it was for the fetus. He further added that it would also help the fetus grow as it should, following that up with another list of pros.

From what Holly could tell, there were no side effects, yet. She would be the first person to try this wonder drug; in essence she'd be a guinea pig. However, she didn't mind in the least. Especially if it would keep her from feeling so horrible.

While Jake held the clipboard for her, she picked up the pen and signed.

"I'll need to keep her overnight—the first twenty-four hours are critical. The medication should start having an effect by tomorrow night."

Stay overnight! Holly didn't say it out loud, of course, but she was none too happy. The last time she'd stayed over was when Jamie was constantly in and out of hospital.

The staff at Downsend, a couple of miles away from P&E

had organized a makeshift bed for Holly, placing it right next to her sister during her last days. It had been an extremely difficult time, and one of the reasons Holly didn't like hospitals. It brought back all those memories of her twin.

"I'm sorry, Bee Puke. If my dad says overnight, it's overnight."

"You said it was just going to be a checkup." Holly's lower lip trembled.

"That was when it was only you we were worried about. But it's not only you, anymore. There is a little bean inside of you, so, I have a different say in all of this."

Holly chuckled tiredly, loving the name he'd come up with. Jake sure seemed very excited about it all, but she couldn't shake the horrible feeling that his mother would never let her forget this episode.

Bernie stayed with her and even accompanied her when she was admitted to the maternity ward. Holly seriously hated hospitals, but she'd always liked the maternity ward. It was the only section of a hospital she loved. It meant life, not sickness or death.

Jake walked into her room at around nine, followed by an ultrasound machine. He was grinning from ear to ear, and she wished that she felt the same way as him.

His father, accompanied by a nurse, walked into the room a couple of minutes later just as Jake was about to turn the machine on.

"Let me do it, before you break the thing," the nurse said, ushering him out of the way.

He moved to the other side of Holly's bed to stand next to Bernie, who shared Jake's excitement.

His father gently lifted up the hospital gown she had been admitted in. She hated those stupid gowns and wished she had her pajamas. He squirted lukewarm gel on to her lower abdomen—which at that point in time didn't even resemble a woman who could be pregnant—before he gently moved a device over her midriff.

There was nothing at first, and then he stopped when he found what he was looking for. He clicked another button on the machine and the heartbeat, sounding like it was beating a thousand times per minute, filled the room.

Holly's eyes grew.

"Don't worry," Bernie assured. "It's normal for it to be fast."

Jake didn't say a thing. He just stared at the sonar like a ten-year-old boy who was watching his favorite cartoon.

Gus was mesmerized, too, as he gently moved the device to see another angle.

Tears welled up in Gus' eyes.

"You are such cry-babies," the nurse announced.

Holly looked at Jake, who at that moment had pinched his eyes closed with the fingers of one hand.

Holly just smiled. She might not feel the same as him yet about the pregnancy, but she loved the way he was so emotional over it.

When the sonar was done and Gus felt happy about what the little bean had shown him, he bid Holly a good night.

Jake and Bernie stayed behind. Both smiling like idiots.

"I can't believe you are pregnant," Bernie gushed.

Holly gave her the raised eyebrow look.

"Okay, relax, will you?" Bernie huffed, raising her palms in defense. "But can I just say this? It was due to happen, Holls. By the way you guys attack each other every time you get together, this is so not hard to believe."

"Bern!" Holly said, but blushed immediately.

Jake chuckled, not ashamed in the least.

"Why don't you go home? I'm fine. I'm just going to close my eyes and sleep."

"You sure? I sort of feel crappy about promising a checkup and now it's a full night."

"In that case, you owe me big time, and you're going to need to make it up to me."

Jake laughed. "It's because of all those making- up sessions that you are in here."

"Seriously!" Not him, too.

Bernie laughed.

Jake bent and gave Holly a kiss. "Be safe. Love you," he whispered.

"Love you, too."

"Night, Bernie."

"Night, Jake."

Bernie stayed for about another hour and then left, too. By then, Holly felt so tired she hardly noticed her friend had left.

Jake woke Holly up early the next morning. He was wearing a doctor's coat.

"You're on duty?" Holly asked sleepily.

"I'm always on duty." He bent down to give her a kiss and touched her stomach softly, which made her smile.

Jake got to work and helped one of the nurses take her vital signs. "You ready, Dr. Peters?" a woman's voice asked from the doorway.

"Dr. Peters," she mouthed, opening her eyes wide.

Jake winked, kissed Holly on the temple and made to leave. Turning back, he ordered, "Just hit the button if you need anything. I'll be back later, but right now I have to do the rounds."

"Go, before they fire your ass."

"I'm dating a funny girl," he teased, and then exited the room.

TWENTY-FOUR

GUS CHECK on Holly late in the afternoon. He took a while perusing the charts and her vital signs before finally signing the release form.

Bernie had gone in to see Holly and took her home right after they'd hunted Jake down to say goodbye.

As happened on a regular basis with doctors, just as they found him, his pager beeped. He quickly rattled off instructions before leaving them. "I'll call you tonight. Take it easy and drink the shake my dad gave you." He kissed her, while cupping her face with both hands. Just before he disappeared completely, he turned. "Bernie?" he called.

"I'll make sure, Jake. But she's old enough to take care of herself and I doubt she'll want to feel shitty."

They could hear him laugh all the way down the corridor.

Once home, Bernie began to prepare dinner. Leo still hadn't arrived.

Holly busied herself and read over the description of how to mix the shake, which Gus had written the proportions of on a piece of paper.

Bern gave her a quizzical look. "So... it's not out on the market yet?"

"Yeah. He's one of the best baby catchers out there, so I very much doubt that my boyfriend's dad would want to poison me or bean here." This was said with a smile and a tummy rub.

Bernie smiled. "They do look like beans, right?"

Holly chuckled at Bernie's sudden change of mood and nodded.

"Jake seems excited, though. How do you feel?"

"I don't know how this could've happened. I was on the pill."

"They come when they come. I've learned that it doesn't matter what you are on. It will happen if and when the right person comes along, and when it's the right time."

"This is so not the right time. His mom is going to kill me."

Bernie giggled. "I'm just glad it's not me. That woman can be crazy."

Holly's smile disappeared. She picked up a cubed piece of carrot from the counter and chucked it at Bernie, who immediately ducked and laughed.

"What type of a friend are you?"

"The one who loves you to bits, but not the one who's going to hold your hand when you share this news with her. That is Jake's department."

Holly smiled, shaking her head. Pulling her hand through her hair, she mumbled, "She's going to kill me, isn't she?"

"His mom is psycho. So she could try but the way that man looks at you, Holly, I'm sure he'll even take a bullet for you, if it comes to that."

Holly giggled again as she popped a piece of carrot into her mouth. "She'll get over it."

"She has to, I mean..." Bernie's eyes grew. "Have you even imagined what this kid is going to look like?"

"You mean... if he or she ends up looking like Jake? Baby contests, here we come."

Bernie snorted. "I feel sorry for all the other babies."

"Me, too. Think I'll go have a bath." Holly couldn't stop thinking about the plus side of being pregnant with Jake's child. Children were never relationship fixers, but whatever happened; Jake would forever be in her life. And if she wasn't going to be with him until eternity, at least he was still the father of her child. She couldn't ask for anyone better. It sure was the silver lining around that dark cloud.

THE BATH DID absolute wonders for Holly, and when she started to feel a bit woozy, she grabbed the shake Gus had given her and spooned four heaps of powder into a glass of milk.

While Bernie was still busy in the kitchen, Holly went to have rest.

Jake called her early in the evening. "How do you feel?"

That was the first question he asked when she answered the phone.

"Much better. Your father's shake seems to be working."

"You don't feel nauseous or dizzy?"

"Nope. It's quite amazing if you think about it. I mean, I was in the hospital for a day and I only had one earlier."

"I'm impressed. And how does it taste?" The taste wasn't anything to write home about, but the fact that it worked was all Holly cared about.

"It doesn't matter what it tastes like, Hooligan. It's working, so that's all that matters."

Jake chortled. "I'm never going to be rid of that name, am I?"

"Let me think. Umm... nope, not going to happen."

Both had a good laugh and continued to talk for a while

longer. Conversation was interrupted by his beeper going off in the background.

"I've got to go, Bee Puke. Talk to you later. If you feel bad again, please ask Leo to bring you in, will you?"

"You know how I feel, Jake. I'll be fine."

"I know. But you have a bean to take care of now. So please, Holls, if you feel bad, come in."

"Okay, I promise," she acquiesced, saying goodbye and hating having to do so. She placed the phone on the nightstand and lay back down.

Holly couldn't help but wonder if she could have become any more pathetic. She was at a stage in her life where she couldn't imagine going on without Jake anymore.

What had become of the Holly who had packed her bags not a couple of months ago, swearing to never go for abs and ass again? Jake most certainly had both, not to mention his Tommy Hilfiger look and those sultry bedroom eyes.

She touched her belly softly. None of it mattered anymore. She was going to be a mommy in less than nine months and whatever happened, happened.

He'd promised to never leave her and she was just going to have to trust that for now.

OVER THE NEXT couple of weeks, Jake spent as much time with Holly as possible. Any time he was off duty, he made a point of visiting her during the night.

It was evident to her that he was dead tired. However, he always went out of his way to keep their conversation flowing.

Yet time and again, she went back to the same question. What was it going to be like when baby arrived?

GUS INTRODUCED HOLLY to Dr. Meyers. It wasn't the same doctor who'd helped her the night she collapsed. Something told Holly that Gus didn't quite trust Dr. Augustus with the woman who just happened to be carrying his grandchild.

Strangely enough, Holly really liked Dr. Meyers. She was in her mid-fifties and of course, of the female persuasion, which was a huge plus as far as Holly was concerned. This bode her well as she'd always struggled to spread her legs for just anyone, other than the man of her dreams—exes excluded—and was glad that having found herself in this situation, she was opening them for another woman.

Holly felt no awkwardness, or not as much as she thought she would have. The first time, however, had been somewhat nerve-wracking only because she'd had no idea what to expect. This was due to the fact that she'd never visited a gynecologist before, knowing full well how stupid of her it had been, what with the risk of cancer, but that was just how it had panned out. Plus, she'd thought that there had been no reason to visit one, really, as starting a family hadn't been in her five year plan.

Attending one of her weekly appointments, which sucked as it should have been one a month— but due to her case, Gus had insisted on once a week—Holly made herself comfortable in the waiting area, along with a few other families.

One in particular, had a little boy who kept looking at Holly. She started making faces at him and smiled, and he in turn kept hiding behind his mom's belly. Holly thought it was really huge.

"When are you due?" she asked the woman, smiling.

"Only two weeks to go," the woman replied, her relief obvious. "It feels like I'm going to pop any minute now."

"I can just imagine. Do you know what it is?"

"The little girl we've wanted," her husband answered.

"Daddy's girl," Holly said, making them laugh.

"I can't wait," the man added, to which his wife chuckled.

"Miss Scallanger?" The girl behind the desk called Holly's name and gestured for her to follow. She returned the magazine to the coffee table and followed her. On her way, she glanced at her watch, and then toward the door. Jake hadn't as yet arrived and she hoped he wouldn't miss their first appointment. She quickly pushed her worry to back of her mind; there was a slim chance that he might not be able to make these at all.

The receptionist opened a door to Dr. Meyers' office and stepped aside to let Holly through. The doctor smiled from behind her desk as she entered. "Thank you, Natasha," the gray-blond woman said. "Good day, Holly, please, take a seat." She gestured to one of the two chairs in front of her desk. "How do you feel?"

"I feel good, thank you," Holly replied.

"Dr. Peters told me that you are one of his guinea pigs."

Holly grinned, nodding. "Thank heavens I don't look like one, yet."

Doctor Meyers laughed. "Are we going to wait for Jake, or do you want to get started?"

"I don't think he's going to make it." Her tone was sad, more than what she'd wanted to show.

"It's not easy having a doctor as a boyfriend or spouse, especially when it comes to appointments like these. I wish I could tell you it gets easier, but it doesn't."

"I'm learning that pretty quickly." She smiled, regardless of how she felt.

"Okay, then. You can change in there"—she pointed toward a small cubicle behind her desk—"and when you're ready, we'll begin."

Holly nodded, got up and walked to the change room. She was feeling miserable, so much so she wanted to cry over Jake not being there to see what their little bean looked like now. There was nothing to be done. Her only option would be to leave the ultrasound photo for him to look at when he had the chance.

As soon as Holly was ready, Dr. Meyers led her to another room where an ultrasound machine was positioned next to a bed. She climbed onto the bed and lay back.

The doctor covered Holly's legs with a blanket, and then scrunched the material of her gown in her hand and moved it upward to expose her belly. Smiling at Holly, she gelled a flat device of sorts.

Hovering over Holly's stomach with the same tube of gel, she smiled. She squeezed quite a substantial amount of the gel onto her stomach, which she then spread using the device; going first up and then down, around, and from left to right.

Dr. Meyers suddenly stopped what she was doing and chuckled, listening to whatever was going on outside the door.

Interested, Holly did the same, and then began smiling.

"Something tells me Jake managed to make it."

True to her words, a knock sounded on the door and it opened.

"You are lucky you made it. Didn't your father ever warn you about ticking pregnant women off?"

Jake sauntered in, smiling broadly. "I'm so sorry, sweetheart." He bent over Holly, kissed her on the lips, and made himself comfortable on the edge of the bed.

Holly's heart beat a tad faster. He looked gorgeous in his sea-blue scrubs. The white jacket was missing, providing Holly with an image of him running out of the ER in order to make it just in time.

"Let's start again, shall we?" Dr. Meyers began to move the device on Holly's belly, back and forth a few times, trying to find their bean.

A million fears ran through Holly's heart in those seconds.

"Here we go," she said, bending forward to turn on a speaker. The sound that reverberated around the room sounded like horses galloping, just like the first time she heard it in the maternity ward when Gus checked bean for the first time to make sure everything was fine."

Using the computer's mouse, she started measuring the bean by clicking on one end of the fetus and dragging a line to the other.

Holly noticed a date on the screen. "Is that my due date?"

"Speculative due date. We never really know the exact date, and it can change at any time. But we'll know more or less after a couple of appointments."

She then looked at Jake. "So, daddy," Dr. Meyers began but then rolled her eyes. "You Peters' are such babies."

Holly looked at Jake, who was chuckling while wiping his eyes.

"Again?" Holly asked.

"Our bean is beautiful," he said, kissing her hand softly.

Doctor Meyers smiled. "Your father was exactly the same. You should've become a gynecologist."

"No, thank you," Jake said, too fast.

Both Holly and the doctor burst out laughing. "I thought you guys were crazy about vaginas?

"That disappears when it becomes one's job."

"Jake!"

"What? I'm just being honest. Besides, I love brains."

"Okay, that is definitely not the kind of conversation we usually have in this room, go back to the crying."

Holly giggled as she looked at the ultrasound's screen once more.

The doctor hit another button, as another knock sounded. All three looked at the door.

Doctor Meyers put the device away and got up to open it. "I should've known. Checking up on me?"

Gus walked in. "I'm just making sure everything is okay. This is my first grandchild, Tiff."

Jake shook his head and closed his eyes for a few seconds. Then he looked at his dad. "Is this going to be a regular occurrence?"

"Shush, unless you want me to tell your mother."

"Mara doesn't know yet?" Dr. Meyers raised her eyebrows at Jake. "Ooooh, I'm so glad I'm not you, Jake."

"It usually takes two to conceive a baby, I'm not the only one at fault here." He sat straight up on the bed.

"Excuse me?" Gus stated with a raised eyebrow in Jake's direction.

Holly saw the smirk Jake tried to hide, as if he had done something wrong. Well, they practically had.

"Okay, fine. Whatever," Jake mumbled.

Gus smiled at Holly. "How do you feel?"

"Good, actually," she replied.

He looked at Dr. Meyers. "How is her blood pressure?"

"Almost normal. I think it's working, Gus."

"It better be," Jake growled.

Gus shot him a look over his shoulder. Jake didn't bother to contain his smile. But when Gus looked at the frozen screenshot of their bean, Holly saw tears well up in his eyes again, just like the last time. He cleared his throat. "Everything okay?"

"Yes, cry-baby, everything is just fine," Dr. Meyers assured him.

Gus mumbled something or other, which no one understood, and promptly left.

"I told you they were babies," she said to Holly.

"Don't care. That's my kid in there. I can cry if I want to, Dr. Meyers," Jake snapped, although playfully.

She hid a grin. "Your mother really doesn't know?"

"I'll tell her, soon."

"Don't put this pressure on Holly, Jake."

Holly raised her hand. "Still here, you know, in case you forgot."

Jake chuckled. "I promise I won't put her under any undue pressure. I've got to go as I only had a couple of minutes." He bent down and kissed Holly again, then retreated toward the door.

"Tell your mom, Jake," Dr. Meyers shouted, before he disappeared.

"Yeah, yeah." Holly heard, as well as his footsteps pounding down the hallway.

"I just hope Mara is not going to get her nose bent out of joint. I hate lying to her."

"We will tell her soon," Holly promised.

"Oh, no, missy. He's the one who needs to tell her. You stay as far away as you can from that woman the day he tells her, you hear?"

"Will she really be that upset?"

"She's a bit over-protective when it comes to her children, even though they are adults and are more than able to make decisions for themselves."

Holly giggled. "I take it you don't approve?"

"Not with some of the things she does, no."

Dr. Meyers helped Holly sit up. "I mean it, Holly, you need to take it easy. You're not going to have a stress-free pregnancy as is, and *any* kind of stress can lead to danger. So relax and surround yourself with loving people."

Holly grinned. She loved Dr. Meyers' humor, getting it the moment she'd started using it on Jake.

"I will."

"So, if all goes well, we are looking at a March baby, but it will likely change to February in the next few weeks.

Holly smiled, got dressed, and made another appointment at reception before leaving. She'd get another peek at her bean the following week. She felt different, as if today had made everything a reality.

When she got to work, Marabella couldn't wait to see the picture of the baby. She gave Holly a hug and jumped up and down. "I can't wait to become a grandmother. I think it's the most amazing feeling ever."

"I doubt that this one's grandmother is going to feel the same way."

"Then it's her problem, Holly. Don't let her stress you out."

"Easier said than done," Holly mumbled.

"By that, I'm guessing Jake hasn't told her yet?"

"Nope, he hasn't." Holly rubbed her face. "Maybe he's waiting until I'm like six months or something, and hopefully by then she's able to put two and two together."

"I doubt that. Maybe he's just waiting for the right moment."

"I'm not sure that with her there is such a thing as 'a right moment' when it comes to this. My doctor was the second one to tell me that she's a psycho when it comes to her children."

"Psycho or not, Holly, what is she going to do?"

Holly thought about it. She knew Jake loved her and wanted their baby. She could see it in his eyes, but then his crying over their bean had confirmed it. "Nothing, I guess."

"Exactly. Then why do you worry about it? Stop thinking and stressing over it. You have the second most important being inside of you as we speak, and that's who you need to worry about and take care of now. No one else even matters."

"I know. Okay," Holly said, adamantly. "No more stressing about what she is going to do or think."

"That's it. Have you told the other grandmother yet?"

Holly shook her head.

"Darling, now might be the perfect time. People do amazing things when the pitter-patter of little feet is expected."

"Even help with alcohol addiction?"

"She told you before she has sobered up."

"I know, but I'm scared of introducing her to Jake and the rest of the Peters'."

"It might not be that bad. Just phone her, tell her the good news and whatever happens, happens."

"Sure, I'll think about it."

"You do that. Now get on those invoices, please. I've got absolutely no idea how to add them onto the computer."

Holly laughed and shook her head. "What are you going to do without me, Marabella?"

"I don't know, but I do know that I'll be lost. Totally."

They hugged each other, after which Marabella left in order for both her and Holly get on with work.

TWENTY-FIVE

"ARE you sure I don't need to go with you?" Holly asked.

Jake wrapped his arms around her waist. "No, I'll deal with this." He gave her a kiss on the lips. "Go drink your shake and I'll see you soon."

"Okay. Just get out of there before she kills you. I can't do this without you."

Jake chortled. "I doubt it will come to that."

"That's what you say now," Bernie interjected, without looking up from the newspaper she had spread on her kitchen counter.

"Nobody asked you, Bernie," joked Jake.

"My house. I put in my two cents if I want to, thank you very much."

That comment made Jake grin broadly.

Shortly after Jake left, Holly settled down and tried to read a novel, but she kept reading the same passage over and over. The waiting was awful, and even worse was the fact that she couldn't help but glance at the clock every so often. And with worry came all sorts of scenarios, one being that she pictured Mara blowing a fuse and promptly driving to Bernie's, where she'd zip up the driveway and come to a standstill on screeching tires.

Bernie must have noticed her friend's anxiousness.

"Stop worrying; it's just a baby. I'm sure Amelia will be in seventh heaven."

Amelia. Holly had forgotten about Jake's sister. She hadn't spoken to her in ages, but knowing Amelia would be on their side made her feel more at ease. She just happened to have a huge influence on Mara, and Jake was like her twin; only eleven months apart.

By noon, Holly still hadn't heard anything from Jake.

It must be going well as he isn't back, or maybe he hasn't told Mara yet.

She decided to take a nap after lunch, which consisted of her gulping down her shake. She was almost out of powder and would need a refill from Gus soon.

It felt as if she'd just closed her eyes when she was woken by someone shaking her gently. Slowly opening her eyes, she looked into Jake's face and smiled. Goodness knew how long he'd been watching her for, but he seemed comfortable lying next to her with his head resting on his hand.

She buried her face in his chest and breathed in the cologne that was him. "Do I need to know what she said?" she mumbled. She could feel him laughing and looked up.

"No." He kept it short and sweet.

"So... it's not good, I take it?" Her facial expression was one of seriousness.

"I didn't say that. It's just nothing to stress about."

"Okay, but does she want to see me?"

"Do *you* want to see her?" He smiled.

"Not really, no. I just want to know what to expect."

He continued to smile. "It's not worth it, Holly. Stop stressing about it. I told you not to worry. It's taken care of."

"Just tell me."

"Okay, fine. She's not happy, chased me out of the house and that was it. I would've been worried if she hadn't reacted that way. She'll cool off and probably want to speak both of us to know what sort of a plan we have. If not, well, we'll just have to show her, then."

Obviously, Holly knew nothing good had come of their 'meeting'. His own mother chased him out of her house. She tried to suppress that thought and hated the fact that he didn't want to tell her, in more detail, what he'd said and what she'd said. And despite his assurance that she needn't stress, she would nevertheless do just that.

"Amelia is quite beside herself. She immediately wanted to give you a call of congratulations, but I told her to hold off for another time. And, she needs to clear it with me first."

"At least one person is happy." She shrugged.

"Holly, stop it. Don't worry about who has a problem or not with you being pregnant, or who's going to love this child or not. Our bean will have its mom and dad, and a wonderful family. I can promise you that."

"Okay," she whispered, kissing his jawline, and then his lips. It wasn't long before the kissing became more demanding. Holly giggled against his lips. "Seriously?"

"What? It's not like we can get pregnant again," he said softly.

"What about our existing bean, Jake?"

"Holly, the baby is just that right now, the size of a bean, really. Besides, it can only be good for it."

"Oh, really? And in what way would that be?"

"Keep the mom happy, and baby will be happy."

Holly burst out laughing.

Soon enough, their lips locked. She rolled on top of him and curled her fingers with his, pushing his arms above his head. His shirt was the first thing to disappear, and then hers.

He rained kisses down both sides of her neck making her body feel alive. She'd never felt that safe in someone's arms as she did in Jake Peters'. She also felt loved and wanted, and never wanted those feelings to ever disappear between them.

His hands caressed the side of her body ever so softly, causing the hair on her skin to stand on end.

Her shorts were soon disposed of, too. But when it came to his jeans, though, he seemed to struggle to get them off, until she lent a hand. That brought on a fit of giggles from both. Holly eventually shushed him, because Bernie and Leo were probably taking an afternoon nap with Sam. God forbid they had to hear.

The sex was, as always, amazing. Nothing hardcore like the other times, but rather gentle and slow; the feeling of him inside her felt like she was going to lose her mind. She just hoped and prayed that he was right and they weren't harming the baby.

When he thrust deeper, she bit the flesh on his shoulder, and nothing was more satisfying than when she heard him groan out of pleasure as a result.

Holly reached her orgasm fast and couldn't believe how much she truly enjoyed making love with Jake. With others, not that there had been many, they'd only cared about themselves—and quite honestly, that had only been sex. There was a difference.

Coming back down to earth, she lay on his chest and listened to his heartbeat as he drifted off to sleep. She noticed the dark shadows under his eyes as he'd worked the night before, deciding to just let him be. She didn't like those circles at all, but knew how tired he'd been lately. If truth be told, she loved being with him like this.

She continued to listen to his heartbeat, imagining hers and his beating as one. They were made for one another, that much she was sure of. She felt it in her blood, her veins, and deep down in her bones. There would never be another man for her, of that she was certain.

THE SECOND APPOINTMENT CAME QUICKLY, like the following week quickly.

Amelia accompanied Holly this time around, because she was dying to see what her nephew or niece looked like.

The minute Holly walked in, Natasha looked up and smiled.

Amelia smiled, too, and greeted her. "Hey."

"What are you doing here?" asked Natasha.

"Just checking up on how my nephew or niece is doing."

"Your nephew or niece?" Natasha gave her a funny look.

"Yes. I'm here with Holly."

Natasha frowned, and all Holly could do was shake her head slightly as she took a seat. The girl was obviously not putting two and two together. Either that, or she couldn't believe that the child Holly was carrying was Jake's.

Amelia laughed at her expression of confusion and disbelief, and then took a seat next to Holly.

"Let me guess, she's one of your brother's exes?"

"She wishes," Amelia mumbled.

Holly sniggered while paging through a pregnancy book, looking at all the baby clothes, cots, mobile toys and strollers.

"These are really expensive."

"Don't worry about the prices, Holly. Besides, we are going to buy you guys the coolest stroller ever."

"Amelia..."

"Oh, no. I googled it. It's the aunt's privilege to get something big and the mom isn't allowed to say a word. Cool, huh?"

Holly just smiled at her.

The waiting room door opened and Holly looked up. As soon as a couple entered, Natasha gave them her million dollar smile.

"What are you doing here?" she asked.

That was when Holly saw Jake closing the door.

"I've got an appointment."

She frowned once again.

Holly watched Natasha's face closely, and it wasn't long before she saw her expression change when the light bulb went on. "Oh! Congrats, I guess."

Jake pulled a face at Holly as he walked over, while she suppressed a smirk. "You are here, too?" he shot in Amelia direction.

Amelia pulled a face, and then mocked him by making sounds when Jake kissed Holly. He scowled at his sister before dropping into the chair next to Holly.

Holly could feel inquiring eyes on her and knew that it wasn't because of the cute couple they obviously made; it was all about the hunk who was occupying the seat next to hers. How he was able to ignore the obvious attention was something she still needed to get used to.

"Look." Amelia practically thrust the book in Jake's face. "I'm going to get that. So don't buy it, please."

"Whatever, Amelia," he returned.

Amelia rolled her eyes at her brother.

"Miss Scallanger?" Natasha called, clearing her throat.

Amelia sucked in her lips as she tried to hide her gloating expression. Holly could tell she didn't like Natasha much. The girl was quiet as she led the trio into the doctor's office.

"Enjoy," Natasha mumbled.

Holly frowned when Amelia raised her eyebrows in Jake's direction before laughing softly.

"Shame, poor girl," Amelia said.

Holly merely shook her head and left them to their sibling shenanigans.

She went in first for a very personal checkup, while Jake decided to keep Amelia company. She changed into a gown and sat on the bed.

Dr. Meyers was still speaking to Amelia outside the office, as old friends did. Holly figured she was her gynecologist, too.

The door opened and Dr. Meyers walked in. After they exchanged greetings, the checkup began. First up were the breasts, and then her blood pressure. When Dr. Meyers double-checked the latter, Holly became somewhat concerned.

"Is everything okay?"

"Yes, yes. Don't worry." She smiled at Holly kindly. "I think Gus' pregnancy shake is working."

"Then, it's all good?"

"It's more than good. It's amazing, Holly. This is a huge breakthrough, no doubt about it, especially for women who suffer from all these ugly symptoms that lead to so many complications, both for mothers and their fetuses. I feel so sorry for you poor things when you have difficult pregnancies. This is really big."

"Thank goodness. That makes me happy."

"Me, too. I was so worried when he asked me to take you on, but he promised that he would assist."

"Well, I'm glad you took me on." She frowned. "I feel like a puppy."

Dr. Meyers laughed and walked back to her office door, opening it. "You guys ready?"

Jake walked in first, followed by an over-excited Amelia, who stood at the end of the bed and then leaned on her elbows to see the screen.

Jake took his normal spot at the edge of the bed. The order

of things was the same; first the gel, and then the device. The heartbeat was just as quick as when she'd last heard it. It still looked the same as last time, nevertheless Amelia shrieked softly; she hadn't seen it yet.

When Holly smiled and looked at her, she too, had tears in her eyes. Turning, she hugged her brother from behind as she wiped her tears.

"Miracles can happen, Amelia."

"Don't make me obsess about it again," she said to Dr. Meyers. "I just found a reason to let it go."

Dr. Meyers laughed as Jake stroked his sister's arm.

"So I take it you told your mother, Jake?"

"Yes, although she still wants to sit down and talk about everything, but at least she knows."

Holly huffed, shook her head and took a deep breath. She felt like crying. Even though she'd known that Mara was going to have a fit, she'd still hoped that the woman would see it their way and be happy.

She concentrated on the lines Dr. Meyers was drawing on the screen again. Her eyes flicked to the due date. It was still end of March.

Dr. Meyers told them how big the baby had grown, and confirmed what Holly had seen in regards to the birth date. What sex the baby was, she didn't say.

Gus didn't make appearance this time around.

When Dr. Meyers was done with Holly, the girls said goodbye to Jake at the exact time his beeper went off.

"Don't worry about my mother, please," he whispered in Holly's ear, while wrapping his arms around her.

"It's not easy to just forget about it, Jake."

"She'll understand when we tell her about our plans, and how we'll get through all of this," he persisted.

"Okay, fine. Whatever."

He kissed her on the top of her head and left.

Amelia hooked her arm with Holly's after she got another tin of formula from Dr. Meyers, and they walked to her car, which she'd parked just outside of P&E's entrance.

"My brother has a point," she said on the way.

"Still. I don't like it when she's like the only one not excited about it."

"It doesn't matter, Holls."

"It matters to me, Amelia."

"He hasn't told me much, but I know she's not ecstatic over the idea."

"She chased him out of the house and hasn't spoken to him since. No, ecstatic is an understatement."

"Okay fine. I would've been worried if she didn't act like that."

That was exactly what Jake had said.

"Believe me, she'll come around. You have nothing to be worried about."

"Okay. But I worry, anyway."

"I know you worry. But seriously, let it go. You're going to have a baby!" she cried excitedly.

Holly's smile was beautiful.

Amelia decided to take her to the nearest mall, where she dragged Holly to every baby shop she could find.

Holly was grateful for the time Marabella gave her off when she needed to go for her checkup. She really couldn't have asked for a better boss.

As expected, she was exhausted when Amelia finally dropped her off at Bernie's around five.

"Take care, mommy-to-be."

"I will, aunty-to-be."

Amelia chuckled, honked twice and drove away, all the while waving out the window.

When she entered the house, she immediately went to prepare her shake. She was hungry—even though Amelia had fed her like three times—tired and dizzy, all at the same time. Holly made quick work of opening the new tin and measuring four spoons of powder into a glass, she added the milk and stirred.

"Where have you been?" Bernie's voice filled the kitchen.

Holly jumped. "Give me a fright, why don't you? Amelia took me shopping. I swear she is more excited than I am."

"Of course she is. So where is the pic? Let me see."

Holly got the picture of the ultrasound and handed it to her.

Bernie's entire expression melted when she saw it. "I can't believe you are going to have a baby. I miss having a baby in my arms. I can't wait to find out what it's going to be so I can buy tiny little onesies, and little baby dresses if it's a girl. I hope it's a little girl."

Holly started to laugh. "It didn't stop Amelia. Tell you what. You can go with her next time, you guys will have a blast. I don't have the energy to go shopping."

"It's normal, you're pregnant," Bernie said, clucking her tongue.

Holly rubbed her face and leaned forward on the counter with her head in her hand. "She's not ecstatic about the idea."

"Who are we talking about now?" Bernie asked.

"Mara. She wants to speak to both of us soon."

"So? Just tell her how you feel, and that both of you want this, Holly, and that you are not sixteen anymore. I'm sure she is human. I haven't seen fangs yet, even though I'm sure she owns a pair that come out when she smells female hormones near her son."

Both girls started to laugh.

"He is a grown man for crying out loud."

"I bet you she wants to kill me."

"I don't think she's *that* psycho."

Holly gave a tired chuckle. "I'm going to have a bath, and then I'm going straight to sleep. My throat is killing me."

"Just your glands, it's normal."

"Ugh! How long is this going to last?"

"About a week or two."

"Yay, me."

OVER THE NEXT TWO WEEKS, Holly became overly emotional and cried over the dumbest things. Sometimes, it would be over a movie, and then it would turn into her missing Jake terribly. Mara being a class A bitch, came next.

Dealing with Jake having to work the night shift didn't help in the slightest. She had to make do with speaking to him over the phone during the day, which couldn't have been good for his cell phone charges. And on top of all that, missing his late night calls made her feel sad and somewhat depressed. Because she was so tired of late, she'd pass out quite early. Jake had even mentioned that they should get a place together.

The times she did manage to see Jake, always turned into him trying to elevate her fears by telling her he was going to speak to his mother. That Mara was ignoring him seemed to be affecting Jake. At least that's what she hoped it was and not him being worried about the baby. One good thing Holly had going for her was that the shake was working.

On the Wednesday, Holly received a message from Jake.

Meet me at my mom's place at 9:00. Sorry for the late notice, but it's important.

APPARENTLY, Mara did want to see them both. Holly phoned Marabella to ask if she could go in at around twelve, and then lied when asked why, saying she wasn't feeling at all well that morning. To her surprise, Marabella gave her the entire day off.

At exactly nine, Holly pulled her Beetle into Mara's driveway. The feeling inside her gut made her want to throw up. She knew it wasn't the baby because she'd had her shake before leaving home. Glancing out the window, she searched for Jake's BMW. It was nowhere to be seen. Reaching for her cell phone, she dialed his number; no answer.

She suddenly jumped as Mara tapped on her window. *Deep breaths, Holly, you can do this*, she told herself, switching her car off and getting out.

"Hi, Mara. Is Jake here?"

"No. He had to leave on an emergency, but I promise you, you are safe." She smiled.

Holly giggled nervously and gave Mara a hug. "I'm so sorry about all of this."

Mara nodded. "Let's go inside. I thought it best to have some iced tea on the patio. And then we can talk."

Holly decided to keep her mouth shut and instead followed Mara. Her Yorkies barked like mad, jumping up against Holly's leg until she picked one up and carried it along. The rest followed and when Mara yelled for them to go to their beds, all three dogs scrambled. Holly quickly placed the fourth one on the floor. It was quite comical how it, too, made a mad dash to its bed.

"Please, sit," Mara said, gesturing to one of the chairs.

Once Holly was sitting, Mara took the seat opposite to hers. She then filled two glasses with iced tea and handed one over.

Holly couldn't help but think that somehow it was

poisoned, so waited for Mara to take a sip before she put the glass to her lips.

"How do you feel?" Mara asked.

"Good, Gus' shake is working."

"Good. I'm glad. Look, I'm must be honest about something."

Holly frowned. "What, exactly?"

"Jake didn't have an emergency. He left a couple of minutes ago because he wasn't quite sure how to tell you."

Her heart began to beat slightly faster and a heavy feeling pressed down on her chest. She took a deep breath. "Tell me what, Mara?"

"He doesn't want the baby anymore, Holly."

Holly gasped and shook her head. To say she was stunned was putting it mildly. "I'm sorry, Mara, but I don't believe that."

"I don't care what you believe!" Mara's demeanor changed in a flash. "I'm just telling you how it is, Holly. He made a mistake and came to me for guidance. He wanted to know what his choices were."

His choices?

As far as Holly was concerned, that didn't sound remotely like the Jake she knew. He would've spoken to her about any insecurities he was having. However, when Holly began to contemplate things, the last couple of times they'd been together he'd seemed distant. The fact that Mara hadn't really spoken to him ever since he'd told her, had worked.

Oh, shit! What if I've misread the signs? What if it had nothing to do with his mother, but everything to do with not wanting our baby?

She shook her head again.

"Holly, you know this is true. He's seemed distant lately, am I right?"

Holly nodded. "I thought it was because you were not happy about it."

"I promise you, it's not. We've been discussing this situation for the past couple of days now. We had a family meeting late last night, where he voiced his concerns."

"Amelia—"

Mara cut her off. "She's his sister. She didn't like what he had to say, but blood is thicker than water, Holly."

"No." Holly continued to shake her head as images of tears filling Jake's eyes every time he saw the sonar jumped into her mind. He was happy, he'd told her he wanted this, wanted their baby. "I don't believe a thing you're saying and to be frank, I don't give a damn what you say."

"He doesn't want you or the baby anymore, Holly. I told you to go on the pill. I know my son and he changes his mind on a monthly basis."

"He wants the baby!" Holly yelled.

"Maybe he did, but I assure you, he doesn't want it anymore."

"No!" Holly refused to believe this. "Bernie was right, you are a psycho when it comes to Jake."

"I'm not a psycho! If you don't believe me, give him a call." She held her phone out to Holly.

All Holly was capable of doing was stare at the phone in Mara's hand, like it was a foreign object she'd never before seen. She hadn't bargained on Mara's challenge, and doubt filled her gut again. But the minute tears began to fill her eyes, her mind filled with visions of Jake whenever he'd looked at their unborn child, and her doubt disappeared.

"Oh, believe me, I will." She got up, glaring angrily at Mara. She was disgusted with whatever it was Mara was trying to pull. Looking at her phone, she touched the 1 for speed dial, which had been programmed to Jake's number. It rang, and rang, and rang until it went dead.

No, this isn't happening. Jake wants me and our baby. I know it!

She dialed his number again, with the same result. Panic was beginning to set in. Tears welled in her eyes as she dialed him again. This time, though, he picked up. She heard a sigh.

"Talk to me, Jake, what's going on?" Holly asked.

"It is what it is, Holly. I've got to go."

She was left with a dead tone. The air left her lungs, as if she'd been sucker punched. The tears dislodged and rolled down her cheeks. She felt Mara's hands gently take hold of her arms, guiding her back to the chair. Holly dropped onto it with a thud. There was nothing she could say.

"I know it's not easy," Mara began, "but you need to make a choice, Holly, and the best one is to get rid of the baby."

Holly's head snapped up. "What did you just say?"

"I know it is a horrible thing to say"—Mara put her hands up —"but Jake has a choice in this pregnancy, too, and he wants you to terminate it. Without Gus' shake and our support, you could lose your life. Hypertension is not a good thing, and even if you get to thirty weeks, it could worsen the minute you contract eclampsia."

Mara shook her head. "It's not something you want for yourself. Without Gus' shake, it's not going to be an easy pregnancy, Holly, not by any means. Google it if you don't believe me."

Holly shook her own head as more tears welled up in her eyes. "You people are unbelievable. Let me guess... this is the part Amelia didn't agree with, but she stands by her brother, right?"

"Blood is thicker than water."

Holly stood up. "Yes, you've made that perfectly clear." She picked up her handbag, wiped at her tears, and left.

How could Jake do something like that? But worst of all, allow his mother to tell her that he didn't want the baby anymore.

"Get rid of it!" Mara yelled at her retreating back.

The hell I will, Holly thought as she ran to her Beetle.

She had never, not in a million years, expected that her wish of wanting to run away would ever become a reality, but for the sake of her unborn child and how events had turned for the worst, she had no choice.

TWENTY-SIX

WHEN HOLLY ARRIVED at Bernie's, she was glad her friend wasn't home. She had no idea what she would do now, but she couldn't stay there anymore. If she did, it was inevitable that Jake would visit that evening and beg her to abort the baby. And she would, she knew it, which meant she would hate herself for the rest of her life and would end up hating him more than she already did.

To hate Jake like that... no, she would never be able to live in a world if that was what she would feel like for the rest of her life. She knew she shouldn't feel any love for him at all, but she did love him; she would die for him, that much she knew. The best thing she could do was leave, never to see or speak to him again.

She slid down her closet door and cried. How could he have been so heartless, telling her that it was what it was, and that he'd had to go? It hadn't even been a conversation. After everything they'd shared, Holly was devastated that he hadn't had the guts to tell her to her face.

She pinched herself for the umpteenth time; none of it felt real, but the resulting pain of that action told her she was definitely awake, and the gut-wrenching feeling inside of her confirmed that it had happened.

She packed her bags—two of them—all the while crying, knowing that it wasn't just Jake she would leave behind, but her best friend as well. She had no choice. Leo was Jake's best friend, and that just wouldn't work.

She left the phone he'd bought for her as there was no way she was going to keep it. For all she knew, there was some sort of tracking device on it. Not that he would search for her, although he might, just to make sure she had gotten rid of her baby.

Still, whatever he would've tried to do, she wasn't going to give him that chance. She placed the phone on the table.

When her suitcases were full to the brim, she hauled them out to her Beetle. Looking at her watch, she realized it was almost twelve. After locking up, she placed her key under the rock and said goodbye to what had become her home.

Once she'd settled herself in the car, she thought about the phone again. Bernie would definitely want to know if she was safe. Holly would have to let her know some way or another that she was okay.

Bernie would eventually understand why she'd run away, because Holly wasn't planning on getting rid of her baby, not in her lifetime, and her only course of action was to do what was best for them both.

As she turned the engine on, she wiped away another tear, and then drove to the nearest bus station where she bought a ticket to Atlanta figuring that once she arrived there, she would decide where it was she would end up.

The only solution she could come up with was in regards to the one person she'd never thought she'd ever again see, but he was only person who could get her through this, the only person who had the means and money to help her; Charles Scallanger.

Holly cried the entire bus drive to Atlanta, and continuously tried to figure out how the hell she could have misread the signs.

Why hadn't she just asked him? Then again, how could she have known?

He'd mentioned that they should get a place, and he'd talked about how much he wanted the baby. That he would never leave them, still... there she was.

Abruptly, her thoughts did an about-turn and began to calculate how much powder she still had left; half a tin as well as a full, unopened one. For the next month she would be fine. What she would do thereafter was in God's hands.

EARLY NEXT MORNING, Holly arrived in Atlanta. She couldn't shake off the feeling of being discovered and covered her head with the hoodie she'd bought when she purchased a ticket to Seattle—where her father lived.

She knew what he would inevitably say when she showed up, but she had no other choice. He would help her, of that she had no doubt as he'd been trying desperately to connect with her again. And there she was, presenting him with that very chance.

A woman sat next to her on the bus, and when the tears began to flow again she asked Holly if she was all right.

Holly ended up telling the stranger her story. The woman, who turned out to be very kind, listened with compassion, even giving her a hug, which was exactly what she'd needed. It had felt really good.

Finally reaching Seattle, she stepped off the bus, gathered her bags, hailed a cab and directed the driver to her father's offices. When he pulled up in front of its glass doors, Holly waited a beat before paying and hauling her suitcases into the reception area.

Duly announcing herself, she was told by the beautiful girl behind the counter that Mr. Scallanger would be out until late that afternoon, so she made herself comfortable in preparation for the long wait.

Her father was filthy rich. It was a life Holly knew nothing about, because Charles Scallanger had left them just before her sister died. Sure, he'd helped with the bills and paid maintenance; he wasn't that heartless, but the last time she'd seen him was at her sister's funeral.

At one point during her wait, Holly went to a corner store and bought milk in order to drink her shake when she began to feel dizzy. With time on her hands—and as one does when time needs to be killed—she began to think about what Bernie might be going through due to her disappearance. But that life couldn't be hers anymore.

She'd even considered phoning Bernie, but knew what it would lead to so decided against it. How sad that out of fear for her baby's life, she couldn't bring herself to phone her best friend to let her know that she was safe, and that there was no need to worry.

Close to four that the afternoon, in walked the man she hadn't seen in over ten years. His hair was gray now. She got to her feet when he stopped to speak to the girl at reception.

He turned around, and when he realized it was Holly, walked toward her hastily. She began to cry and was surprised when he folded her in his arms and hugged her.

"Don't worry, Holly, whatever it is, whatever you need, I'm here," he said, hugging her tighter.

Deep down, she hated being there. He was the last person she wanted to see, but Mara had been right about one thing. Blood *was* thicker than water.

"Have you eaten anything?"

Holly shook her head.

"Let's go to the cafeteria then, shall we? We can talk there."

Holly nodded and followed her father into the most beautiful cafeteria she'd ever seen. He was one of the most successful architects in America, and thank heaven his company name didn't include his surname. It was called CDS Developments.

She hadn't told Jake what her father did for a living because before now, she'd wanted nothing whatsoever to do with Charles Scallanger.

"Emery, may I please have a glass of orange juice?" he said to the waitress. "What would you like, Holly?"

"Milk, please."

Charles frowned, but added, "I'll have the chicken as well."

"Just a toasted chicken for me, please."

For a while, neither said a thing to the other. When the drinks were placed in front of them, Holly tried not to gulp hers down.

Charles looked at her with concern. "Holly, what is going on?"

"I'm pregnant," she whispered.

"Who's the father?"

"Does it matter? He doesn't want me anymore, and wants me to get rid of it."

He narrowed his eyes. "What do you want to do?"

"Abortion is out of the question, Charles."

"Okay, I understand that. Your mother and I didn't raise you that way, but Holly you have to think this through clearly. Having this child will tie you to this man forever."

"There are way too many women out there who haven't a chance in hell of having children. I can't, and I won't kill it."

"So... you're thinking about giving it up for adoption, then?"

"No, I'm most certainly not. I don't care how he feels about the baby, or me. I'm going to keep it."

Charles took a deep breath.

"Charles... Dad, please. I've never asked you for anything. I just need your help until the baby is born." She wiped at her tears. "Nobody will hire a pregnant woman who's likely to faint at any given moment."

"What do you mean? Why would you faint at any given moment?"

"It's not going to be an easy pregnancy. I'm taking medication; a trial formula, but it will finish in a couple of weeks. And then crap's going to hit the fan."

"So, I'm to be your piggy bank, is that it?"

"I came to you for help. You can look at it any way you want. If you are serious about making amends, Dad, this would be the perfect time. I promise you, you won't get another chance like this one." Tears rolled down her face again.

Charles got up and crouched in front of her. "Shh," he whispered, putting his arms around her. "Don't worry. I'll take care of it."

Holly couldn't contain her tears. "No abortion, please."

"No abortion," he promised.

"Thank you, Dad."

He took her face in both hands and looked at her. "I know I fucked up, okay? But I do love you, always have, and I loved Jamie, too. Your mother made it difficult for me to see you both."

Holly didn't believe him for one minute, but she had no choice.

Charles kissed the top of her head just as the waitress arrived with their meals. "Eat," he said, "and I'll take you home afterward."

She did as she was told and ate as if she hadn't eaten for a week.

During the meal, Charles discussed his course of action.

"I'll phone my doctor first thing in the morning. I'll need recommendations as to who's the best in the country. We'll get you through this."

Holly swallowed past the lump in her throat, because she knew that the best was Jake's dad. She didn't say anything, though. Her father could never know who the baby's father was.

If Charles Scallanger found out, she was scared he would not only sue the living crap out of Jake, but the whole Peters' clan while he was at it. If there was one thing Charles was superb at, it was winning.

Should that happen, Jake would then find out that she'd kept the baby and he might just change his mind. She wasn't going to let that transpire, either. If it hadn't worked out the first time, it would never work out the second. That was something else her grandmother had said. Holly huffed inwardly thinking about what her cousins—once removed—would have to say. She'd always thought they'd been her aunts growing up, but now she knew better. Thank heavens she didn't need them.

THE DRIVE to her father's mansion took only a couple of minutes.

Holly's eyes grew wide as they pulled into the driveway. She found herself gawking at a semi-palace with glass windows built high on a cliff. It was gorgeous.

Having given orders for her bags to be taken inside, Charles led her through to the patio.

Gabriella, her father's wife, was sunning on a lounger next to the pool. Holly had only seen her a handful of times when she was a little girl, but as soon as Gabriella noticed Holly standing next to Charles, the look on her face said she wanted to scold him over who the hell the strawberry blond slut was.

Charles knew her all too well. "Relax, Gabriella. It's only Holly."

She squinted and looked at Holly. "Holly? As in—"

"Yes," he cut her off, "she will be staying with us for a couple of months."

Gabriella finally smiled. "Welcome to our home, Holly. It will be nice to finally get to know you."

"Likewise," Holly lied. She hated this woman with every fiber of her being, but needed to remain on her good side otherwise her father would throw her out, and then where would that leave her?

The woman standing before her in gorgeous open-toed shoes was in her mid-forties but still looked twenty, only because of all the plastic surgery her father had obviously paid for.

Money that should've actually helped raise me and Jamie, Holly thought, shaking her head. If her current situation was going to work, she needed to rid herself of such thoughts.

"Come, darling." Charles motioned for her to follow him. "Let me show you to your room."

Holly gave him a soft smile, although it was really hard to muster one after the last two days. A part of her had always known that the situation she now found herself in was bound to happen, that the day would come when Jake would not want her anymore.

She still couldn't believe it, but the words had come directly from the horse's mouth, so to speak. Words that would stick in her head for years to come.

She wiped at a tear, then followed her father through one of the side doors into his mansion. They walked up the first set of stairs. Another led them to the upper level. It was huge, which made her wonder who had more money; him or the Peters'.

A small dog ran out of one of the rooms and barked hysterically as they passed by him. Holly jumped because that had to have been the ugliest dog she had ever seen. It was completely hairless.

"Pimples, quiet," Charles demanded in a thick voice.

The dog backed off, but continued to growl, letting it be known he wasn't happy with the new stranger coming into his home.

"Sorry, he's old. I can't wait for him to die."

Holly giggled, although she was a bit taken aback with him wanting the dog to die. "He's not the prettiest dog I have seen, that's for sure."

"It's Gabriella, she's got a thing for ugly mutts. Have to love that about her, otherwise she would never have gone for me." He raised his eyebrows, and Holly only smiled.

I don't think it was your looks she was after, dearest Dad, Holly thought but didn't dare say out loud.

They continued down a hall. Numerous picture frames had been hung along one wall, all showing photos of Gabriella, but none of her father.

The door at the end was their destination and when Holly entered, she sucked in a huge breath. It was stunning, the stuff dreams were made of. At its center was the biggest four-poster bed she'd ever seen, covered in the most beautiful satin linen.

Surrounding the room were ceiling to floor glass windows, framed by the softest, white curtains. Almost all opened up onto a balcony with its own breakfast corner, and amazingly what looked to be an honest to goodness hot tub.

She shook her head. That kind of opulence was something she wasn't used to, but as her father was the only one with the means to help her through this mess, she would make herself get used to it.

"I hope the room is to your satisfaction. If you'd like the linen changed, I can ask Penelope to come sort it out—"

"It not necessary," she interrupted. "It's simply beautiful. Thank you, Dad."

He smiled and looked at the carpet. "I'm glad you've stopped calling me Charles. It's nice to have you here, Holly. Really."

She smiled at him, feeling somewhat guilty. It wasn't like she really wanted to be there anyway, but beggars couldn't be choosers.

"I'll let you settle in, then. I've a couple of things I need to see to in my office. If you are hungry, let the chef know and he'll make you something."

Chef! He's got a freaking chef?

"Thanks, Dad. For everything."

Once he closed the door, she began to unpack her clothes. Her mind ran rampant again. All the times her mother had struggled to put food on the table, he'd had someone making it for him. He'd never been there. Even when Jamie died and her mother drowned herself in alcohol, he hadn't been there. He'd never even bothered with threats toward Jane regarding taking Holly away from her if the alcohol bingeing continued.

What Holly had now done was without a doubt the lowest she'd succumbed to in her life; ask the man she despised most in the world for help. She'd never in her wildest dreams thought that that was where she'd end up, that that was what would happen to her. But the end result was her only option. She was in the one place where she'd be safe.

Bernie knew her mother, but Holly wasn't certain if her friend was privy to her whereabouts. Sure, Holly had spoken to her from time to time. She'd even, shockingly, given money toward Holly's now doomed wedding to Brandon. But she was the one person Holly couldn't have gone to. It would have been too easy for Bernie to find her.

She was safe in Seattle. No one, not even Bernie would find her.

She wondered if Bernie would be upset with Jake for not wanting the baby. But Holly knew the answer to that; she most definitely would be. However, as far as Leo was concerned, that was another matter entirely. Jake would never sever his friendship with Leo. They'd been friends practically since the day they'd been out of diapers. That kind of friendship shouldn't be broken, and those kinds of friends shouldn't have to choose. In the end, Holly had been the one to make the choice instead.

Her hands began to tremble as she pulled the tin that held the last shake out of her bag. Thank heaven she had another full one, but it would only last her half a month, and then everything would go haywire once again.

Her fear of hospitals was such that she couldn't imagine what she would end up going through. If Mara was right about dying, there was nothing to be done. She'd rather die for her unborn baby than contemplate aborting it. Her life felt meaningless, anyway. She was convinced she'd never find love again. She'd known it the first time she'd kissed Jake, and if by some miracle the baby and her survived, it would have to be happy with only one parent.

TWENTY-SEVEN

THOSE FIRST FEW weeks went by quickly. Holly spent most of them in her room.

Gabby, as her father called his wife, tried her utmost to be friendly, but after the umpteenth time of short answers from Holly—who had absolutely no interest in either being her friend, much less go shopping with her—that's when the fighting started. Her father's house wasn't big enough for Gabby's shrill voice.

To her surprise, her father didn't interfere, demanding that she give Gabby a chance. Instead, he tried his best and was nice to his daughter, which Gabby didn't approve of.

One day, she noticed that her father had been sleeping in one of the guest rooms for at least two nights. A part of her felt awful, but she really had nothing in common with Gabby, neither was she interested in what kind of plastic surgery she was thinking of getting next. Actually, Holly wasn't even sure if any of the woman's body parts were real anymore.

Time wasn't the only thing that went by quickly. Holly's last tin was also diminishing with every passing day. She had more or less one week of the supplement left, deciding to stretch it as far as she possibly could. She'd only drink it when she felt she really couldn't cope with the dizziness or nausea anymore.

She would also drown the powder with milk and would skip the next dose, which needed to be taken every eight hours. She hated the whirlwind thoughts going on in her head. Worry was a constant companion.

That evening after consuming her shake, Holly took a bath and went straight to bed, after Al, Charles' chef, made her something light to eat.

At around two in the morning, a crazy nauseating feeling interrupted her sleep; she barely made it to the bathroom.

She couldn't stop what was happening and began to cry as she dry heaved over the toilet bowl.

Eventually, her father must have heard. When Charles saw the condition his daughter was in, his face was a mixture of horror and worry.

"We need get you to the hospital."

"No. Just get the tin from my closet. Four scoops into a glass of milk. It will help."

She listened to closet doors opening and closing as her insides burned.

"Which one, Holly?" he yelled from within her bedroom.

"The one closest to the wall, Dad, third shelf."

The sound of the closet opening again, followed by her father exiting her room and walking to the kitchen came next. She took deep breaths and wiped her mouth. The dizziness was horrific.

If she wasn't capable of skipping eight hours, how on earth was she going to make the tin last? And then it hit her. The tin wasn't going to last—it meant that Mara had been right. Holly didn't want to die, but she didn't want to abort the baby, either. She couldn't.

She'd walked that horrible marathon with Amelia against

abortion. And even if Amelia had managed to change her mind about the baby, Holly still wouldn't have been able to go through with it. It wasn't right, and she would never be something she wasn't just to get Jake back. Whatever they'd had wasn't love, because he'd basically discarded her and their baby.

Holly began to cry as she thought about Jake and the mess he'd left her to deal with. He was a coward, a word she never would have used to describe him before.

He'd broken her heart. No, he'd shattered it and it would never be able to heal. She would end up like her mother, alone with a tiny baby.

Charles returned, holding the glass to her mouth so she could drink. He then picked her up and carried her gently back to bed. "Are you going to be okay? Don't you think we should call for a doctor, Holls?"

"No, Dad. I'll be okay now. If it worsens, I'll go see a doctor."

"When is your next appointment?"

"I made one with Gabby's doctor. She said he's really good."

"Dr. Rikus is one of the best. I've checked him out and Gabby trusts him, so he must be really good."

Holly managed to chuckle. Her father's humor reminded her of Dr. Meyers. It was dry, but she could read between the lines.

Charles smiled and stroked her hair. "Sleep tight, and if you don't feel better in an hour, you call me and we'll go to the hospital, you hear?"

She nodded. Even though she hated the fact that her father had just told her what to do, she had to admit that it felt good to be taken care of.

WHEN SHE WOKE the next morning, Holly was forced to drink the shake. Al now made sure she didn't skip even one. He took a photo of the tin and said he would try to get her more.

Holly didn't like it one bit and worried that somehow Gus would find out, especially as it wasn't on the market, added to the fact that she was carrying his 'grandbaby', so to speak.

The bean was almost three months along now. Holly was proud that they'd both made it that far. Just a little farther to go. At least her father had her back, and she knew that should the day came when those she was trying to avoid interfered, he would fight them tooth and nail in court.

She didn't want a single thing from Jake, but for some reason she loved him still, even if she hated his guts. She often wondered if she'd ever go back were he to beg. But she'd counter that thought in the negative; he'd made his choice and that was where it would stay. Her grandmother had always told her to never take someone back if the relationship hadn't worked out the first time around. Although, where Brandon was concerned, she'd given him a number of chances. With Jake it was different, though. She was carrying his baby, one he didn't want and because of that, there would be no second chance.

'It is what it is, Holly. I've got to go.' Every time she heard his words in her head, tears would stream down her face and she would hide her face in her pillow, ashamed that she still cared for him.

TWO DAYS LATER, her father entered her room. "Holly, where did you get that formula?"

"It doesn't matter anymore, Dad."

"If it's the only thing that keeps you healthy, please. If it's money—"

"It's not about the money," she cut him off hastily. "Thing is, it's not on the market yet, and the doctor who's experimenting with it won't give you any."

"Honey, we've got to try."

"Dad, please, let it go."

Charles sighed. "We need to help you somehow. Please, let me help you. It's why you came to me."

Holly merely nodded. She didn't want to fight with him, and God knew how scared she was of Jake finding out about her keeping the baby. But she had no choice, not if she didn't want her father to find out who the baby's father was.

"When is your appointment with Dr. Rikus?"

"Tomorrow."

"We should ask him about this, maybe he'll be able to get his hands on some."

"Sure, I'll ask him."

Charles eyed his daughter both patiently and warily, and then left.

After dinner, Al prepared her last shake. She cried as she finished it, the end had come.

There were still six months left in her pregnancy, and Holly could just imagine in what kind of a state she was going to be in when it was time to deliver the baby. She just knew she had to.

She slept through the night, but when she woke it was with a mind that wouldn't stop swirling. It felt as if her thoughts were smashing up against each other in her head, and when she sat up in bed the nausea hit her like a ton of bricks. Hurling herself out of bed, she ran to the toilet and threw up bile, just slime and water.

Al knocked on the door. "Miss Holly, are you okay?"

Between breaths she croaked, "I'll be fine, Al." Which was an outright lie.

As the nausea abated somewhat, Holly pushed herself up

from the toilet and stumbled back into her room. She dressed in a T-shirt, jeans and a coat. Her belly had started to extend slightly but not by much, which also told her that something wasn't right. Women usually began showing at around three months, right?

She knew she was over three months now, according to her last visit with Dr. Meyer's five weeks ago.

Grabbing a brown paper bag out of the pantry as an afterthought, she made her way out to the waiting car. The driver opened the door for her and introduced himself as Bennie. Once seated, she rested her head against the window's cold glass, hoping it would help with her hot flushes.

Holly thought about having skipped that one shake; it had influenced the progress she'd made. If she hadn't skipped it, she probably wouldn't be feeling as horrible as she was at that moment.

Pulling up at the hospital, Bennie stopped the car, got out and opened the door for her once again.

Holly thanked her lucky stars he was close by when she climbed out, as she almost tumbled over from the dizziness.

"Don't worry, I've got you, miss," he reassured her. Turning, he yelled for assistance.

She was settled into a wheelchair and taken to the emergency room by a man wearing scrubs, and was immediately attended to.

"What seems to be the problem?" a woman asked, shining a light into Holly's eyes.

"I'm pregnant and I have gestational hypertension," Holly answered. "I'm here to see Dr. Rikus."

"Page Doctor Rikus, stat. We've got a bad case of hypertension," she yelled.

Holly was immediately moved onto a bed.

"Do you have any insurance?"

Holly shook her head. "You'll have to call my father."

"I already did, Miss Scallanger."

The doctor looked at Bennie.

"Charles' daughter?"

"That's correct, doctor," Bennie confirmed.

"Get her up to the maternity ward, now. Private room," the doctor barked.

Holly was wheeled away whilst still on the bed and into an elevator. Nurses fiddled with her arms, while she pinched her eyes closed as a needle pierced her skin.

"I'm pregnant," Holly stated, sounding tired.

"We know. It's okay," a male voice answered. "Once you get that line open, let's get her that labetalol. Start with 20 mg," he barked his orders to another man who'd joined them in the elevator.

The nausea began to slowly disappear as did the lightheadedness, but not completely. *This is manageable. I can work with this,* she thought.

It wasn't long before they were exiting the elevator. By then, fatigue had consumed her and she fell asleep, only to be woken by the doctor.

She looked around and found herself in a small private room. Her father was standing in the doorway with his coat hanging over one arm, and his phone in the other at his ear. He was talking to someone, rescheduling an appointment it sounded like.

"Miss Scallanger?"

"Please, call me Holly."

"How do you feel now?"

"I'm okay. Much better than this morning."

The doctor smiled. He was somewhere in his mid-fifties and had kind eyes.

"Your father tells me that you were on some sort of supplement which helped with your symptoms. Do you know what it's called?"

"It's not on the market yet. It's still in its trial stages, but I've now run out and can't get any more."

"Did it work?"

She nodded. "It did, but the one who gave it to me..." she trailed off, casting her eyes downward.

"Is he related to the baby?"

She nodded again.

"Holly, I need to know what happened, and I need to get my hands on this supplement. If he can give us—"

"He won't. Believe me, he won't," she cut in.

"So, I take it that somewhere along the line someone didn't want you to have the baby?"

"Yes." Holly gulped.

"I must still try to get the supplement, Holly. Without him knowing who it's for, of course. We need to get you back on it as soon as possible. Who is he?"

She hesitated.

"Please. I promise your name will be kept out of it."

Holly sighed. "Dr. Gus Peters."

He stared at her for a minute, dumbfounded. "You are telling me that he started with the p47 trial?"

"Correct."

"I'll see what I can do." He smiled. "We've been waiting for him to start with this very trial for the past year. And you say it's worked for you?"

She nodded. "Very well, actually."

"Terrific. I'll need you to stay overnight. All we're going to do is observe you both. I'll make a couple of phone calls, see if we can get you sorted, okay?"

"Thank you," she whispered.

As soon as he left, two nurses entered, one pushing a monitor. Smiling down at Holly she connected a belt over her slightly extended belly.

Please let there be a heartbeat, she begged.

The nurse hit a switch and Holly immediately heard the baby's heartbeat, confirming that the bean was okay. However, she was worried, too. The heartbeat wasn't as fast or as strong as it had been in Dr. Meyers' office.

The nurse, who'd been standing off to one side, left the room immediately, while the other tried to assuage Holly's fear.

"It's okay, it's low but no danger yet. We'll wait for the doctor to come and have a look."

Right on cue, Dr. Rikus entered and went straight to the monitor.

"That isn't normal, is it?" Holly asked.

"Holly, don't worry. The baby is doing fine. Get me an ultrasound. I want to see what is going on," he commanded, and the nurse made a hasty retreat.

Her father entered, finally having finished with his phone conversation.

"Dad, you don't have to stay if you have business to attend to. I'm in good hands."

"I'm not going anywhere until I know you are going to be okay," he uttered softly, kissing her on the top of her head.

Why couldn't he have always been like this? Why now?

"Doctor? What's the verdict?" Charles queried.

"I'm trying to get that formula as we speak. My assistant is making a few calls." He glanced at Holly and then back at Charles. "She'll be okay."

"And how's the baby doing?"

"We are about to find out," Dr. Rikus replied, just as the nurse returned with the ultrasound equipment. He switched it on, squirted warm gel onto Holly's stomach, and began his examination.

She felt better now that she was able to see how the bean looked. The fetus was still relatively small, but the limbs had grown a bit thicker, and one could see the outline of a tiny baby.

"Hmm," Dr. Rikus murmured.

"What is it?" Both Holly and Charles asked simultaneously, which had them both smiling.

"Nothing bad. Would you like to know the baby's sex?"

"You can see that already?" Charles was taken aback.

The doctor nodded.

"Amazing. That is entirely Holly's choice, of course."

Holly smiled and nodded her ascent.

"It's a little girl."

A solitary tear escaped and Holly closed her eyes. It was going to be a little girl who would look just like her father. She was convinced of that, because that was how Murphy's Law worked. She was going to look exactly as Jake had when he'd been a four-year-old toddler, just like the photo she'd seen when they'd vacationed as his parents' home.

The doctor's voice broke into her musings. "She's not in distress yet, but she is very close to it. What do you want to do, Holly?"

"What do you mean?" she asked, slight hysteria building within her.

"You can still abort—"

"Never! That's exactly what they wanted. I cannot and will not abort my baby."

"They?" her father queried, an angry look on his face.

"Don't, please, Dad. I'm never going to see them again."

"Holly if I can't get that shake, you have no idea what we are going to be up against. I can tell you what you can expect, but not many of my patients have shown symptoms as early as you have and still managed to make it to term. By the looks of things, you are on the severe end of the scale. You aren't alone, though.

There are a handful of women going through the same thing. But the extreme cases I've read about... sadly, either the mother, the fetus, or both don't survive."

"What!" her father shouted.

"Dad, I'm not aborting this baby."

"Holly, think this through carefully. You're putting your life at risk here. I've already lost one child. I do not plan on losing another."

Holly was furious. All she wanted to do was yell right back in his face that Jamie had never mattered to him. He hadn't once visited her when she fought for her life at the bitter end, just paid the bills, but she kept quiet. Instead, she said, "I am not getting rid of this baby, Dad."

"But... what if you die?"

"Then I die, okay?"

"You don't know what you are saying."

"Just go, please." Tears rolled down her cheeks.

Doctor Rikus had a few words with Charles, practically ordering him to go.

Relenting, Charles finally acquiesced. "I'll be outside if you need anything. Do whatever is in your power to help her. I will not lose my daughter."

"You know I will, Mr. Scallanger."

Charles kissed Holly softly on the head again before leaving.

"Doctor Rikus, give it to me straight. What are these women going through?"

The doctor pulled his chair closer. "Severe headaches, nausea from hell itself, high blood pressure, weight loss, not to mention the strain it puts on the baby. Babies are usually born premature and struggle to stay alive. But if you really want to carry on with this, I promise to do all I can in my power to help you through it."

"How do the women die?"

"Oh, a number of ways. They die of strokes, heart attacks, or clots in their lungs. The pressure is terrible on the kidneys, so even those who manage to survive sometimes have to go on dialysis for the rest of their lives. Even after delivery, you may still suffer with hypertension and develop heart failure."

Holly nodded.

"It's not going to be easy, Holly."

"I know. But nothing worth keeping is ever easy, is it? And I want to keep my baby. Please."

"Then we'll do everything to see that that happens. Okay?" He smiled, patted her hand reassuringly, stood up and turned to speak to one of the nurses.

"I'll see you later tonight. Rest now."

"Thank you, Doctor Rikus, for everything."

Closing her eyes, she listened to the voices outside her door. Clearly, her father and Doctor Rikus were having a discussion of sorts.

"No," her father answered whatever had been asked, adamantly. "She came to me for help and that is exactly what I'm going to provide."

What was Doctor Rikus asking of him?

She was pulled out of her thought when one of the nurses injected liquid from three separate vials into her IV, fatigue washing over her once more. Her eyes closed. She was swept away into the darkness of her mind

TWENTY-EIGHT

HOLLY WOKE with a startle and found herself tucked into bed at her father's house. She jumped out of it quickly when the nausea hit, making it to the bathroom in the nick of time. She was sick for what seemed like forever. Taking deep breaths, she cleaned up as best she could and went back to bed. Her head seemed to spin out of control.

She'd lost a couple of pounds in the past month, and had been admitted to hospital three times by Dr. Rikus.

She also cried a lot, which could have been due to a number of things; hormones, Jake, and the baby who was struggling just as much as she was.

The day she reached 20 weeks was one she celebrated. She was halfway through the hell she'd fallen into.

Where peace and quiet should have reigned, it seemed like her father was constantly fighting with her of late.

On the plus side, she'd finally started looking like a pregnant woman, even if her highly defined shoulder bones and cheek bones made her look like she was on drugs. She hated looking sickly, but it wasn't like she had a choice.

Holly needed baby Jamie now more than ever; she wouldn't

lose her, too. She'd decided to name the baby after her sister, as well as her best friend; Jamie Bernice. Bernie was a sister to her, so it was appropriate to name the baby after the two most special people in her life.

Lying in bed, her heart beat like drums at a rock concert. She felt hot and bothered, and knew that her blood pressure had shot sky high again. The tablets the doctor had given her weren't working anymore. It made her think of what Jamie had experienced when she had been alive. A particular drug would work for a month and then it would just stop.

Holly decided she had no further choice in the matter, she needed to go back into hospital again. They weren't really as bad as she'd thought, since they always treated her kindly and with care.

It took a huge amount of effort to turn around and locate the buzzer that had been left on the nightstand in order to call her father. It was something he'd installed a couple of weeks back when she needed him in the middle of night.

She was feeling weak, but managed to turn nevertheless, swinging her arm out toward the nightstand. It was there, somewhere, all she had to do was find it. Her hand felt around the top a few times until it connected with the buzzer. Relieved, she pressed the button. A siren, not a very loud one, went off farther down the hall.

Not a minute later, Charles burst through her door and picked her up. She could feel him move quickly, yelling for help at the same time. Lights went on throughout the house, and more hands appeared to help. And then Gabby's screeching made its way to them. Luckily for Holly, she couldn't make heads or tails over what the bitch was going on about.

The cold air outside was a breath of fresh air, offering some relief to her hot body. But the minute she was settled in her father's SUV, the heat returned, making her feel ten times worse.

Penelope, one of her father's staff members who thankfully resided on the property, held Holly's head in her lap. The old woman stroked her hair as her eyes closed, whispering words Holly couldn't make out.

The drive to the hospital felt like it was taking ages, and just as she thought that, they suddenly stopped. Charles' voice barked demands for help, and soon hands seemed to come from nowhere, pulling her out of the SUV, placing her on a bed and wheeling her into the emergency room.

Lying flat on her back, Holly saw ceilings and lights whizz by, hurting her eyes. She was thankful, though, for the hand holding hers. Her father's.

All too soon, Charles released her hand when Dr. Rikus and a few nurses needed to attend to her. Whatever she'd been given —not that she'd felt anything during all the commotion—began to work as her symptoms settled.

Dr. Rikus waited until her body reacted to the medication she was given, upon which he began an examination of the baby.

Holly waited and prayed to hear the tiny heartbeat, when it finally came. The sound was exactly as previous times; soft and far from the tempo it should be but it was there, hanging on, just like her mommy.

Both were fighting to live for the chance to see what the other one looked like.

Hold on, Jamie, please, she prayed softly, before all went silent.

WHEN HOLLY WOKE, a dark figure was sitting in a chair next to the bed.

"Dad?" she whispered.

"Holly..." It wasn't Charles' voice as she had expected, but rather her mother's.

Holly closed and opened her eyes a few times in order to focus. When her mother came into view, her face was both riddled with worry and relief.

"Mom? What are *you* doing here?" she croaked.

"Why didn't you phone me, Holly?"

"Too scared to."

"Of what? You went to your dad, after everything—"

"Don't," Holly interrupted. "I wouldn't be here if it wasn't for him, Mom. You've got to give him that. He came through for me this time. It counts."

"Don't ask me to forgive your father, Holly. Not after everything he put us through."

"Have you forgotten what you did when Jamie died?"

"I can't."

"Try, Mom. I'm still here."

"You could've died, and then what?"

Holly didn't answer.

"Holly... why don't you abort—"

Her scream cut her mother off. "No! I will never abort my little girl. Deal with it."

Her mother's bottom lip trembled, she was crying. "It's a little girl."

Holly nodded. "Her name is Jamie."

Jane stood up and bent to hug her daughter. A loud sob escaped her. "I can't lose you, too. Promise me that I won't lose you, Holly."

"I'm trying my damnedest to live, Mom. Believe me, I don't want to die."

Jane sniffed, running the back of her hand up and down Holly's cheek softly.

"Did Bernie phone you?"

"Bernice?" her mother asked.

Holly nodded.

Jane shook her head. "My phone was stolen and I don't think she has my new number. Your father called in one of his detectives to track me down."

"Detectives don't come cheap, Mom. That should be reason enough for you to forgive him."

"He's an arrogant bastard, Holly. I'm far from forgiving him yet, but I'll try. For you. Okay?"

"Okay."

"So... who's the bastard that put you in this position?"

"It doesn't matter now. He will never see or meet her. His loss. She's mine."

"I swear, I will kill him if I ever find out who he is. To leave you like this..."

"Mom? He's a coward. Besides, you didn't kill Dad, so I very much doubt you'll have a personality change and become a murderer."

Her mother giggled. "Why didn't you phone me?"

"Truth?"

Jane nodded.

"I needed money. I knew this was going to happen, and I know you don't have the kind of funds I needed lying around. Besides, I still owe you that wedding money."

"Holly, we could've made a plan."

"No. There comes a time in one's life when we have to suck whatever up and move on."

"And this was one of those times?"

Holly affirmed with a nod.

Jane stroked her arm. "Well, I'm here for the long haul."

"What about your job?"

"It's just a job. You are what's important to me. Besides, there will always be hospitals looking for nurses and I'm quite the nurse, I'll have you know."

Holly chuckled.

"What is it they have you on?"

"No idea, but whatever it is, it's working."

"Do you know where your chart is? They're usually at the end of a patient's bed."

"Right there on the wall, next to the door," Holly said, pointing in its direction.

"Dear me, why I never looked there is beyond me," Jane mumbled, clicking her tongue.

She made her way to the metal casing affixed to the wall and pulled out Holly's chart. The light seeping through the door outlined her slender body.

For an older woman, one who'd drowned herself in booze for years, she still looked like a million dollars, even though she didn't have the funds to back it up. It was one of Jane's strongest traits; she knew how to look good.

Why her father had lost interest in her mother was beyond Holly's knowledge.

Jane read through Holly's chart carefully, and eventually returned to her daughter's side.

"Did you find what you were looking for?" Holly asked.

"Yes, and it's really expensive stuff."

"See why I needed him?"

"Still. I wouldn't have asked him for a dime."

Holly sighed tiredly. "The way you feel about Dad is exactly how I feel about Jamie's dad. I wouldn't ask him for a dime."

"Please, Holly, tell me who he is?"

"Some big shot."

" Don't tell me he's married."

"No, you raised me better than that." Her eyes were closed, but she was smiling.

"What's the problem, then?"

"He changed his mind about being a father."

"How long have you known him?"

"Not long enough, apparently. But it was perfect while it lasted, Mom. The kind of love you only read about in Jane Austin novels."

Her mother gave her a sad look. "So why didn't it last?"

A tear rolled down Holly's cheek. Jane dabbed it away.

"Because that kind of love doesn't exist, Mom. It's why it only happens in fiction."

Jane shook her head. "What is this p47 in your chart, Holly?"

"Sorry, the what?" Holly hadn't fully paid attention to her mom's question.

"Your doctor has drawn a huge circle around something called p47. I've never heard of it. What is it?"

"Oh. He circles things that are important. That's the formula he's trying to get."

"What formula?"

"Something another gynecologist was working on to help women like me," she lied.

"Hang on a second. Are you talking about the formula Dr. Gus Peters has been working on?"

"You've heard of it?"

"Yes, it's the one trial every hospital in the US has been hoping for. I didn't even know it had a name yet, or that work had started on it."

"It has started, but nothing is official yet."

"Then why has Dr. Rikus written it down?"

"I received a couple of containers."

"You got your hands on a few containers? How? From who, Holly?"

"It doesn't matter, Mom. I don't want to talk about it."

Her mother was silent. "Holly Scallanger. Do you know Dr. Peters? Was he your gynecologist?"

"No, he wasn't." Holly hoped her short reply would end Jane's questioning. It didn't.

"Then... none of this is making any sense."

"I don't want it to make sense, just drop it, please."

Jane gasped, a hand to her chest. "That son of a bitch. Dr. Peters is the baby's father, isn't he?" she blurted, her tone angry.

"No! Are you insane? I told you Jamie's father wasn't married."

"Then how did you get the supplement?"

"Mom, really!"

"He has a son..." she trailed off.

Holly froze. Her mother had untangled the riddle her father had been bugging her about.

"It was him! That little asswipe. He's just been nominated for an award, you know that, right?"

"What? He's only an intern."

"Holly, P&E is a family business. He performed major head surgery, removing four tumors with some doctor from China. It was a huge medical miracle, one where the patient woke without any complications. They felt they needed to give him an award for his assistance."

Holly felt the air leave her lungs. *Breathe,* she ordered herself.

"What is it, baby girl?"

"Further confirmation that he's gone on with his life, winning awards and whatnot like nothing else has happened in it, and here I am fighting for mine and our baby's."

"Is that why you are going through all of this?"

"No, Mom. I want this baby. I don't care how he feels about me, and even though in the beginning I didn't want her as much as he did, our roles reversed."

Jane frowned. "He wanted the baby?"

"Don't, please."

"It doesn't make any sense, Holly. Men don't just—"

"Mom, please!"

"Fine, I'll leave it. But if he crosses my path, rest assured, I will strangle him."

Holly giggled despite the situation when a picture formed in her head; a deranged, older woman attacking a much younger man and strangling him, whilst hanging on for dear life off of his back.

Apparently, Jane had the same vision and she, too, started to giggle. "Why do these things happen? You know this baby will more than likely be the spitting image of that rat bastard?"

"I've made peace with that."

"Honey, I'm truly worried about you."

"You, Mom, aren't the only one."

By now, Jane was sitting on the bed. She leaned forward, resting her head close to Holly's. "Well, I'm here now. It's going to be okay."

"Thanks for coming, Mom. Means more to me than you'll know. Don't ever say anything, but Dad isn't one of the most understanding beings out there."

"I don't know how you've managed to live with him. I can just imagine what Gabriella is like."

"You mean Gabby. Or Plastic Gabby, as Penelope calls her."

"Penelope?" Jane queried, eyebrows raised.

"A lovely lady. She's an employee of Dad's, runs the house, while Gabby sips on cocktails and goes for spa treatments."

Her mother shook her head. "To think of all the things I did for that man."

"Don't think about it, Mom. It's not worth it."

"I bet he has it all, right?"

"Don't even get me started. It would only infuriate you more, and then you might turn into a serial killer."

Her mother laughed out loud. "He's so not worth it. But Jake Peters is."

"Don't tell Dad, please. You know what he's like, and I really don't want Jake to find out I've kept the baby. I don't have the money to sue him."

"No, you don't. But your father does."

"Mom, forget it. He's done more than enough, and I am grateful. Still, I can't help but wonder what he's going to want in return when all this is over."

"Hopefully, nothing. Or I will fucking kill him."

Holly snorted.

"Just be thankful right along with me for now. Pretty please?" Holly smirked.

"Oh, okay. I promise." Jane rolled her eyes.

"Where are you staying?"

"Nowhere, yet. I'll book myself into a motel or something."

"I can always ask Dad—"

"Hold it right there, young lady. I can think of four words. Over. My. Dead. Body." Jane punctuated every word with her index finger. It was quite comical.

Holly giggled. "I'm sure that can be arranged."

"Funny," Jane replied, sarcastically. "You need your rest, and I desperately need coffee. Try to get some shut-eye."

"Thanks, Mom." Holly watched her mother get up and walk to the door. "Mom," she called.

Jane turned back. "What is it, sweetheart?"

"Thank you for coming. I've really missed you."

"My pleasure. And ditto that, baby girl."

Holly smiled and closed her eyes at her mother's words.

TWENTY-NINE

HOLLY WASN'T RELEASED from hospital the next day as she'd hoped. Doctor Rikus requested she stay as she'd been admitted four times in the past month. In case she took a turn for the worst, he wanted her close by so he could attend to her immediately.

By the third week, Jane busied herself in trying to make Holly's room a bit more homey, buying a crystal vase in which she arranged a variety of beautiful and bright flowers. She also made sure that the staff replaced the flowers every second day, and that the cost was to be added to Charles' account.

Holly thought it hilarious. She also thought her father would bitch and moan about it all, but he uttered not one word.

Gabby miraculously appeared for a visit every time her mother happened to be there. She really was a shallow bitch. Jane, however, took it all in her stride and made herself scarce by announcing she needed coffee or something to eat every time they waltzed into her room.

The four weeks Holly spent in hospital went by ever so slowly, at least that's how it felt, but when Holly finally reached twenty-four weeks in her pregnancy, she felt as if the hospital's walls were going to suffocate her.

Dr. Rikus did everything in his power to make it as comfortable for her as possible. He'd really turned out to be one amazing doctor, for which Holly was deeply thankful.

One morning, Holly woke up to the sound of the alarm on the fetal monitor, and a terrible pain in her lower abdomen. The heartbeat seemed much more rapid than usual. She knew it was supposed to be fast but somehow that didn't make her feel any better. She reached for the emergency button and pressed it.

Two nurses immediately ran into her room.

"What's wrong?" one asked.

"Look." Holly pointed at the monitor, which had both nurses smiling. "And my belly hurts."

The expression on their faces changed rapidly.

"Call Dr. Rikus," one nurse said to the other, who immediately rushed out of the room.

Holly continued to stare at the monitor. Something deep inside her didn't feel right, though. The pain in her abdomen was constant, not like a Braxton Hicks contraction. Whatever it was, she couldn't even guess at.

Dr. Rikus ran into her room, closely followed by Jane.

The look on her face was one of question, showing that they hadn't come together. Her eyes widened the minute she saw all the doctors and nurses in the room.

"What is going on?" She ran to Holly's side.

"Baby's heartbeat picked up."

"That's a good sign, sweetheart." Jane smiled at her, holding Holly's hand tightly, while Dr. Rikus checked the monitor.

"I'm not feeling too well, though. It hurts."

"Where?" asked Dr. Rikus, his face serious.

"My abdomen hurts."

"I need an ultrasound, now!" he barked, to no one in particular.

"Is something wrong with the baby?"

"No, it sounds good, but I have to make sure that she's doing okay."

Holly breathed deeply and smiled. "She's getting better."

"It seems like that's the case, but we will confirm it shortly, Holly," he reasoned, just as the ultrasound machine was rolled into the room.

Doctor Rikus began examining her belly.

Jane didn't take her eyes off the monitor, smiling when she saw the baby, but gasped a couple of seconds later.

"What is it, Mom?" Holly asked, panic setting in.

Dr. Rikus looked at Jane, concern lacing his eyes. "You have twins in your family?"

"Twins?" Holly was dumbfounded.

"Holly had a twin. We lost Jamie to leukemia about ten years ago. Is that..."

Dr. Rikus nodded, an expression of shock and surprise on his face.

"What? I am here, you know!" By now, Holly was frustrated and worried.

"There are two, baby girl."

"Two what?"

"Babies! You're pregnant with twins."

"What! How is that even possible? There was one just a minute ago."

"No," said Dr. Rikus. "There were always two. It's just that one sometimes hides behind the other. And that makes it hard to pick up as in some cases, their hearts beat in synchronization. Just let me check a few things on the sneaky one."

The doctor suddenly cussed, which wasn't good practice. It

had to have been something worth swearing over. His entire posture changed.

"What now? I don't think I can handle any more revelations!" Holly felt like she was going to pass out.

"It looks like the second baby's placenta is separating from your uterus. She can't get oxygen without it, and you, my dear, are bleeding. Get me the other monitor, like yesterday, people!" he barked.

The poor nurses jumped in fright and scrambled out of the room at his command.

"What's wrong, Doctor Rikus?" Charles eventually asked, having joined them without anyone noticing.

"We have to find what caused the change in heartbeat."

When the second monitor was brought in—one that had the ability to detect both heartbeats—the doctor immediately strapped the band around Holly's belly, removing the first one.

Holly, Jane and Charles simultaneously gasped at the difference in the girls' heartbeat. One was clearly struggling.

"We have to get them out."

"What? Are you insane? It's only twenty-four weeks!" Holly couldn't contain her tears.

"We have no choice, Holly. This is their only chance at survival. We need to deliver them, and now."

Holly's own heart beat uncontrollably.

"It's okay, baby girl. Deep breaths," her mother whispered, holding on tight to her daughter's hand as the nurses began preparing Holly for what was to come.

Holly tears turned to heart-wrenching sobs. "They aren't going to make it. How can they? They are too tiny."

"They?" asked Charles in apparent shock, eyes widening, clearly not having cottoned on to the fact that two babies were being talked about.

Nodding, Holly sobbed her confirmation. "I'm pregnant with twins, Dad."

Charles' eyes seemed to widen even further, but he said no more.

Jane had tears in her eyes, too. And all Charles could do after the news he'd just received was rub his hands together. If he kept that up, he'd rub all his skin off, so much was his worry.

"Shh, don't think like that. It's a miracle you carried them for this long. They will be fine, Holly. I know it. I can feel it, and I'll pray like I've never prayed before. Just stay strong, okay?" Jane smiled down at Holly, albeit if it had ended up being a wobbly one.

Holly nodded, but she didn't feel as her mother did. She was terrified, not for her life, but for the lives of her babies. Should she live and the babies not, she didn't know how she could possibly be able to handle such a tragedy, if she'd handle it at all. If that happened, fate was a cruel motherfucker.

Holly was wheeled into the operating room. Everything was happening so fast; her head was spinning, her heart was beating erratically, and she was praying all the while that her babies would be saved.

The anesthesiologist arrived and began his preparations. The only other doctor they were still waiting on was the neonatologist, Dr. Edwards.

"Don't worry, Holly. Dr. Edwards is one of the best, if not the best in the world. If he can't pull these two babies through, nobody can."

Holly managed a nod and felt her body going numb, the epidural was kicking in. They connected her to a fancy surgical monitor while they waited for Doctor Edwards.

The anesthesiologist was on the phone, saying something about needing blood.

She caught Doctor Rikus' eyes. "Can my mom come in, please? She's a nurse."

He nodded once, and one of the nurses led her mother to another room to change into scrubs.

Everything happened extremely fast after that. The room was spinning out of control, and Doctor Rikus' voice, as well as the nurses' turned into dull sounds.

Holly took a couple of deep breaths, all the while keeping vigil on the door. She had never panicked like that before. Her heartbeat pounded way too fast, yet it felt as if she could hear every single beat.

The last figure she saw before the world went quiet and black, was Jake hurtling into the room and into view. Then a beep emanated from the monitor.

HOLLY WOKE IN A PANIC. She wasn't in the OR anymore, nor was she in her private room. She didn't feel the ache in her heart, quite the opposite in fact—peace. It was the most amazing feeling ever.

But there was something she needed to remember which was odd, but she couldn't recall what that something was. The feeling inside her was wonderful, she couldn't explain it other than the fact that it was pure serenity. She usually only felt that for a mere second before her reality crashed down on her, but what that reality was she didn't know, either.

A gentle hand touched her shoulder and she moved her head to the side. It was like she was looking in a mirror, but when the image smiled, Holly shook her head.

The image, however, didn't mimic her action.

"Jamie?" Holly whispered.

Her sister laughed, tears evident in her eyes.

"How is this possible?" Holly grabbed her sister around the neck.

"You know it's not normal if you're able to see me, Holls Polls."

Holly's heart skipped a beat at the nickname Jamie had always called her by. "I don't care. I've missed you so damn much."

"I have missed you, too. But you can't stay. You can still go back."

"Still go back? Where?"

"You know where."

Holly tried to think, but it was like her mind was blank. She looked at Jamie and shook her head.

"You know. I haven't been with you for a long time. Think about what happened to me, Holls Polls. Think, please. It's important."

An awful sadness filled Holly, and then images of Jamie's coffin filled her head. She saw her mother crying and screaming while she just stood there, watching her best friend and sister being whisked away from her.

"No! It can't be. Am I dead?"

"You can still go back. Your babies need you, Mom needs you, and he..." Jamie trailed off, closing her eyes.

"He? Who are you talking about?"

Jamie opened her eyes. "Secrets; there are a few you need to unlock. You need to go back, Holly, and figure out the truth. You *have* to go back. You must take care of those beautiful girls and find your happiness again."

"I'm happy now."

"Follow Mom's path, it will lead you to the truth."

"Mom's path? What do you mean?"

"You will know when you wake up."

All of a sudden, Jamie screamed, "Now, wake up!"

Holly's eyes flew open.

"She's back," she heard Dr. Rikus say with relief.

What the hell just happened?

She could've sworn she'd seen her sister, however unlikely that was. But she knew she had... somehow.

What had they been talking about? A path. What else? Her thoughts disappeared faster than she could hold on to them, until the only thing she remembered was the distant memory that she had definitely seen Jamie.

Her eyes closed again, and that was the precise moment she remembered the last thing she'd seen before she'd slipped into that serenity.

Jake. He's here!

THE NEXT TIME she woke up, her chest hurt, as if someone had cut into it with a knife. A stronger pain jolted through her body.

Jamie. Jake.

Her eyes flew open and landed on her mother, who was asleep in the chair next to her bed.

"Mom," she whispered, but Jane didn't move.

"Mom," she called again, slightly louder this time.

Jane jumped in her chair. When she focused on Holly, she promptly burst into tears, got up and held her daughter tightly. "Oh, thank you, Lord! I thought I'd lost you. I just got in when the babies were delivered... that horrible noise filled the room..." She bit her lip and let out a sob. "I thought I'd lost another daughter."

"Where are they? My babies? Is Jake with them?"

Her mother frowned, and then shook her head.

"Mom, I saw him."

Silence filled the room and her mother closed her eyes.

"Mom?"

"He's not here, sweetheart."

"I don't believe you. I saw him, right before—"

Jane halted anything further by putting her hand up. "He didn't come, Holly."

"He's not here? But I..." The ache of missing him, and the reality of him still not wanting them made her feel as if she wanted to die.

"In near death experiences, sometimes our mind plays tricks and it makes us see the people we want to see the most."

Holly shook her head and started to cry. It felt as if her heart had broken all over again. He wasn't there, he'd never come. What a cruel trick her mind had played on her this time.

"Shh, now. The babies are fine, but they need you, Holly."

She nodded, her lips wobbling, unable to subdue her tears.

Why? Why, fucking why did my mind play such a dumbass trick on me?

She was sure she'd seen him right before she'd exited the world. He'd been right there. All she was left with now was the fact that he'd never been there at all. She thought about her babies again. They were all alone. Nobody was with them. Nobody.

"Can I see them?"

"I'll go ask Doctor Rikus."

As soon as her mother left, Holly wiped the last image of seeing Jake running into the room from her mind. It hadn't been real, only her deepest wish her mind had tried to turn into reality, but the reality was that he would never be there for any of them.

She needed to let him go and take care of the two precious babies he would never get the chance to know. His life would be empty, even though he didn't know it yet. It would be empty with no real love again, because nobody would ever love Jake Peters the way she'd loved him and nobody, except for her two girls, would ever receive her love ever again.

Dr. Rikus walked into her room accompanied by Jane. Relief washed over his face. "You have no idea how happy I am to see you alive and breathing."

"Me, too. How are they doing?"

"They are tiny but fighting, Holly. Dr. Edwards is doing everything he can. He's been working for 48 hours straight."

"Two days? I was out for two days?"

Jane grabbed hold of her hand. "You're awake now, sweetheart." Turning to Doctor Rikus, she pleaded, "Can she please see the babies?"

He shone the light into her eyes, did a thorough checkup, which felt like it lasted for hours when in fact was merely minutes, and finally acquiesced. "I'll get her a wheelchair," he stated, then disappeared.

Jane touched Holly's cheek gently and looked into her eyes. "Sweetheart, he wasn't joking when he said they are tiny. There are quite a number of tubes attached to their little bodies. You need to be prepared. No crying you hear? Just give them lots of love so they're can feel how much you care and want them."

Holly nodded. "Just take me to them, please, Mom."

"Okay," she said, mentally sighing on her daughter's behalf.

Dr. Rikus had brought her a wheelchair, and both he and Jane helped Holly into it. Placing his hand on her shoulder, he squeezed lightly. She was wheeled into NICU, which was where babies who needed extra care, or were battling serious issues were kept.

Holly found her father sitting between both incubators, reading *Sam I Am* to his granddaughters in the softest tone he could muster.

Holly sucked her lips in when her eyes caught sight of one very tiny baby. *Why couldn't I have carried them longer? Why?*

"Charles," Jane whispered.

When he looked up, his eyes were filled with tears. He closed the book, stood up and placed it on the chair he'd just vacated. He then walked toward Holly, leaned over and hugged her. "Thank you for waking up."

"Thank you for reading *Sam I Am* to them."

"It's a grandfather's duty." He winked.

Holly smiled at her father. *Gus... no,* she stopped her thought immediately. Those people did not matter anymore. Her family consisted of her, Jamie Bernice, and Romalia. She froze.

Where did that come from?

Robyn Amelia—Romalia—her other little girl's name just popped up without warning. She'd never thought of it, or even said it out loud. It was as if a higher power had inserted it into her head. It was meant to be. Jamie's twin would be named after Amelia and Robin.

Charles stepped behind Holly and wheeled her between the incubators.

Her lips trembled when she looked from one precious baby to the other. They really were tiny. However, they had one thing going for them; Scallanger blood ran through their veins. They'd pull through. Holly believed that with her whole being. She already loved them more than life itself.

A doctor, who seemed to be as tall as Holly was, stopped directly in front of her wheelchair.

She looked up at him. He had gray hair and the friendliest face she had ever seen.

"Miss Scallanger, I'm Dr. Edwards. May I have a word with you, please?"

Holly looked at the incubators, reluctant to leave her babies.

"I promise it won't take long, but there are a few things we need to discuss."

She nodded.

Jane pushed her into the room next door, filled with chairs and a coffee machine.

"One thing you need to know, and I say this to all my patients' parents, miracles do happen. But, there are times when they don't. Where the latter is concerned, one has to be strong enough to let go."

Holly's lip began to tremble.

Dr. Edwards crouched in front of her. "I'm only trying to prepare you for the worst. Your twins are extremely premature... anything can happen."

Holly nodded.

"You need to be strong, because in that room it's a no-crying zone. They are very sensitive and are able to feel every single emotion emitted. What you want them to feel is an abundance of love, which in turn will give them the strength to fight."

"Okay," she whispered.

"One more thing. Your mother wasn't able to share any information with me regarding their father."

"He's not a part of our family, nor do I want him to be."

"I respect that, Holly, but I do need his details in order to complete their birth certificates."

"Dr. Edwards. He has no interest in his daughters, so he is nothing in their lives. As far as I'm concerned, he falls under the 'not applicable' category. They will bear my name."

He frowned. "I'm sorry to hear that. These situations always sadden me. He wasn't interested in them at all?"

"His only interest was in wanting me to abort them."

Dr. Edwards stood up and rolled his shoulders in an agitated manner. "Not applicable it is."

"Do you need anything else?"

He shook his head. "That will be all for now, thank you. I'll see you soon."

Jane took her chair by its handles and rolled her back into NICU.

Holly was given an anti-bacterial liquid for her hands, and when the nurse was satisfied, Jane moved her between the incubators once again.

Smiling, although what she really felt like doing was cry, Holly stretched both arms out and pushed her hand through into each incubator. "Hi, Jamie Bernice. Hi, Romalia. It's your mommy. I want you both to know that I love you so, so much. But, you've got to fight and be strong, okay? Think you can do that?" Her voice was gentle and sweet.

She touched their tiny hands softly and closed her eyes. She didn't know which had been born when, but she knew that Romalia was the one who was struggling the most. It was evident, as she was smaller than Jamie Bernice.

Please, God, don't take them away. I'm not ready to let them go... I never will be.

Holly closed her eyes. Unbeknownst to her, Charles had sat down once again. She only realized how close he was when she heard his voice, soft and gentle. He'd begun to read *Sam I Am* again to her two tiny, precious miracles. Tears formed in her eyes, but she refused to let them fall. Looking at her father, she smiled.

THIRTY

ROMY WASN'T DOING VERY WELL. A few days had gone by and every time Holly saw her fragile little body fighting hard to stay alive, she just wanted to break down and cry. Jamie Bernice wasn't faring any better, but she was indeed the stronger of the two.

Her dad had pulled through big time, paying for everything without any complaint or requests for return payments, which he usually did when anyone borrowed money from him. He even stayed late into the night, keeping Romy and Jamie company.

Both were allowed human contact where Holly was concerned—breast-to-breast—Dr. Edwards called it. He was a sweetheart, and she wasn't the only one who thought so. Holly had seen her mother's eyes sparkle every time he made an appearance.

He was one of Holly's heroes, too. His help with the girls was immeasurable, and he did everything in his power to make sure that they would pull through.

The mental picture of what her babies looked like at this poignant time in their lives would stay with her for as long as she lived. The number of tubes protruding from their little bodies were so much, it was a wonder they managed to breathe at all. Still, they improved almost daily.

Jane and Charles would take turns sitting with Holly and the babies.

She was beyond tired, mostly due to lack of sleep. Her worry that something bad would happen the minute she closed her eyes prevented her from getting the much needed sleep her body so desperately craved. She was adamant that she wouldn't let that happen and drank copious amounts of coffee, one cup after the other, until it got to a point where her body was no longer able to function. So it happened that one evening she passed out cold in her chair, right next to the incubators.

When Holly opened her eyes, she realized she was back in her private room. That startled her, and then panic set in.

She hastily climbed out of bed and rushed to NICU, stopping dead in her tracks when she found her father sitting with one of the twins in his arms. Further contact had been extended to both Charles and Jane. By the size of the baby and dark fluff at the nape of her neck, she knew he was holding Jamie.

"Why did you let me sleep?" she whispered.

"Holly, you were dead tired. You needed it. No way can you go on without rest. Besides, your mother and I are here to help you."

"Dad, anything could've happened! I can sleep some other time."

"Nothing happened. Calm down," he reassured softly, giving her the gentlest look he could muster.

"Thank you, Dad."

"That has to stop. Stop thanking me, Holly. I should be the one thanking you for allowing me be a part of both my granddaughters' lives."

Holly swallowed the lump in her throat, but sent a smile his way as she softly brushed her lips against Jamie's head.

Although contact was allowed, it came with a time limit. So, when the allotted ten minutes were over, the nurse placed Jamie back in her incubator, while Holly handed her father his shirt. The breast-to-breast rule applied to Charles as well, except Dr. Edwards called it chest-to-chest, for manly reasons. He was truly one of the kindest men Holly had ever met.

"Has Romy had her time yet?" she asked, watching her lying in her favorite position.

Charles shook his head, tears glistening in his eyes.

"What's wrong, Dad?"

He cleared his throat. "Dr. Edwards said she's too critical for one-on-one contact at the moment. It's best to leave her in the incubator."

Holly's heart skipped a beat and her bottom lip began to quiver.

Please, Lord, don't take Romalia from me. I know I'm being selfish, she prayed softly, *when I have two babies, where others who only want one aren't capable of having even that. But... I love them so very much; they are my heart and my soul. You gave them to me for a reason, so please let them fulfill their destinies*

She felt her father's hand take hold of hers. "I know how you feel, Holly. I don't think I've ever prayed so much in my entire life."

She covered his hand with her other. "Thank you. I know you don't want me thanking you, but I don't know what would've happened if you hadn't been there for me."

"Holly..." Charles paused and lowered his head, chin to chest. When he looked up, his eyes were sad. "I know I fucked up, big time, and let both you and Jamie down. I was a coward. It's time I admit that. But I can't go back and fix my wrongs, no matter how much I wish I could. But I can step up to the plate now and do right by you. I... I just want a second chance." He all but choked up with every single word he uttered.

"Dad. Everything you've just said? Hit me right here." Holly pointed at her heart. "You can't even begin to comprehend how much that means to me. You've more than stepped up to the plate. I could not have done any of this without you, and I'm not solely talking about your financial help. So, Dad"—Holly smiled at him tearfully—"you more than deserve a second chance. And, in case you haven't noticed, I even think Mom is going soft on you."

That made Charles chuckle. "I really need to make amends with her too, don't I?"

"It would be a start."

Charles reached out for Holly and pulled her into a bear hug of note.

Her arms automatically wrapped themselves around him, too, and her body shook with sobs she wanted to let loose so badly but couldn't. Not yet.

"Shh, this is a no-crying zone, remember? It's not good for the babies."

She stood up straight, wiped her eyes and smiled. "I know. I need to stay strong for them." She pushed her hand inside of Romalia's incubator and stroked her back softly. Her skin was so delicate and Holly imagined that it could break and tear at any moment.

Charles stayed with her, making up for old times, until Jane relieved him at around five in the morning. She smiled at him as he said goodbye, and then kissed Holly on her head before she sat down.

"How are my grandbabies doing?"

"Romy is not in a good place, Mom. Dr. Edwards suggested we hold off on the one-on-one for a while."

Jane stroked Holly's cheek. "He knows what he is doing. They say he's one of the best neonatologists in the country."

"I certainly believe so, and he's just wonderful with them. I guess I'm just scared."

"Nothing can ever prepare a mother for this type of situation. It's not the way it was meant to be."

Holly nodded. She understood a little of what her mom had gone through now with Jamie's death. It was time she stopping judging her for drowning herself in booze for so many years. The thought of losing either Romalia or Jamie, or both, was so hard to contemplate, she could only imagine what it must feel like to really lose a child. All Holly could do was pray day and night that it wouldn't happen to her.

Then she had another thought. It just zapped through her mind, and she asked her mother for her phone.

Jane handed it to her without any question, at first.

Holly started typing his number.

"Who are you phoning, baby?"

"Him, to tell him what a fucking mess he's left me in."

Jane grabbed the phone out of her hands before she could type in the last number.

"What good is that going to do, Holls? He left you, didn't want anything to do with you. A baby isn't going to change that. You know that."

"I know, but he needs to know how I feel, Mom."

"He doesn't care, sweetheart. As much as that hurts me to say to you, he doesn't care."

"What if—"

"Holly, *what if* doesn't exist, not for us Scallangers."

Tears rolled down Holly's cheeks. She got up and left. Next thing, she felt a pair of arms wrap around her shoulders. Somehow, she knew it wasn't either her father or her mother. She looked up to find Dr. Edwards looking at her sadly.

"It's okay. You need to cry." He stroked her back. "Who did you try to call, just now when your mom grabbed the phone?"

"Nobody." She sniffed.

"Was it the father?"

"It doesn't matter, he didn't want us. It's not going to change."

She stepped out of his embrace and wiped her eyes with the sleeve of her robe.

"Holly, who is he?"

She smiled. "I told you before, he's not applicable, and that is exactly how he's going to remain, Dr. Edwards."

He nodded, and thankful he wasn't going to push, she went back inside.

A while later, when she returned to her babies, her mother wanted to know everything, and since her father wasn't there anymore, Holly shared every detail she could with her. How he used to make her feel; how he'd said that he was going to get them a place together, and how it had all sounded like a dream.

"He sent me a text that morning, telling me we needed to go see his mother, talk to her, and basically sort shit out."

She recounted what took place once she arrived at Mara's.

Jane listened intently, and by the end was totally shocked. "That was it? He told you that it was what it was and he had to go? Not even an apology or explanation?"

She confirmed with a nod.

"That fucking bastard!"

"Tell me about it."

"You can never try to phone him again, you hear? That can never happen, baby. He was a coward and no coward is good enough for you."

She stroked her mother's arm. "Yeah, I know. I really appreciate your support, Mom."

Just then, Dr. Edwards entered the NICU to checkup on the twins.

Holly and Jane had been so immersed in their conversation, they hadn't noticed the small spots on Romy's arms and legs.

Noticing Dr. Edwards looking closely at Romalia, Holly became alarmed. "What is that?" she queried, her breath catching in her throat.

Dr. Edwards gave her a sad look. He was visibly shaken.

"No!" Holly began to cry. "Please don't tell me there's nothing you can do for her."

"Let's go outside, Holly."

"It's okay, baby girl. I'll stay with them."

Holly sobbed quietly as Dr. Edwards led her out of the ward. "Please... is there nothing you can do? What are those spots?"

"Normal under the circumstances. But, she is fighting for her life, Holly. And although she's been the fiercest little trooper I've come across, her body is just too weak."

Holly's hand went to her stomach and she doubled over, almost as if she'd been stabbed, and the other covered her mouth. Tear careened down her face freely, dotting the floor where they fell and splattered.

Dr. Edwards took her in his arms, holding her close to his chest. "I'm so sorry."

"How long?"

"It's only a matter of days now. She will worsen, and the spots will grow. She's not in a good place, Holly."

"What can I do?"

"Help her go."

"You're asking me to kill my baby?"

"I would never ask that of anyone, let alone a parent. No, I'm asking that you to let her go. She's fought a long, hard battle for her tiny body. Babies go straight to Heaven, you know."

"I don't want her in Heaven, I want her to stay here."

"I know." He held her tighter. "Believe me, if I could do anything further, I would. Her organs are failing."

Holly merely nodded. She didn't want to let her baby go, but she had no choice. Romy was suffering and there was absolutely nothing any of them could do. She could give her everlasting life, elsewhere, and she could make sure that Romy knew how much she was loved.

"Can I hold her?"

"For as long as you want."

"Thank you." She wiped her tears as she tried to regain her composure. "My father's not here. Can we wait a while so he can say goodbye, too?"

"Of course. She's not going anywhere just yet."

Dr. Edwards handed Holly his phone.

Holly admired his perceptiveness. Taking the phone from him, she dialed. By now, she knew his number by heart. It rang and rang, and just when she thought it would go over to voicemail, he answered.

"Charles here."

"Dad? It's me." She sniffed into the phone. "Romy is not well... she's not going to make it." She started to cry all over again. "Dr. Edwards just told me. We need to say goodb..." She choked on the word, and couldn't speak to her father anymore. Her sobs were uncontrollable.

She heard Dr. Edwards speaking to her father. When she'd broken down, he took the phone from her.

Holly sagged against the wall and slid to the ground until her backside connected with the floor.

She felt Dr. Edwards' arms around her shoulders again; the call must have come to an end. She finally succumbed to the immanent tragedy on the verge of unfolding. She wept for her little girl. For the baby she was going to have to let go. And the wonderful man at her side, Dr. Edwards, cried along with her, too.

"...miracles do happen. But, there are times when they don't. Where the latter is concerned, one has to be strong enough to let go."

Those had been the exact words he'd uttered to her the first time she'd seen her babies. She knew she needed to be strong now, but it was a damn near impossible task, an almost fucking impossible one.

One of the nurses who'd helped her throughout the past week took Dr. Edwards' place as he excused himself. She sat down next to Holly and wrapping her arms around her body, cried right along with her, too.

Holly allowed her to be the comfort she so desperately needed. Along with her pain and sorrow, rage began to fester. She hated Jake Peters now more than ever, and hoped to never see or hear from him again as long as she lived.

She had been so fucking stupid for almost having called him earlier. He was a coward, pure scum of the earth forever even thinking she would be as hollow and shallow as to contemplate abortion.

Mara had been right; he wasn't ready to be a father, and as far as Holly was concerned, he wasn't fit to be a human being, either.

It was inevitable that the day would come when he would find out what happened. She just hoped she wouldn't be around anymore, because he deserved every ounce of unhappiness when he met the woman who would introduce herself as his daughter. And then, he'd be dealt a further blow when she explained to him what had happened to her twin.

That day would come, of that she had no doubt. As was often said, what goes around comes around. She wondered if he'd be mature enough to embrace the pain she was feeling right that second, in that very moment.

Holly cleared her mind and pulled herself together.

"No mother should have to go through this. I can't imagine what it must feel like. What you're going through."

"Do you have children?"

The nurse nodded.

Holly squeezed her hand. "Just love them with everything you have, because we never know what fate has in store for us."

"Oh, I do. Believe me, I do." The nurse helped Holly up.

Just then, the elevator opened and her father walked out.

Holly ran into his arms.

Charles embraced her tightly. He didn't shed a tear, but it was clear from his red-rimmed eyes that he'd cried his heart out. He took a deep breath and walked with Holly back into NICU.

Dr. Edwards was waiting for them by Romalia's incubator, trying just as hard not to cry again.

"Are you ready?" he asked.

Holly shook her head. "I'll never be ready. But I don't want her to suffer anymore."

Dr. Edwards opened the incubator, removed the tubes from her nose, and from her tiny body. She'd looked like a robot baby for nine days. When he was done, he picked Romy up and gently placed her in Holly's arms.

Holly kissed her forehead and the tip of her nose before settling into a chair.

Charles crouched beside her, and kissed Romy's head softly.

Holly struggled to keep the tears at bay, but she tried, nevertheless. Love was the only thing she could think about if she was to convey to Romy how much she meant not only to her mother, but to everyone whose heart she'd crept into.

Romalia's attempts at breathing escalated as she struggled to take in air. And it was at that precise moment that something monumental entered Holly's head. Romy had shared the same confined space with her sister, all curled up, for five and a half months. That was exactly the manner in which she should leave this world.

"Dr. Edwards?" Holly called.

He'd been standing to one side, respecting Holly's time with her baby.

"Can I put her with Jamie? I think it's the way she should leave... it would be the right way. Would that be okay? With all of you?"

She looked at her parents.

Charles nodded while looking at the floor.

Jane kissed her on the temple, and then bent to place the softest kiss on Romy's head. "I think that's a beautiful idea. Very grown up." She smiled at Holly.

By way of answering Holly's question, Dr. Edwards opened Jamie's incubator.

Holly stood up and carefully took the two steps she needed to reach the incubator. Whispering words of love only meant for Romy, she settled her precious bundle down next to her sister.

Dr. Edwards fastened the lid and stepped back.

Jane and Charles, with Holly between them, looked at the fragile little bodies lying against one another.

Romy suddenly shied away, as if she wanted to hide behind Jamie.

Holly knew that that was exactly what she was doing, because that was why she hadn't known about Romy until she had been ready to show herself.

The end ultimately came about ten minutes thereafter; little Romalia left the world.

Holly jumped up and ran out of the NICU. She just couldn't be strong anymore and she hated, hated, *hated* every single member of the Peters' family. Sadly, even little Ben, because he would grow up exactly like the rest of his siblings.

As far as she was concerned, they'd killed Romy by not giving her what she'd so desperately needed to keep her babies inside of her longer.

Holly found the nearest empty room and once inside, a rage the likes of which she'd never felt before overpowered her. Chairs flew against the wall, one after the other, she kicked a cabinet and attacked anything she could get her hands on. This went on until her father wrapped his arms around her, holding her tight; both crying uncontrollably.

At one point, Holly screamed as if she was being burned alive, trying to get rid of the emptiness within her. It was the most torturous scream Charles had ever heard. She would never, as long as there was breath in her body, ever forgive the Peters' for what they had done.

Never.

THIRTY-ONE

ROMY WAS GONE. Holly had the death certificate to prove it.

She'd decided on cremation and would keep her ashes in the tiniest, teddy bear vase her father had gotten her. Such was her heartbreak, she couldn't find it in herself to go back to NICU; there was just too much sadness inside of her, and that would do Jamie no good.

Having given in to exhaustion, Holly slept after the small ceremony her father and a couple of the staff attended. She desperately missed Bernie, ached to have her friend close by for support, but she couldn't phone her. It would be a mistake of huge proportions.

She'd dreamed of Jake again, the kind Jake with tears in his eyes as he'd looked at his daughter's ultrasound—at the time, they'd only known about one of the babies. She missed that Jake, but she knew he didn't exist. He'd purely been an illusion all along, some sort of sick act or joke. And to prove what, she didn't know. She would never know.

When she woke, she had a second of peace until the ache of losing Romy crept into her gut, consuming her entire body. She cried for what seemed like years, until she felt a soft touch and her mother's arms wrapping around her.

Jane cried along with her daughter. It was unbearable, and a part of Holly felt like dying, too. She didn't want to be on this earth.

Face it, Jamie is going to die, too, she kept telling herself. She believed it would only be a matter of days, so felt it was better to disconnect herself from Jamie—the sooner the better. She had to do it, even if her thoughts were the cruelest ones she'd ever had.

"Holly? Jamie needs you, now more than ever. Please, won't you go to her?"

"I can't, Mom."

"You've got to."

"Like you did?" Sarcasm laced her words.

Jane stared at her. Not in shock or anger, only sadness. "That is exactly why you need to get out of this bed and be there for your daughter, because I know what it's like not to. It's the one thing I regret most in my life, Holly. It eats me up on the inside, every single day. I don't want that for you."

Holly cried again. "Just leave me alone, please."

"Baby," Jane begged again.

"One hour, Mom. I need to find a place within me that won't affect Jamie, please."

Jane got up and kissed her daughter on the cheek.

Holly didn't glance her way. She prayed hard to find peace, love, and all things that were still beautiful in her life. For Jamie's sake. It was over an hour before she managed to leave her bed, and another hour of pacing in front of the NICU before she even attempted to go in.

Dr. Edwards smiled upon seeing her, and then opened the incubator.

Holly was too scared to look at Jamie, terrified that the same black spots marred her tiny legs. But when he placed Jamie against her chest, she couldn't help but look at her baby's legs. No spots were visible, and sighing in relief she prayed, giving thanks. She began to hum softly, gently rocking in the chair.

Contact time had increased to fifteen minutes, a good sign, or so she'd thought. It was over all too soon, as it had felt more like five seconds when Dr. Edwards returned, picked Jamie up and placed her back into the incubator.

This time, though, Holly didn't leave her side. From that moment on, she stayed with Jamie, day in and day out.

BY NOW, four weeks had passed, and Jamie was still with them. She'd struggled, but for some reason continued to pull through. Jamie, being the first born, or so Dr. Rikus told her, had always been stronger than Romalia and had even grown a couple of inches.

Holly had been pumping breast milk for the nurses to feed the babies, and now there was only one.

At first, they'd had to feed Jamie through a tube in her stomach, but of late Jamie had begun to drink from a bottle, not without some struggle. The nurses found it hard to sometimes get 5 milliliters into her little body as most of it spilled, but they'd eventually managed to get a fair amount in.

Throughout the time she spent with Jamie, she'd force Romy from her mind. She just couldn't think about the ache in her heart when she spent time with Jamie. The only peace Holly had where Romalia was concerned, was that she believed she was still with them, even though she was now in the afterlife; the plus side of having a twin in Heaven.

Jamie had looked exactly like Holly, and she knew that her sister would take care of her baby as if she were her own.

When Charles showed up one day, it was with a pacifier,

which he handed to Dr. Edwards. "I know I'm not a doctor, but I've read that pacifiers help with breathing and sucking." He hadn't sounded too sure when he shared his explanation, but Dr. Edwards had nodded his approval.

"We'll see if she will take to it. You got the smallest one, too, I see."

"I'm a man of many talents, doctor."

For the first time in a long time, Holly chuckled.

Charles took the chair next to hers. They watched as Dr. Edwards coaxed the pacifier gently into Jamie's mouth. She spat it out a couple of times, but around the fifth time it stayed in.

Holly's heart flip-flopped when she noticed the sucking movement on Jamie's jawline. It had worked.

"Thank you so much, Dad."

Charles gave his daughter a hug and kissed the top of her head. "It's a start. She's going to make it, Holly. I can feel it."

"She'd better make it."

"Oh, she will." Charles smiled, while watching Jamie sucking on the tiniest pacifier either had ever seen.

ANOTHER MONTH FLEW by in a whirl. Holly continued to stay at the hospital, but occasionally went to her mother's motel, which was thankfully close by, to take showers and catch up on sleep.

Jamie improved weekly and if progress continued in that manner, she would soon be allowed to go home. She had finally made it out of NICU and was now in the nursery.

Holly would cry for Romalia when she wasn't with Jamie, which would turn into a cursing session where the Peters' were concerned.

Jane and Holly had settled into a pattern; when one needed rest, the other would take over and sit with Jamie.

Holly came across many women with preeclampsia, most in week 32 of their pregnancy, and almost none in their first trimester. The more she spoke to them, making friends along the way, the more she wanted to help them. But she couldn't.

She didn't have the knowledge Dr. Rikus or Gus Peters had. He still hadn't given the go-ahead for the supplement to released, and by Dr. Rikus' as well the nurses' reaction during one of their discussions, he wasn't going to.

He'd apparently found something not to his satisfaction and terminated production entirely. Whatever he'd found to be wrong, Holly more than likely hadn't used it long enough to feel its side effects.

When she finally came across the press release and his reason as to why p47 had been terminated, he simply stated that it wasn't a good supplement, it didn't work, and wasn't fit to be consumed by anyone. Perhaps it had caused severe side effects with another of his patients, leading him into believing that it was too risky a chance to take.

Whatever his reason, Holly would remain grateful that she'd at least had a couple of months' worth in supplies, and as far as she was concerned it had worked in the short time she'd taken it.

Still, she wanted to help those women so badly. Seeing them suffer, scared of going through what she had was too painful for her. Until one day, something totally out of left field hit her. She might not have had the knowledge at that moment, but she was adamant she could gain it.

What if she studied to become a doctor? She'd always been a bright student, achieving mostly As in certain subjects. And her grandmother had always said that one was never too old to learn something new. Was it possible that she could very well become a doctor?

Those thoughts occupied her mind space quite a lot. Uppermost in her mind, though, was the fact that it would mean her path would cross with Jake's eventually, and that was one of the things she really didn't want. However, she weighed the pros and cons every second she spent with those women, it was a small price to pay.

Jake stood out in crowds, where she faded. But she'd always know when he'd be too close for comfort; the female doctors would alert her to that fact.

In the end, though, he'd surely find out. Word would spread, somehow, especially as she was determined to enter the exact field Gus was in, and work to achieve what he had so readily discarded—a supplement to help women through the situation they were in.

Still, it was a small price to pay. What she would have to do is be insanely careful not to mention Jamie. Her professional and personal lives would be poles apart. It could definitely work.

Holly couldn't hide the smile that spread across her face. She knew that it was the right thing to do. It was what she wanted. She was going to medical school. She wanted to share her good news with her mother, but came to the conclusion that she'd probably think Holly was wanting to step into Jake's shoes in the hope of seeing him again, even if that was the last thing she wanted. It was something her mother should by now know.

The day Charles Scallanger somehow found out who Jamie's father was, or what he did for a living, would be the day he would surely blow a gasket.

Instead, Holly waited for just the right time to tell her mother.

JAMIE WAS FINALLY DRINKING all her milk, and the best part was that she was drinking it from Holly's breast. She had to admit that it hurt like hell the first couple of weeks, but she was convinced that a mother's milk was best for babies. Also, her breasts needed the relief as she had milk for ten babies, not just one.

The women in the nursery all smiled as Holly walked in. Grace, the nurse who'd helped Holly the night Romalia passed on, had become a really good friend. She picked Jamie up and handed her over to Holly. As she looked down at her little girl, who at that moment was yawning, her lips formed a perfect O.

Holly cursed Murphy's Law, because little Jamie was the spitting image of her father; her skin such a gorgeous color it looked like she had a permanent tan, and her head was adorned with a bush of black hair.

"Ooh, that feels so good, yes it does," Holly cooed, as Jamie stretched, her tiny hands balled into fists, arms reaching past her head. She yawned once more, letting out a cry that sounded like a lamb's. It was too cute for words.

"I know, you're hungry. Just hold on, my little angel." She made her way to another room, one with a bed. Her mother had shown her an easier way to breastfeed, and it was much more comfortable than sitting in a chair.

She lay down on the bed with Jamie at her side, watching in awe as her mouth sucked, doing overtime. Holly couldn't help but stare at her.

Jamie really was one of the most beautiful babies in the ward, everyone said so. Even Dr. Edwards would look at her for hours and when he saw Holly, would always tell her how beautiful she was.

FINALLY, the day came for little Jamie to go home. Holly was a wreck, and her mind filled with worry. What if something happened and they couldn't get Jamie to the hospital in time? Or worse, what if she died in her sleep? She voiced her concerns to Dr. Edwards.

"Calm down, Holly. Her lungs are stronger than most babies', and she's already had her fair share of a hard time. No more. She'll be fine. Now go and raise your baby," Dr. Edwards assured soothingly.

Holly smiled at him, and then looked down at Jamie. She was sleeping all cozy in the sling her father had bought. It was like a little hammock that attached to her body and stretched from around her back to her chest, the perfect place in the entire world for little Jamie to be. "Okay. But if anything happens..."

"You'll have your mother there, who just happens to be one of the best nurses I've ever met. I doubt she would let her granddaughter want for anything, including the best care. Trust her."

"You're right." Holly finally relented, giving Dr. Edwards a hug, and trying not to squeeze Jamie between them in the process. "Thank you. For everything. None of this would have been possible without you, you do know that, right?" she added as they broke their hug. "I don't know what I would've done if I'd lost them both.

"It was with absolute pleasure, and she really is a gorgeous baby, Holly."

"That she is." Holly smiled.

"Will you do me a favor?"

"Sure, anything."

"Tell your mother I'm still waiting for her answer."

Holly's eyes narrowed. "You asked her on a date?"

He laughed. "I would be so lucky. No, I asked her if she

would consider working here at Seattle Memorial. We need more women like her."

"I will... wow! When did this happen?" Holly's expression was a mixture of astonishment and shock.

"A couple of days ago, but she told me she needed some time to think it over."

"I'm sure she will."

Dr. Edwards said goodbye, just as his beeper went off. "Got to go, sorry, duty calls."

"Go save some babies."

He smiled at Holly and waved as he walked away in the opposite direction.

Bennie had been sent to pick them up, and Holly smiled when she saw a big ass, expensive baby seat in the back of the car. Her father had really become the dad she'd always wanted, and she hoped to God he wouldn't change when she shared her future plans with him. Or when he found out that a doctor was the twins' father.

Bennie dropped them off at the motel Jane was staying in. When she walked in, she was overtly surprised.

Jane had arranged for a cake and a homemade banner, which read 'Welcome Home, Jamie' and had been hung on the wall. Even though it wasn't their home, her mother's gesture meant a lot.

They had tea and a slice of cake as they talked about their next steps.

"Mom? I need to tell you something," Holly said, whilst playing with her last bite of chocolate cake.

"What is on your mind, baby girl?"

"I've thought long and hard about this, so don't go thinking it's a spur of the moment kind of thing. I want to go back to school."

Jane smiled. "Children have the tendency to do that to a

person. Rethink their goals for the future to make sure they have a better one than you had."

Holly returned her smile, but it soon disappeared. "Don't judge me when I tell you what it is I want to do, please."

That made Jane frown, but before she could utter a single word, Holly blurted it out.

"I want to go to medical school."

Her mother's entire body puffed up.

"It's not what you think, okay? I don't care about him in the least. He's less than the dirt attached to the soles of my shoes. And especially not after what he's put me through, us through. I promise you that if our paths ever cross, I will run my legs off in the other direction. He will never know."

"Then why, Holly?"

"I want to help the women who are in the same position as I was. They don't need to go through that. They shouldn't have to go through that."

"You want to become a baby catcher?"

Holly laughed. "There is nothing wrong with being a baby catcher. I want to prevent what happened to me from happening to them. You said it yourself, no mother should go through that."

Jane nodded. "As long as you do it for the right reasons. But it's clear that yours are. I'm just not sure if, or how, you'll manage to hide from the Peters', Holly. They're a huge family, and each one wants to be smarter than the other. I mean, Jake really made a name for himself. There are even rumors that he has been offered an internship in China with Dr. Huyo, not to mention the rest of the Peters'."

He's going to China?

"I don't want to talk about them. Please. They are the scourge of the earth and have no clue what life is about. As far as I'm concerned, they're in the wrong profession! I'm doing this for the right reasons, Mom, and I'm doing it for me."

"Okay, Dr. Scallanger. How do you propose we get you through medical school? 'Cause I can promise you this, Charles Scallanger is going to close his hands if he discovers who the father is."

"Yeah, I know. I'll find a way, study hard, get good grades, get a scholarship. If that doesn't happen, then I'll borrow it. I really want to do this. No, it's more than want, I *have* to do this. It's like this has been my purpose all along."

Jane caressed Holly's cheek, a sad smile on her face.

"I'm going to need your help too, Mom."

"With what?"

Holly laughed. "With getting this one big."

Jane smiled. "Now that, my darling daughter, would be my pleasure."

SECRET LOVE

ONE

4 years later

The suitcase sat open on the bed.

The past four years hadn't been easy for twenty-eight-year-old, Holly Scallanger. She'd lost one child, and raised another on whatever she had.

If it hadn't been for Jane, her mother, she wouldn't have known how life would turn out. Her decision to become a doctor hadn't made life any easier, either. It was with thanks to the Lord that he'd created her with a good head on her shoulders, and placed people in her path who saw talent when it stood in front of them, hence being awarded a scholarship.

If it hadn't been for all the good that had ventured her way, well, she wouldn't have had the very suitcase that sat open on the bed that day.

"How many sleepies, Mommy?" the curly black head asked.

Her ice-green eyes made Holly's heart skip a beat every time she looked into them. Jamie truly looked so much like her dad, but as hard as it was, Holly thanked the Lord every night for having Jamie in her life. The almost four-year-old had been nothing but a blessing, and Holly couldn't imagine life without her.

"Did you find the calendar?"

Jamie hopped off the bed.

She really should get a haircut, Holly thought. The girl's black curls almost reached her bottom. *Just a trim though.*

If there was one thing Holly loved, it was Jamie's curls. She had them, too, but because of all the pulling and tugging caused by Jamie as a baby, Holly had cut it all off, so short she could barely put it into a ponytail.

Jamie returned with the calendar, one almost as big as she was. She flopped with it onto the bed, out of breath. "Here you go, Mommy. That thing is heavy."

Holly laughed as she went to the drawer next to her bed, retrieving a black marker, and went back to the calendar. She paged through the first five months until she got to June.

"That's your birthday date, and I promise I will be here, okay?"

Jamie's eyes continued to stare at the round circle her mother had drawn, her tiny lips pulled down in a frown.

"What is it, peanut?"

"That is a lot of sleepies." Jamie looked into Holly's eyes, her bottom lip now trembling a little.

"I know," Holly said, picking Jamie up and setting her on her lap. She gave her daughter a big hug. "Remember what we spoke about?"

Jamie nodded.

"I need you to be a brave little girl, and also be good for Nana."

"You won't go into the rainbow, too?" Jamie asked with a squeak in her voice.

"I promise. I'm staying as far away as I can from any rainbows, except when I'm chasing one. But I would still keep my distance as nothing, and I mean nothing, would ever take me away from you." Holly's heart turned into a knot as she thought about the rainbow.

Jamie was smart, too smart for a three-year-old, but it was to be expected. Her father was a genius, and Holly thought she had a pretty good head on her shoulders, too. She'd gotten it from both sides.

Ever since she was two, she'd asked the daddy question. Holly couldn't bring herself to tell a two-year-old the truth; Jamie wouldn't have understood, anyway.

So instead of telling Jamie that her daddy hadn't wanted her, she did the opposite. She told Jamie that he loved her, but he was stuck in a rainbow. The story evolved as she got a little older and Amelia, Robyn, Grandpa Gus, and all the others made their way into the rainbow, too. Every single one of them lived in a rainbow.

She was grateful that the Peters' were easy to google, so she ended up printing their photos. She'd stuck them in a book with their names above each respective picture. It was the only thing Holly had been able to do as Jamie's questions kept on coming. She wanted to know everything.

In the beginning, it had been extremely hard. Holly would end up crying every night before she went to bed. Angry tears would eventually turn into sad ones. Sad where Jake was concerned, because he was missing out on the most beautiful little girl, both on the inside and out.

At the time, she hadn't thought too much about her story, or even contemplated introducing her to Jake and the Peters'. But Jamie had wanted to know where her father was and what he looked like, and Holly had relented. Now, it seemed to be biting her in the ass.

She had been going to do her internship at Seattle Memorial, but a couple of months ago they had been told that there would be no internship program anymore, because they'd lost their status as a teaching hospital.

Holly and Rodney, her best friend who was gay but one would never say so, had to take whatever was available. She'd almost told Rodney the one day who Jamie's father was, but was thankful she hadn't.

As for the rainbow stories, she managed to keep those from him as well; the meaning of them that was, although he knew about them in a whole different way.

Rodney wanted to be a neurologist, and the best one around was Jake. It came as no surprise that he'd fast made a name for himself and became known as the doctor who'd take risks with tumors nobody else would. It all began with that first operation her mother had told her about. The one where he'd scrubbed in with a doctor from China; Dr. Huyo, who'd sort of become Jake's mentor. He'd even spent a year in China, which made Holly silently wish he'd never returned, but he had. Since then, he'd taken on patients who were close to death and added another twenty-five years to their future.

It was by no means easy to study to become a doctor with the Peters' receiving awards for practically everything, as well as attending lectures where their names popped up constantly. And it wasn't just Jake. They were all masters in their chosen fields.

Robyn had reached a huge goal, too. She'd become an oncologist and invented some kind of synthetic colon. She'd also found a cure for pancreatic cancer, and had won the Gillepsy Award.

If Rodney ever found out that the Peters' were the ones who'd left her in her time of need, and that Jake was Jamie's father, he would not want anything to do with him. He would only be second best, and Rodney needed to become the best. He deserved to be trained by the best, and he'd been wanting to meet Jake for a long time.

So, Rodney went to P&E, and Holly to Downsend. The distance between both hospitals was only about fifteen minutes, but she would find a way to steer as clear away from P&E as she could. That had been one of the reasons why she hadn't taken Jamie with her. She now knew what her father looked like, what all of them looked like, and Holly was scared that Jamie would accidentally run into one of them.

Holly breathed deeply just thinking about it all. Jake would be livid with her for having kept Jamie, but had he to meet her he'd also fall deeply in love with the little girl who had the tendency to crawl into one's heart, dirty feet and all. He would surely take her away.

One thing Holly didn't have was the money to fight Jake in court, and she doubted very much that grandpa Charles would hand it over in order to fight him, even though her father hated Jake's guts.

Charles had found out that Jamie's father was a doctor, the minute she'd told him about her great plan to become one herself.

Everything had stopped.

Charles had gone on to tell Holly that she needed to start paying him back. It was something Charles Scallanger just didn't understand. He didn't want that for her, and the only way he could keep her from her goal was to overpower her with the bills. Bills she'd somehow found a way to repay by working nights as a cleaning lady at an up-market hotel. She'd almost paid a tenth off but was convinced that once she became a doctor, it would be easier to pay her father in full. And then, she could finally tell him to stuff it.

Jake would definitely win should she ever come to that

crossroad. Even if his case was weak, Jake would always find a way to win.

Though Holly had made up the rainbow story, she would eventually tell Jamie the truth. But for now, her little girl lived in a dream world where her father was some sort of hero, saving lives in a rainbow world.

Jamie's arms released Holly's neck, bringing Holly back to the present. The two looked at one another, their noses touching softly.

Don't cry, Holly, she begged herself.

"Where are my kisses?"

Jamie giggled and started kissing Holly all over her face. She gave her one long kiss on the mouth. "That one counts for ten sleepies."

Holly laughed. "Okay, but I think you should give me about ten of those and you'll be that much closer."

By the seventh kiss, Holly could tell Jamie was really getting bored.

"Two more long kisses and they count for twenty."

"Okay," Jamie said, giving Holly the requested quota.

A knock on the bedroom door made both of them look up.

"And where are my kisses?" Rodney asked, walking into the room.

"Uncle Rodey!" Jamie yelled, jumping off of Holly's lap and into his arms.

Jamie could never pronounce the 'n' in his name, which made Holly laugh every time she called him Rodey. He was the father she'd never had.

To Holly, he was the brother she'd never had and one of her best friends. He loved kids, and she was sure that had he not been gay, she would have married him. His mom was African American, and his dad Caucasian, which left Rodney with soft brown skin and beautiful blue eyes. He was handsome, but he didn't come close to Jake. Still, the guy that one day captured Rodney's heart would be the luckiest man ever.

Jamie began to get bored all over again, squirmed out of Rodney's hands, and half skipped and half ran to her room.

"How are we holding up today?"

Holly looked at him, tears glistening in her eyes.

"Come here, sweetheart."

When she complied, he wrapped his arms around her. "You are leaving her for a good reason. To give her the best future any child could have."

"I know, but it's so hard."

"Of course it is. But think of the end result. It's only for a year, and the following year we'll be back, somewhere close to Seattle. Hopefully, the pay will be better and we can finally get a house where she can have a damn puppy."

Holly giggled through tears.

"It is going to be fucking hard, though," he admitted.

Holly slapped him. "Watch your language."

"Ow! Sorry." He rubbed his chest. "Okay, it's going to be fudging hard, but she's going to love you tons when you get back."

Holly couldn't help but burst out laughing, while wiping a stray tear from her cheek. "News flash, she already loves me."

"She loves me more." He winked.

Only because you don't say no to her."

His face scrounged up. "You're the only one who can tell her no."

Holly laughed again.

Just then, Jamie ran back into her room. "Look what I made you."

Rodney crouched in front of her and looked at the picture. "It's you and mommy, saving lives," she said in explanation.

"And what is that?"

"That is a kidney, and a heart, and those are brains."

"Okay..." Rodney gave her a playful, raised eyebrow look, then gave Holly an insane look, which made her giggle. He looked back at the picture. "And that?"

"It's blood."

Rodney laughed. "You are watching way too much Grey's Anatomy with your mother."

"Are you insane? She's not watching Grey's Anatomy until the day she's twenty-one! There is way too much... coloring in there."

Jamie's body bent over as she crouched simultaneously, laughing uncontrollably at what Holly said, but having no idea what it was really about.

"Well, maybe mommy should color in again."

"Oh, shut up. My coloring days are so over."

"Are not, you colored in with me last night," Jamie spoke up, still having no clue what they'd been talking about.

"Cheater," Rodney teased.

Holly chuckled at his antics. "Fine, I cheated, so what?"

Jane entered the room. "It's time you guys hit the road, otherwise you are not going to make your first day. You still need to hunt for an apartment."

Rodney dangled a set of keys on the end of his finger. "I'm way too organized for you Scallangers." He shook his head in a taunting motion, earning him a slap on the chest from Jane.

"What is it with you women and slapping?" He rubbed his chest.

"Those thanks to daddy?" Holly snorted.

"Whatever. You are going to live like a queen because of my daddy." Rodney wiggled his eyebrows.

Jane laughed. "At least your daddy pays for things like that."

Holly rolled her eyes.

"I don't get your father. He still wants you to pay him back?" Rodney queried.

"Every month."

"He sucks."

Both women laughed.

"Grandpa Charles doesn't suck."

"Okay, missy, he doesn't suck *that* much," Rodney teased again.

Jamie loved her grandfather, but then she got away with murder every other weekend when she visited him.

Holly blew out a breath and her lips quivered as she tried to push back tears.

Rodney grabbed her suitcase, and Jamie helped by taking hold of the smaller bag.

Holly picked up her handbag and slung it over her shoulder, and then tucked a pillow under her armpit for the long trip.

Both Jane and Jamie walked down to the ground floor where Rodney had parked his Toyota. It was a typical 'doctor starting out' type of car; it huffed and puffed when starting it, but it got you where you needed to go.

He placed Holly's suitcase on the back seat with the rest of her stuff.

She snorted when she thought back to when she'd left Boston. The situation was practically identical, and now she was going back in a similar fashion.

Holly turned to Jamie and crouched down to her level. Her baby had tears in her eyes, so she pulled her in for a tighter than tight hug. To keep her voice from breaking, she cleared her throat. "Remember what mommy told you?"

Jamie nodded, while still in Holly's arms.

"I'm going to miss you so much, but I promise to speak to you every day over the phone and to chase down every rainbow I can find, okay?"

Jamie smiled and every time she did so, Holly smiled back. How she was going to break the truth to her one day was a conundrum she'd have to figure out. She just hoped that when the time came, Jamie would understand why she'd lied.

"Love you, Mommy. Be good."

Holly snorted. "You be good, and no ice cream after eight."

"What we are going to do is none of your business," Jane butted in.

Jamie giggled. "Yes, it's our little secret, Nana."

Jane covered Jamie's mouth playfully, making everyone laugh.

"I'll know," Holly said, closing the door, and then rolling the window down.

"Love you, Mommy."

"Love you more."

"Love you more than more," Rodney said, picking Jamie up. "I'll see you on your birthday, okay?"

"Promise?" she asked.

"I'll try my damn best."

"Rodney!" both Holly and Jane yelled.

"Oops! Sorry." He glared at Holly. "I'll try my damn best," he whispered in Jamie's ear, but Holly knew exactly what he'd repeated.

She merely shook her head.

"Big kiss, and a biiiiig hug." He made a grunting sound and Jamie flung her arms around his neck, squeezing tightly.

Jane winked at Holly.

Holly winked back. "Love you," she mouthed.

"Love you more," Jane answered softly.

Rodney put Jamie down and climbed into the driver's seat.

"Drive safe and call me the second you get there."

"Will do," Holly promised.

"Last touch." Jamie snapped her hand out, grazing Holly's elbow just before the car pulled slowly away.

Holly tried to touch her back, but Jamie had squirmed away, giggling loudly.

"I love you, Jamie!" Holly shouted, halfway down the road.

"Love you more, Mommy."

Holly watched her little girl until Rodney turned a corner. When the coast was clear, she finally broke down and bawled her eyes out.

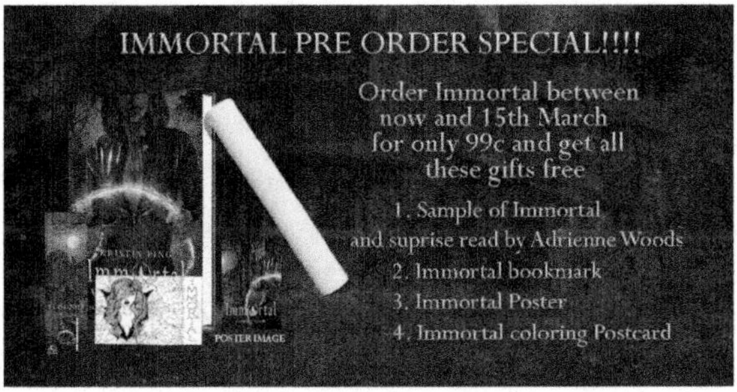

Click on image to go to landing page of Immortal

Natasha's life begins the night she is turned. With the ability to channel fire, a gift that only belongs to the witches, she becomes a terror— not only to the packs, but all the supernatural breeds. She's known as Blaze. The deadliest vampire out there.But Blaze has a secret. She didn't want to become a vampire, she needed to become a vampire, and her reasoning is lost. It died the night her human life did.Her conscience activates when two varcolacs visit the covenant, looking for allies for the Great War. What was it about the Varcolacs that made her grow a conscience? And will she be able to outrun it to keep the title of terror?

Buy Immortal for only 99c and get all these gifts

Click on image to go to Pre Order deal for Ghost Slayer

Twenty-one-year-old Kaelyn has spent half her life hunting ghosts and killing them. But she's not like the other ghost hunters who have to rely on spells and curses to banish ghosts back to where they came from, hoping that they don't come back. When Kaelyn kills a ghost, they stay dead.

But in Mortimer Hall, a behemoth of a house, Kaelyn is about to face the most powerful and life-threatening ghost she ever met, and what she doesn't know is that the ghost has been waiting just for her...

GET GHOST SLAYER FOR ONLY 99c AND GET A BOOKMARK AND FREE SHORT STORY FREE

ABOUT THE AUTHOR

Isabella White lives in South Africa with her family.
She writes many genres under many aliases. Her first debut novel was written under the name of Adrienne Woods, which she uses to write her YA/fantasy series.
Imperfect Love is her first contemporary romance (new adult) work, and is part of a three novel series.
If she isn't writing, she spends her time with her family and friends, loving life.
You can find out more about Isabella White at

Subscribe to her newsletter Here

For more information about Isabella's books

www.authorisabellawhite.com

Printed in Dunstable, United Kingdom

63776585R00231